THE JESSIE KESSON OMNIBUS

THE JESSIE KESSON
OMNIBUS

The White Bird Passes
Glitter of Mica
Another Time, Another Place
Where the Apple Ripens

Jessie Kesson

Chatto & Windus
LONDON

Published in 1991 by
Chatto & Windus Ltd
20 Vauxhall Bridge Road
London SW1V 2SA

A CIP catalogue record for this book is available from British Library

ISBN 0 7011 3783 5

Phototypeset by Intype, London
Printed in Great Britain by
Mackays of Chatham plc

THE WHITE BIRD PASSES

Bright is the ring of words
When the right man rings them
And the maid remembers

R. L. S.

For
My Dominie, Donald Murray

CHAPTER ONE

OUR Lady's Lane; that was what the Monks had called this thoroughfare eight hundred years ago. The name may have fitted it in their time; perhaps it had been a green and cloistered place in those distant days. But, in this Year of Grace 1926, it was no longer green, although it still remained cloistered.

Lady's Lane was a tributary of High Street, one of many such tributaries of long, narrow wynds that slunk backwards from the main street, gathering themselves into themselves, like a group of women assuring each other proudly, 'We keep ourselves to ourselves', and, at the same time, usually knowing more than most people of what is going on around.

If you rushed down High Street in a hurry, you wouldn't notice Lady's Lane at all, so narrowly and darkly does it skulk itself away, but Lady's Lane would most certainly see you. At all hours of the day a voluntary look-out lounges against the entrance to the Lane. It may be Poll Pyke, Battle-axe, or the Duchess. For those ladies of the Lane are in some mysterious way self-appointed guardians of the Lane. The Duchess is the supreme guardian of course. Poll Pyke and

Battleaxe are merely her faithful henchwomen, competent enough to take over temporary command on these not infrequent occasions when the Duchess is forcibly removed to Barclamp Jail for ten days without the option, and wary enough to step down from office the moment the Duchess's 'time' is up.

The less ambitious occupants of the Lane were quite content with this order of things. It meant that they could swipe the bugs from the walls of their sub-lets in peace, in the sure and certain knowledge that, if anything exciting and untoward was taking place in another part of the Lane, they wouldn't miss it; they would receive a clarion call from the Duchess to come and bear witness to such goings on.

Only the children of the Lane were irked by such vigilance. To get up through the Lane unnoticed took on the face of an adventure, and became triumph indeed, if they could reach their own doors without the Duchess confronting them with a pillow-slip, threepence, and a threat: 'Run up to Riley's back-door for a stale loaf, tuppence of broken biscuits. And see you that the loaf isna' too stale.' Or Annie Frigg trapping them with her tin plate, her persuasive voice, and a promise: 'My fine queanie take a runnie down to Lossie Will's for a tanner of herrings. Your legs are younger nor mine. And I've got something for you. A great big ball. All the colours of the rainbow it is. Blue, red, green, and yellow. And there's something else about this ball that I've got. It will never burst. Run on now, for my herrings. That's a queanie!'

And though the Lane's children knew from experience that Annie's promises never came true, they grew up and they grew old before they finally lost their hope that one day Annie Frigg might really give them a ball of all colours that would never burst.

Janie was one of the children who never quite lost faith in Annie.

'Annie Frigg's giving me a doll,' she shouted to Gertie Latham, as she struggled up the cobbles with a pail of water. 'If I carry her water for her, she's going to give me a doll.'

'Some doll,' Gertie responded. 'Annie Frigg's just an old twister. It's Salac's night, Janie. Let that old bitch carry her own water, and come on. We'll play the Salacs up for a laugh.'

'But the doll,' Janie said reluctantly, 'it's a fairy one.'

'What about the toy piano she promised you? and the skipping rope? And all the other things she was going to give you for carrying her water?' Gertie went on relentlessly. 'What about all those things?'

'She just couldn't lay hands on them,' Janie explained. 'She's got them all, Gertie. Somewhere in her room, I'm sure she's got them all. She can tell you every bit about what they're like. She couldn't do that if they weren't there at all. Could she, now?'

'O.K.' Gertie became resigned to the inevitable. 'Be a soft mark if you like. I'm away for my supper. Hurry up out, Janie. It's Salac's night.'

Trauchling up Annie's stairs with the pail of water, now almost half empty, Janie recalled her Mother's verdict on Annie: 'There's one thing about Annie, she'll never send you away with a sore heart.' Nor did she.

'Here's your water, Missis Frigg,' Janie shouted, bracing herself against the smell of cats that was going to rush out and catch her breath the instant Annie opened the door. 'It was awful heavy that water. I thought I'd never get up here with it.' Like Jack in the Box, Annie's head popped round the door, a grey, curly head, like a golliwog grown old, and a mouth that looked as if it had a black moustache above it, but Janie knew it wasn't a moustache, it was just the snuff that Annie took to clear her head.

'My fine queanie. There's no' a better queanie in the Lane.'

Annie's eyes twinkled, and Janie, a willing prisoner, stood caught again in the spell of Annie's promises. 'About that doll you're to get, I've got an idea it might be lying under some bits of things that's come from America. Some bits belonging to my cousin's bairn; just your size she is. And my word there's some bonnie bits that will fit you. There's a blue velvet frock for one thing. And a ribbon to go with it. I'm having a sort out just now. And when I've sorted out, you're the queanie that's going to get the fine surprise, or my name's not Annie Frigg!'

Janie emerged as always, empty handed but full-visioned after an encounter with Annie, and with but one small doubt, how to share the delight of this new promise with Gertie, who could never see that something to look forward to, and something to dream about, were such glad things, even when you knew within yourself that they might never come true.

It was Janie's day to be 'caught'.

'That you, Janie?' Mysie Walsh's voice called to her from across the landing. 'Run a message for me, luv?'

Janie needed no second bidding. Doing something for Mysie Walsh brought its own reward, and it wasn't the threepenny bit she always gave you either. She was big and bright and safe. And next to Janie's own Mother, Janie thought her the loveliest woman in the Lane, with a smile that sucked you right into the core of its warmness, and plump arms that caught you and squeezed you when she was excited, and left your small body trembling with something of her own sudden excitement. Sometimes, with a sudden impulse to please the women grouped round the entrance to the Lane, Mysie Walsh would dance to the music coming from the chip shop's gramophone, her petticoats whirling, her garters showing, real and silk, her voice rising above the gramophone; and, like her smile, her voice gathered you right into it, so that her song seemed to come from you, too:

> Yes, I'm goin',
> Yes, I'm goin',
> And soon I'll be hullo-in
> That coal black Mammy of Mine!

In moments like those the Lane became so alive and full of colour to Janie that she felt suddenly and intensely glad for just being alive in a world of song, and colour, and whirling petticoats and warm, dark women like Mysie Walsh.

'What message do you want me to get?' Janie sniffed the room. It smelt, as always, different from all the other rooms in the Lane, of powder and cream and scent, all mixed up together and coming out in one great sweet smell, which Janie thought of as the smell of a woman that's lovely.

'Cheese. A quarter will do, luv.'

The request, as much as the tone in which it was requested, aroused Janie from her contemplation of the room. Mysie Walsh lay on the top of her bed, her face hidden in the pillow. Janie had never seen Mysie Walsh without her face, dark and laughing. She sensed there was something wrong.

'Have you been taken ill?' she asked the head on the pillow.

'No. Not ill. You'll find money for the cheese on the mantelpiece, or on the table somewhere.'

'You're awfully sad, then?'

'Real sad. Hurry, Janie, or you won't catch McKenzie's open.'

'Just cheese? Nothing else?'

'Just cheese. Just a quarter. Shut the door behind you.'

Cheese. Not like Mysie Walsh's usual messages, Janie thought to herself, as she ran up High Street. Mysie Walsh's messages were usually as delightful as herself. Phulnana from the chemist's, a smell of it, a little on your own cheeks, rubbed well in by Mysie Walsh herself, and the promise of the jar to yourself forever and ever when the cream was done. Or a comb from Woolworth's, the brightest one you could find, with gold stars on it, that shone through Mysie Walsh's hair, even when it was tucked away, and her old comb with only some of the teeth out for yourself. Or cream buns, not stale ones either. 'And we'll have one with a cup of tea together when you come back, luvie.' All the other people in the Lane bought a quarter of cheese, or polony, or a tin of condensed milk. 'And tell McKenzie to mark it on the book.' But not Mysie Walsh. You never had to get it marked on the book for her, because amongst all her other enchantments, Mysie Walsh also always had money.

Twenty minutes later Janie stood in the Lane debating what to do with the money in her hand. Two shillings. The biggest amount she had ever had. More than Mysie Walsh had ever given her before. 'Keep the change, Janie,' Mysie Walsh had said, when she delivered the cheese.

'But there's two shillings change,' Janie pointed out. 'The cheese only cost sixpence, and I took half a crown.'

'Keep it,' Mysie Walsh had insisted. 'Run off now, Janie, and bang the door behind you.'

There were so many ways to dispose of two shillings, that Janie couldn't decide on one of them. Hide it away till my Mam's broke and give her a real surprise. Or just give her a shilling and me a shilling. Or don't say a word to anybody at all, and spend it myself. Gertie waving in the distance solved the problem and gave Janie a small moment of triumph. 'I didn't get the doll from Annie Frigg. But, do you know what, Gertie, I got two bob from Mysie Walsh. As sure as death I did. Look at it.'

CHAPTER TWO

DAY had ended in the Lane. But it was not yet night. Night didn't come till the lamp in the causeway was lit. The hooter from the tweed mill had sounded twenty minutes ago; like the belated echo of its dying wail, the mill workers began to clatter up the Lane. This was one of the regular periods in the Lane's existence when Poll, and Battleaxe, and even the Duchess herself, were dispossessed. They ruled their contemporaries, old and bound to the Lane like themselves; they awed the children whose youngness bound them to the precincts of the Lane; but the workers, coming through the causeway in little groups, were impervious to the Duchess's dictates. The Lane was their bed, their supper, their tea and bread and dripping in the morning. Their lives began beyond it. In the Rialto with Pearl White on Monday nights, with the Charleston at the Lido on Tuesday nights, nearer home with a threepenny poke of chips, and *It Ain't Gonna Rain No More* scratched out for nothing at Joe's chip shop round the corner. Thursdays were zero nights in their lives. The one night that the Lane could hold them, and even then on unflattering terms: the lack of the price to get beyond it.

The Duchess and her coterie diminished on Thursday night, leaning against the causeway with silent disapproval while the Lane's up-and-coming race held the cobbles and, even more galling, held them in an idiom alien to her Grace; flaunting overmuch of that tin jewellery from Woolworth's, that new store, Nothing Over Sixpence, that had just opened in High Street; drunk with the novelty and prodigality of jewellery so cheap; hands on their hips; shimmying their bodies, like new-fangled whores, for the old-fangled ones like Mysie Walsh and Liza MacVean still just kicked their legs and showed their garters; and the daft tunes they shimmied in rhythm with:

> But yes,
> We have no bananas,
> We have no bananas today!

They had no feeling of protocol either. Didn't care tuppence which lavatory they used. When it had been the Duchess's rule for years that Right Laners used the lavatory by the causeway, and Left Laners used the one up beside the ragstore. They simply used the lavatory nearest their moment of need. And the Duchess strongly suspected, that, as in one other ancient time of need, they also went in two by two.

Fortunately the Duchess's peace of mind was disturbed only on Thursdays in particular, and for this short period of time which was neither night nor day but a transition between. Up the causeway they clattered, this little group of Laners, unknown to either Poll, or Battleaxe, or the Duchess.

'That's wee Lil's Betsy. She's shot up some in this past year.'

But they didn't know Betsy. Not now. She had outgrown them. She wasn't old enough to be behind with her rent. She

wasn't young enough to have the School Board Man searching her out. And so she eluded them.

'You've got home again, young Betsy?'

'Aye.'

'They're saying you're all being put on half-time at the
mill. Is that right?'

'*You* tell me!'

'Well!' The Duchess felt weary. 'Did you ever hear the
like of that for cheek?'

'It's this picture-going!' Poll reflected. 'It's making them
all like that. They'd bite the hand that feeds them.'

'I've never put foot in a picture palace in my life,' Battleaxe
concluded. 'And I've no intention of starting now.'

Hugh, the lamp-lighter, set night on its course with one
flick from his long pole, and Melodeon Mike set the final
seal on it, the clop of his wooden leg distorting the sound of
all other passing footsteps. The women round the causeway
relaxed. They had come into their own again.

'It's *The Home Fire's Burning* and *The Long Long Trail
Awinding* for them tonight, Cocks!' Mike shouted his greeting, knowing that the Duchess had no objection to the rest
of the world being cheated as long as she was 'in the know'.

'I'll just squeeze them out of the old box, give my gammy
leg a jerk behind me. And before you can spit, the coppers
will be landing on my bonnet. "Poor Bugger" the folk will
be thinking as they eye my leg. "Poor Sod" that's what the
war did.' Not, mind you, that I ever blamed the war for the
loss of my leg. I wouldn't have the lie of it on my soul. But
if I were to tell them the truth now, Poll. If I were to turn
right round and say I lost my leg in a brawl at Aikey Fair.
What do you think they'd say? They'd say, 'Drunken Brute.
Serves him right.' That's what they'd say. Folk's minds work
queer. Dead queer. If they think I lost it in the war, they're
glad because I lost it in a good cause. Or sorry because I lost

it in a bad one. All according to how they feel about war. Either way they fling the coppers. What they don't see is that the loss of your leg is the loss of your leg. And it doesn't matter a damn how you lose it. It's still a loss to you.'

'And a gain too, though, Mike,' Poll pointed out, but without rancour. 'I bet you make more out of that gammy leg of yours and that squeeze box than Dodsie Jenner makes out of his lavender bags. And him went through the Dardanelles and all.'

'I'll grant you that,' Mike agreed, the love of an argument growing big within him. 'That's granted. But what has Dodsie Jenner got to show for being through the Dardanelles? Damn all, Poll. If he'd lost an arm now. Or even a coupla fingers itself, his lavender bags would go like nobody's business.'

'But Dodsie Jenner lost his mind,' Poll protested. 'Or at least what mind he did have. I knew him years before the war, he never did have much in his top storey. But what he had he lost after the Dardanelles.'

'But a mind's a different matter altogether, Poll,' Mike urged. 'Nobody knows if you got much of a mind in the first place. So how to hell can they tell when you've lost it? Outsiders I mean. Now I know a cove. He's brother to Bert Wylie's wife. He went through the lot. Got half his face blown off. He sells oranges down in the Green.'

'Oh, I know *him*!' Battleaxe broke in. 'He's called Pippins for a by-name.'

'The same. Pippins. That's him. Well . . .'

'God knows the poor soul can't help only having half a face, but 1 can never bring myself to buy his oranges,' Battleaxe went on. 'His face puts me off. I stick to Ned Wheeler when it comes to buying an orange, and of course that's just at the New Year.'

'Maybe that then.' Mike was impatient of interruptions.

'Now, where was I? Oh aye! This cove told me himself one night in The Hole In The Wall . . .'

'I thought Pippins was Pussyfoot,' Poll protested. 'He was a great one for the Salvation Army for a while.'

'He's not that now then,' Mike was patient. 'Though I did hear tell that it was the Army that helped to set him up in the Green. But when I saw him, he was in The Hole In The Wall. God, Poll, did you ever see a man with his nose shot away down a pint? You don't want to either. But, as I was saying, he told me himself that he makes more money now than he did when he had got all his face. It's proof folk want for their charity, Poll. Something they can see. No. I'll say till my dying day that Dodsie Jenner would have been better off if he'd lost a hand. My luck was just in, I lost my leg in 1916. If I'd lost it in a brawl at Aikey Fair in 1902, I'd have been a dead duck. That's what I mean by "luck", Poll.'

Luck. It was the invincible argument. Even the Duchess was wordless against it. Mike trailed himself away from the safety and comprehension of his own kind, out into the High Street. Only the sound of his melodeon echoed back to them:

. . . to the land of my dreams.

'Where the nightingales are singing.' Poll sang in solitary accompaniment.

'There was a lot that didn't come back,' Battleaxe ventured.

'And them that did come back, came back worse than they went off,' the Duchess added. Even the Duchess, who knew the truth, unconsciously accepted the lie of Mike Melodeon's wooden leg.

Up the Lane at 285 Janie, too, contemplated the results of her 'luck'.

'Mysie Walsh must be doing all right to give you two bob all in a once,' her Mother said, through the hairpins in her teeth. 'Did you see my side combs anywhere, Janie? Was Mysie Walsh getting ready to go out, did you notice?'

'I don't know.' Janie was absorbed in clearing the table to find room for her book. 'She hadn't got her curlers in. She was just lying on top of her bed. She looked fed up. There's a new word for meadow, Mam. A Red Indian word. Musko-day. On the muskoday. The meadow. Muskoday. Musk-o-day. It's in this book. It sounds right fine, doesn't it?'

'Was that what you bought with your two bob?' Liza sounded amused.

'And your tobacco!' Janie protested against this forgetful-ness. 'You are glad about the tobacco, aren't you, Mam?'

'Yes, of course I am. Get a lace out of one of my other shoes, Janie, this damned lace has snapped!'

'You'd hardly any tobacco left, had you, Mam?'

'No, hardly any. Not out of that shoe, Janie! Use your eyes, that's a brown one.'

'Your black shoe must be under the bed then. If you'd had one wish, it would have been for tobacco, wouldn't it?'

'Yes, Janie.' Liza's voice came slow and quiet and clear. 'I'm glad you bought tobacco. I had hardly any left. And if I'd had one wish, it would have been for tobacco. Now. Have you found my shoe?'

The surprise of Mysie Walsh's two bob was over. Dimly Janie realised that her Mother's gladness at getting, just didn't equal her own gladness in giving.

'Is this the right shoe, Mam?'

'That's it. That's the one.' Liza sat absorbed unlacing it. Janie, watching her down-bent head, thought, It's strange, I can hug Mysie Walsh. And smell her hair and I can't do that to my own Mam. Though she's much bonnier than Mysie Walsh. If Janie had been suddenly stricken with blindness she would have had a perpetual picture of her Mother in her memory. Not a photograph. Her Mother had so many faces.

But a hundred little images. Each of which was some part of her Mother. And her Mother some part of each. The way her red hair glistened and crept up into little curls when it rained. Her long legs sprawled across the fender. Her tall, swift stride. And her eyes that looked as if they were smiling when the rest of her face was in a rage.

'I'll maybe get diphtheria like Gertie did,' Janie thought, watching her, 'and have to go away in the ambulance. Maybe my Mam will hug me like Mysie Walsh does, then.'

'The Salacs are here, Janie,' Gertie shouted from the lobby below. 'There's going to be testimony and saving. Hurry up, or you'll miss it all.'

'Well.' Liza's eyes were smiling. 'That's something, Janie. Aren't you going?'

'I was going.' Janie was undecided. 'But there's a penny for the gas now. And I've got my book. The only thing is the Salacs only come on Saturdays. If I don't go tonight, I'll miss it all for a week.'

'And you want both things at once, Janie?' Liza was quizzical. 'Well. Nothing like it if you can get it. I'm away now. If you're in your bed before I get back, see and leave the sneck off the door.' Liza, remembering something, popped her head round the door again: 'Take my tip, Janie. If you go to the Salacs tonight, you'll still have your book left for tomorrow. That way of it, you'll get both things. But not at once, that's what makes it tough. Don't forget. Leave the sneck off the door for me.'

Five minutes later Janie and Gertie were pushing their way through the crowd gathered round the street lamp.

'You've made us late,' Gertie grumbled. 'And you've got an awful smell.'

'I know.' Janie was unoffended. 'It's cats. I'd to crawl under our bed. And Mysie Walsh's cat always comes in and does it under our bed. O look, Gertie, Annie Frigg's got a good shot in. I bet you anything she'll cry tonight, and give testimony, and kiss the Salacs. I love it when she does that. She's so funny.'

The crowd gathered round the Salvation Army was unchanging. The old Laners, who preferred the light of the lamp and the company to the darkness and loneliness of their rooms. The deformed Laners. White, fanatical, and selfish, not only laying claim to the best position round the lamp, but forcing a prior claim on God Himself, whining their Hallelujahs right up to the top of the lamp, where they thought the Mercy Seat must lie. And of course always the children of the Lane who loved a noise anyhow. Later the drunks, reluctant to go home, would join the group. And if testimony wasn't over by the time they arrived, their testimony would be the most fervent of the lot. Beyond the group, leaning against the causeway, were the objective spectators, the Duchess, Poll, and Battleaxe. Without need of salvation in their own opinions, they nevertheless enjoyed the antics of their neighbours who were so very obviously in need of it.

He's the lily of the valley.
He's the bright and morning star.

Despite themselves, the objective spectators hummed the chorus. It was familiar. Like saying God bless you. Or God curse you. Something you had always said.

He's the fairest of ten thousand
To my soul.
To my soul.

But Janie knew that she would always remember the sudden green and silver image the words had brought to the Lane at dusk. Gertie, unmoved by words and images, was becoming irritable.

'I thought they were going to be saving us tonight. It's a damned shame if they don't. So it is.'

'Wheesht,' admonished Chae Tastard, normally one of the best cursers in the Lane, but momentarily under the spell of the Salvationists. 'It's terrible the language that's on you two bairns. And the napkins hardly off your arses yet.'

And even more terrible the crowd's sudden and complete desertion of the Salvationists. It was Betsy's young Alan, who started the whisper:

'Mysie Walsh's done herself in. Hanged herself. The bobbies are up at 284 now.'

'Making a right barney about her being cut down before they got the chance to do it themselves,' Betsy added to the information.

'Who cut her down, Son?' Battleaxe demanded like a furious general who had been overlooked, but still had a right to know. 'Who was it that cut her down?'

'Chae did. Chae Tastard, with his sharp cobbler's knife.'

'Liars!' Janie screamed in a small panic. 'She isn't dead. I took cheese to her.

'Yeah?' Betsy's young Alan shot his tongue out at Janie and passed on, anxious to spread all the news to the more important grown-ups. 'And do you know what? A bit of cheese was stuck in her mouth when they took the rope off.'

Ted Howe, only drunkenly comprehending the news, forced his way through the crowd. 'Take my boots off when I die. When I die.' And beneath the lamp the Salvationists sang for their own edification:

> Dare to do right.
> Dare to be true.

> God who created you
> Cares for you, too.

For the crowd had deserted them and were following Ted towards the door of Mysie Walsh who was.

'Them,' Poll was saying, watching the police-guarded door morosely. 'Them that takes their own lives, don't get to rest in consecrated ground. It's yon bit of common ground behind the gaswork for them.'

'I saw this coming,' Battleaxe added, with the pride of a prophet whose vision has come true. ' "Mark my words," I said to my man just the night before last, "Mysie Walsh will come to a bad end. She'll never die in her bed." '

'Not with the life she led,' the Duchess agreed. 'Running around with every Tom, Dick, and Harry. Enough to drive you mad, through time. And that time she was in hospital with the poomonia. I know what she had. And it wasn't poomonia either. I cut my wisdom teeth too early to be mistaken.'

The next of kin pushed her way through the crowd. Battleaxe, furious at her prerogative in getting past the Bobby unchallenged, spat out her commentary:

'See her? No show without Punch. Last time she saw Mysie Walsh she was pulling the hair out of her. Said she wouldn't spit in Mysie Walsh's direction because she owed her ten bob.'

A sense of fear took hold of Chae Tastard's small wife. Fear of what lay beyond the police-guarded door, fear of Battleaxe's anger, fear of everything. 'Death pays all debts,' she said in a quiet and already defeated attempt to escape.

The Duchess began to laugh harshly. 'That way of it, Lil, the sooner we're all in our wee, black boxes the better.'

The next of kin was coming out. 'Is she dead?' shouted

Battleaxe, waving aside personal differences out of a zeal for truth.

'Stone dead.' The next of kin was glad of a truce which lent her an attentive ear. 'As dead as a door nail. You wouldn't know her. You wouldn't know a bit of her. Her face black. Her tongue swollen twice the size of your fist. And a lump of cheese fit to choke her on its own stuck in her gullet.'

'I took the cheese to her,' Janie shouted from amongst the women's shawls. 'But I didn't know. Honest to God I didn't.'

The shawls wheeled round in attack.

'You shouldn't know either,' Battleaxe shouted, jealously eyeing the small girl who had last seen the corpse alive. 'You're too young to give evidence, anyhow.'

'You should have been in your bed long ago,' the Duchess added. 'If you were mine! But, thank God you're no' mine. Standing there all eyes and ears. Beat it now. Before I take the lights from you!'

The policeman saved Janie from sudden extinction. 'The show's over for tonight,' he said, with just the amount of humour needed for the crowd's mood. 'You lot got no homes to go to?'

'Only just,' cried Battleaxe, speaking for them all. 'The rent's behind.'

The crowd had gone, taking with them the cover which they had flung over the tenement. Mysie Walsh's window, covered with a blanket, lay exposed to Janie and Gertie. Gertie who lived two doors away flaunted her own safety: 'I'd just hate to be you, Janie, having to pass Mysie Walsh's door tonight. Maybe she'll jump out on you.'

'She can't. She's dead.' Janie used reason to fight fancy,

but didn't succeed. 'Come on up with me, Gertie. Just till my Mam comes home.'

'I can't, I've got to go home or else I'll get a belting. But she can't touch you, Janie,' and as if regretting her reassurances, Gertie shouted over her shoulder as she disappeared: 'I wouldn't be you for anything. Janie. She might just jump out on you.

All black and her tongue purple, Janie thought, as the wooden stairs creaked beneath her feet. Ready to jump out on me when I reach second landing. For death, and this was Janie's first, near experience of it, could suddenly translate the loved and the living into the ghostly and the frightening. The scream poised itself in Janie's throat, ready for its flight through the tenement, the moment Mysie Walsh jumped out of death, through the door. And not really ready when the moment came. Only the figure who leapt from beside her door, heard the cry that was a substitute for the scream.

'Shut your mouth, you little bastard. Do you want the whole house woken up?'

The dead don't speak so. The livingness of the words calmed Janie into surveying the speaker. It was a man. Her Mother suddenly appeared from behind him, annoyance in her voice. 'Leave the bairn alone.'

'Yours?' the man asked.

'Aye. My first mistake. And my last one.'

The man jingled coppers in his pocket. 'Like to go and get yourself some chips, hen?'

'I can't. Chip shop's shut,' Janie said, contemplating him gratefully, since, whoever he was, he just wasn't Mysie Walsh back from the dead.

'Find out the time for us, then.'

'It's gone eleven. Gertie and me heard the clock not long since.'

'Scram then.' The man was growing angry. 'Make yourself scarce for God's sake.'

'She's my bairn,' Liza said resentfully, coming towards Janie. 'Look, luv, run into Mysie Walsh's for some coppers for the gas. Here's sixpence. Move over, you. Till the bairn gets past.'

'I can't,' Janie stood impassively. 'Mysie Walsh's dead.'

'Don't be daft. Don't act it,' Liza said harshly in the darkness. 'I spoke to Mysie Walsh when I went out.'

'She's dead since.' Janie stood small and impregnable in the safety of truth. 'She hanged herself. The bobbies were here and all. Chae Tastard cut her down with his big knife.'

Liza stared at Mysie Walsh's door, and backed away from it, no longer aware of the man: 'Come on, Janie. It's high time you and me were in our bed. Mind your feet on the first step. It won't be there much longer.'

'What about me?' The man's voice came plaintively behind them.

'You can keep,' Liza called down, as if she had forgotten him.

'What about my dough? I paid you, didn't I?'

'And I should have got you between the eyes with your lousy dough.' There was anger in Liza's voice. But Janie sensed that this anger wasn't directed at her. It was as if herself and her Mother were in league, against the man. 'Mind your feet now, bairn,' her Mother said. Warmly, intimately. The two of them taking care of each other on the stairs.

'You damned two-timer. You prick tormentor.' The man's voice came furiously from below. 'I paid you, didn't I?'

'And here's your money.' The sudden clatter of coppers in the darkness, the anger in Liza's voice, frightened the man. He mumbled himself down, and out of hearing.

'You stay here, Mam,' Janie cried, when he had gone. 'Just

wait for me here, and I'll look for the money you threw. It's on the landing somewhere.'

Liza waited without protest. Throwing the money had been a sincere gesture, but a reckless one. 'There was two bob. A two-bob bit, and sixpence of coppers,' she shouted to Janie. 'Can you see, or will I light the lobby gas?'

'I've found the two-bob bit,' Janie answered. 'Maybe the pennies have rolled under Mysie Walsh's door!'

But Mysie Walsh was dead. At the other side of the door. Her face all black and her tongue all purple. Janie had forgotten. Now she remembered, and ran upstairs without the pennies, to where her Mother waited.

CHAPTER THREE

THE Lane came reluctantly to life. Its occupants, unwilling to face the first shock of early morning coldness, were even more unwilling to miss a moment of Mysie Walsh's funeral.

No one was sure of the exact time of this event. 'Before dinner-time,' Battleaxe said, tilting her tea-leaves into the dustbin. 'Before the sun rises full.'

'Myself now,' maintained Poll, waiting in the bin queue, 'had the idea that suicides were buried after the sun goes down. I know that the sun hasn't got to shine on them. But one can never be sure about that.'

'I know one thing,' the Duchess concluded, 'if Pinner has the undertaking, and he usually has the Poor Law burials, he'll want it over and done with by the time The Hole In The Wall opens.'

Nothing was sure at this grey time of the morning, except that the burial of Mysie Walsh would be a sly, dark thing. As hurried and as secret as her death had been. The women round the dustbin felt that she had cheated them by dying without first informing them. But, by Christ, they weren't going to be done out of her funeral too.

'Not if I stand holding up this wall till midnight,' vowed Battleaxe, planting her teapot firmly between her feet, settling her back comfortably against the causeway and casting a resentful glance over the other women, arriving to stake for themselves a place with a view.

Wee Lil, flopping down the cobbles in her man's shoes, felt Battleaxe's resentment rush towards her and directed it away from herself with panting haste:

'You lot hear the shindy, last night? That Liza MacVean and one of her pick-ups. You wouldn't have thought there was a corpse in the tenement. Chewing the fat like hell they were. Sounded like they were both up against Mysie Walsh's door. No shame in the world. Some folk haven't. And Mysie Walsh stone dead on the other side of the door.'

Poll felt suddenly ribald. 'Well. What's the odds? Mysie Walsh couldn't take it herself anymore anyhow.' Poll's laugh rose solitary and, shamed by its own loneliness, darted thinly into silence.

'There is,' admonished the Duchess, 'a time and a place for allusions to other folks' weakness. And Mysie Walsh is dead.'

'And me thinking Mysie Walsh came alive, last night,' Janie confided to Gertie, on the way down to join the watchers. 'As sure as God. I thought it was her when the man jumped out on me.'

'What man?' Gertie asked, with the sleep still over her.

'Just some man,' Janie answered swiftly. 'After Mysie Walsh likely.' For it was known that men went for Mysie Walsh. And Janie hoped it wasn't known that men went for her Mother, too.

'And her dead,' Gertie said, completely sidetracked. 'No wonder my Mam says men are just beasts.'

Battleaxe was right. Before the sun rose full, two horses, pulling the hearse, drew up in front of the tenement.

'Only two horses.' Janie was disappointed. 'Balaclava had four, with black feathers over their heads when she was buried.'

'That's because this is no' a real funeral,' young Alan shouted, knowing everything, loudly.

'No. But the corpse is real enough, Son,' Chae Tastard answered. And he should know, Janie thought, watching him curiously, for he had cut down the corpse. He had seen somebody dead. She stared at his face to find the imprint so strange a seeing must have left upon it. His face looked the same as it always did in his dark, cobbler's shop, his eyes pale and peering, with yellow stuff stuck in the corners. And when Chae spoke again, there was no more wonder to him.

'I could hardly get near her to cut her down. She hadn't opened her window for weeks, surely. Her room stank to Heaven.'

As the undertaker's men shouldered the coffin, past condemnation turned to present pity.

'She wasna' the worst.' Battleaxe dabbed tearless eyes. 'If she'd got a bob she'd break it, and let you have the tanner.'

'And that time my Ned was knocked off the mill, she never saw him without a Woodbine,' Poll said, edging Gertie off the kerb, to get a better look at the coffin. 'What a sin. Not even a flower allowed on it.'

Battleaxe assented sadly. 'A funeral's no' a funeral without a flower.'

'What you never had you never miss,' Janie's Mother broke in, appearing so suddenly behind the coffin, that she scattered the crowd. 'And, what's more, Mysie Walsh's in the best place.' She didn't give the surprised women time to sharpen their tongues for the defence of such callousness to a corpse, but strode through them. Not even having the decency to stand still in that moment when Pinner crowned himself with his long, funeral hat and lifted his black cane to motion the hearse forward.

'Well,' said the Duchess when she had got her breath back. 'Of all the hard-hearted bitches, that Liza MacVean takes the cake.'

'She'll miss Mysie Walsh for one,' Poll prophesied, 'She always knew where to go for the price of a bag of cinders. And that young Janie of hers always knew where to go for a bite.'

'What's more,' Battleaxe said, looking furtively round to see where young Janie was, 'what's more, you'd expect Liza to cut up rough. Her and Mysie Walsh being partners in the business, as you might say. When one has too many clients, she handed the other the overflow.'

Janie had at last caught up with her Mother. Furiously. Accusingly. 'You didn't cry once, Mam. Everybody was sorry for Mysie Walsh, and cried, except you.'

'There's nothing to cry for.' Liza didn't look at the child. And didn't slacken her stride. 'Nothing at all. Death's the poor man's best friend. Burns said that. And do you know something? He was quite right. I'll be back a bit earlier tonight. Here's tuppence for you. And I've left coppers for the gas.'

'How much?' Gertie demanded, closing in.

'Tuppence.'

'But she said she left coppers for the gas, Janie.'

'So she did.'

'Well, you won't be needing the gas for ages. We can have the lot between us. Birnie's have got gingerbread men. Great fat ones. They only cost two a penny.'

The Lane settled down into an apathy edged with restiveness. Mysie Walsh's funeral had ended too soon, leaving the rest of the day to stretch interminably before the women, leaning against the causeway, with their arms folded across their bosoms.

Janie and Gertie were not caught up in the surrounding apathy. The Lane was the world. And, being so, ever willing to offer up some new distraction. Like the Duchess's scillas in the window-box. A blaze of blue.

'It's bound to be summer soon,' Janie said, spying them. 'The Duchess's scillas are out, now. And then it'll be Waifs and Strays' picnic. I'm going to eat till I burst, this year. I was too excited to eat last year. And I wished for days after that I'd eaten everything.'

'Me too,' Gertie agreed. 'I'm going to get tore into all the stuff this time. Only it'll be a long time till it comes.'

'And I'll have new boots, soon,' Janie went on, trying to reach the picnic sooner, by marking time off with small landmarks. 'I'm due for a ticket for new boots soon.'

'My Mam won't apply for a ticket any more.' Gertie was rueful. 'Because the man that gives you the tickets tried to put his hand up her clothes. My Dad wasn't half flaming. Said he would knock him into next week. But Mam said not to. He gives the tickets for Free Coal too, you see. And he mightn't have given us one. Not if my Dad had bashed him one.'

An old envy of Gertie's Dad crept over Janie. That big coal carter, with a voice that could frighten Cruelty Inspectors and Sanitary Men, making them small and wordless and quick to disappear. Gertie didn't know what it was to sneck the door and hide under the bed when they came. Her Dad was there to attack the attacker, shouting right down the Lane after him:

'She'll go to school when she's got boots to her feet. And that'll be when I can afford them.'

Not like us, Janie thought. My Mam is afraid of them all.

And I get frightened for her. And there's nobody to knock the Free Boot Man into next week if he tries to put his hand up our clothes.

Janie had created a Father for herself. It was easier to make a completely new Father, than to build from the scant facts she knew about the original:

'You've got your Father's eyes,' her Mother would say when she was in a temper. 'Real wicked eyes. And he was a bad one. By God he was.'

Or, when her Mother was in a mood, mellowed sometimes by the Lane's own mood, warm and kind, gathering its occupants round its causeway in an expansive oneness, with Poll's voice singing over them:

> Abie, Abie, Abie my boy
> What are you waiting for now?
> You promised to marry me
> One day in June.
> It's never too late,
> But it's never too soon.

Janie's Mother would squeeze Janie's hand, whispering through Poll's song: 'Your Father could take music out of a tin whistle. That he could. He had so much music to him.'

It had been difficult to take these solitary, contradictory facts and build one complete Father out of them. So Janie, perforce, had given life to a new Father. And death too. Death eliminated awkward questions to which Janie hadn't got the answer. Gertie had accepted it all as if it wasn't a lie at all:

'So that's why you and your Mam go up to the Cemetery every Sunday?'

'Don't be daft!' Janie had protested, momentarily forgetting her fabrication. 'My Mam just goes for the walk, and I go to pinch the flowers out of the green bins. Yon little white angel we have on our mantelpiece, I took that too, once. We do look at my Father's grave,' she added hurriedly, remembering. 'Do you know what it says on his stone, Gertie? It says *Asleep In Jesus*. You can come with me one Sunday to see for yourself.'

Dusk had drawn the Lane into its folds. The women at the causeway had become part of its pattern, absorbed into the greyness of the walls they leant against. Battleaxe leapt in sudden protest against this loss of her individuality. 'It's gone six,' she said, bending to retrieve her teapot between her feet. 'My Joe's due home.'

'What's more,' the Duchess cried, coming to life and darting for second place at the pump, 'this perisher of a pump's froze, or choked up or something. We'll be all night squeezing a drop of water out of it.'

'Not me!' Battleaxe defended her nickname. 'Not if I've got to rattle the guts out of the damned thing. My Joe works for his supper, so he does. Not like some I could name.'

Poll rose glinting-eyed to the bait: 'My Hughie would work too, if he'd got work. But he was never the one to lick the Town Council's arse. If he'd licked a bit more, he might have still been on the dust-cart.'

'Meaning what?' Battleaxe's ears flew back and flicked. 'If you're insinuating that my Joe's a Yes Man.'

'I'm insinuating nothing.' Poll was beyond fear. 'I'm saying straight out that your Joe wasn't knocked off with the rest of them, because his wife's tongue's handy for the Council's ears. Who was it that nipped up to the Town Hall and reported wee Lil's bugs to the Sanitary? Tell us that!'

Wee Lil, proud of being the sudden centre of interest, gasped pink-faced and pleadingly: 'I don't know who reported my bugs. I only know that I've lived in the Lane all my days, and I've never reported nobody. You all know that.'

'Because you haven't got the guts. That's why!' Battleaxe's skirt wheeled round wee Lil. 'None of you have got any guts. Except when the beer's inside you!'

'There's going to be a fight,' Gertie prodded Janie excitedly. 'Poll and Battleaxe are getting tore into each other at the pump. Come on and watch. Come on, Janie. Don't be such a fearty.'

Janie was a fearty. Feared of so many things that left Gertie unafraid. Like the women when they fought. Not looking like women any more. But dark and furious and whirling like witches Janie had seen in story books. Janie's fear was never for the actual, but for the imagined. It could have been her Mother, lying there mauled and vulgar with her clothes up round her head, and blood trickling from her mouth. But that will never happen, Janie vowed to herself. Because I would fight for my Mam. I'd be so frightened for her, that I wouldn't have fear left for myself at all. I'd become as strong as anything. I know I would. I'd batter the women's heads against the cobbles, and squeeze their faces, and trample all over them with my feet. I'd just kill them, if they ever touched my Mam.

'Here's Sam's Ernie coming to throw sawdust on the blood,' Gertie said with regretful finality, as if this ritual truly ended the fight. 'Anyhow, Battleaxe won, Poll had to get stitches.'

'Ten stitches,' young Alan assured them in the passing. 'My mother went with her in the ambulance to Casualty. Said she didn't half bleed.'

'Come on, Janie,' Gertie urged. 'The sawdust's on the blood now, there's nothing more to see.'

But there was. Through the sawdust Janie still saw the

blood, a small, dark loch submerged between cobbles that had become mountains.

'Come on. Down to the Green to see Beulah.'

'Don't you two be going and bringing lice back from that lousy tinker,' warned the Duchess, overhearing the suggestion. 'We've got enough troubles without getting some of her lice into the bargain.'

'Anyhow,' wee Lil contributed, 'you won't find Beulah down on the Green, she's doing time.'

'Wee Lil's a liar,' Janie hissed, as they ran towards the Green. 'Beulah's out. I saw her in the street cadging rabbit skins.'

Chapter Four

THE Green was as much part of the Lane as the communal pump in the causeway. If you weren't in the Lane you were 'down at the Green'. There was no third alternative. Even if there had been, you would have been out of your mind to have chosen it in preference to the Green.

The summer through, the Green's chair-o-planes, whirling high, blistered with colour and blared with music. The Devil's Own Din was how the sedate residents of Hill Terrace described it in a protest to the Lord Provost and Town Council, but to the Laners who were the true lovers of the Green it was music.

It was *If you were the only Girl in the World* sung in a frenzied, birling chorus by the angels and cherubs painted on the awnings of the chair-o-planes; it was the voices of spielers imploring, hectoring you into seeing The Strongest Man in The World, as crowned heads of Europe were privileged to see him, and You that wasn't a crowned head of any place at all, what in the Name were you standing waiting for, when you could walk right in. A tanner a time. And the best tanner's worth you'd ever be likely to see this side of heaven, that is if you were ever likely to get there at all.

It was thin men at coconut stalls wheedling you into three balls for tuppence, and a prize every time.

It was the show's women in bright head-scarves shouting to each other from the steps of their caravans about their washing and their children; of how liver had been ninepence at Auchnasheen last week, but would be less by the time they got to Auchnashelach. Auchnasheen and Auchnashelach, Udale Bay and Duirinish. The bright, far-sounding names of places drifting up through streamers and balloons as bright and remote as themselves.

It was the sound of a smack on a child's bare bottom and a rising scream of protest.

It was all noise gathered into the chair-o-planes in the centre, held there, and flung over and outwards in a singing crescendo of adoration:

O, O, how I love you,
How I love you,
My dearest Swanee.

The Green had its own social scale. Lord John Sanger's circus was the cream of its aristocracy. When the circus arrived, the chair-o-planes, the Strong Man, the coconut stalls, withdrew from the centre of the Green and huddled themselves away in a more remote direction, like younger sons knowing their proper place but still dependent.

When winter came and the last circus elephant had trumpeted its way to the station, and the show's last caravan rumbled along the North Road, leaving only faded, brown circles on the Green's grass to prove that they had ever been there at all, the tinkers, the third and last grade of the Green's society, took over.

The show they put on was less spectacular than that of their forerunners. Their caravans were still horse-drawn, shaped like wagons and made of green canvas. Their tents were small and brown. But the tinkers also had the magical facility of rolling far-sounding places round their tongues.

Aikey Fair, 'Where the ale cost only tuppence and a tanner bocht a gill.' Raffan Market, its horse sales with brown, furtive tinkers 'wheezing gajes for jowldie' – taking country men for suckers. Blairgowrie, the great trek southwards to the berry picking, and 'I'll show ye the road and the miles to Dundee, Janie.' Still southwards but nearer home, to the farming lands up Donside way, 'There's no place like Aberdeenshire, Janie, and no folk so fine as them that bide by Don.'

And, though Janie had never been beyond the Lane, through her own imagination and through close companionship with Beulah the Green's oldest tinker, she knew their ways and their meeting places almost as well as she knew the Lane.

Janie's ambition was to be a real tinker someday. Meanwhile, under Beulah's expert eye, she had learned to 'pick rags', cadge rabbit skins, stock the 'swag' in Beulah's basket. And given money, Janie could have purchased Beulah's swag herself, in correct proportion to its selling powers. Shoelaces, buttons, reels of cotton, a line that even the harassed, hard-up cottar wives would not close their doors against. Milk bowls and fancy butter dishes for the more opulent farmers' wives, brooches and hair-slides for her brosy servant girl, for the great secret was to get round the servant before you attacked her mistress. Bluebirds flying from long sticks for the lawful bairns of both cottar and farm wife, and the unlawful bairns of the servants. It was a fact, garnered from Beulah, that even when money was scarce, it was never so scarce but it would be taken out from the hoard, hidden in some antrin jug, to quieten the roar the bairns set up, when they caught their first glimpse of a bluebird flying from a stick.

One of the intensely happy moments in Janie's life was a moment like this, when she saw Beulah's caravan rising high out of the dusk, with the fire burning redly outside it, and Beulah herself coorying over it, stirring her pot.

'I told you Beulah was out of the nick, Gertie. She's making rice. I can get the smell of it.'

Janie suddenly realised that she was very hungry. 'We'll get some if Beulah's had a good day gathering rags. She'll be in a right good humour.'

Beulah *was* in a good humour. Her release from jail lay largely and benignly over her, smiling in the brown creases of her face, dancing defiance in the jingle of her long, brass earrings. She greeted Janie and Gertie exuberantly:

'God bless us. Over the bones of my poor Mother that's dead, I thought you'd gone clean off the face of the earth, Janie. Gospel truth I did. Did you forget your road to the caravan? Or, was it maybe that you found a better friend than old Beulah?'

A protest against such treachery rose to Janie's lips to be stifled by the smell rising overwhelmingly near and sweet from the pot.

'No, Beulah,' Janie struggled for an explanation that wouldn't offend Beulah too deeply. 'We didn't come because we heard you was away for awhile.'

'A while!' Beulah protested, scandalised by such under-statement. 'Fourteen days without the option of a fine. That's what I was away for. Fourteen days. And me with no more than a wee hauf and a brown inside me. Not another drop passed my lips. And there's the God's truth for you. There, sit you down on the rabbit skins, and I'll tell you dead straight – between you and me and the mare – without a word of a lie, what's behind me and the fourteen days.'

Beulah's spoon stopped stirring, she thrust her face nearer the fire, and Janie held back her breath for the momentousness of a secret.

'They lift me to spring-clean their jails for them,' Beulah whispered, her whisper cracking with the injustice of it all. 'I can be as drunk's a Lord in November, or even in February for that matter of it, and the Bobbies turn a blind eye to me, but, this is the Gospel truth, the moment the first ray of spring sun blinks through and shows up all the dirt in Barclamp Jail, every Bobby in the force is on the look-out for me. Folk can be robbed in their sleep. Or murdered in their beds. Does the Bobbies care? No! They're too busy looking for me. They know it will be a feather in their bonnet for lifting me. For there's none that scrubs out their jail as thorough as I do. Free gratis and for nothing. But it's the last time they'll lift me in the spring. I vow that to my Maker. The flat-footed bucks!'

Beulah's spoon went whirling into action again: the renewed thick smell of rice rising into the air keened Janie's hunger into a pain. The solution to Beulah's problem suddenly seemed so much simpler than the solution to her own hunger.

'But you could go away in the spring, Beulah. Miles away in your caravan. They couldn't catch you to spring-clean the jail then.'

The solution didn't appeal to Beulah. 'My reputation,' she said in an offended voice, 'my reputation as a scrubber has gone before me. South to the Border country. And as far north as John o' Groats itself. I've spring-cleaned all their jails for them in my time. But this is the last time. The very last time.'

'I'm glad you're never going back to the nick, Beulah.'

Janie was anxious to atone for offending Beulah, and even more anxious to taste the rice. 'Honest I am. You're always so good when you're making your rice.'

Beulah stared intently at her pot as if all prophecy lay inside it, then lifted her head sharply up from the pot and fixed Janie with her bright eyes:

'You're byordinar fond of rice, aren't you, Bronian?' Janie, trapped by the glint of Beulah's eyes and the bright gleam of her earrings, said, staring:

'I do love your rice, Beulah. It's the best and sweetest and hottest rice in the world.'

'I know you love it. Bless you,' Beulah answered, smiling contentedly into her pot. 'And because I know that, something happened to me the day. I was just turning into Birnie's for my half ounce of black twist, when a thought took hold of me there where I stood, on Birnie's doorstep. And a voice said to me, Beulah, you can't have your half of twist this night: You just can't have it. Do you know something? Janie is coming to see you tonight. And she's the bairn after your own heart. And you know how fond she is of a tattie of rice. If you buy your twist you won't have a brown farthing left to buy rice. And Janie won't get the fine taste of it on her tongue this night. So I bought the rice and went without my roll of twist.' Beulah sighed and stirred her pot in silence before she lifted her eyes to Janie. 'And do you know something, Janie? God above and my Mother that's dead knows that I didn't begrudge buying the rice for you. But, all day, my tongue's been like a bit of bark in my mouth for want of a smoke. And it's a queer dwamie feeling I've got in my head. As if I'm going to fall down on my face any minute. And not rise again. I wouldn't be sorry to be not rising again with the dwam that's come over me. I'd be glad. For peace to my bones.'

'Would a smoke take the dwam away from you, Beulah?' Janie asked in a panic.

Beulah considered this: 'It might just help. Might just take the edge of the dwam away from me, like. Give me my second wind back to fight against the terrible things that's killing me. But where in the world is even a pipeful to be had?'

'I'll beg some tobacco for you, Beulah. My Mam's got some. But she's out. But I'll beg some for you.' Janie sprang to her feet. 'I'll beg it from the first man I see. I just won't come back till I've got a pipeful for you.'

Beulah looked swiftly up from her pot as if anticipation had already lessened her dwam.

'Say it's for your Grandmother, Janie, Bronian. Her that's just at death's door. Say it's the last thing she'll need from Man. Or from God either, for that of it.'

Janie flew across the Green, spurred on by Beulah's promises: 'Your rice will be done to a T by the time you get back, dearie. And I'll leave a McPhee's mark on this little friend of yours, if she knocks back one bit of rice that was meant for you.'

Begging, in Janie's eyes, was the one distasteful aspect in the tinker's otherwise perfect way of life. There was no adventure to it, and the only ability it needed was the instinct to pick out the 'right' face. Janie had never to beg for her own needs. There were better ways of satisfying them. The surest way to get a penny was to scour the football grounds for empty beer bottles and sell them back to the beer shops at half rate. A fair bargain, since the bottles hadn't belonged to you in the first place. More remunerating, but less infallible, was to stand outside The Hole In The Wall on Saturday night, bump into the first drunk man you saw, weep loudly, pretending he had bumped into you. That was usually a sure threepence forced into your palm. Sometimes it was sixpence if the man was drunk enough. For her other needs, Janie confined herself to the dustbins in High Street. The paper she scribbled on came from the bin of MacFarlane, Stationer and Bookseller. Her fruit, usually well out of season, from the Greengrocer's bin. Her dolls came from further afield, from the City dump. Being completely unselfish, Janie dragged home most of the bits that furnished her Mother's room from the dump, too. Gertie was truly the sleeping partner, in this business of existing; she shared the profits, while Janie put in most of the capital required. Discrimination, and being on the spot at the right time. Standing here, watching for the 'right' face to come up, had none of the excitement of discovering a new shop and its new, unexplored dustbin.

Meanwhile Gertie was curiously watching the renewed energy with which Beulah stirred her pot.

'You're feeling a bit better now, Beulah?'

'A thochtie better maybe, bairn. A thochtie,' Beulah agreed with some reluctance. 'The thocht of getting a bit of tobacco. Mark you, that's nearly as good as the tobacco itself lying tight in the bowl of my pipe, and myself drawing away fine and regular, with the good rich spit to it. Now, this is what the thocht does.' Beulah relaxed, talking slowly and comfortably in rhythm with her stirring. 'My old Father could break in a colt with the best of them; the Williamsons, the Robertsons, aye, and the Stewarts. Now, when he was lying at death's door at Raffan Market that was. A wild market that. Such as you won't see again. At least one of our breed getting killed at it, and a dozen getting broken heads and needing the hospital or women's care in the tents. That is if we weren't needing care ourselves. For we fought each other too, you see. God above we did. Nothing personal in it. Nothing at all. Each just for the sake of sticking up for her own man. At the end of the night we were so muddled up that we fought both friend and foe alike. And no offence taken when it was all over. None. We'd bid each other God speed. Tell each other of the best farms for a "touch" on the road. Roll away in our wagons and forget everything till a year passed and Raffan Market came around again. Then we'd suddenly remember what this cove had called us last year, or the names this manashe had spat at us the year before. And, God bless you, before we knew what had happened, we were in the middle of another fight. But it was all just part of Raffan Market, the fights were. And the thing you've got for Raffan Market now is a poor thing at its best. No murders. No broken heads. Not a Man Jack in it that does more than commit a breach of peace. A poor thing compared to the Raffan Market I knew.'

'But what about your old Father, Beulah? Him that started the story? Him that was lying at death's door?' Gertie asked, eager for Beulah to go on with her story.

'Oh, him is it?' Beulah was not to be distracted from her vision of bygone Raffan Markets. 'He died in his bed, that's all. The only McPhee for ninety years to disgrace us by dying in his bed. That was at Raffan Market too.' Beulah stared into her pot again as if seeing within it all the Raffan Markets she had ever known. 'Mind you, he was a smart man, my father. None his marrow when it came to making an old mare look as young and lifey as a two-year-old, tarring its grey hairs, till the rains came or the heat of the sun came and the tar melted leaving the grey hairs and the bald patches for even the blind to see. But of course he'd sold the horse by that time, so it was imagination that made us laugh when the sun came, at the thought of the gaje who had bought the horse. Oh, and he could blow a thin horse up too. Simple enough to do that. But you've got to sell the horse quick. Before it does its natural function, and blows out all you've stuffed its behind with. But that's another tale.'

'I've got tobacco for you, Beulah,' Janie shouted from the

distance. 'I told you I'd get some for you. Look, there's more than a pipeful here.'

Beulah sniffed the tobacco suspiciously, 'Scented dirt. Too fine altogether,' she said, rubbing it between her fingers. 'It hasn't got the body in it to lie dour and dark in my pipe. This dirt will blaze up like shavings.'

'A gentleman gave it to me,' Janie protested, 'with a hat on and gloves and everything, a real barrie gaje he was,' she emphasised in Beulah's own language, proud of her knowledge of it. 'And I had an awful job to get it from him at all. I'd to tell him my name and address and everything.'

'And did you?' Beulah looked up sharply. 'Your real name?'

'Yes,' Janie answered, 'I haven't got another name.'

'You could have given yourself another name,' Beulah grumbled. 'Folk that know you don't need to ask your name. And them that don't know you have no right to ask it. Mind on that and you'll walk safe. It wouldn't have been one of "them", would it?' Beulah asked in a furtive whisper.

Janie cast her mind's eye over 'them'. 'No. No, Beulah, it wasn't one of "them". This was a big gentleman. The Cruelty Man's wee with a moustache, I know him. And it wasn't the School Board Man, he's got a uniform. And the Bobbies have got uniforms. It wasn't any of them.'

'I'm not so sure.' Beulah was unappeased.

' "They" dress up different to catch folk out. Did you tell him it was for your Grandmother?'

'Yes. He asked her name. I gave your name, because my Grandmother doesn't smoke. She just hates pipes. Even my Mam has to hide her pipe in the top of her stocking when we go to see Grandmother. He took it all down in a wee book.'

A sudden fury took hold of Beulah. Her wooden spoon clattered into the pot.

'In the name of God. The Sheriff will have me up in front of him for aiding and abetting. Thirty days I'll get this time. Haven't you got a Grandmother of your own, without taking the McPhee name in vain. I wouldn't spit on the breed of you, bairn. What about your own Grandmother's name for the gaje's book?'

'I couldn't give her name.' Janie was frightened by the anger in Beulah's voice. 'I just couldn't give my Grandmother's name. She doesn't smoke. And she's a lady, you see.'

'A *lady* is it?' Beulah's face closed nearer till it almost touched Janie's own face. 'So it's Grandmother is a lady? But the McPhee has to feed it. Highland pride and scab and hunger!' A harsh quality had entered Beulah's voice. 'The lady Grandmother doesn't give you rice, does she? No. No fear of that.'

Janie's fear left her, she was filled with an incomprehensible anger against Beulah. 'My Grandmother gives me soup. She gives me it in a blue bowl with roses round it. And a spoon that shines like anything. My face looks twice as fat when I look at it in her shining spoon. When we have pudding we get another clean spoon. She would give me rice too, if I stayed with her. But it's too far away for me to stay with her. I don't know her address, but I know the road to her house. It's away in the country. In Grandmother's country.'

'We would have got some rice too,' Gertie grumbled, when herself and Janie were safely away from Beulah's curses. 'We'd have got it if you hadn't said that your Grandmother's a lady. That made Beulah awful mad. Besides,' Gertie went on suspiciously, 'it's a funny thing, Janie, I've never once seen your Grandmother. She never comes to the Lane, does she now?'

'No. And do you know why she doesn't come, Gertie, she doesn't like the smell of cats. She lives in a red house on top of a hill. It shines like anything. I'm glad she doesn't come to the Lane to see us. Someday I'll ask her just to pass by the causeway. I'll ask her hard to do that. Just so that you can see she is real. She'll be wearing a black hat with a purple feather, and she carries a stick with a gold handle. And she's got a dog called Bruce. You'll see all that when my Grandmother comes.'

'Do you know something, Janie?' Gertie asked, anxious to make up for her unbelief. 'That old bitch Beulah wasn't in a dwam at all. She just wasn't ill at all. Janie, she winked to me after you'd gone to beg tobacco for her.'

Janie knew that now. And with the knowing, also knew that she didn't want to be a real tinker any more.

CHAPTER FIVE

THIS was the time to catch the Lane unawares. This early hour. Before day took over. The Lane still slept. Its grey face relaxed; a fine mist drifting up through the causeway mellowed its gaunt tenements. Soon the dustman's cart would clang and alarm the Lane into wakefulness, but now only furtive cats padded across its cobblestones.

Leaning from the high window at 285, Janie watched it all. Excitement had banished her sleep. More, her frock and her liberty bodice, washed in the dying minutes of the previous night, hung over the window-sill to dry. It wasn't the first time that Janie's sole wardrobe had fallen from this drying place on the window-sill into the gutter below. This was one time when no such risk could be taken. Today she was going to visit her Grandmother.

The rarity of a visit to Grandmother magnified it into a high occasion. And although such visits never lasted longer than a day, that one day encompassed so much that was strange to the Lane, that Janie looked on it with the apprehensive sense of seeing it for the last time.

Her liberty bodice still felt damp. That didn't worry her,

44

it could dry when it was on her, and nobody saw your liberty bodice anyhow. And, if the worst came to the worst, her print frock would dry in front of the gas-ring.

The first of the workers went clattering past now; then the bairns would follow with their pillowslips, in a great rush to Riley's back door to get the first chance of yesterday's loaves. Janie watched impatiently for a sight of Gertie. Like a genie, fretting to get out of his bottle to work his magic. It seemed so long in coming, that moment for shouting: 'I'm off to see my Grandmother today, Gertie. Didn't I tell you last night that she was real?'

Last night Janie had arrived home, after her encounter with Beulah, to find her Mother home before her, sitting wiggling her toes and silently watching them wiggle; this was one of her Mother's 'thinking' attitudes, so it wasn't really a surprise to Janie when her Mother stopped wiggling and announced abruptly: 'I was thinking we'd go to see Grandmother the morn. A day away will do us both good. You'd better get your clothes off and nip into your bed, till I give them a wash through. You ought to have been home long since. Where did you get to till this time of night?'

'Just down to the Green. To Beulah's caravan.'

'Not one word out of your head to your Grandmother the morn, about Beulah,' Liza warned.

'God only knows what she'd think about you hobnobbing with all the tinkers in the town.'

'Not a word, Mam,' Janie agreed, struggling out of her bodice and beginning to share her Mother's anxiety over the visit. 'There's only one button on my bodice. I always think Grandmother can see right through my frock to the lost buttons on my bodice.'

'Hardly,' Liza laughed. 'Your Grandmother can see far, and deeper than most, but she just can't see through your frock. I'll stitch your bodice together when it's on you, tomorrow.'

The bairns were running down the Lane now. Gertie stopped under the window. 'Coming, Janie? Betsy's just got back from Riley's with loads of stale cakes with pink ice on them. We won't get none if we don't hurry.'

'I can't.' Loads of stale cakes with pink ice on them momentarily clouded Janie's other prospect. 'I can't, Gertie. I'm standing here mother naked. All my clothes are washed.'

'What are they all washed for?' Gertie shouted up curiously.

'Because I'm going to see my Grandmother today. That's what. If it's appletime at Grandmother's, I'll bring you back loads. There's hundreds of apple-trees.'

'Come away from that window,' Liza grumbled from the bed. 'And pull it down, you're letting the draught in and I'm freezing. What time is it?'

'Gone seven. The mill hooter went a while back. It'll soon be time to go to Grandmother's.'

'What like's the weather? If it promises rain, we'd maybe better bide at home,' Liza said, beginning to regret the necessity of getting up so early.

'It's not raining, Mam.' Janie was alarmed. 'There's a mist. It's going to be a fine day. And you promised we'd go.'

'Oh, all right. Fling over my corsets. They're under the chair somewhere.' Anger crept into Liza's voice. 'And my stockings, there! On the fender. It's the damned last time I'll promise anything.'

Janie searched unbidden for her Mother's shoes and skirt, quietly, wordlessly. In moments like these it just took one word, one false move to wreck a promise.

The real business of going to see Grandmother had begun. Liza sat on a corner of the table counting the money in her purse. Janie, watching her, prayed silently: Let there be enough money for two train tickets. Please let there be enough money for the two of us. If not, I'll have to hide under the carriage seat again and I'm afraid that the Ticket Man will catch me one day.

'There's enough for my ticket,' Liza said. 'You'll just have to hide under the seat. Or, maybe,' she considered, looking out of the window, 'maybe we could walk there, and have enough for both our train fares back.'

Janie seized the alternative, before her Mother could change her mind.

'That's a good idea, Mam. If we walked we'd have enough for your tobacco then. You can smoke all the way to Grandmother, and sing *Rolling Home To Bonnie Scotland* all the way back in the train without having to worry about the Ticket Man.'

'We'd better get on our road then,' Liza agreed, still looking out of the window. 'It's a sea mist that's in it. Mist from the hill brings grist to the mill. But mist from the sea brings honey to the bee.'

It was spring along the road to Grandmother's country. Not the dusty, daffodiled, yellow spring that Janie glimpsed on the barrows in High Street, but a spring that was sharp and white. Star of Bethlehem flowers clustered together in groups, like milestones flashing along the way. Hawthorn wound itself in thorny whiteness, smelling like heart-break, if heart-break could smell. The great fir wood of Laveroch shadowed the road; yellow primroses and blue vetch lost their own colour in its shadow, pale, like the wood's own wild, white anemones drifting down the banks.

'This is Grandfather's wood, isn't it, Mam?' Janie knew the answer, but wanted to hear it all again.

'Aye. Every inch of it,' Liza said, wanting to tell it all again. 'There's no one so acquaint with a tree as your Grandfather. He can tell if it's in good heart just by listening to it. When I was little, I used to think he could speak to the trees.'

'He never speaks to me,' Janie remembered. 'Not once ever. He just looks at me.'

'That's his way,' Liza said casually. 'He seldom spoke to us as children. And we never spoke to him until we were spoken to.'

'Was he a wild man, then?' Janie asked, thinking it very possible that he was.

'No. Your Grandfather never lifted his hand or voice to any of us in anger in his life. It was never necessary. A look from him was enough.'

'Was Grandmother afraid of a look?'

'Never her.' Liza laughed. 'Your Grandmother could manage him. She always knew the right moment to speak. That was all that was to it. And Grandmother knew it.'

'I like Grandmother best,' Janie said decidedly. 'Did you like her best when you was little, Mam?'

'No, Janie. I was Grandfather's favourite. He tried not to show it. But you just always know when you're somebody's favourite. I was always Miss MacVean to Grandfather. 'Where's Miss MacVean?' he'd shout, when he led the men and horses home. He'd lift me up beside him and I'd ride home on the first horse as proud as anything. We'll take the short cut through the wood now,' Liza concluded abruptly. 'Mind your feet jumping that ditch.'

Janie wondered at her Mother's easy intimacy with this country; her quick recognition of the flowers in the wood-workers' gardens, with names unheard of in the Lane; Snow in Summer, Dead Man's Bells, Love in a Mist, Thyme, yellow St John's Wort, pink-starred bramble-blossom. 'There's going to be a good crop of brambles the year.' Liza cast an experienced eye over them. 'We'll need to come for a day in autumn for the bramble picking.' They wouldn't of course. But Janie had learned to enjoy the prospect more than the reality.

The wood thickened and dimmed. Great patches of wild hyacinths waved darkly blue. The sky was crowded out. Moss sprang beneath their feet, and the dust of it rose like thin smoke. The foosty guff of an ancient wood drifted over and past in great imprisoning waves. The Hangman's Tree loomed high in this dark heart of things. 'Tell me all about it again, Mam,' Janie pleaded, fearful but fascinated.

Liza, in one of her rare, enchanting moods, willingly complied:

> There was a man that wadna' hang
> Three times upon a tree.
> Three times they strung him up aloft
> But never hang wad he.

'Why couldn't they hang the man, Mam?' Janie kept the question till well away from the darkness of the Hangman's Tree.

'I'm not sure.' Liza considered carefully. 'It may be, you know, that he was so bad a man that even the Devil didn't want him.'

But there were others, less wicked, who had hanged on the gallows tree. MacPherson was one. The fiddler. 'And anyone that had music as deep as he had couldn't be all that bad, with the exception of your Father of course, Janie. And there was none badder than him.' Burns told of how MacPherson had gone to the Tree. You could hear MacPherson's fiddle in the way Burns told of it:

> Sae rantingly, sae wantonly, sae dauntingly
> Gaed he.

He played a spring and danced it round,
Beneath the Gallow Tree.

Those rare moods of communication between Janie and her Mother more than made up for the other things lacking in their relationship. And yet, if these moments had never existed, it would have been so much easier for Janie in the years to come.

Meanwhile the path through the wood widened. The sky pierced its way through the trees again; hyacinths blazed truly blue. And the light of the world outside the wood surprised the eye with momentary blindness. Primroses took on their own colour again, and vetch shouted in masses along the bank.

Grandmother's house stood high and red as Janie had remembered it. Where the sky met the fields marked the end of the world. But Grandmother's house stood safely in the centre, looking down over all the world. And all the world looked up and saw Grandmother's house.

'We're nearly there,' Liza warned, tucking her pipe down the leg of her stocking. 'That's the men yoking their horses. Thank goodness, Grandfather's had his dinner.'

'If he's had dinner there might be none left for us,' Janie said, alarmed at this prospect.

'There'll be plenty left for us in the pot,' Liza assured her, 'only, it's easier. Grandfather won't go without his dinner now.'

'Why would Grandfather have to go without his dinner?' Janie asked curiously. 'If there's plenty in the pot.'

'Not from necessity,' Liza answered. 'From choice just. Once anyone does anything wrong to Grandfather, he never sits down at table nor breaks bread with them again.'

'We didn't do anything wrong to Grandfather,' Janie protested. 'I've never even spoken to that man.'

'He thinks we did.'

'Grandmother takes her tea with us then?'

'Grandmother sees things differently. If she didn't, Janie, I can assure you we wouldn't be walking up her roadway this day.'

The last steps to Grandmother were harried with last-minute warnings: 'Mind now! Say please and thank you, Janie. Don't blow on your broth if it's too hot. Just have patience till it cools. And say "No, thank you" if Grandmother offers you a second helping. Don't be gorging into you as if you hadn't seen food for days. And giving me a red face. And give your nose a good blow. And not sniff, sniff, sniff into your bowl all the time. And come here till I give your face a dicht. It always gets as black as the Earl of Hell's waistcoat.'

The last and most important warning came more slowly and more clearly: 'And, for the love of God, Janie, don't be asking to look inside your Aunt Morag's box.'

'It isn't a box,' Janie pointed out. 'It's a treasure chest, Mam. Aunt Morag's got beads and hankies and pencils and scent and books. And she never gives me one of them.'

The white flowers were coming out on the Butcher's Broom. Liza stood amongst them, explaining carefully: 'Your Aunt Morag is a poor thing. She hasn't got a treasure chest at all. She's got a box. That's all it is, a brown box. And all the things she has inside it are just things her brothers and sisters gave her, because they're sorry for her. And mind, don't you go asking her to open that box. Because you won't get anything out of it.'

'She's just greedy then,' Janie concluded, pushing her way through Butcher's Broom, with its faint, bitter smell. 'And I hate my Aunt Morag.'

'She's a poor thing,' Liza said in her voice that you never argued with. 'And don't you forget that.'

It was dim in Grandmother's kitchen. The uncles' long, sprawling legs broke up the pattern of her red stone floor. Grandfather sat in his corner chair, his face hidden behind a newspaper. Aunt Morag in her wheelchair, sat staring out of the window, not turning her head to look upon the visitors.

The first dimness passed. The eyes sought out familiar brightness; the glinting brass-work on Aunt Morag's treasure chest, the shining top of Grandmother's bellows; the gleaming face of the wall clock, ticking away the timelessness of this wait on the threshold.

'You've got here, then?' Grandmother's voice startled the uncles' long legs into their right places; the floor lay clear and red and patterned. Aunt Morag turned her head to stare on the visitors and looked away out of the window again. Grandfather stayed hidden behind his paper, and Grandmother bustled into a noise. 'Sit you both down then. You'll be tired after your long travel.' Her black apron rustled, so stiffly starched that it could have stood on the floor by itself without Grandmother being inside it at all. Liza found her voice and talked through the new, comforting noise.

'We thought we'd be better of a day away. A neighbour of ours died last week. Sudden kind. Janie and herself were very thick. And, to tell the truth, I felt a bit lost myself. We were so used to her.'

'Poor soul,' Grandmother said. 'What would have ailed her like?'

'Nobody was rightly sure,' Liza answered. 'Some said this and others said that, but no one was sure.'

It's Mysie Walsh Mam's telling of, Janie realised with surprise. But it wasn't like that at all, she thought excitedly. I could tell Grandmother all about it and what it was like. Something in the atmosphere prevented Janie from doing so; words that you volunteered got lost here, somehow, drifted up out of you, foundered in the air, and hurried back to the safety of your secret self again. Perhaps it all sounded best the way her Mother was telling it. Unreal. Just as the Lane and Mysie Walsh seemed unreal and far away in this kitchen.

'No man knows his dying hour,' Grandmother said, never dreaming that Mysie Walsh had chosen her own hour. 'And that's a true mercy. I'll away to the milk house for a bowl of buttermilk for the quean, it'll put body in her, till the broth comes to the boil again.'

Grandmother took away with her the large safety she had thrown over the kitchen:

'She's no' at her school the day, then?' Uncle Hugh spoke for the first time.

'You can see that she's no',' Liza answered shortly.

'She'll never be a scholar.' Grandfather's paper rustled in sharp agreement with Uncle Hugh. But Grandmother had returned, filling the kitchen with her tall self, and darkening the sun each time she passed the window.

'Come in about to the table now.' And soon Grandmother was throwing all Liza's careful forewarnings to the wind: 'Sup up now, Janie. Just you blow on your broth if it's a bit on the hot side. There's plenty more where that came from. Sup up, now. Never mind your Mother nudging you under the table there. Your belly maun be gey teem after your travel.' Grandmother's voice rose roughly and comfortably. Soon Grandfather and the uncles would go out to Laveroch Wood with their horses, leaving a legacy of freedom behind them. Freedom to explore the milk house, dark and cool, with its great stone slabs, its bowls of yellow cream, basins of brown hens' eggs and green ducks' eggs, its pale, shining rhubarb laid out on green leaves; its smell of an imprisoned summer, grass and clover and cold well water.

Freedom to peep into the 'best' room, curtained against the light of day, its willow-pattern plates behind doors of glass, its chairs standing as if they had stood so for a hundred years. The piano that set up a quivering wail of protest when you ever so quietly pressed one of its yellow keys, and all the whiskered men and ringleted ladies on the photographs above stared down in silent reproach. 'When Grandmother first got the piano,' Liza once told Janie, 'she was so excited about it till Grandfather and the men came home at night to carry it into the house. She sat and played it under the trees; all the wood-workers got great fun out of that, but Grandmother didn't care, and she sat and played all afternoon. We children thought the world had come to an end, it was such an odd thing for Grandmother to do. She was always so tall and strict and busy.'

Janie loved this picture of her Grandmother. Her piano had known the wood once and had made music for it. Now the wood was shut out with great, green curtains, and the piano had grown grumbling and old.

The uncles looked as if they would sit forever, till Grandmother got her broom and furiously swept amongst their feet. Her busyness shamed the long men into going. Their going stirred up the quick smell of fir resin and loam. For a moment the kitchen might have been Laveroch Wood itself.

'I'm away to throw the hens some corn,' Grandmother said casually. 'I'll maybe have a look in bye the black pig too. Anybody like to come?'

Janie jumped at the invitation. Inside the house Grandmother was old and very wise, knowing the best cure for this ailment, and the worst weather for that ailment. Knowing what Paul had said to the Corinthians. And what someone ought to say very soon to that Geordie Scobie for underpaying country folk and overcharging town folk for their eggs. Outside the house was a different matter altogether. No ailments existed round the garden, out by the steading or in the wood. No one cared what Paul had said to the

Corinthians. According to Grandmother when she got outside, Paul had once said something quite different:

> Paul said and Peter said
> And all the saints alive and dead
> Swore she had the sweetest head,
> Bonnie, bonnie Bride of the yellow, yellow hair.

Grandmother knew that the secret of her other self was safe
in the keeping of the black pig and Janie. Neither of them
thought it in any way odd for Grandmother to kilt up her
apron and trip sedately round the sty to her own singing:

> And she slept for a hundred years,
> Years, years.
> And she slept for a hundred years,
> A hundred years.
> Till Prince Charming came and kissed her
> Long ago.

They stepped easily into this other world, the child and
the Grandmother. Pondering over a new word for meadow.
Muskoday. Musk in the garden now. And small, yellow
musk roses waiting to come in summer. High afternoon, the
stable doors open, the stables empty. No great, black wood
horses there now, to flick their tails, and stamp their feet,
and roll their wild and searching eyes round a visitor. The
whitewashed byre, dark stone drinking troughs. An intruding hen whirred out of her nest in the manger, cackling her
resentment, and rousing the sleeping afternoon. 'We'll go in
bye now,' Grandmother said, 'I'll make a baking of scones
for our tea. You can have a hot one with milk. Hot scones
are ill for the belly they say, but I never died of eating one

yet. And, for an ill thing, a hot scone's got an unco fine taste.'

The bellows roared the fire into redness. Grandmother, huge and hurried in her white baking apron, had become old and wise again. Aunt Morag, still and quiet by the window, shaded her face with her thin hands and lifted her damp hair from her forehead. Only her eyes had life in them. Blue. Like the sharp blue flames that shot up through the fire, when Grandmother threw salt in it to guard against ill-luck. The firelight glimmered along the brass work on Aunt Morag's treasure chest.

'Can I see all your treasures again, Aunt Morag?' Grandmother coughed harshly through Janie's sudden request. Liza creaked in her chair, and mentioned some flower that Janie had yet to see. 'Please, Aunt Morag, just one more look.'

Aunt Morag smiled her first, small smile. Her eyes became more brightly blue, her great box creaked open, lovingly and separately she took out its contents, holding them up against the light of the sun. Beads that flashed. Scent bottles blue and green and yellow, their scent remaining forever secret. Books with vivid jackets, pencils, and the blue bird brooch with pearls flashing on its wings. Soon the table was as crowded and coloured as the stalls in the Green. 'I only want the blue bird brooch,' Janie thought, staring at them all. 'Just the blue bird brooch, but if I don't get that, I'd like anything else at all.'

'Get that litter off the table, Morag,' Grandmother commanded, roughly and fiercely. 'I want to get the tea set up.' Janie watched Aunt Morag return each treasure to its own corner of the box, her face pink, her eyes triumphant. The lid clanged down with ominous finality. And Janie's hopes clanged with it. Aunt Morag looked white once more, her hair damper than ever, and her eyes sought and held the window again.

Grandmother's voice sounded fiercer than ever: 'Heaven only knows why you keep tormenting yourself with that box, bairn. You know fine there's nothing in it to spare for you. Or for anyone else. Come on and see if Grandmother's got something for you. And it's high time you were getting out of the sun for a while, Morag, you're taking up all the light.'

Grandmother wheeled Aunt Morag into a corner, the geraniums stood revealed now, on the white window-sill, the light caught and danced across the row of Aunt Morag's medicine bottles. Janie turned and followed Grandmother, not even worried about the sharp, sly kick Liza gave her in passing. Aunt Morag was in disgrace. And Janie was glad.

'Haste ye back now, soon,' Grandmother's voice came to them all the way past Butcher's Broom. Liza lit up her pipe with a great sigh of relief. It was good to be going back to the Lane again. Grandmother's country was frightening in the dusk. Wheeling curlews cried out in their loneliness. Wood cushats grumbled in their sleep, flapping crows screamed in last angers. Janie ran on in front to have a Think, and having thought, relayed it all to Liza:

'Mam, I wish the man that owns Woolworth's would give me the biggest sack in the world, and let me choose all the things I wanted off his counters. I'd fill the sack as full as anything. With beads and books and scent and things. I'd show every one of them to Aunt Morag. Then I'd put them all back in my sack again and not give her one thing. That's an awful good Think, isn't it?'

Liza took the pipe from her mouth and stared at Janie. 'That's just about the wickedest Think I've ever heard tell of,' she said. 'Just the wickedest. If Grandmother knew you'd think like that, she'd never give you eggs and butter and jam to take home with you again.'

'But that's what Aunt Morag does to me,' Janie insisted.

'Nothing of the kind, Janie,' Liza said with finality. 'Your Aunt Morag's a chronic invalid. Don't you forget that.' Liza put her pipe in her mouth again, the smell of it rose homely and comfortingly in the air. The lights of Kinloch Station twinkled in the distance. Janie was glad there was enough money to take the train home.

CHAPTER SIX

THE morning after the visit to Grandmother possessed no time in its own right. It became this time yesterday on the road to Grandmother's house, or this time tomorrow when I'm back at school, and my name's on the register again. It became any time at all, except its immediate, worrying self.

'Janie had a bad cold and couldn't come to school,' Liza scribbled hurriedly. That this was a lie didn't worry Janie. That Teacher would know it was a lie worried her exceedingly.

'Hurry up, Janie. You'll be late today, as well as absent yesterday.' Liza, too, had morning after regrets. 'Take this rhubarb in bye to Betsy in your passing. We haven't got the right pot for it. Get a move on. It's nearly ten to nine. And don't be standing there sniffing at the rhubarb. It hasn't got any smell.'

But it had. A smell of yesterday. Of Grandmother's milk house. A small, intangible smell of far-off safety.

The line to Teacher lay on a corner of her table. Janie kept her eyes fixed on *High Summer*, the huge painting on the opposite wall. Staring at it with the desperate single-mindedness of shutting out all other sights. Especially the line to Teacher on the corner of the table. Any moment now, Miss Sim would say:

'Janie MacVean, take this line to the Headmaster.'

High Summer, blazing down from the wall, withheld the moment in a great maze of greenery.

A voice more ominous than the voice of Miss Sim broke through *High Summer*. Janie saw the startling figure of Nurse Conduit in the doorway, her list of Names To Be Examined in her hand.

Janie's first impulse was to shoot her hand up in the air: 'Please, Miss Sim, may I leave the room?' And rush through the door and away out of the schoolgates altogether. But that means of escape from Nurse would have been too obvious. It wouldn't have worked.

Other means of escape crowded swiftly in on Janie. It wasn't Nurse Conduit who stood in the doorway at all. It was Mr Thompson, the Headmaster, smiling and hurried. 'Excuse me, Miss Sim,' he said, 'but I would like to speak to my daughter for a moment, if you don't mind.'

'Certainly, Mr Thompson,' Miss Sim replied, all pink and puzzled. 'Children, the Headmaster would like to speak to his daughter. Where is she?'

Everybody got a great surprise to discover that Janie was really the Headmaster's daughter all the time. Especially Gertie. She just stared with her mouth open when Mr Thompson put his arm round Janie's shoulder and led her away, saying very loudly: 'Janie, my dear.'

Now it was Grandmother, dressed in her Sunday clothes, who strode through the doorway, tut, tut, tutting Nurse and Miss Sim out of the way and making straight for Janie's desk, singing as she had sometimes sang in the black pig-sty:

Off we'll go to London Town,
Yo Ho, my lads. Yo Ho, my lads.
We'll see the King wi' the golden crown,
Yo Ho, my lads. Yo Ho, my lads.

Not knowing that this was just Grandmother's way, everybody in the class would think that Grandmother was really going to see the King and taking Janie with her. In her Sunday clothes Grandmother looked as if she could go anywhere at all.

'Janie MacVean.' It was Nurse Conduit's voice that dispelled all images of escape. At least, thought Janie, as she walked forward to join the group of children on the floor, my frock's still clean from yesterday. So is my bodice. And I haven't got knickers to worry about. But I've still got nits in my hair. Nurse Conduit will be sure to find them. She always bone-combs my hair so well. She just flicks her fingers through other folks' heads. Lucky other folk, Janie thought, as she watched Connie Morne and Isla Skea and Shona Coolin, whispering and laughing easily together, enjoying Nurse's visit as a break in lessons. Shona Coolin, that's a lovely name for such a horror to have. She never once lends me her rubber. My name's Shona too. My real name. Only it's Grandmother's name as well. But Grandfather will never let us use it. So I've got to be called Janie instead. It's the English name for mine. Janie. A terrible name.

'Gertie Latham.' Nurse Conduit's voice brought a gleam of comfort. Janie wouldn't, now, be de-loused alone. More, they both had the secret of 'nits' to keep together from the rest of the children.

'It isn't fair,' Janie confided to Gertie later, 'everybody in the class must know that we've got nits. That stuff Nurse put on our heads smells terrible. It makes my head itch all over. And I think I'll kill that Connie Morne if she goes on sniffing the smell out loud and laughing and whispering about us.'

It was a mystifying day. Nurse hadn't given Janie a note to take home to her Mother. 'And that's a funny thing, Gertie. Because you've got one. And I always get one too.'

Nor was any word spoken about the line for being absent. Not even by the Headmaster when he came into the class-room. He seemed quite unaware of the existence of his 'daughter'. The news he brought was momentous.

'You all belong to a city with the oldest and loveliest Cathedral in Scotland. I'd like to discover just how much you all know about the subject. To the pupil who writes the best essay on the Cathedral, I'm going to award a prize of one shilling. Find out all you can about it. Better still, go down to see it, and tomorrow you'll write your essays.'

'That bob's mine for certain,' Janie informed Gertie, without conceit. 'My Mam knows everything about history, if I can just catch her in the mood for telling.'

Liza *was* in the mood for telling. 'We're off to see some old friends of ours. Quiet folk down bye,' she said cryptically to Poll, as herself and Janie walked through the causeway. 'You see, the dead that lie in the Cathedral are awful quiet folk, Janie,' she explained, twinkling, when they were out of Poll's hearing. 'But of course we don't tell Poll that, we just leave her guessing.'

Janie had often seen the Cathedral looming darkly through the trees. It stood close by the Green. In summer charabancs drew up in front of it. Flower-frocked women stared at it from beneath large hats, clicked their cameras, and made their way to the fair on the Green. Old women of the city drowsed beneath the Cathedral's trees. They knew every inch of the Green and every aspect of the Cathedral, and the time for staring at both was over. Old men pottered and bent amongst the Cathedral's tombstones, then they too sheltered and slept beneath its trees. In Janie's mind the Cathedral was a resting place for the old, and a thing of curiosity for the stranger. Until now. Until Liza gave it a vivid, personal life of its own, and Janie began to see it through her Mother's most curious eyes.

'The Wolf of Badenoch, swooping down from the high hills behind Forres. The clang of his horses' hoofs ringing on the cobbles, wakening the sleeping townsfolk and sending them scurrying out into the streets, curious and frightened. Their curiosity diminished but their fear heightened when they saw the flames rise red and high from the airt of the Cathedral. The whole town was aglow, Janie. Everybody in the world must have known where our town lay, with the red sky of fire that was above it. Quiet monks in brown cassocks chanting their queer, Latin words on this very spot, maybe. Hearing the nearing noise of the Wolf and his men. But like as not the monks had gone on singing till they came to the end of their song. The burning torches, the flash of skean dhus, the cries of the wounded, an old monk hiding beneath a tree, watching the Cathedral blacken and crumble and fall all round him, knowing that it would be built again, but he would be too old to have part in it again. And unco sad in heart at the knowing. The plunder over, the destruction done, the Wolf of Badenoch clattering out of the town again. His loot lighting up the darkness; golden chalices and silver crucifixes. Townsfolk lurking in the shadows, crossing themselves at the devilish departure of holy things. And, mind you, Janie, I've not got muckle meed for Popish things. But it was the first, old faith of our land. Though your Grandfather will never allow mention of that. His religion lay in a chield by name of John Knox. Him that put the clampers down on Mary Queen of Scots. She was Queen of Bonnie France. But that's a story for some other time. And, Papes or no Papes, the monks were fine craftsmen. You've only got to look at this Cathedral to see the truth of that. They gave our Lane its name too. Our Lady's Lane. They must have walked through it often, and been byordinar fond of it, to give it a name like that. You wouldn't think it to see the Lane now. But maybe it was all different four hundred years ago.'

'It's different sometimes now,' Janie remembered. 'But you've got to see it early in the morning, when it's all misty, to catch the difference.'

'Just one last thing,' Liza said, as they made their way out of the Cathedral, through the tombstones. 'It's hard to tell whether the Bishops and Archbishops all lying here were good men or bad, because all that's told about them is written in Latin. But here's a stone that I like. Everybody can understand it. Listen to it, Janie:

> Here lies Martin Elginbrod,
> Have mercy on my soul, Lord God,
> As I would have, were I Lord God,
> And You but Martin Elginbrod

A fine man that,' Liza concluded, closing the gate of the Cathedral behind them. 'And mind you, Janie, hurry home with my shilling for the essay the morn.'

'There was a man looking for you, Liza,' Poll greeted them, when they arrived back at the Lane. 'I didn't see him myself, but wee Lil here was speaking to him. He came back and fore three times.'

'It was the Cruelty Man,' wee Lil broke in, 'asking me questions about you and Janie, there. But I'm not the one to meddle with my neighbours' affairs. He got small change out of me,' Lil ended quickly, frightened by the sudden tallness and glint that had come over Liza.

'He couldn't get much out of you, could he, Lil?' Liza burned Lil up in a look. 'Nor from you either, Poll.' Her anger extended itself to Poll. 'Because none of you know anything about Janie and me. Do you, now? Except, of course, the kind of things that would interest the Cruelty. And I bet you let him have the lot. I bet you did. You'd have licked his boots all right, and would have licked his arse too, if your tongue had been a bit longer.'

Liza strode up to 285, declining Janie's company. 'You run and play yourself for a while.'

'She's a dark horse that, and no mistake,' Poll condoled with wee Lil. 'I can't make her out at all. But you'll see, she won't get herself out of his lot. She's lost that Janie. It'll be a Home for her. Or my name's not Poll Pyke.'

'And the bairn would be better in a Home,' wee Lil agreed. 'She'd be sure of a bite and a sup. And God only knows there can be no example for a bairn up at 285. There's no' much of a life for any bairn in the Lane, if it comes to that.'

If Janie had heard Lil's sentiments she would have been entirely out of agreement with them. The Lane was home and wonderful. And even more home and more wonderful in moments like these, when it seemed at stake. A long line of men drifted out of the Labour Exchange, throwing their usual sallies over to the women in the causeway: 'Where's your Ramsay MacDonald now, Poll?'

'Up my clothes,' Poll flung back in kindred mood.

'By God, he'll get fair lost there, then, Poll.' Their rising laughter covered Janie's apprehension. A group of bairns, showing off, chanted their ball game on the cobbles:

> One, two, three a-leerie,
> Four, five, six a-leerie,
> Seven, eight, nine a-leerie,
> Ten a-leerie. Postman!

'I've been looking for you all over, Janie,' Gertie's voice broke through the noises. 'Where did you get to?'

'Down to the Cathedral for the essay,' Janie said quickly, for the essay no longer seemed important. 'I think I'll have to go away to a Home,' she added, partly to shock Gertie, and partly to put her own apprehension into real words. 'Cruelty Man was looking for me. He was up here three times.'

'That's nothing.' Gertie remained disappointingly un-shocked. 'Cruelty Man's often up at our house. He looks through all the blankets, then inside the cupboards, and if he catches you he looks in your head as well. He's never catched me. My Dad bawls him out of it. Come on, Janie, I've something to show you down High Street. There's going to be a ball in the Assembly Rooms. They're all lit up. And there's a new frock in your shop. But the Frock's mine because I saw it first.'

Down High Street took the edge off apprehension. Gertie and Janie 'owned' many of the shops in High Street. Owner-ship of the same being acquired by merely being first to reach and touch a shop window, laying the formal vocal claim: 'My Shop.' Janie's proudest property was a small dress shop, which only displayed one dress at a time, a grown-up, Cinderella creation, at which Janie and Gertie would stare, snub-nosed and appreciative, seeing themselves so adorned in the miraculous, but far-off time of grown-upness. Today, the dress in the window surpassed its predecessors. It was white, glowing and glimmering with silver sequins. Passing girls stopped to look at it, oh-ing and ah-ing in little groups, edging the children away, to get a better look, never dreaming that Janie owned the shop and Gertie owned the white dress because she had seen it first.

Down at the Assembly Rooms, the lights lit up she street, dancers flitted past the windows, sudden whirls of bright colour. The music drifted down to those watching from the street. *When You and I Were Seventeen*. Some of the girls sang the words, some of them waltzed on the pavements to the tune, the policeman edging them away, to let the lawful dancers pass through. A new distraction arrived on the scene. Forty Pockets, with his barrel organ and his monkey in its bright red petticoat. Janie and Gertie, delighted to see him, forsook their hard-won position with its view of the Ball. The music from the barrel organ drowned out the music from the Ball. Back to the land where the skies are so blue. Please give the monkey a penny, too.

'Move along,' the policeman shouted. 'No obstruction here, now. Keep moving, all of you.'

'And don't you follow us,' Gertie threatened some children from a rival lane. 'Because Forty Pockets is more ours than yours. Him and the monkey stays in the next Lane to us.'

'Beat it,' Forty Pockets snarled, unmoved by Gertie's loyalty. 'Don't you two be trailing after me all night.' The monkey stared at them brightly, his red bonnet on one side, his red petticoat hanging on one side too.

'I bet you Forty Pockets beats that poor monkey,' Gertie said as they ran towards the Lane. 'And he smells terrible with all that dirty old coats he's got on. No wonder everybody calls him Forty Pockets.'

Back at the Lane the children bounced their ball to a perpetual chant. A week ago they had skipped to *A Big Ship Came to the Eelie, Ilie O*. Next week they would be running round in rings to *She is the Girl of the Golden City*. But no chant ever overstepped its own mysterious season, and this week it would be a bouncing ball and *One, Two, Three A-Leerie*.

'Can Gertie and me get a game?' Janie asked the owner of

the ball, formally, as strict etiquette in the matter of street games required.

'If you take the last turn,' the ball owner answered, 'because you two joined in last.'

To be a leader in street games required not so much personal ability, as personal possessions. The owner of a ball or a skipping rope invariably got off to a good start in the race for being 'Boss'. Janie had savoured the powers of leadership for brief spells, usually broken by some irate mother: 'You and your bloody Ghost in the well! My Rosanna didn't get a wink of sleep last night.' You had to be very humble when you were not the Boss of a game. The least unwitting word of criticism brought forth the dreaded and irrevocable judgment: 'Out of this game, You. It's my ball.'

There were rare moments, though, needing much self-denial, when you could take the initiative first, and shout: 'I'm not playing. It's just a lousy game.' More, the Boss of a game could always cheat and get away with it, saying that it was a bad turn of the rope or that the ball was thrown too low, too high, too fast or too slow. This you patiently endured for the sake of getting your turn. When your turn was over you could get your own back by deliberately throwing the ball too hard, too fast, too high all at the same time and getting the Boss 'accidentally' but firmly in the place where it hurt her most.

Janie seldom resorted to such brutal methods: she had a more subtle and effective method of dealing with the Boss: 'I know a game. A new one. You don't have to wait your turn, you can all play at once. Who's coming to my game?'

They all came, of course, lured by the promise of an equal share, except the Boss of the previous game. 'And you can't come,' Janie would inform her, becoming as much of a Boss herself, as the Bosses she thought she despised. 'You can't come, because this is *my* game.'

When your turn was last, as Janie's turn was now, no such tactics were practicable. The game might end long before your turn came, and then, of course, it wouldn't matter. On the other hand if the game didn't end, you didn't want to ruin your chance of a turn. In those eternities of being 'last' Janie stared at the walls of the causeway and at the cobbles round her feet so long and hard that, in after years, she could still recall the patterns of cracks on the walls and the shapes of the cobble-stones in the Lane. Meantime, the voices of the Lane's women drifted through and over the chant of the ball game.

'I can tell you one thing,' the Duchess was affirming, 'and I'll tell you it for nothing. If this strike goes on, they won't be sitting so cooshy on their thrones. I heard Nelly's Bert vow just the other day that he'd tear Royalty to bits with his own two bare hands. And you know what Bert's like when he's in a paddy. And he's been in a paddy all right since the tweed mills had to close down. What's more, he's off now on the hunger march to London.'

'You can never tell what will happen,' Poll marvelled, as if Nelly's Bert might both end the strike and 'do' the Royal family the moment he arrived in London. 'If the mines don't start up by winter, we'll all die off like flies.'

'It's bad enough,' the Duchess agreed, 'when you haven't got the price of a bag of cinders, but it's even worse when there's no cinders to be got, even though you haven't the price of them. It's them not being there that gets you down.'

'My Hugh's old man won't last through another winter,' Poll cheered up. 'I can see him failing under my eyes. Mind you, he's had a good innings. And I'm not going to pretend I'm sorry he's going. There'll be more room left for the rest of us. I've put up with a lot from the old cove. But it's his spitting and slavering all over that I just can't abide. It's all on account of his catarrh. But still, you forget that when you've got to clean up after him.'

'Do you know something?' the Duchess broke in, with the eagerness of discovery. 'It's just a week tomorrow since Mysie Walsh did for herself. And, by God, I haven't had time to miss her yet.'

'It all happened so quick,' Poll agreed. 'That you still kind of expect her to come jazzing through the causeway, acting the goat, the way she used to.'

'My Mother went off sudden,' wee Lil recalled. 'It was her heart though. One moment she was as living like as you, Poll. She'd been down to the Ham Factory for a tanner's worth of pigs' trotters. It was a Saturday. We always had pigs' trotters on Saturday. She got home with them, slumped down on her chair, and died there and then. I've never been able to eat pigs' trotters since. What with the shock and one thing and another, the worry of getting all her relations on the spot for the funeral, and getting the Insurance money from her death policy to bury her, for she'd got a week or two behind with her payments. And you know what like the Insurance are when you're a bit behind. Especially if you die. Though God knows she'd paid it regular for over thirty years, enough to bury three folk. And what with Pinner the undertaker, and you know him. Has to see the colour of his money first, before he measures you. No cash and you can keep your corpse. And scurrying around everywhere looking for a cheap bit of black, since I was chief mourner, of course. My Mother was buried for weeks before I realised she was really dead. I picked up her coat one day, it smelled all of her. That was the first time I knew she was dead and gone. I cried terrible when it came home to me.'

'Death's always worse when it hits sudden,' the Duchess assured them. 'Because it just gives you a wee push at first, then it gets tore right into you and knocks you flat on your face.'

'You can have the rest of my turn, Janie. My Mam's shouting me. I'm at "Open the gates, and let me through, Sir".'

The rare thing had happened in the street game, an accidental and 'preferred' turn. 'Janie's got to get the rest of my turn,' Maikie Stewart informed the Boss. 'Because I've got to go. And I've just had half a turn. And that's fair, because I waited here for ages.'

The game came to a standstill, while the legal aspects of such an infrequent contretemps were debated.

'That's fair enough,' Poll suddenly refereed the squabble that had arisen, threatening to become a free-for-all, from the vantage point of her grown-upness. 'It's fair enough. If you're due a thing and can't take it yourself, you can hand your due over to anybody you name.'

'All right,' the Boss agreed reluctantly, her personal wishes thwarted by such a powerful adversary as Poll, but still holding on to some of her dignity of office. 'But Gertie Latham still has to wait till last for her turn.'

Gertie didn't have to wait till last. But neither she nor anybody else knew that, as Janie caught the ball for her turn.

One, two, three a-leerie.

'Not from the beginning, Janie! Maikie did that.' The squabble rose renewed. 'You've only got half a turn. It's from "Open the gates".'

Open the gates, and let me through, Sir
Open the gates.

The causeway was very quiet. Even the women had a sudden

interest in this controversial turn. The watchful quietness unnerved Janie. The end of the chant seemed so far away:

Open the gates, and let me through, Sir
Open the gates.

'The ball's down. Janie dropped the ball at "Open the gates". She's out. She just went and dropped it.' The cries rose through the causeway in mingled accents of triumph and regretfulness. Gertie's voice rising in admonishment. 'Getting to "Open the gates" and going and dropping it, Janie. Your turn's gone now.'

'I meant to drop it,' Janie informed them, 'because I'm needing the lavatory in a hurry. Gertie can have the rest of my turn,' she cried as she flew up the causeway. An argument which not even Poll had the power to settle rose fierce and furious behind her. But Janie flew beyond it all, as if compelled, to the lobby of 285. Only to the lobby, apprehensive of her Mother's reception of this most urgent question.

'Mam,' she shouted up the stairs. 'Will you die soon?' And lest the answer should be in the dreaded affirmative, added: 'Just say this one time that you won't die soon.'

The answer, when it came, was hurried and irritable.

'I don't know when I'll die. For goodness' sake run and play.'

Janie didn't. She stood for a long time in the lobby, getting her face quiet and ordinary again, to meet the other bairns. It took a long time to get your face ordinary so that no one would know anything had happened. And, in the longness, Liza's voice came down again, with laughter and assurance in it: 'Of course I won't die soon. What on earth would I do going and dying?' Janie ran from the lobby, lest death should change its mind again.

'I thought you was off to the lavatory,' Gertie was accusing. 'Did you get a penny?'

'No. I had to go to speak to my Mam, that's all.'

'You look as if you'd got a penny or something.' Gertie's suspicions were unallayed. And although Gertie was Janie's very best friend, Janie sensed that not even to Gertie could she confide the truth: 'I've just got a promise from my Mam that she won't die soon.'

A promise that lit and warmed the Lane for the rest of the night, that put the apprehension of the Cruelty Man completely out of mind, that made Woolworth's bangles shine more brightly on the young girls' arms, that whirled herself and Gertie faster round the street lamp than ever, singing as they whirled:

> We're two little piccaninnies,
> Real gems you know,
> We're the real dusky diamonos,
> Only from Iohio.

CHAPTER SEVEN

THE worst had happened. Liza stared silently at the blue summons in her hands. She had sat there staring at it for a long time now, discovering from it that Janie was neglected, and in need of care and protection.

To Janie it seemed that Liza, numbed and white and bewildered, was really the one who needed care and protection. Janie found herself able to provide both.

'We'll go away, Mam. Miles and miles away together. Where nobody will ever find us. They can't take me away from you if they can't find us,' she reasoned.

'They'd catch up on us sometime,' Liza answered dully, but not dogmatically.

And Janie pressed her 'prospect' home.

'Not for years and years, maybe. We could sell bowls and bootlaces, like Beulah does. Nobody worries about tinker children. So they wouldn't worry about us any more. Not if we become real tinkers.'

'I know a place,' Liza said tentatively. 'It's a long walk from here. But I know we could get a cheap bed in this place.'

It was dusk when they slipped together away from the Lane. It was difficult to hear Liza say casually to Poll as they passed through the causeway:

'I've got one of yon heads of mine coming on. I thought we'd take a turn round the Green for a bit of air.'

Difficult not to blurt excitedly out to Poll:

'We're really going away forever, Poll. You'll never see us again ever.'

Difficult, because that was the only exciting bit of 'news' they had ever had to impart to Poll.

Each familiar landmark loomed up in supplication of farewell. Janie said good-bye silently to the chip shop and all the buildings that couldn't speak and report them to the police, and still gave them a sense of 'belonging', till they reached the Toll Booth on the outskirts of the town.

'We're real tinkers at last,' Janie thought, with a great sigh of relief, when they had passed through the gates.

The relief of being a real tinker communicated itself to Liza. She lit her pipe. The first 'light up' for a long time.

The road they took was strange to Janie. 'It leads to the next town,' Liza explained. 'There's a Diddle Doddle there. With a bit of luck, we'll get a bed for ninepence.'

Janie lagged behind, eyeing the children playing round cottage doors, with a sense of triumph and pity. They were confined to their doors, they weren't going on to 'the next town'. Passing carters grumbled good-night and rumbled out of sight up farm roads. Clusters of lights foretold another village, enclosing and cheering the travellers, letting go of them suddenly out into a darkness intensified by the remote glint of a lamp in an isolated farm house.

'I'll carry you on my back for a while,' Liza offered, when the next four villages didn't turn out to be the 'next town'.

The darkness was more frightening from the height of Liza's shoulders than it was on the ground. Branches tugged at Janie's hair. The one shadow the two of them cast was taller than the trees themselves. A long hunchbacked stranger loping beside them.

'Let me down, Mam,' Janie begged. 'I'm not tired now. Honest I'm not.'

'I can see the lights of the next town now,' Liza said. 'We'll be there in no time. And mind, Janie, when we reach the Diddle Doddle, we're just there because we missed our last bus home. And our name's Sinclair. Mind you don't forget that if you're asked any questions.'

The Diddle Doddle was filled with light and noise and people. A hot-plate glowed redly, sizzling with frying pans, the overpowering smell of onions tantalised hunger. Men spat on the sawdust on the floor. Women clattered enamel mugs on a table. Voices rose in laughter, song, oaths and temper. The owners of the voices were all vagrants. Janie instantly and warmly felt at home. An at-homeness which helped to cover Liza's bewildered lostness.

A small tinker mended dishes on the table, her slim, brown fingers controlled her whirring, whirling mending wheel, setting her eyes free to watch the ever-opening Diddle Doddle door. She seemed to know everyone who came through it, greeting them like an unofficial hostess who also happened to be a true friend. The rare combination lit her with charm.

'Strike me down stone dead, Mairi,' she greeted a newcomer. 'I thought you was bound for Mosstowie. The last time I saw your face it was set in the direction to Kinross. And is Lindsay with you this time at all, now?'

'Never him.' The newcomer resignedly slung her pack on the table. 'He got himself mixed up with some whoreson of a McPhee at New Pitsligo. They were all set up to hawk the Bullers of Buchan airt when I last saw them. And I'm no' sorry. I can tell you that, Aggie. I had my bellyful of the breed of him.'

'It's as I've always said, Mairi.' Aggie's wheel purred round with contentment. 'The road's always easier and faster when you take to it on your own. And there's always a man to be had when the need for one comes over you. But the need's not always over you. And, when it isn't, any cove's just a dead loss to you.'

The Diddle Doddle dimmed down with heat. Thick pipe smoke curled round it, padding its noise into a hum. Its occupants looked as hazy and relaxed as Janie felt. Voices made the most comforting sounds in the world.

'You're going to cross water within a three, my dear.'

A fortune teller peered down into Liza's tin mug.

'A sad crossing, my love. But you'll survive it. I can see that in your face, as well as in your leaves. There's a dark man here, too. He has crossed your life before. He's in your path again. Still after you.'

'That's the Cruelty Man,' Janie realised to herself. 'He's got a great big black moustache.'

'This dark man has got an S in his name,' the fortune teller continued. 'You wouldn't recognise a man with an S in his name, would you, now?' she urged.

'It isn't the Cruelty Man.' Janie turned away with relief. 'He hasn't got an S. His name's F. Murray.'

A man with no legs startlingly propelled himself through the door.

'It's the Railway Tramp,' the Dish Mender shouted gladly. 'Bless you, Thoomikies, my wee love. You all set for the Timmer Market too?'

The legless man grinned. A great, black hairy grin.

Thoomikies is taking the short cut to the Market. Aren't you, old Cock? Nipping over the sleepers, and all round the junctions,' a man teased. 'And don't you fall asleep on the slag heap either. Old Thoomikies did that one night, and felt so burned up that he thought he was in Hell at last. Didn't you, son?'

The Diddle Doddle lifted up one voice and laughed. The Railway Tramp grinned in echo, squeezing himself compactly into the corner by the hot-plate and the wall, filling it so exactly that the room seemed only to be completely furnished at this moment. Janie stared at him fearfully. Their equal size brought their eyes level with each other. The tramp held a penny between his teeth. His great head nodded, beckoning Janie to come for the penny.

'Go on, Littl'un,' the Dish Mender coaxed. 'It will please Thoomikies terrible if you take his penny. He's fond of littl'uns, but they're all so feared of him.'

But Janie couldn't. Not even to please Thoomikies. She turned frightenedly away from his eyes.

With the entrance of Blind Jimmy, the Diddle Doddle began to sing.

> The summer's gone
> And all the flowers are dying.

Led by Blind Jimmy, they all sang. As if in a sleep, their eyes closed, their bodies sagging across the table, or stretched in corners by the hot plate.

'He can sing like an angel,' the Dish Mender said sadly, 'especially when you consider that he hasn't got his sight. But for all that, Jimmy's a bit too free with his hands the moment he gets within an inch of a woman.'

'Aye,' the Fortune Teller agreed drily. 'Blind or no' blind they always know their road in that direction.'

But the blind street singer's voice transcended his natural instincts:

For I'll be there
When summer's in the meadows.
Or when the valley's hushed
And white with snow.

The entrance of two policemen with the Warden of the Diddle Doddle brought Danny Boy to a premature close. The singers loved the law too little to serenade it. They closed up, condensing themselves along the forms, busying their fingers with the tools of their trades. The policemen examined the backs of their heads, recognising one here and there:

'Been taking a turn through Balvenie woods lately, Joss?'

'No, Sergeant. To tell you the honest truth, I've gone kinda off rabbits these days. They don't agree with my digestion no more.'

'You'll no' have gone off venison too, Joss?' the Sergeant asked heavily.

'I'm no' sure, Sergeant. It's so long since I've tasted a steak, that I forget if it speaks back to me now or no'.'

'All signed in for the night, then?' the Sergeant turned to the Warden.

'Aye. Here's the book. House full the night. Most of them are moving on the morn, though.'

'The Bobbies have come for me and Mam,' Janie thought, afraid, watching the policeman gaze down on the signatures in the book. Her fear communicated itself to them. They looked down at her curiously.

'You're a bit on the young side for this game, are you no'?'

'She's mine,' Liza said. 'She's with me. We missed our last connection home.'

The policeman stared down on the book again:

'Is your name MacVean?'

'Yes,' Liza answered with a voice that had no fear in it. 'MacVean of Laverock.'

'I thought we were Sinclairs now, Mam,' Janie said, as they followed the Dish Mender and the other women up long stone steps to bed.

'I know, Janie. I shouldn't have told them who we were. But I just had to. It made me feel real for a minute just hearing to myself who I really was.'

The Diddle Doddle folk said good-bye to each other in their good-nights:

'If I don't see you in the morning before I go, Aggie, I'll be catching up with you again at the Timmer Market.'

'Aye. Or on the road to Foggie, maybe. I havena' hawked that road for years now.'

Their reunions were chance. Their good-byes, being chance too, were without the regret that tinges ordinary good-byes:

'Good luck, Mairi, if you're on the road before me in the morning. I'm bound for the herring town myself. I hope to get there before the season starts up.'

'Janie,' Liza whispered, when the lights were out. 'Are you sleeping yet, Janie? You and me are going to give ourselves up the morn.'

Diddle Doddle life, wonderful to Janie, had frightened Liza more than the summons to court.

'The years will birl bye in a blink,' Liza assured Janie, as they sat together in the anteroom of the Courthouse, waiting for the Vigilance Officer to come and take Janie to a Home.

'You've just got no idea how quick the years fly,' Liza insisted, thereby also reassuring herself, as she sat there, carefully picking small digestible scraps off the bare bones of the Court's decision and handing them to Janie.

'The Home's a hundred miles away. Three hours' journey

by train. The longest time you've ever been on a train. You're
going to like that fine, Janie.'

Liza's voice increased the desolation of those last moments
together. The anteroom smelt sharp and clinical as all Janie's
preconceived ideas of 'a Home'. Its austerity more fearful
than any pool of blood that had ever incarnadined the Lane.
Its silence more ominous than all the curses coursing through
the causeway.

Liza, feeling the chill of the anteroom too, floundered
through it, falling back on a more familiar facet:

'Poll and them fair got one in the eye. Thought all they had
to do was to flock down to the Court and cock themselves up
in the gallery, getting an eyeful of everything. But, no faith
you. Nothing doing. They werena' even allowed a foot across
the door. I bet you a pound to a penny though, they've all
draped themselves along the railings outside. Just waiting to
gape when you come out. And that's another shock in store
for them. Like as not you'll be taken out by the side door.'

Liza chuckled at the small triumph of it. And Janie was
momentarily lifted out of bleakness into importance. I don't
want to go out by the side door, she thought protestingly. I
want them all to see me. I'll just cry and kick up something
terrible, if they're all there looking.

The Lane's instinct both to provide and appreciate 'a show'
was deeply ingrained in Janie. Such a moment came only
once to the children of the Lane. Like the time when the
Probation Officer had come to take Tom Shoggie to a Training Ship. How the Lane had lifted up its voice in lamentation:

'God help us all. Mind you, there's no gainsaying but that
Tom was a bit on the wild side. Still, he was just Maggie
Shoggie's craittur for all that.'

One would miss one's epitaph completely, huddled out by
a side door!

'The Home's in Aberdeenshire,' Liza was saying. 'Just a

small home it is. Though all I can mind about Aberdeenshire is a hill called Lochnagar. There's a song to that hill:

O for the crags that are wild and majestic.
I sigh for the valley of dark Lochnagar.

The Home's in a place called Skeyne,' Liza went on, 'though I've never heard tell of Skeyne myself.'

Skeyne. Janie turned the sound of the place round and over in her mind. It was familiar. Like the bed-cover that the Duchess crocheted on summer days. It had never reached an end in all the summers. Blue skeins. Yellow skeins. Red skeins. 'All out of stock,' the Duchess would grumble, 'just when I needed skeins of that colour for my pattern.' And the bright bed-cover would disappear, bereaving the causeway of colour. But, on some other summer day, it would blaze back to the causeway, shimmering and rippling against the Duchess's large bosom in triumphant folds. 'I got the right skeins at last,' she would inform the Lane. 'And no' before time neither.'

There was some magical quality to the Duchess's bright bed-cover. You felt it would never come to an end and turn into a real bedcover. And all because of some elusive skein. Skeyne. Janie liked the sound of the place where the Home was.

CHAPTER EIGHT

SKEYNE never had the colour of its sound. It lay on the threshold of Deeside, a doormat against which hurrying tourists wiped their feet, their eyes straining ever forwards towards the greater glories of the Moor of Dinnet and Lochnagar. Skeyne lay sulking eternally under this slight, its grey face lined and loured with the perpetual shadow of the Cairngorm Mountains.

The Orphanage of Skeyne folds itself back from the main road, withdrawing into a huddle of trees. Tall trees, top-heavy and shaggy with crows' nests, loud with their rancour. Trees that shuddered and whined throughout Janie's first night in the Orphanage, twining their shadows across the walls of the dormitory.

It had been a long day. Still spring. But it seemed to have been spring in Grandmother's country ages ago. A white, quiet spring, then. Now it was loud and yellow. The glare of daffodils crowding out the Orphanage garden still beat hotly under Janie's heavy eyelids; the smell of them hovered through her senses. The suddenness of their impact had imprinted itself in her being. I'll never smell a daffodil in all my life again without minding how I first saw the Orphanage.

So many things lay in mind. Urgent elusive scraps. she sense of lostness when the train screamed past Loch Na Boune, the last known landmark in Janie's world. Screaming out of time and place altogether. I'm leaving my Mam. I'm leaving my Mam, it had panted. A loud thing in a living hurry. The places it had flashed through focusing in fragments now. Bending boulders like old men groping round a high hill. Dead Man's Bells fleeing whitely from their own wood, shivering down the banks, bowing the train out and past. OYNE in big white letters on a small, black station. A strange name for a place, the only name I remember now. I'm sure I saw it though. Some day I'll go back to see if it's real.

All things seemed unreal to Janie. The dormitory most of all. She looked anxiously over to the chair beside her bed. Her new hat lay safely. So huge that it hid her small bundle of underclothes. She felt her head, still with a small sense of shock, although it had been shaved hours ago, after she left the Courthouse. This morning. Or was it yesterday morning? Time had leapt out of bounds. She lay trying to catch time and return it to its proper place. Its hours eluded her. How enviably Peggy's long hair scattered itself on the pillow there. If I got one wish I'd just ask for all my hair back again. No, I wouldn't. I'd just ask to get home to my Mam again. Not having any hair wouldn't matter if I could just get home again.

But home lay too raw and tender to the piercing touch of thought yet. There was escape from thought in listening to the whispers flitting frighteningly like small bats through the dim dormitory.

'Did you have to read the inscription above the front door, Janie?'

'Yes.'

'You've got to remember it by heart as well, though.'

'I do. "Proctor's Orphan Training Home 1891".'

'If ever you don't do your work right, Mrs Thane will take you round to the front door to read it again.'

'She makes you say "training" three times. That's so's you'll never forget.'

'And you've got to learn Table Manners off the Card as well, Janie. But you'll get a week to learn them in.'

'I've learned a bit of them already:

> I must not talk about my food,
> Nor fret if I don't think it good.'

'Do you know something, Janie? We get porridge for breakfast every morning except Sundays.'

'And we get fish on Sundays. Haddocks. I just can't abide them. You get an egg on Easter Sunday though, Janie.'

'And an egg on Christmas morning. Don't forget, Peggy, we get an egg on Christmas morning.'

A panic seized Janie and forced her upright in bed:

'When will I get home? I've asked everybody. The Court Man and the Vigilance Officer and Mrs Thane and just everybody. They all let on they don't hear me. But somebody must know *when*?'

'When you're sixteen, most likely.' Peggy's casualness distressed Janie. 'At least that's when I'm getting home. When I'm sixteen.'

'But that's ages!' Janie's distress increased. 'That's just years and years. I'm not nine yet. Not till October. I'll have to stay here for eight years.'

'Only seven and a half years, Janie,' Peggy corrected. 'If you're eight and a half now.'

'But it's still years and years.' Janie was disconsolate. 'My Mam could die by that time.'

'You can write a letter to her once a month, Janie.'

'Mind what you write though. Mrs Thane reads all the letters before they go out.'

'I know what I'll do. I'll mark every day off on the calendar till I'm sixteen. It will pass quicker that way.'

'That's what I thought when I first came, Janie. Then I just forgot.'

'I won't forget.' Janie felt very certain. 'I'll never forget to count the days off.'

'Wheesht! Janie!' Peggy admonished. 'The boys' dormitory has gone quiet now. Mrs Thane will be shouting up for silence if we don't go quiet too.'

Janie pulled herself down under the sheets, and lay staring for a long time at the changing flecks of colour that always danced into vision when she shut her eyes very tightly. 'I won't forget,' she thought, staring. 'I know fine that I'll never forget to mark the days off.'

CHAPTER NINE

'YOU'RE right lucky, Janie. Leaving and everything.' The wistful whispers had echoed enviously through the kitchen all morning.

For eight years, Janie had dreamed of such whispers, troyed within the limited landmarks of Skeyne. And waiting, had forgotten to mark off the days on the calendar. Except, of course, days that had marked themselves off, cutting their inscriptions deeply on the small, memorial cairns of the mind.

How angry Mrs Thane had been when Janie had discovered a 'secret' way of commenting on the food. Orphanage Table Etiquette ruled that you must not 'talk' about your food. But there was no law against composing 'forewarning' chants.

> Pease brose, Pease brose,
> Pease brose again, Chris,
> They feed us a' like blackbirds.
> And that's a bloody shame, Chris.

And how annoyed she had been over the desperate postscripts added to the letters home:

'Be sure not to die soon, Mam. Try hard not to get into any fights with Poll and Battleaxe.'

'Don't send any more *Love Stories*. Mrs Thane says they're rubbish. But mind to tell me in your letter when William Corder gets catched and hanged for murdering Maria Marten.'

But that was long ago. Janie still added desperate postscripts, but transferred them now to the tail-end of her prayers in the Kirk.

It had taken her longer to learn to part with her dirty underclothes to 'the wash' on Monday mornings, and even longer to give up sleeping with her vest and knickers huddled to her in a bundle, because they had smelt homely and personal, an antidote to the sterility of Jeyes' fluid that pervaded the Orphanage.

'I've lost the best chamois, Janie. The new one. The impregnated one for the front windows.'

Chris worried into the kitchen:

'She'll go off her head when she finds out. She's at high doh already, all because it's Trustees' Day. I was sure I put the chamois into this press with the brooms.

'Stay quiet, Chris,' Janie advised with the calm objectivity of the safe onlooker. 'Stay awful quiet for a long minute, you'll be able to look for it right when your belly stops heaving up and down.'

'You'd better get a start to your front windows.' Mrs Thane stalked into the kitchen, dropping through its apprehension like a stone that sent Chris wheeling round and round amongst the brooms.

'What on earth are you rummaging there for, Chris? And it's high time you set off down to the village with the morning milk, Janie! You can take Craig's milk. The shop milk, the police milk. And you'd better take Mrs Mudie's milk too on your first round.'

'But Donnie always takes Mrs Mudie's milk now, Mrs Thane. You said . . .'

'I *know* what I said, Janie!' Mrs Thane shot up tall. Her black frock stiffened. The small spots on it leapt out large and white. 'I said that if there was a bit of dirt lying anywhere around, you'd be sure to stop and pick it up. I can't spare Donnie this morning. And if you haven't learned yet at your age to close your eyes and ears to improper things, you'll never learn now. Get your coat on, and I'll away and fill your milk pails.'

'What's all that about Mrs Mudie's milk?' Chris's curiosity momentarily overcame her anxiety.

'I told you, Chris.' Janie's mind had already flown off at a more intriguing tangent. 'Mind? About Mrs Mudie having "the change". Chris. Chris. Some folk would be a lot nicer if they never wore any clothes at all.'

Chris stood shocked into stillness, considering the strangeness of the idea.

'Not everybody,' Janie explained incoherently. 'Just folk like Nurse Conduit in the School Clinic at the Lane. And the Green Ladies. And the Cruelty Man and Mrs Thane. I once saw her without her frock on. She was rushing to the lavatory. She had bowdie legs, Chris. And black silk knickers. I could have spoken to her about anything when she hadn't her frock on. She just looked ordinary. I bet the School Nurse and the Green Ladies are just ordinary too, when they haven't got their frocks on.'

'Haven't you got a start to your front windows yet, Chris? Well, get on with them. Don't stand gaping at me with your mouth open. Your head's in the clouds this morning!'

But Janie knew that Chris was just trying to imagine what lay beneath Mrs Thane's frock.

'And you get going too, Janie. Don't you dawdle down

in the village all day either. The Trustees will be here by two o'clock. And mind! No gossiping with Mrs Mudie!'

'High,' Skeyne whispered Mrs Mudie was. Though, God knows, other Skeyne women just took 'the change' in their stride. Whiles a bit cantankerous right enough. Whiles going clean off their men folk altogether. But never going clean off the Kirk instead and taking to singing dirt or Evangelistic choruses, like orra town's folk at street corners, the way the Mudie wife was doing now. Her that was not only country born, but Auld Kirk bred into the bargain.

Despite that, Janie had missed her morning encounters with Mrs Mudie. They had ceased abruptly one morning when Mrs Thane had inquired about Mrs Mudie's health. And Janie had told her, had just said: 'Mrs Mudie's got hot flushes coming all over her, Mrs Thane. And she says she's losing something terrible every month now.' Donnie delivered Mrs Mudie's milk after that, leaving Janie with a bewildering sense of disgrace. She had learned over her years in the Orphanage that tact was as important as truth, but had not yet learned to combine them successfully. Nor had she outgrown her affinity with what Grandmother would have called 'Ne'er do weels', the Lane 'Riff Raff', and Skeyne 'Ootlins'. Skeyne's word was the best word. The most accurately descriptive. Ootlins. Queer folk who were 'oot' and who, perversely enough, never had any desire to be 'in'.

Entering the low doorway of Mrs Mudie's cottage, Janie always felt the enjoyable apprehension of Gretel entering the Gingerbread House, uncertain whether Witch or Fairy Godmother was in occupation.

Witch this morning. Transforming Mrs Mudie into a tiger dimly pacing the cluttered kitchen. Blind to Janie and the morning milk, but bright and beckoning to her own reflection in the overmantel mirror. Urging it shrilly:

There is life for a look at the crucified one.
There is life at this moment for thee.

The whole room throbbed in dark quick rhythm with its owner's mood. The grandfather clock gasping the seconds over and past; the kettle hissing on the crook, curled, ready to spring. The dresser still but wary, the saucer eyes of its blue china glinting and watchful.

'Here's your morning milk, Mrs Mudie.'

Janie spoke to the face reflected in the mirror. It seemed the realest face. It stared at its own origin, without recognition. Abjuring it in a shrill, high voice:

> Look, Sinner, look
> Unto Him and be saved.

Janie tried to put the milk pail down very quietly. But the table quivered with life too; the milk pail rattled in protest. The face reflected in the mirror went on exhorting, as Janie backed swiftly out through the low door.

> Unto Him who was nailed
> On the tree.

The village had lost all its own livingness since Janie had last looked on it, short seconds ago. Its cottages stood as small and still as the images of themselves, for sale on postcards in Beaton's shop in summer. Or like dolls' houses. Craig's car a toy car now. Craig himself, a tiny tin man at its wheel. Mrs Mudie's garden shot up round Janie's feet. A jungle of boxwood, wild and pungent and bitter. A ladybird, huge and red and clockwork, ticked and hummed across the bewildering boxwood in a blind, mechanical panic.

> Fly away home.

Your house is on fire.
Your children all gone.

The sound of her own voice soothed Janie. The childishness of her words shamed her. No wonder Mrs Thane was always puzzling about what was to become of her when she 'got out into the world'.

Here she was, almost going, and part of her still half believed that ladybirds could interpret and understand. Strange thing, Mrs Thane was either annoyed because, 'You're far too knowing for your years, Janie,' or anxious because, 'You're going to find the world a tough place. I'm sorrier for you than for the other bairns I've brought up.'

'You're all behind with your milk this morning, Janie!' Schoolchildren rushed round Leuchar's corner, shouting in their going, 'It's gone ten to nine, Janie. You'll be late,'

'None of the Orphanage is coming to School the day,' Janie shouted to their retreating backs. 'The Trustees are coming. And it's my last Trustees' Day!' Her triumphant words missed their targets vanishing down Barclay's Brae. But the normality of the words set Janie's feet free now. Willing them to carry her out of Mrs Mudie's garden. Out through the village, thinning down into scattered crofts. Out towards the Cairngorms, slinking behind their own protective mists with every step she took in their direction. She could have seen the whole of the world, if the Cairngorms didn't rise immense and blue, shutting Skeyne away from it all.

O Cairngorms, sae heich and blue
I'd see the warld
Were't na for you!

Long ago Janie had thought that if she ran very fast and

hidden, along by the side of Leuchar's Wood, she could catch up on the Cairngorms. Rush right into their foothills and take them by surprise, before they had time to hide behind their mists again.

'Aye, Janie. It's a right fine morning.'

But no matter how fast she ran nor how hidden her race was, no matter, the Cairngorms were ever swifter, ever more wary, and she had never caught up with them.

'I was saying that it's a fine morning, Janie.'

Lower Hempriggs peered over his byre door, his eyes staring out into the fine morning.

'But mebbe your mind's no' on the weather the day at all now, is it?'

'No.' Janie reddened under the crofter's twinkling stare. 'No. I was thinking about something else.'

'Some lad or ither, mebbe?'

'Not that either.' Janie's embarrassment increased. 'I was just watching the Cairngorms.'

Lower Hempriggs turned sidewards and watched the Cairngorms too.

'Aye faith. But they're gey hills, the Cairngorms,' he concluded thoughtfully, bringing his keen stare round on Janie's face again. 'And so you're just no' for letting on your thoughts at all this morning, Janie?'

'No. Not this morning.' Janie laughed herself awkwardly out of reach of the crofter's curiosity, and into the safety of Leuchar's Wood.

'I'm leaving the Orphanage, Mr Tocher!' she shouted back, remembering suddenly. 'The Trustees are coming the day. And I'm leaving soon!'

Her shout startled the wood, set all its cushats off on the scold, its insects hurrying on the hum. Janie stood till the hot, scattered haze subsided. And the wood gathered itself together again in still, dark concentration. Listening. Staring absorbed at its own reflection in the loch below.

Two woods there always were, on fine, mist-threatened mornings like this. One stood high and sentinel over Skeyne. The other, down and distant in the loch.

> Twa woods there was
> Before ma een,
> But yin lay drooned
> In Loch of Skeyne.

The play of thoughts and words carried Janie to the end of Leuchar's Wood. To where it gave up its own large being with tortuous reluctance. Tearing itself apart and flinging its tattered pieces all over the hill in a blind frenzy. Its remnants rose in sullen copses. Dark and disconsolate.

All else that was broken and rejected by Skeyne lay here too. Crushed beer bottles bejewelled the dump. Jags of emeralds still uncut, glistening through smithereens of crockery, myriad-coloured and many-shaped. Swift and acquiescent to the imagination. The rusted frame of a bicycle rose grotesquely up out of the moss. Rooted there in mounting position, awaiting a strange rider. Some mad man or wise child, to whom the desire could always become the deed.

Lost civilisations had been discovered down under the earth, Janie remembered, as she stood fiercely absorbing the dump. Maybe that's why dumps were always so exciting. Always like coming across some small, lost civilisation too.

'I've found an old world. Older even than the Roman world. What if it *really* was so?'

The largest of Leuchar's copses, the Duck's Wood, dipped down towards the Orphanage. It closed in on Janie. Its waves of near-memory surging up and over her, dark and ice cold!

And old worlds red with pain.
And old worlds . . .

She fixed her mind to the image of the dump, desperately, a
drowning man grabbing a drifting flotsam –

And old worlds . . .

For once a poem refused to come to her rescue. Its author,
origin and ending eluded her, crying Halt! Only its sparse
words rose baldly in the mind:

And old worlds red with pain.

Black with pain. That's what the Duck's Wood was. Ever
since the day that Liza had arrived from the Lane, setting
the seal of her suffering upon it.

'I thought,' Chris had accused, after Liza had gone, 'that
your Mam was awful bonnie, Janie. You was always telling
us that. And I thought it was just my Mam drunk, when she
came staggering up the avenue.'

'She wasn't drunk!' Janie had defended wildly. 'My Mam
never never got drunk. She always hated drunk folk. She was
just ill, Chris. Awful ill. She had a doctor's line to prove it.
I saw it. So did Mrs Thane. You can ask her. My Mam
wasn't drunk.' Janie brought out the name of Liza's illness
triumphantly, completely vindicating the shameful accusation of drunkenness. 'She's got an illness called chronic
syphilis. That's what made her stagger. And that's what made
her white and not bonnie any more.'

But Liza had been beautiful, Janie remembered. Almost
like Shelley said. Her beauty made the bright world dim.
Not quite the same though. All the other women of the
Lane had been grey. Prisoners clamped firmly into the dour

pattern of its walls and cobblestones. But Liza had always leapt burnished, out of her surroundings. And in the leaping had made the dim world bright.

Her Mother's changed appearance had shocked Janie into numbness. The Lane, and the dream of returning to it, disintegrated in the wrecked reflection of Liza's face. Dulling in the dimness of her eyes, withdrawing into the pale hollows of her cheeks. Not easily though, nor suddenly. They had sat here in the wood, crouching over the smouldering ashes of old loyalties, trying to coax them into flame again.

'And Poll and Battleaxe and the Duchess?' Janie had inquired, her question sounding from the voice of a stranger. 'How are they all?'

'Fine. Just fine.' Liza had cheered at the deceptive narrowing of a gulf. 'Aye, asking for you, all of them. Did I mind to tell you that poor old Annie Frigg is dead and gone? She never got over a fall from the top landing to the bottom. One Saturday night with a good shot in. The one and only conscious word Annie ever uttered after that was a swear.'

'Did it begin with F, Mam?'

'Aye. It did that.'

'I thought that.' Janie congratulated her memory with a smile. 'That was always the swear that Annie used.'

'At least she wasna' a hypocrite.' The old Liza, amused and satirical, peeped out for a brief instant. 'Not like old Balaclava when she kicked the bucket, cringing and whining to God at the last minutes. Annie, game to the end, went out with a curse. It was gey pitiful though, when you come to think of it. Annie had just been "saved" again. But I've no doubt that your soul saved is of little comfort till you when your body's sel' is coming to its end. Your soul's a stranger to you, like. But you ken your body's sel' awful well.'

'Who got Annie's room, Mam?' An old wonder had

prompted the question. The one room in the Lane into which Janie had never penetrated, thereby still retaining its probability of all Annie's bygone promises redeemed.

'None got it.' Liza had shattered probability. 'And deed it was fit for none when Annie was through with it. We had the Sanitary on the top of us for days. Fumigating and disinfecting. Before any of us could get by her landing without getting knocked down with the stink that come from her room. And that's another thing, Janie.' Liza's voice had allowed no period for mourning. 'We're all getting new Council houses down by the Cathedral. Another good reason for you coming home again. The Duchess's moving into her house next week. She managed to wangle herself to the top of the list. Her cry aye being the loudest, like. And there was Poll, all set to step into her shoes. All ready to take over the rule of the Lane, when she got a notification about her new house too. Poor Poll. She didna' ken whether to mourn over the loss of power, or rejoice over the acquisition of property. Anyhow it left the road fine and clear for Battleaxe. There's a queer kind of truce in the Lane just now, Janie. Its rulers are no' on speaking terms at all. And their subjects are fair going mad with new freedom. Oh, and you mind on wee Lil? She got the chance of a new house too. She turned it down flat. Said that she would never be able to pass herself amongst a crowd of complete strangers. And that she preferred to stay on in the Lane amongst her old friends. The pathetic thing about that, of course, is that wee Lil hasna' got one friend in the Lane. But she doesna' realise that. And I hadna' the heart to point it out to her. It would have been a real unkindness. Because wee Lil's happier no' realising.'

But Liza, who had always realised things, began to realise then that the road back to the Lane was not going to be so easy.

'We'll have a house in the country, Mam. Mind, we always

wanted that. With a garden and nasturtiums and a goat. We'll never live in the Lane again. We'll have plenty of money when I'm educated, you see; that will only be a few years now.

Janie's words lapped against the grey, unseeing rock of Liza's face.

'The Lane will do me fine,' she had said bitterly, 'for all the time I've got left now.'

A vividly remembered fear of death had clutched at Janie's mind.

'You're not going to die, Mam? Not for a long, long time?' She had almost pleaded, 'Promise me that you won't die. Just promise this one time.' But, knowing now that people couldn't truly make such promises, had sat quietly, filling her eyes and mind with the long lengths of the great trees and shutting out the brooding image of death.

'I'm no' so sure. The doctors dinna' hold out much time for me.'

It was then that Liza had groped in her bag for the certificate.

'You can see I'm that, that I'm gey ill,' she had said quietly, proudened by the impression the unfamiliar name of her illness had made on Janie.

'But the doctors can cure you, Mam? Surely they can cure you?'

'I've left it some late for that. They say I need somebody with me all the time now. It's my sight that's failing fastest.'

You could pray your intensest prayer ever, stricken by blindness yourself. Your eyes wide open, staring through the wood without seeing its trees. And without words at all. Just the heart beseeching in hurried incoherent beats:

> O say what it is that, thing called light
> Which I can ne'er enjoy.

What are the blessings of the sight?

That had been one of the first poems that Liza had ever taught Janie on the long road to Grandmother's house. The sudden recollection of it lit dim corners of her mind, revealing small half-forgotten things.

All the things I know, she taught me, God. The good things, I mean. She could make the cherry trees bloom above Dean's Ford, even when it was winter. Hidden birds betrayed their names the instant she heard their song. She gave the nameless little rivers high hill sources and deep sea endings. She put a singing seal in Loch Na Boune and a lament on the long, lonely winds. She saw a legend in the canna flowers and a plough amongst the stars. And the times in the Lane never really mattered, because of the good times away from it. And I would myself be blind now, if she had never lent me her eyes.

'And if that Matron gets thrawn about you coming home, she's got this to contend with.'

Liza had waved the doctor's certificate preciously, gently, smiling over it as secretly as if it had been a magic wand and she only had the awareness of its power.

But the magic hadn't worked with Mrs Thane. The spell had exploded in the magician's face, confounding the onlookers.

'*That*,' Mrs Thane had shot back from Liza, handing the certificate to her, finger-tipped, a spill rescued from the flames and still smouldering, 'is about the very last reason why Janie should return to live with you again. It is certainly the last reason the Trustees will ever recognise.'

Liza had cursed them. Striving for utterance in words that were familiar enough to her ears, but harsh and uneasy on her tongue:

'You smug bastard! You're born, but you're not dead yet! You . . .'

Poll and the others swore slickly. Could say F and B and C smoothly, as if they weren't swears at all, but part and parcel of the Lane's own language. But even ordinary words had always come to life on Liza's tongue. They writhed now through the dim reception room, stabbing it with light each time she swore.

'And God doesna' pay his debts wi' money. But that's something you've still got to learn yet, you . . .'

The fir tree in front of the window closed in on the room. I've never properly heard a swear till now, Janie had marvelled. Mrs Thane hasn't heard one before either. And her face isn't really angry. Not half as angry as it sometimes gets with me for just saying Damn. She just looks fat and lost and bewildered with arrows. The fir tree began to swim in front of Janie's eyes. A great blur of green. 'I'm sorry.' Her eyes had tried to find Mrs Thane to tell her, 'I'm sorry she's swearing at you.'

The shame of that day was less now. Janie felt guilty about this. 'It should never get less,' she protested to herself, 'I ought to feel ashamed about it forever and ever.'

But the pain of that day remained. My Mam went away without knowing I love her. The words wouldn't come till she was getting on to the bus. And then it was too late.

Unleashed by the desolation of Duck's Wood, Janie raced down into the ordinary world again. Its large brightness rushed upwards to meet her, its fields panted past her, a great haste of green. The Orphanage down in the hollow was the only solid thing in the whirling, sunlit world. It had gathered all its own within it. There was neither sight nor sound of its children.

They'll be polishing the floors like mad. Getting all stickied up. And creaking, every time they rise off their knees.

Janie stopped in her race to enjoy the moments of not having to polish. To recall with apprehension how the house would put out its dark, cold claws and claim her again, catching at her breath with the smell of beeswax, whispering roughly in Scots. And speaking aloud in polite English.

This was true freedom. Out here beyond beeswax. She shut her eyes to feel the sun groping warmly over her and hotly finding her. You could know an invisible world if you were blind. You could feel its being trembling. Smell its nearness. Hear the thin murmur of its voice.

'You'd better make your feet your friends, Janie! There's a gey bit steer going on down in the house.'

The Mannie shouted across from the lythe dyke, slanting above it like a shadow cast by the trees. 'They havena' missed me yet, down bye.' He nodded towards the house, his felt hat clinging to the back of his head by a miracle. 'But they'll have noticed by this time that you're no' there yet, Janie.'

The useless ones. A knot of laughter unwound itself, wriggling through Janie in little smiles. Weary Willie and Tired Tim. Ike and Moe. All the funny folk I once knew in the comics. That's us. That's me and the Mannie. Leaning over a dyke in the sun, till a big, fat policeman moves us on with a kick in the pants.

'And I'll warrant you've been on the dawdle again, Janie.'

The Mannie unconsciously but severely withdrew himself from the comic strip. And Tired Tim had never been funny, left on his own. Aware of this Janie volunteered seriously:

'Hempriggs is going to scythe his inroads the morn.'

'Is he, by God? Did he mention it, like?'

'No. Not exactly. But I noticed. I saw his scythe. He'd been sharpening it. And he was keeping his eye on the weather.'

'Mphmmmm.' The Mannie turned his eyes towards the weather too. Even the Cairngorms were free of mists now. A small flock of gulls put a cloud in the sky. They watched them dipping and rising and borrowing a sheen from the sun.

'I'm no' so sure about the weather,' the Mannie said. 'That's the first of them flying inland. From the Brock, likely. There'll be others to follow. I'll warrant it's rough at sea. And we'll land wi' the hinner end of the storm. But mebbe thae chieldies werna' in flight, when Hempriggs took his survey.'

'His oats are gey and thin.' Janie was enjoying the rare experience of being accepted man to man, in broad Scots, and with authority. 'He's got some gey rank-like stuff in yon park.'

'And small wonder at it,' the Mannie agreed. 'Hempriggs should have stuck to concreting. He kens a lot about cement, but deil all about the rotation of crops. And so his corn's shargared, ye think, Janie?'

They stood contemplating the fat, bearded ears of their own corn. Still green over by the Glebe, but yellowing south-wards down to Hardhillock.

'I'll maybe mak' a start to the inroads next week, if the storm bypasses us,' the Mannie concluded.

He'll be a windmill on the hum then, Janie thought, remembering past harvests. Flailing his long arms above the scythe, and singing the hot afternoons over and past.

'This will be your last hairst wi' me then, Janie.'

It was just a statement. But, somehow, it needed a reply. An expression of regret.

'I'll miss outside,' Janie said truthfully, 'I'll miss outside terribly.'

The clang of a distant door prevented elaboration. It shot

the Mannie up into straightness, and turned his face to Leuchar's Hill.

'I'm taking a turn up bye to look at the gimmers if onybody speirs. And you had best be making tracks for the house, Janie.'

Dear Mannie. He was none other than Mrs Thane's husband. But the children had no name for him, other than the Mannie. He hovered on the fringe of Orphanage life. Clumsy, and 'in the road' of everybody in the busy kitchen. Ill at ease in the best room. And positively uncomfortable in his stiff, black Sunday suit in the Kirk pew.

His was the shadow that would whiles slope round the back door, wondering 'if he could get a bairn or two to give a hand with the tattie lifting?'

The children vied with each other to work for the Mannie. He made slight demands on them, and was so grateful for so little.

'And what's *your* name, lass?' he would inquire with great bewilderment. Never quite sure if the Mannie had really forgotten the name, or if this was a signal for fun, the children would shout protestingly:

'That's Janie! Janie MacVean. She's been here for years and years!'

The Mannie would lowp startled up into the air, knocking over the tattie pails in his surprise.

'God be here! So it is. Of *course* it's Janie. Can ye sing, Janie?'

And without waiting for a reply, would go striding down the furrow, past the children bent double with laughter, singing out of him:

> There was a wee cooper
> Wha lived in Fife
> Nicketty. Nacketty. Noo, Noo, Noo.

Without ever probing, the Mannie knew when any of the children were 'in disgrace' with his wife.

'How can ye no' work your work right in the house?' he had once asked Janie, as sadly as if her unhappiness belonged to him too. And the Mannie was the only person to whom she had ever tried to explain it:

'I do try. Truly I do. I start to dust fine, then something comes into my head, and I think about it so long that the time passes, and the dusting isn't done.'

Peering over the calves' loose-box, which was momentarily the confessional, Janie had awaited the Mannie's verdict with all the apprehension that sometimes overtook the Kirk on Sunday mornings when the Minister, tired of beseeching God, attacked his congregation with cantankerous cunning: 'Can any good thing come out of Nazareth?' That the Minister didn't really want an answer, relieved the doubt on the faces of his congregation. But Janie *had* wanted a reply and, in supplying it, the Mannie had somehow relieved her too.

'The happiest chield ever I kent, Janie, was a chield who hadna' two thoughts to crack between his ears. But God preserve us! Folk couldna' thole to see him so happy about nothing at all. They couldna' comprehend it, ye see. So they just up and lockit him awa'. On the t'ither hand, folk with owre muckle thoughts in their heads, they've been lockit awa' as well. Nothing riles one human being so much as the ither human being that they canna' understand.

'Like the brute beasts, by God! Tak' you a calf that's been born wi' two heads or one leg. That's no' the beastie's wight. It was born that wye, poor vratch. But the ither calves, in the same loose-box, mark you! They'll hound it down and butt it to death. That's the beasts. And whiles human beings are no' muckle better, for all that they've got minds to think things out with. And never comprehending that it's gey ill for some to find the balance, and aye just hell and all to keep it. Do you no' think now that it might be easier to work your thinking in with your other jobbies? It *can* be done, ye ken, Janie. Between you and me and the roan calf there, I do it mysel' all the time.'

Janie was vividly to recall and interpret the Mannie's words a short year later: meanwhile they seemed to cover herself and the Mannie with a conspiratorial kind of comfort.

There had always been comfort to the Mannie's being. A smell of dung as coarse and complete as that of the dustbins in the Lane, when you had first lifted their lids. You still sometimes escaped to the fields, just for the smell of him. To gaze on his glorious grime, to hear him sing in the loud uninhibited accents of the causeway:

> For the Minister kissed the fiddler's wife.
> And he couldna' sleep for thinkin' o't.

The Mannie had set his singing seal on Janie' growing-upness. Had marked the passing of the years with a signature tune. Gently, teasingly at first:

> For Nancy's hair is yella like gowd.
> And her e'en are like the lift, sae blue.

Now that the gentle preliminaries were over, that skirts were longer, and legs had become a mystery beneath them, the Mannie's song of growing-upness echoed with virility in the early morning. byre and in the fields that lay the furthest from the house:

> O my lass, ye'll get a man.
> And syne ye'll need a cradle.

Furtive, but exciting were his theme songs now. Like the

gleam of young girls' thighs once glimpsed in dark corners of the Lane. Mysterious and thrilling and quite unlike the dark, growling sound, 'whoring', that the Duchess had applied to it all.

Janie would have got all the blame if the Mannie's songs had ever been overheard. She knew that surely, in the dim, instinctive way that she realised blame had been borne in from some bewildering airt, with her first breath. And, though a sense of blame was ever present, the sins which gave rise to it could not easily be defined, confessed to God, and absolved. God could understand everything, even incoherent guilt, but you were only really sure about this on Sundays. Everybody believed in God on Sundays, then laid Him carefully away with their best clothes for the rest of the week.

Old and forbidding as the Kirk was, it was one of the few places in which Janie's spirit thawed in its narrow cocoon. Bursting out to meet the Word of God according to the prophet Isaiah. Blossoming, as it had blossomed in the Green, to the enchanting sound of far-flung places. Racing through desolate Sharon and Lebanon ashamed. Through Tarshish seas. Up Tyre and into Babylon bloated and be-damned. Down Ephraim and over Idumea.

But the cormorant and the bittern shall possess it; the owl also and the raven shall dwell in it.

And it might have been Leuchar's Hill itself that Isaiah told of, for all that he had ever excited the faces of the congregation, folding their thoughts darkly down into the furrows of their own fields:

God help the poor Israelites if ever they were as deived wi' reiving hoodie craws as we've been over Leuchar's way the year. According to Isaiah there, the bodies of his time had more than their whack of pests and plagues and the like. You would have thought now that such mischances would have quelled the perverse craitturs. But deil the bit o't! Isaiah ranted on of worse to come.

And thorns shall come up in her palaces, nettles and brambles in the fortresses thereof and it shall be an habitation of dragons, and a court for owls.

Thorns and nettles, by God! Skeyne had known its share of both. Though the Lord in his wisdom had keepit the dragons for the fear of foreign folk in far-off times and places. Knowing, no doubt, that a dragon crawling over the Cairngorms would fair bewilder a decent Skeyne man.

But Isaiah's dragon had never bewildered Janie. It was something she took from the Kirk, a weapon of the imagination which she whiles sent writhing in through the back door, to breathe its fire through the coldness of Mrs Thane's disapproval.

Chapter Ten

THE shrubbery which walled the Orphanage round parted to reveal Mima, the newest Orphan, sitting on the shaft of the wheel-barrow, staring bleakly at the long length of yard which she still had to rake clear of leaves.

'I hate raking this yard.' She spoke dully, as if Janie had been standing beside the barrow forever. 'It's the hardest of all the jobs in the Orphanage. You never come to the end of it.'

That was allowed.

'You finish raking one bit of it' – Mima felt encouraged by the allowance – 'then the leaves fall down and you've got to go back and rake it all over again. It's always me that's got to do the raking.'

'Because you're the newest. That's why,' Janie explained. 'That's the job we're all put on to, when we first come here. It teaches you perseverance and self-discipline,' she added, echoing Mrs Thane's own words.

But I hated raking the yard too, Janie remembered silently, staring at its grey length and at the treacherous trees and rhododendron bushes that surrounded it. Especially in autumn. I used to sit on the shaft of the barrow and cry sometimes, because the wind nipped my face all the time, and the leaves kept whirling down, and it was like trying to rake the whole of the world clean, in a wind that had taken a spite to you and never ended. I was right glad when Donnie came and I wasn't the newest any more. Because he had to take over the raking of the yard.

'Never mind, Mima,' Janie consoled aloud. 'You'll soon get off the raking now. I'm leaving. Somebody else will be coming in my place. They'll be the newest, and you'll get promoted to another job.'

'To running down the village and doing all the messages?' Mima asked hopefully.

'No. Of course not.' Janie guarded her present privilege jealously. 'This is the very last job you get promoted to. You've got to be old like me and almost leaving the Orphanage, before you get to go down to the village amongst other people. Your next job,' she continued severely, 'will just be to scrape the mud off all the boots in the boiler house. It isn't really a bad job, Mima,' Janie added, touched somewhere by the desolation on the small girl's face. 'I used to be awfully happy scraping the boots. The Mannie boils all the hens' tatties in the boiler house. It's lovely and warm in there in winter. And he always gives you a hot tattie in its jacket, when he finds you there. You could,' Janie added, viewing the stretch of yard still to be raked, 'you could say to Mrs Thane that you've got an awful gripping pain in your belly, Mima.'

'But I *have* got a pain in my belly, Janie.' Mima looked up wonderingly. 'Honest I have. Just here.'

'I know.' That was accepted. 'I sometimes used to get one there too, when I had to rake the yard. Mrs Thane will likely give you a dose of senna though, but it's better than raking. Don't you tell that I mentioned it now. And don't say your belly,' Janie warned over her shoulder. 'That's vulgar. Mind and just say your stomach!'

The stir had reached its height in the kitchen. That moment when the confusion is so great that nobody cares any more, and everybody is light and hilarious with the burden of caring suddenly gone from them. The mood provided cover for Janie's belated entry.

'You'd better get down to the printing of the place names for the table, Janie.' Mrs Thane spoke as if Janie hadn't been away for a long time at all. 'Your best printing mind! And write 'The Reverend Mr John McLaren.' Not just plain 'Mr McLaren' the day.'

'Yes, Mrs Thane.' Relief at not being scolded for lateness made Janie expansive. 'I'll print them in two different colours if you like. They'll look extra good in black and red.'

The offer was almost accepted.

'But Donnie spilt all the red ink,' Alice remembered smugly. 'That time when he was doing his graph.'

'Yes. And the stain hasn't come out of the desk yet, I see.' Mrs Thane examined the desk frowningly. Her finding jolted her out of good humour. 'You would all be a sight more careful if you had to pay for all the stuff you waste and destroy. You'll just have to use black ink, Janie. And get on with it now.'

The task had a certain prestige. Janie studied the list of Trustees' names with an importance that impressed the children busied with much humbler tasks.

'Is the Head Trustee coming the day, Janie?' Chris peered over Janie's shoulder with suitable deference.

'He's my favourite,' Alice admitted, approaching the desk curiously.

'Mine too,' Janie agreed. 'He's so quiet. He hardly ever

says anything. But you've got a feeling that he understands about everything.'

'You'll be left behind with them on your own today, Janie. I wouldn't be you for anything.'

Donnie's commiseration sparked off a thought in Janie's mind.

'I'm excited in a way about that,' she confessed. 'I think I'll feel like a real person when I'm alone with them. Not just one of the crowd. And I'm glad because the Dominie went to see the Trustees about preparing me for the University Prelims. I bet they never even knew I was good at lessons, till he told them.'

'That's one good thing, Janie,' Chris pointed out. 'I bet the Dominie didn't tell them one bad thing about you. He's always liked you.'

'He might just say one thing that's not too good,' Janie admitted. 'And he's always saying it to myself, that my essays are the best in the School, but my endings are always sad. And I just can't write happy endings,' she explained, 'because things don't end that way.'

Strange thing that. Janie sat pondering it quietly. You knew the instant you were sad. But happiness always lay either in the past or in the future. I was happy this morning, Janie realised with surprise. About nothing. Just walking along watching the mists steam out from the seams of the Cairngorms. And I know I will be happy when I leave the Orphanage. But I can never pin the actual moment of happiness down in an essay, and recognise it. Saying it is *now*.

The reception room was loud with coughs and nervous with the scraping of chairs. The children in the back row fumbled for the touch of each other's hands and found little reassurance in the contact. They fixed their eyes anywhere, except upon the Trustees' faces. Each trying to find calmness in the contemplation of ordinary things.

But familiarity itself had turned into strangeness. The Wife of the Founder of this Orphanage stared down over everyone from her large canvas above the fireplace, as if she was really seeing them and felt slightly surprised by what she saw.

The Mannie had put on the unease of Sunday with his stiff, black suit, strumming his fingers along the window-sill, tapping his foot in rhythm to a tune heard only by himself.

Mrs Thane was the one person whom the children could see without setting eyes on. Stand erect. Don't stare at your feet. Her warning signals trembled on invisible wave-lengths. Your eyes rested on no particular face, but you were intensely aware of all the faces slanting around you. Most of them familiar. But each of them isolated.

'*Well! Well! Well*! You're to be congratulated, Mrs Thane!'

The small Trustee's greeting riveted all eyes frontwards.

'A fine, healthy crew! A fine, healthy crew indeed!'

The smaller children, not yet familiar with the exuberance of his greetings, stared wide eyed and puzzled, as if he were referring to Sinbad and his Sailors and not to themselves at all. The older children took a sudden, collective interest in the fir trees outside the window, steeling themselves against a fit of the giggles.

If I look at the Mannie now, Janie realised, turning her face swiftly towards the fir tree too, I know he'll wink. And that will be the end of me for certain.

'And this *can't* be Alice, Mrs Thane! You don't mean to tell me that this is Alice! When you think of the scrap she was.'

The children's minds scornfully rejected the small Trustee's assumed ignorance. But their eyes slanted, compelled, in the direction of their unfortunate companion. Groping unwillingly over her. Reluctant to discover Alice enlarged and transformed.

'And. My word! Alick's spectacles certainly improve him.'

Alick shot into focus now. Ping Pong. Ping Pong. Ping. And we're coiled up quiet in our inner selves. Pong. And we spring quivering out into a glancing space.

I wish I could change when my turn comes, Janie thought. Into something big enough and strange enough to fit the small Trustee's vision.

'Goodness! Hasn't Donnie shot up in the past year.'

If Donnie turned into a giraffe right now, Janie's thoughts raced, the Trustee would get such a surprise that he wouldn't be able to utter another word. The ridiculous thought got out of control, spreading itself grinningly across Janie's face.

Of his bones are coral made . . .
Nothing of him that doth fade.

The lines rushed to Janie's rescue. She steadied her thoughts against them:

But doth suffer a sea change
Into something rich and strange.

Her grin wrecked itself on the wide and wonderful phrase. Into something rich and strange. She could look with serious face now at the small Trustee. At Mrs Thane. At all the Trustees. She wouldn't have changed places with one of them. Not for anything. They were all so old. Nothing was ridiculous, or rich, or strange to them any more.

'And Janie? We're going to be losing Janie soon. How many years, Mrs Thane? How long have we had Janie?'

The Head Trustee rose to his feet. The gesture signalled

the dismissal of the children, and cut off the flow of the small Trustee's words.

'Stay behind the others,' Mrs Thane whispered in Janie's ear. The children filed past her, their small, sidelong glances of awe lengthened her in spirit and in stature. The door closed behind them. Its click separated her from childhood.

'We've had a visit from your Schoolmaster, Janie.'

The Head Trustee was speaking long enough for Janie to know the sound of his voice for the first time.

'He tells us you have made excellent progress at school.'

'Did you know,' Mr McLaren, the Minister, leant forward, cutting Janie from the scene, 'that her English papers were the best in Aberdeenshire? Most unusual,' he explained, 'I read the particular essay. The lifetime of an old woman, complete in a single page. It was difficult to understand how anyone so young could have written it, without having possibly experienced it.'

'I didn't realise that Janie was in any way . . .' The small Trustee faltered, his eyes searched Mrs Thane for aid. 'I always had the impression that she . . . well, that she . . .'

Mrs Thane came to his rescue.

'She's a puzzle. She can be as crude and knowing as they come. And, at the same time, she's less sophisticated and more sensitive than any of the other children, who haven't had such a deplorable background.'

'A disintegrated personality?' the Minister suggested.

'I'm afraid so,' the Head Trustee admitted. 'That's why this question of further Education presents a problem. The pity is that we sometimes get them too late to adjust the balance.'

'How old was Janie when she came to us, Mrs Thane?' The small Trustee put the question.

'Nine. Just on nine.'

'Give me a child till it is seven,' the small Trustee deplored.

'After that, anyone can have it. What's bred in the bone, you know.'

'Well! What have you got to say for her, yourself, Mrs Thane?'

The Head Trustee's breeziness drew Janie into their circle again.

'She's honest,' Mrs Thane agreed. 'She's very good with the younger ones. She's got a nice nature, she never sulks. She's an excellent milker. She can turn out a room well. Indeed, Janie can do anything well when she likes. But she doesn't always . . . like!'

'We're all inclined to be a bit like that, sometimes,' the Minister confessed. 'It s a very human failing.'

'What about an under-housemaid's job for her, Mrs Thane.' The small Trustee was struck with the idea and urged it lovingly.

'In some good household you know. Where they'll take an interest in her.'

'I'm no' so sure about that,' the Mannie intervened for the first time.

'Good, Mr Thane.' The small Trustee sounded as if he were aware of the Mannie for the first time, and was anxious to make up for it. 'It's excellent to have the practical opinion of a plain man. What would you suggest?'

'If Janie has to go into service at all,' the Mannie spoke unperturbed by Mrs Thane's alert attitude, 'I suggest that she works at a local farmhouse. She likes outside work. And she's good at it. She'll know where she is, and the folk that she's amongst. At least till she gets another year over her head.'

'What do you think, yourself, Janie?' The small Trustee put the question.

Don't fly up. Mrs Thane's eyes pleaded. Don't fly up just now. I tried to prepare you for this.

Janie found the small Trustee's face.

'I don't want to dust and polish,' she told it. 'And I don't want to work on a farm. I want to write poetry. Great poetry. As great as Shakespeare.'

Janie dismissed herself from the room. Surprise rooted Mrs Thane from preventing her. Her last Trustees' Day was over.

There had been no haste about that night's delivery of the milk. No haste at all. It was the last time. And, last times, Janie was gradually beginning to discover, gave you a large sense of freedom. The largeness of the freedom that was over her had diminished the approaching village. World enough until then, Skeyne seemed to have shrunk small and down into the foothills of the Cairngorms. Even the Cairngorms themselves had lost their terrifying immensity.

'I'll be beyond them next week,' Janie had thought contemptuously. 'I'll know at last what lies beyond the Cairngorms.'

The outlying cottages of Skeyne had stood rooted in tansies, sloping forward as if they had grown up out of the earth itself and were moulded in its slant forever. Women lounged outside their doorways in untidy ease, conscious that the night had a lot of wear in it yet.

'It's yoursel' then, is it, Janie?' Kirsty Withan had peered round her bourtree bush. The fine autumn night had resurrected her.

'For I thought she died long ago.' Janie had felt resentful somewhere.

'My faith ye! But ye've shot up, Quean! Ye was just a bairn the other day, when I set eyes on ye! Just a bairn.' Kirsty's voice had gabbled urgently. As if it hadn't uttered for years and was desperately making up for lost time. 'And how are all the folk up bye at the Orphanage? Old Thane is still to the fore they tell me. Deed aye! Me and Thane will stick them all out yet. We'll see them all in the Kirk yard down bye.' She had chuckled as if this triumph was her own and secret. Janie had been glad to escape the old woman's eyes, detaining her with their dumb pleading . . . Speak to me, speak to me, they had urged. I only know that I am truly alive when *other* folk think it . . . Had been glad to strike down through Carron wood to the Orphanage again.

The threshing mill had flung its gaunt grotesque shadow across the corn yard. The mill men had hovered round it like ghosts. Their voices drifting upwards, a dirge in the dusk.

'Roon. Roon. Roon.'

'Roon wi' her.'

'Roon yet.'

'Roon. Roon. Roon.'

The younger children, condemned to play outwith the radius of the dangerous mill's shadow, had leapt defiantly in the light. Outcrying the mill men's dirge. Dusk and distance distorting them into little demons, and the words of their familiar game into some weird incantation:

> Queen. Queen
> In paraffin
> Was seventeen
> Caroline.

Losing their otherness only when she had come within hailing distance of them.

'It's Janie! Come on! We can go inside now. We can all go in with Janie. She's big!'

The kitchen at a loss, with the harvest workers huddling inside it. The straws off their boots wisping forlornly across the highly polished floor. The smoke from their pipes curling guiltily upwards. Their great feet scraping in incoherent embarrassment for the coarse, sharny smell of themselves that tussled with the refined but persistent smell of beeswax. Janie, sniffing an aura of battle, had smelt danger. Mrs Thane struck the first blow, opening all the windows with a snap that sent Claystone's voice rushing in to cover the sudden, humble silence.

'Mind you! We've had weeter harvests! A damned sight weeter! Ye mind on that, Kinmyles? Surely to' God ye mind on that? Yon year we were gatherin' in Burnie Boozle's corn. By God we were weet! We were baith weet then. Weet up till our verra . . .'

'So you got back at last, Janie!' Mrs Thane's voice had cut into Claystone's recollections with a lash. He had sighed his story back into a silence broken by Kinmyles venturing tentatively:

'I hear that Janie's to be lowsin the sheaves for us, on top o' the mill, the morn.'

'Aye. Deed aye!' The Mannie, grateful for some safe and 'proper' topic of conversation, had become voluble. 'Her first time abune the mill. And her last,' he explained. 'Janie's going to Kingorm. They've decided to mak' a scholar oot o' her. They have that!'

'Aye, then, Janie?' Kinmyles had said. 'So ye'll no' be kennin' ony o' us in a year or twa. They'll be makin a Kingorm lady o' ye!'

'They'll have no need!' Mrs Thane had snapped, straightening up from picking the straws off the floor. 'She thinks she's that, already. Kingorm. Kingorm. There's been nothing else in her head or on her tongue but Kingorm, this past week!'

'It's an odd thing about youngsters hereaboots and nooadays,' Kinmyles had begun pondering diplomatically, 'they all seem to think that the world begins and ends at Kingorm. Though, God knows, I never needed to go further than Skeyne for everything and onything that life has to offer at Kingorm.'

'Aye. God knows!' Claystone had agreed banteringly, suddenly forgetful of his austere surroundings. 'God knows, Kinmyles! Ye've experienced twa three things that life has to offer at Skeyne. God aye, Man! Ye could just tell a gay story, if aince ye get crackin'.'

'Cry the mill men in for their supper, Janie!' Mrs Thane's command had prevented such an exciting possibility. 'Run on, now! You'll get yours when they're finished.'

'So the brose is up, then, isn't, Janie?' The mill men had emerged in a cloud of dust from the dark mysterious caverns of the mill. Shaking themselves and straightening up into livingness.

'You're to be lowsin' the sheaves till's the morn, Quean?'

'Keep an eye on auld Hughie here, then! He's an auld man, Janie! But he's no' short o' young ideas. He'll hae ye coupit down in the mill, head first!'

Their words had struck and faded.

'She'll be a fine change fae auld Maggie Hooch!'

'Nothing the maitter wi' auld Maggie Hooch!'

'Damn all the maitter wi' her, Dod. Except auld age.'

'An ill enough thing, auld age!'

'It's fairly that! It's a thing ye can do nothing wi'!'

'Such as, Dod? Come on now, Man! Dinna be shy. Out with it!'

Their laughter had belched upwards. The dusk had questioned it quiveringly, then dismissed it. But Janie had stood holding on to it. Holding on to her awareness of the possession of her body. She had been aware of it before, had glimpsed it in the smirks of the boys at school, had overheard it in their whispers. A mild awareness. But grown men were beginning to acknowledge it now. There was something cruel and fierce in their knowing.

The Cairngorms had begun to close in and were pressing down on the howe. Carron wood had crept upwards till its trees stood rooted against the sky. Silence had circled all the landscape, and held it trembling prisoner. A peesie had cried through the silence, weeping its grief across the stubble field. Some long, long grief that had found an echo in Janie herself. Her pain became submerged in the peesie's cry. Herself and the landscape had stood in some ache, waiting for release.

> Guard us, we pray
> Throughout the coming night.

It was then that she realised why the Minister always chose that hymn to end the Evening Service. Because the aloneness of night was beyond the bearing of the land itself. It caught you, the land did, if you walked it at night. Held you hostage. Clamped and small within its own immensity, and cast all the burden of its own aloneness upon you.

The wind had begun to threaten the air. Passionately she had longed for the wind to come. To blow herself and the landscape sky high into movement and coherence again. Almost she had been aware of the wind's near fierceness. Ready to plunge the furious hillside burns down into Cladda river. To hurl the straws over all the dykes. To toss the chaff into the eyes of the protesting people, bending before it, flapping in their clothes like scarecrows. To sting the trees in Carron wood into hissing rebellion. To give the land some loud, loud cry, other than that of pain.

'Aye. But the wind's hoverin'. She's goin' to rise.'

The mill men were clanking out now. Pausing by the back door. Sniffing the night.

'Think ye that, then, Dod?'

'I wouldna' wonder at it. We could do wi' a breesie o' wind to dry out the stooks.'

'A breesie, man! No' a bloody gale, though! And that's what's in it. She's on the road! A muckle North-Easter!'

They had dragged themselves reluctantly away from the contemplation of the night.

'Well then, Janie! This time the morn's night, Quean, ilka bone in your body will be hippit, after a day at the mill!'

'God aye, Janie! You'll feel that sore, ye'll have to lie on your belly!'

'Never mind, Janie! The first day at the threshing mill is aye the worst day.'

'To say nothing of the yavins. They'll have ye itchin' a' night. Belly and all!'

'Coarse things, yavins, Janie! Ye ken the cure for them, though, Quean?'

'Hardly, hardly, Dod, Janie has never lowsed on the mill before.'

'Ye tell her, then, Jeems! Ye ken all the answers!'

'Na, hardly. I dinna' like.'

'All right! I'll tell her masel! It's like this, Janie. Ye tak' off all your clothes. Sark and all. No cheating. And shak' yoursel' in front o' the fire. Just mind that auld Hughie here doesna' nip up bye for a wee peep when you're doin't.'

Their laughter had shaken the darkness again. They had carried their joke with them, along the stubble field.

'She's risin' already! We're in for a gale the morn, right enough. You'll need your goggles on the mill, Hughie. The chaff will fair blind ye!'

'Never him! Never Hughie! He likes to wink to a bonnie lowser wi' his bare e'en. That so, Hughie.'

'Na, na. Na faith ye! Janie's just some young for winkin' to yet!'

'Janie! Janie!' The Mannie's voice had assailed the sky. 'Janie! Where have ye got till?'

'She's no' that young.' The mill men began to laugh amongst themselves. 'Harken till auld Thane cryin' awa' there. She's old enough for him to be anxious, now. She'll soon be ready for the knife.'

'Janie! O, there ye are! Where are the ithers? Chris! Alice! Donnie! Come on in, now. Come on! The hale jing bang o' ye! Come on awa' in . . .'

GLITTER OF MICA

for
Elizabeth Adair

This is the shape of a land which outlasts a strategy
And is not to be taken by rhetoric or arms.

G. S. FRASER *Hometown Elegy*

THE parish of Caldwell lies to the east of our shire. It has moved neither poet to song nor tourist to praise. It has little to give or lend but much to sell; Ayrshire and Friesian cattle pastured out for milk, Aberdeen Angus cattle reared for fattening, for this is cattle and barley country, and both, and second to none, are flaunted in the face of the world.

On Soutar Hill, to the north of Caldwell, you can, on a fine clear day, see the figure of a horse carved out in stone from Pictish times, and whatever the weather and from any direction you can see the old Free Kirk, one of the first of the kirks to break away from the Old Established Church, in the Disruption of 1843. Although it stands as intact now as it stood then, the Free Kirk has become a granary, for the people of Caldwell are less kirk conscious than were their forebears. The Misses Lennox, retired from Town, bought the Free Kirk Manse and the wood surrounding it, renaming the latter 'Lob's Wood', but to those who were born and bred in Caldwell, it stubbornly remains 'The Free Kirk Wood'.

Caldwell is surrounded by old 'Houses' occupied by old names: Forbes-Sempill. Seaton. Hamilton. And by castles whose owners are of Norman origin: Farquharson. Gordon. Grant. Duff. So, considering its proximity to ancient aristocracy, the wonder is that Caldwell has neither legends of its own, nor the ballads which arise from them. It is content to borrow these from its neighbours, so it laughs in recollection of the Laird of Udny's Fool, reminiscing satirically . . . 'I'm the Laird of Udny's Fool. Whose Fool are *you*?' . . . Weeps in its cups over Fyvie's *Bonnie Peggie*, or goes singing in its stride with *The Irish Dragoon* who died for love of her.

Early in the morn they set out for Aberdeen.
Early in the morning O!
And when they marched across the bonnie brig o' Gight
The band it played 'The Lowlands o' Fyvie', O!

Long long before they reached Old Meldrum Town
They had their Captain to carry O!
Long long before they reached bonnie Aberdeen
They had their Captain to bury O!

And drunk or sober it becomes bawdy over *The White Cow of Turriff*.

Caldwell also borrows the neighbouring gentry to declare open its Summer Fetes and Shows. A token gesture this, to those who feel that they 'have come down in the World', and an incentive to those who still hope to 'get on in the World', though, to most of its inhabitants, Caldwell *is* 'The World'.

Last summer it was Lady Grizelda Beaton who was 'honoured and privileged' – or so she herself maintained at the time – to declare open Caldwell's Summer Show. Indeed, Lady Grizelda got so carried away on the platform, that a few close observers, with no sense of occasion, gravely doubted whether Charlie Anson's carpentry, makeshift at the best of times, would hold its own anent all the prancing and gesticulating that was over her Ladyship. And when she stretched out her arms as if to embrace the whole wide world, vowing to Caldwell's inhabitants, gooking below, that they were 'indeed her ain folk', those who lived on their avowal of 'Better Days' were deeply moved, although the same declaration had been examined closely and suspected strongly by God Knows and his fellow farm-workers; for Caldwell is first and foremost the land of the farm-worker.

'It's our vote yon one's swarming after,' had been God Knows' considered opinion, but then, he belonged to a race which not only suspected everybody outwith the farm he worked on, but most of those within it too. 'For yon second son of hers is just down from Oxford,' he had recollected, 'and going in for politics. Or so they say.'

'But it's No Ball. And Up the Liberals!' Dod Feary had shouted in his cups, which slogan had visibly cooled down the remainder of Lady Grizelda's speech, for had her claim that they 'were indeed her ain folk' been true, she would have known this much about them at least, that the odds were always on the farm-worker's vote going to his farmer's Party, just as in older times when his forebears with native sagacity had attended the Kirk of their farmer's religious persuasion.

This was a conditioning which had come down through the centuries and was automatic and, in its way, a kind of comfort. For the farmer was their 'Fatherhood', good or bad, and the farm-workers took the fierce privilege of sons in passing judgment on this issue, either way he was their own, so rooted that he became identified with the land itself, his name absorbed into the very title of the acres he farmed. Even the old hereditary aristocrats of the countryside needed a double identification; Forbes of Rothiemay, one said. Hay of Seaton. Gordon of Huntly. Grant of Monymusk. Cowdray of Dunecht. But the farmers had need of no such prefixes to become landmarks, for though they died at last, their earth abideth and their identification with it was simplified and perpetuated – by – the syllabic title of their farms : Auchronie. Ardgye. Balblair. Balben. Calcots. Clova. Drumdelgie. Delgaty and . . . Darklands.

Darklands is one of Caldwell's largest farms, its productivity high, its soil fertile, its landscape bleak. The kind of place will cause a Townsman in passing to thank God for the fury of his factory or the fuss of his fishmarket, but to the men who work on Darklands farm, even the two or three isolated landmarks on its landscape become unnecessary at last. Occasionally, they will lift their eyes towards Soutar Hill to verify that the Pictish horse still stands in stone – always aware that it could rear nowhere else. Whiles, too, they will straighten their backs and gaze on their other landmark, Ambroggan House, for it isn't every parish that provides asylum for the wealthy mentally ill of the land. It was the Plunger who long ago had puzzled it all out for his fellow farm-workers:

'Just you take Chae Finnie. Him that was Handyman over there at Balwhine. And yon night that he up and chased the Vet in his shirt tail with a scythe in his hand. Clean mad Chae had gone, we all said. And until the Authorities came and carted him off to the Asylum, not a man, woman, chick or child of us opened our mouths to Chae for fear of the madness that had come over him, for all that we had known him all our days with him as sane as ourselves. But yet, mark you! We pass the time of day with the patients from Ambroggan House, and them with us. As happy as if we were all in our right minds. You see, it's all just a question of money again. If you're poor you're plain mad. If you're rich they've got an easier name for you. A Nervous Break-down. And yet, the odd thing about it is we *were* all far more scared of poor Chae Finnie than ever we are when we run into the Daft Dominie from Ambroggan House, just speaking away to himself by the side of the road. It would near look as though money mellows the degree of madness itself. Or maybe it's just that our respect for money makes a rich madman less fearful than a poor madman!'

Hugh Riddel, Head Dairyman at Darklands, stood remembering that now. Minding, too, how he had thought at the time that there maybe was something in what the Plunger had said, though he had laughed it off, and had ordered the Plunger to stop speaking stuff and nonsense, and to keep on plunging the milk bottles in the tank.

Hugh Riddel tried to keep his eyes averted from the wooded outline of Ambroggan House, for when time and tide stood still, place itself could petrify you within it, allowing you to escape into the future, and always less than you were. But even had he foreseen that, Hugh Riddel realised, he could not – nor would not – have averted it. Strange how a man, a man like Hugh Riddel, could have compelled himself forward so far and fast, till at last he had lost his bearings and could only grope his way back through a bleak knownness.

This surely was the bleakest landscape in Scotland. Morayshire now. Ah! But there was a mellow country for you. Hot to the sun and comforted by trees. A lass of a land and comely. Hugh Riddel's memories of Morayshire were brief, but safe and warm in recollection. Then his people had moved south to work on a farm near Stonehaven. Bleak land there too, with the sea biting always at hand. Still, it was on that farm near Stonehaven that he had grown old enough to realise that all the comings and goings to work on different farms were not for his parents the fine adventures they had been for himself.

A farm-worker was fee'd to work on a farm for a year only. At the end of the year the farmer would either 'seek' him to 'bide on for another year', or remain ominously silent on the subject. If his silence remained unbroken when lambing-time came round, the farm-worker knew that his services were no longer required. The sack without words. Hugh Riddel could marvel over the simplicity of it still. And the re-engaging of a farm-worker was equally simple. No written contract; just the passing of 'Arles' – a sum ranging from half a crown to ten shillings – by the farmer to his prospective worker, to seal and 'wet the bargain'. Hugh Riddel could marvel over the simplicity of that too.

His father had seldom been asked to 'bide on' at any farm when his year was up. It was always his mother who took this so much to heart. He could see her now, shrunken by memory, a small body forever wringing her hands, so that she fluttered tiny and distressed in his mind. He could see himself too, a small boy speeding perpetually through spring mirks, always the apprehensive – but excited – bearer of the bad tidings.

'The First Horseman's just been asked to bide on. I heard the farmer seeking him in the stable!'

His father banging his fist on the table and shaking the silence in the kitchen.

'What of it, then? Good God, it's but early yet. We're only into Februar'. The farmer's got till March to seek me to bide on.'

'But you are the *Cattleman*, Father.' He heard his ten-year-old self insist. 'You are the Cattleman. And the Cattleman is always asked to bide on before the First Horseman.'

Hugh Riddel knew now exactly what his wife Isa meant, when she accused him of not only 'Baking the cake' but 'Icing it as well. And putting on all the decorations, so that there is nothing left for anybody else to do at all, except to admire it and eat it.'

Even at the age of ten he had allowed no loopholes, and could remember how his father had always struggled to find one.

'What of it, then? There are *other* farms in Scotland. And I have never yet been feared of bending my back. There are other farms I tell you!'

'Aye. And we've tried a gey few of them,' had always been his mother's brief and bitter response.

'What of it?' His father had demanded again. 'We haven't been happy here. Not a one of us. It's too near the sea for one thing. And we are inland folk for another thing. Not seafarers. God Almighty, woman. Even Robbie Burns' father couldna thole this part of the country. That's why he upped it and made for away down the South, yonder!'

The smile broke into Hugh Riddel's thoughts. His father had always tried to translate his failings into strengths, through comparison with Burns. A comparison which never moved his mother, for Burns, as she often said, 'just never won round her at all'. Come to think of it, though, for all Burns' reputed success with 'The Lasses' of his day, it was the women of the countryside who now remained more immune to his 'Memory'. 'The men,' as his mother so often remarked, 'just uses Burns as an excuse for theirselves.' And that had been another of the times when the excuse hadn't worked with his mother.

'I don't give a tinker's curse for *what* Robbie Burns' father thought of this part of the country,' she had protested. 'He's no concern of mine at all. All I'm concerned with is that you have lost this job too. Just as you've lost every job you've ever had. I'm sick and tired of it all. And of you and your light fingers! We are no better off than the tinkers. We are always on the top of the road.'

'Do you imagine, woman,' his father had flared, 'do you imagine for one minute that I am the only man on this farm that helps myself to a pucklie oats for my hens? It's just that I always happen to get found out.'

Oh, and then the spring would grope forward towards the Term, and into the month of May with its small Feeing Market Days. It was then you could see the farm-workers who hadn't been asked to bide on mount their bicycles and go slanting down the roads that led to the little Market towns, whistling with all the defiance in the world, syne standing clustered round the Market Cross, trying to look as likely lads as possible, while waiting for the farmers to size them up and approach them with the offer of another year's Fee.

'Just like a curran Clydesdale horse taking round the ring,' as God Knows had once recalled it. Except that the brute beasts had their natural dignity. For they never kenned that they were being sized up. And they wouldn't have cared a docken if they had kent.

It was then, too, that you could see the farmworkers who had been asked to bide on, planting out their 'yards' – never 'gardens' – with the bare essentials, curly kale and first early potatoes. There was never enough security to plant anything as frivolous but enduring as a lilac bush. Hugh Riddel's mother had always had an awful hankering after a lilac bush, yet never enough faith to plant one. 'Not for *other* folk to get the good of,' as she often explained. For that was another deeply ingrained aversion. The fear of other folk getting the good of anything outwith their own efforts. It wasn't until they had come to Darklands, here, that his mother began to take any interest in the yard, and started to call it by the name of garden.

Hugh Riddel could remember as clear as anything the night on which his father had come home from the market, fee'd to Darklands. 1939. The year the war broke out.

'*Well* now! Who was it said I would never get another fee to another farm?' his father had demanded, jocularly, but with fierce under-currents of pride. 'Who was it, then? For you can just swallow your words, and take a right good look at this for a start-off!'

'This' was a ten-shilling note that his father had wagged under their noses. And his mother and himself *had* taken a good look. For money – paper money, that was – was something they only set eyes on twice a year, on Term Days.

'Well may you both stand there gooking,' his father had said, pleased with the wordless spell the ten-shilling note had cast over them. 'And that's only the Arles that Darklands gave me to wet the bargain. Truth tells twice, you see!' he had added with the wonderful simplicity of one who had just found that out.

'It's a wonder to me you didn't go and drink the lot,' his mother said, when she recovered herself. But there had been no barb in her voice, and they both knew by the way she fussed around getting the supper that she was pleased too.

'But I had a drink,' his father expanded, conscious of the geniality in the air. 'For I had something to drink to. You'll both grant that, when you hear what else I've got to tell you. This is my Fee now.' . . . Even his mother, who so seldom stood still, stopped fiddling about with supper to listen, while his father counted everything off on his fingers.

'Meal. Six bolls of it. Tatties. Ten bags. Not counting two bags of First Earlies. Coal. A ton. And another half-ton extra for calving times. Now, Mother, just you consider that extra half-ton itself! There's not many farmers take into account the coal we burn up night after night sitting up waiting for the cows to calve. So *that's* not to be sneezed at. Syne there's two quarts of milk a day. All the skimmed milk you care to carry home. And of course the first milk after calving is mine, so we'll have plenty of calfie's cheese. And you're both gey fond of calfie's cheese. That, then, that's our perquisites for the year. Now for my Fee. Oh, but you'll never guess my Fee, Hugh, son. Never in a month of Sundays. So I may just as well tell you what it is. Seventy-six pounds a year. Seventy-six pounds. The biggest Fee I've ever been offered.

What do you think of it, then? Well? Have the pair of you gone and lost the use of your tongues?'

Hugh Riddel couldn't remember his own Fee exactly. It had gone up by leaps and bounds. Somewhere in the region of seven hundred it would be. Strange that it was his father's Fee of twenty years ago which lit his memory with golden numerals. Six feet high. Seventy-six pounds a year.

What a perfect night that had been while it lasted. For nothing lasted long, least of all – perfection.

'And there's another thing!' His father had remembered. 'And it will please you as well. I'll never again lay unlawful hands on an ear of corn. Darklands herd is T.T. Tested, so we're not allowed to keep hens.'

'What? No *hens*?' His mother had protested dismayed. 'But I've always had my two three hens. Always.'

'I can make neither head nor tail of you, woman,' his father had puzzled. 'You were always complaining that your hens died in debt. Look see! I'll tell you what. We'll sell the lot. Bantams and all. And we'll buy a bit of new linoleum with the price of them. For you've been making a sore enough cry for new linoleum. How's that, my quean? Come on, now. Come in about to me till I tell you something else!'

'Get away with you, man. You're drunk!' had been his mother's invariable reply to such overtures from his father; and her reaction to scurry away out into the scullery, beyond reach of husband or plea of son.

'I'm far from drunk, woman,' his father would protest to her disappearing figure, turning to confide in the small boy he had been. 'What would you make of that, Hugh, son? Your mother says I'm drunk. I come home to her with a bonnie Fee to a bonnie farm, and your mother shows no pleasure. Though she would be the first to make fine lament if I'd come home without a Fee at all. I try to say a bonnie wordie to her, and she turns and tells me that I'm drunk.'

'The only time your father ever does say a bonnie wordie to me,' his mother's voice came from the scullery in defence, 'is when he is drunk.'

It was true, too, Hugh Riddel remembered, but only as a *kind* of truth. For his father's words of endearment had always been spare and difficult, needing high moments for utterance, and his reaction to rejection, blustering but help-less.

'Now, now, my quean. That's just enough of that. Come here now. Come on in about to me. God, but there's just a handful of you. And I could lift you clean above my head with one hand, if I'd a mind to.'

He could, too. Hugh Riddel remembered that as well, although he had seldom seen it happen. He remembered it because it had feared him. His father spanning his mother's waist with his two hands and lifting her clean over his shoulder in a whirl of petticoats and skirling. It had feared him as much as if they had been in anger with each other, but it had strangely excited him, too.

'My God,' he had thought. 'When *I* am big!' With no other words to expand the thought, or define and clarify it. Only small wordless images and sensations, like his memories of Morayshire; the coarse comforting smell of sharn, the bare firescorched legs of the farmhouse servant girls, their laughter, and the dark skirls of them coming from the hay lofts. Himself high up on the turnip-sowing machine, the turnip seeds running between his fingers. He had always felt very safe, seated on the sowing machine, playing in the darkness with the turnip seeds, yet always apprehensive, as though he were on the brink of something still unknown, but which he would one day discover, and feel as much at one with as he felt with the tiny dark seeds that trickled through his fingers.

He was always greatly relieved – and just as greatly surprised – that at such times his parents hadn't simply lifted the lid clean off all his private thoughts, and stood staring at them, shocked and angry. They never did, of course. He was so often simply a means of communication between them; particularly with his mother. He could hear her yet.

'Ah well, Hugh. Darklands, or no Darklands, Fine Fee or no Fee at all, we are for the top of the road again, as usual. That will mean some other new school for you again. My! But you should be a clever man yet, with all the different schools you've attended in your time.'

'But I like new schools fine,' he had mumbled. Partly out of complete truth, and partly from a desire to side with his father. 'And maybe, maybe, Father, there will be tractors at Darklands farm.'

'Maybe there will be at that, then.' His father had grasped the lifeline. 'That wouldn't surprise me one bit. Mind you, Hugh, tractors are fine enough for clay soil and rough going, but for a bit of company in a long day, give me a pair of horse. God, Hugh. Did ever I get round to telling you about a Horseman I once kent? He always insisted on sleeping out in the stable with his pair. I wight he did that! For he always vowed that he preferred the brutes' company to that of the chield he was bothied with. A terrible man it appeared for snoring and wetting his bed. Though, come to think of it now, I believe I'd prefer the company of a pair of horse to a man like that, myself!'

And, as always, it was his mother who disrupted such moments with the flick of her tongue:

'Good grief, man. Have you nothing better to do but sit there and stuff Hugh's head with a lot of dirt!'

But nothing quite diminished the glow that their minds had cast over Darklands, the new farm that they were going to work on. Even now Hugh Riddel recollected their antici-pation, as through some bright upstanding springtime. Darklands, they had gathered from the farm-workers' grapevine, was a Farm of Farms.

'Not a single pair of horse on yon place,' the Second Cattleman had informed them. 'It's all tractor work there now. And Darklands himself is a gentleman farmer at that. Oh, but you'll have a good enough sit down with him, Riddel. For there's no side to yon man at all. And devil the chance of *him* ever trying to catch you out, by creeping up behind you on a mirky morning, looking like one of ourselves.'

If Hugh Riddel had ever been asked to define comfort, he would have described it as standing young in that spring, under the cover of an old men's voices, his face towards the sea, and half his mind on the mysterious life of the trawlers, drifting westwards to the Bay of Nigg. His remembrance on the strange turns of their speech, and lingering on the high whine of the fisherwives' voices.

... I cast my net in Largo Bay. And fishes I caught nine ...

And drawing his cold face into the warm stable again, lending his ears to accents that were familiar, and to arguments that never varied in context.

'They say that Darklands doesn't hold with the Farm-workers' Union, though.'

'Name me the farmer who does, Duggie.'

'I'll go one better than that. I'll say again as I've said before, if every farm-worker upped and joined his Union, we'd have one of the strongest Unions in Scotland.'

'All right, Duggie. All right. We know all about that, sd don't you get going on Unions again, or we'll be here for the rest of the night! All *I'm* trying to do is to put old Riddel here wise to the bee in Darklands' bonnet. And that's not the Union, though I've heard tell he's not too struck on it. It's the cream off the top of his milk. *That's* what you've got to guard against, Riddel! For he'll come down on you like the hammers of hell if he catches you interfering with his cream. They tell me he never grudges a bit of firewood lifted from the steading on a dark night. And whiles, they say, he'll even turn a blind eye to the paraffin dwindling in the drum. But if you're ever found helping yourself to the cream off the top of his dairy cans, it's just God help you, and down the road with you. No explanations given. And none sought – if you're wise. For, you see, Darklands reasons that the customers who buy his milk are entitled to all the cream that rises on top of it.'

'And sound enough reasoning at that! It's coming as I am aye trying to tell you all. It's coming on both sides. And it would all come a damned sight sooner if you just had the horse sense to join your Union.'

'You and your Union again, Duggie. Bloody fine do you ken that it isn't so easy for a Union man to get a Fee.'

'Fine do I ken that, Charlie. So for God's sake keep your hair on! The two three you've got left. All I'm *trying* to say is this, if we were *all* Union men the farmers would have to Fee us. They'd have no option. For I'll grant you that they could put the army in to lift the tatties, aye, or to hoe the turnips at a stretch, but could you imagine Colonel McCombie yonder calving a cow?'

'Whiles, Duggie, whiles you do make me wonder. For you speak an awful lot of dirt! We're tied hand and foot. We always will be as long as our houses are part of our wage. Lose your job and you lose your house.'

'Maybe. Maybe so. But it's coming. That I'm sure of. You and me may not live to see that day, Riddel. And Charlie there will certainly never see it, for if the drink doesn't kill him, the women will! But our sons might just see it. Your Hugh there, maybe he'll live long enough to see it, and benefit from it, when it comes.'

And Hugh Riddel *had* seen it come. It came with the war. A revolution as complete as the Industrial Revolution, but quieter – and bloodless. If Hugh Riddel's father had still been alive he would not have recognised the farm of Darklands now. For, though it had been a farm of farms in his day, it was now a Model farm, bathrooms and electricity in all the cottar houses. A day off a week, a week-end off a month. Farm-workers running their own cars. And Superannuation. Not even the rabid Duggie of childhood memory could ever have visualised such a benefit as a farm-worker with the security of a pension.

For most of his working life Hugh Riddel's father had known but two days off in the year. The 'Term Days', at the end of May and November.

Golden days though. Hugh Riddel could recall them still with an uprising of excitement. The unfamiliar smell of bacon filling the kitchen, his mother clucking around the range, warning and worrying in the same breath.

'Dip your bread in the fat, Hugh. But the bacon's for Father. He's for the Town.'

And his father big with the good humour that was over him.

'My best suit. The blue, the day. Pressed beneath the mattress three nights hard running. And how's *that* for a crease in my trousers, Hugh? It would just cut your throat, wouldn't it not now? It's as sharp as that! My bonnet, Hugh. Jump to it, son. Not *that* bonnet, you gowk! My Sunday bonnet. For I'm for the Town.'

Even now, such excited preparation seemed just as it should be to Hugh Riddel. For it was a wild town, a wanton town, that farm-workers set out for on Term Days, and wide-eyed on the watch for country men. Though blind, its nose could still have sniffed them out with sharn for sweat, and deaf, its ears could still have recognised their tackettbooted tread, and their laughter rising ribald in Dobb's Café, and Dobb's market too, where siren women lurked behind the stalls, big bosomed, blonde, and honey-mouthed, or so they seemed to farm-workers on Term Days, luring their hard-won penny Fees with tartan trinkets.

'Come on now, Jock. This pouch should hold your six months' siller. In your own tartan too. 'By Dand', and *up* the Gordons!'

And teasingly, with bits of fripperies, would confront the lumbering red-faced men, whose hands had seldom fumbled anything finer than flannelette.

'This pair should fit your best lass, Jock. Think of the fun you'll have fitting them on her. Come, buy – for love's sake!'

Dobb's market was all for love's sake. Post-cards showing How. Books telling When. 'The Chemist' – Quack – doing business all day long with herbs and pills and special advice in after hours. But dark and dear. And not for country men, grinning but stubborn, rejecting such abortive practices.

'We'll risk it yet. For the pill was never made would empty Bogie Bell of what Tom the Ternland gave her, six months come Friday, at Boynlie Ball.'

Free of Dobb's market. Swerving to Baltic Cross – traditionally their own, and freemen of the Town for this one day. And down by Baltic Cross, teeming but islanded alien townsfolk caught in hurried passing the warm dissenting talk of cattle.

'We're tackling Ayrshires up our way.'

'Dangerous vratches. Far too fond of hooking, Ayrshires. They rip each others' flanks to bits.'

'For safety, give me a Red Poll.'

'*Never*, man. Great fat hornless lumps, the Red Polls. Granted they don't hook each other, for they've got damn all to hook with. But, by God, they – make up for that by lashing out. For a quiet-natured cow, now, give me the Guernsey.'

'Too delicate a brute for this part of the country. A Guernsey needs as muckle care as a thoroughbred horse. Fair-weather beasts, Guernseys. No, no. For a good all-round cow there's just nothing to touch the Shorthorn. They're tough beasts and their yield's aye consistent.'

And in the more exclusive haunts, the farmers talked of this and that. Of subsidies and costs, and how they were rising all the time. And never once, not even in trust amongst each other, confessed to profit. But down at Baltic Cross, made bold by beer and strengthened by each other, their workers claimed the leases of their lands by right of deed, and tenanted them with new ideas.

'If I was in Clayacre's shoes, I'd sell at Whitsun. For yon land's souring. It's fair worn out.'

'High time too that Lower Ardgye grew less grain. Yon's not mixed farming. It's just grain forever up in yon place!'

'He'd need to let such land lie fallow for a while.'

The last bus home. The thought of it settling in their minds, like chaff that itched against their skins on threshing days. And all eyes eyes cocked against the sky for a reprieve, or even extension. Then watches, turnip-faced, dragged out to check the stars; their minds would stray to that wild pub down by the docks, and linger there, where women were as bold as brass, offering you all they had for one and sixpence. Near forcing't on you. It was just such women's haste, and the price they put upon it, made it immoral in farm-workers' eyes. Since they preferred it given, just for the love of it. Or, for at most a dozen new-laid eggs, and that but hansel. And, though their thoughts might linger in such places, their feet invariably but unsteadily led them buswards, yet with a kind of virtue. 'For, God Almighty! You never can tell. With women such as yon, you never know what you'll get left with.'

But it was his father's homecoming on Term Nights that lay within Hugh Riddel's own remembrance, and still could move him in the minding of it.

God! But what a difference a drink and a day off had made to the man. Hard to reconcile the dour everyday father of the fields and byres with the huge genial man who stood swaying and singing in the doorway, flanked by his fellow farm-workers on Term Nights.

> Her brow 'tis like the snowdrift.
> Her neck 'tis like the swan.
> Her face it is the fairest
> That e'er the sun shone on.
>
> And dark blue is her e'e.
> And she's a' the world to me.
> And for bonnie Annie Laurie
> I wad lay me doon and dee!

That was another of the times when Hugh Riddel, the boy, had felt all the glamourie of manhood tugging at himself. The *Annie Lauries* and *Bonnie Peggies* of his father's songs had come across to him even then as something more than idylls of time gone past; they became the lush promises of his own future. Strange, though; strange that they should still have remained idylls when the future had become the present.

> Like dew on the gowan lying
> Is the fa' o' her fairy feet.
> And like wind in the summer sighing.
> Her voice is low and sweet!

'Keep *your* voice down, then. And come on inside the house with you. For it will be the clash of the countryside that you couldn't stand on *your* fairy feet on Term Night.'

Down all the years Hugh Riddel could still call up his mother's capacity for diminishing his father. Not even the presence of his father's fellow-workers had ever prevented her from putting on the hurt, white face of martyrdom. A right bad wife could ease a man's conscience, and so set him free. But a good wife could bind you prisoner forever, with the swaddling bands of her goodness. God! but I had to burst myself out and free, Hugh Riddel thought. His father had never brought himself to do likewise. For this, his son could pity but also envy him, and saw him still in all his huge, blustering futility.

'Well, well, woman. If everybody's tongues are clashing about *me*, it stands to reason that they will be leaving some other poor sinful bugger to a bit of peace. And *that's* surely a something to be thankful for! Come in, about then, all of you. Come on, now. Draw your chairs up to the fire, and we'll have a bit of a crack and a song to ourselves.'

That was another of the times when Hugh Riddel had felt insulated in a comfort of spirit. Curled up in the kitchen bed, in the dim flicker of firelight and lamplight. Within hand's touch of a world of men. Yet still safe onlooker, with the voices of his father and his father's friends droning over and round him.

Oh, never were harvests so wet and wild as those they recollected in their cups on Term Nights. And still miraculously ingathered. For they could see themselves in their young years, through such a space of time that personal identification left them altogether. And it was giants, immune to wind and weather, who rode the rigs; and scythed the 'inroads' to epic harvests.

But, despite all their exaggerations, and for all his own

youngness at the time, Hugh Riddel had instinctively recognised their underlying truth. It was simply that words had
caricatured their thoughts. And, by God, words could do
that, right enough. Look and touch and feel should suffice
to allow you walk wordless all your days. Hugh Riddel
remembered one small such instance of his own, on the farm
near Stonehaven, where the hill slopes had lain under grass
through living memory, till one morning on his road to
school he had stood arrested, staring at the sharp gleaming
coulter of the plough cutting into the hill slope and leaving
the first dark furrow. That had struck him with an almost
physical sense of pain. And the image of the virgin land with
the gash of a wound across it had lain unvoiced in mind for
a long time. Small wonder, then, that with the nowhereness
of words, his father and his father's friends had grabbed them
and twined them and stretched them this way and that, in a
kind of anger at their impotence.

But there was the other side of it. The times when threadbare words could cast a shadow, far greater than the substance of their meaning, across your mind, mantling it for
the rest of your days. A small memory too, and gleaned on
a Term night.

'Oh, but he was a hard farmer to work for,' God Knows
had said. 'You durst never be caught straightening your back
when yon one came in sight of you. And God knows, many's
the time I have seen myself, after ten hours' forking to the
threshing mill, bend down just to pick up some straw, knowing that the wind would blow another in its place, when I'd
hear the sound of his footsteps.'

That was when High Riddel had first known the true
meaning of physical tiredness, even before experiencing it.
And, ever afterwards, the ultimate weariness was indeed just
to 'pick up some straw, knowing that the wind would blow
another in its place'.

But he had been infatuated by the speak of the life on the land on those far-off Term Nights. For those nights were Hugh Riddel's initiation into a society to which one could only obtain membership by right of birth. A comparatively secret society too. One which had its being scattered unmarked on the teacher's map at school, where Scotland was made up of Highlands and Lowlands, mining and ship-building, cathedral towns and university cities, and all their world ending abruptly 'over the Border'.

It was his father and his father's friends who crammed the blanks of that map on Term Nights, till Scotland became a continent on their tongues and famous for things that never found their way into the Geography lesson at school. The fine tattie-growing soil of Easter Ross. South of the Mearns where the land was more mellow, the farmers easier, the darg lighter, and fees higher. Up Inverness way, where the last battle fought on British soil was forgotten, and only the democracy of the 'folk' remembered.

'I kent a ploughman once,' Dod Feary had pointed out, as impressive proof of this to his incredulous listeners, 'who used to get blind drunk every Saturday night with the local Doctor, up Culloden way.'

For nowhere was 'Keeping one's proper place' so strictly adhered to as in our shire. Even his mother, Hugh Riddel remembered, had once commented on this:

'If the farmer's wife passes the time of day with the cottar wives, it just makes their day. Poor, silly bodies! You would think that the Lord above had looked down from Heaven, and greeted them personally, so overcome are they.'

Hugh Riddel smiled at the recollection. But there was a kind of pain and protest at the heart of his amusement.

. . . Oh, Burns. Was it to suit the fine sentiments of the Edinbro' Gentry, once cursed by you, and always half despised, that you wrote such smarm as *The Cottar's Saturday Night*?

From scenes like these
Old Scotia's grandeur . . .

The lines grued in Hugh Riddel's mind. It was easily seen that such a poem was written by a man who Ploughed his *own* furrows. Never by a fee'd ploughman. And although farm-workers' conditions had improved beyond all recognition now, Hugh Riddel's pain, though momentary, was ever recurring. It was just that no man could come into good estate free of that which and those who had preceded him.

Far more true of their way of life were the songs of his father and his father's friends on Term Night. Songs of their own countryside, composed by themselves for themselves; and having their origins in the very farms they worked on.

When I gaed doon to Turra Market
Turra Market for to fee
I met in wi' a wealthy fairmer
Frae the Barnyards o' Delgaty!

He promised me the twa best horse
That was in a' the country roon
But when I gaed hame to the Barnyards
There was nothing there but skin and bone!

It was when they reached the singing stage on Term Nights that they really tried his mother's patience. It was then that they sent her sighing 'God be here' round the kitchen, and 'there will be no word of this in the morning'; and, as the night advanced and the songs grew coarser, would set her to redding up the kitchen. As if by the very act she could also redd up the dirt rising round her ears. For how the men loved dirt. That which his father had always protested was 'Clean dirt, woman!' And Hugh Riddel himself had always been in alliance with the men over this.

> She let him in sae cannily
> To do the thing you ken, Jo!
> She chased him out syne cried him back
> To do it once again, Jo!
> But the bottom fell out o' the bed
> The lassie lost her maiden-head
> And her mither heard the din, Jo!

It always meant some other new song for Hugh Riddel to go racing schoolwards with, the wind in his face; and a pack of loons panting behind him to hear the rest of it, syne flinging themselves face downwards on the grass with the exhaustion of their laughter, and laughing long after they had forgotten the cause. Pure laughter that, Hugh Riddel realised now, for it had needed no reason.

God! you could stand out here in the dark, and listen to the youngness of your life singing away past you there, as if it had been conceived in song. His mother had never realised it was like that with him, though. She was always protecting him from his father and his father's cronies, their songs and their talk.

'*That's* fine language to be on you all! And the bairn Hugh there, lying in his bed.'

'Well! Hugh's got to find out for himself one of these fine days,' his father would defend. 'For fine he knows that he wasn't found at the back of a cabbage plant, as you would like him to believe!'

And fine he did know. Ever since he could remember, Hugh Riddel had discovered that sex was the great topic and the huge laugh, the joke that the farm-workers seldom tired of, and rearing itself up at all odd times in all kinds of places. The bulls serving the cows. And the stallions serving the mares. And ill-favoured Annie Coultrie, whom no man had tried to tempt for years, drawing her cardigan fierce around her shoulders, like to protect her virtue, and screeching across the steading.

'There's the stallion man. Just coming up the road yonder, with that great muckle brute of a stallion. But I'm not going to put *him* up for the night. Not *me*! He can just go to the bothy for a bed, or to some woman that's his own like. For they're saying that the man has gotten as randy as that stallion he treks around the country with. They have it that no woman under sixty is safe with him now.'

And the deep satirical laughter her indignation evoked in the men.

'*You'll* be safe enough then, Annie, for you'll not see sixty again. Though you was always safe enough, Annie. Even when you was sixteen!'

But there was always a quality of cruelty in the laughter evoked by sex. A quality which Hugh Riddel recognised in himself, and which was maybe contained to an even greater degree in men far beyond the parish of Caldwell. Take the war years, now, and the time when the Polish airmen were stationed over there at Balwhine. What a clash of tongues *they* had caused in the countryside. God Knows had been fair flabbergasted by their methods. His fiery denunciation of the Poles still burned in Hugh Riddel's recollection.

'The Cottage Hospital is fair full of queans with festered breasts the now! For it seems that plain fornication is just not good enough for that Polish chields. Na. Na. They've got to bite as well. And that, mark you, with all their fine polite words and ways, their kissing hands and all the rest of their palaver. Surely to God a decent man can have a quean without wanting to take bites out of her.'

Laughter shook Hugh Riddel at the recollection, and metaphorically flung him face downwards on a grassy bank, thirty years away in time. But, like laughter of that kind and quality, it left him empty enough for tears. *O! My love Annie's wondrous bonnie.* It was the idyll one's spirit always wept for.

'It's when there's neither lust nor liking,' his father had once confided, 'that a man's marriage has got nothing.' Lust nor liking. He had never heard his father use the word 'love', except in song. But it was all going to be very different with him. Hugh Riddel had made up his mind early about that.

'A quiet decent lass,' his mother had said, approving his ultimate choice of a wife. Though, come to consider it now, Isa was not unlike what his mother had been. It was her small white quality of chastity that had first attracted Hugh Riddel. Novel enough in a time and place where there was nothing for the young to do in the little free time they had to themselves but 'Away to the whin bushes, and into it', as the older men still described it.

Strange that he had been so deluded. The onlookers weren't.

'Isa Mavor! Yon mim-mouthed quean. God, Riddel, but I'd imagine yon one would be on the cold side to bed with, if her thin pernickity walk is anything to go by.'

And his own resentment of their unsolicited opinions.

'There are other ways of judging a woman. It's not a heifer that you're sizing up.'

They had been right, though. Hugh Riddel had to admit that to himself. Times he had felt like contradicting his daughter, Helen, when she came home weekends from her work in a Youth Centre in the Town, with words on the tip of her tongue, like labels, ready to be stuck on to all human faults and frailties. As though the correct word for them could cure them. Words like Delinquency, Hereditary, Environment, Behaviour Patterns. Whiles he felt just like boring through that wall of words with which Helen had surrounded both herself and her vocation, and blowing them sky high with the anger that would be over him.

'Take murder now, Helen. Aye murder. Whiles I Just feel like murdering your mother with my two bare hands. And not even for the big things that are wrong between us. Just, God help me, for the smallest thing of all. Like times when your mother's standing silent by the window. And you know the look that's on her face, by the back of her head. And I go clattering through to the sink to wash my face, making a racket to cover up the wordlessness that falls between us. Syne putting my head round the corner of the scullery door to see if the din I've made has stirred into movement, though Hell let loose itself, could scarce do that! My eye takes in the whole of her – against its will. But when it reaches the stockings wrinkling round her legs, it's then that I could kill her. For the disgust that's on me for having chosen such a woman. What name have they given to *that* in your Youth Centre, Helen? What word is there for the wrinkled stocking that can incline a man to think of murder?'

And, since doubtless Helen would have had the cool clipped reply, but never the answer, he had never deigned to put the question to her.

God! but it was damnable. A man could slip his boot off in the bottling shed, and hold his bare foot out for inspection – his *foot* – that most ridiculous intimate part of him, urging his workmates:

'Take a look at that, now. At that great brute of a bunion! What would you do with a muckle thing like that? It has given me agony for weeks. Pure agony just!'

And advice would pour forth thick and fast, for it would

seem that all the dairy workers would have had a bunion the
like, at some time or another, so it would prove complaint
but common enough.

But there was never time, nor place, nor person to whom
you could confide this deeper agony:

'Was it this way with you when you got married? Did your
wife lie in a cold clam beside you? And for her youngness did
you restrain yourself, feeling but brute and guilty. Yet hoping
the time would come – and soon – when hugging and kissing
were not enough even for her. And when time came, it was
reluctant. And as time passed, became as cold as charity
bequeathed from duty, so that your hunger for it left you
altogether; and appetite itself turned to distaste, so that even
were it *offered* to you now, you couldn't stomach it.'

That too, if aired within the bottling shed, might prove to
be complaint but common enough, though one that was for
Riddel beyond enduring.

It came back to him now, as near as yesterday, his father's
voice, bewildered and defeated: 'What would you make of
women folk, Hugh? I can never say a bonnie wordie to your
mother but she tells me I'm drunk. And maybe she's right
at that of it. For it is only when I am drunk that the words
come to me, and the notion takes me.'

And his mother's bitter response:

'The trouble with you is you should have married some
great roaring quean who was more your like.'

But it was senseless standing here, regretting. Hugh Riddel
realised that. For regret neither eased an old pain, nor taught
you how to avoid a new one. Live and learn, that's what
they said. He lived all right, but he just never seemed to
learn, since experience itself but taught you not to make the
same mistake twice. And sometimes, not even that.

. . . Darklands' milk lorry, roaring in the distance, was
taking the Tienland Corner now, its headlights picking up

the landmarks on the road, lifting them up into the light and dropping them down into the darkness again. Hugh Riddel still stood, reluctant to brace himself for the ordeal of facing the Dairy. For, although the degree of a man's fault is known only in part, even to himself, the exact opinions of that fault can be accurately gauged in the eyes and attitudes of his fellow-men.

Not that he cared a tinker's curse what his fellow-workers thought of him, Hugh Riddel assured himself. Far from it. He had always been indifferent to their opinions. And his knowledge of them had ensured this attitude. Good or bad, top dog was always top dog to them. Oh, it might bite them and they'd yelp out with pain; but the instant it barked out in more genial salutation, they would come panting, their tongues hanging out, and their tails wagging. It was only when one no longer proved to be top dog that apprehension might well set in. For then the pack – always bold on top of their own midden – would set about you, tearing you to pieces.

The thought of that angered Hugh Riddel, but braced him into movement. Damn them! Damn them all. He would go up into the dairy as if nothing had happened. He would supervise the loading of that milk lorry, as if last Friday was still some future date on the calendar above the bottling machine, circled in red, for nothing more important than a reminder to 'Order more Quart Bottles'. And he would do that, too. By God he would! For, at this moment, he was still Hugh Riddel, Head Dairyman, Darklands.

The conviction took such a hold of him that the need for haste left him altogether. And it was with the slow loping stride of habit that he began to make his way up to the dairy, pausing only to interpret the night.

There was an orange glow round the last quarter of the moon, and the Mother Tap of Soutar Hill was hidden in the mist that was starting to come down. The smell of ground frost rose dankly up from the nether park. Real Judas weather, and this now into February. Still, Darklands would cope with all that in its own good time.

The Dairy was loud with the speculation of last Friday night. For it was the lund of night which should have found itself head-lined in the Sunday paper, although it hadn't done so, to the chagrin of God Knows.

'Bloody near a murder!' he shouted across to the Plunger, above the din of the bottling machine.

'Forbye a try at suicide, and the Lunatic Asylum!'

'Not the Lunatic Asylum!' Lil Jarvis contradicted from her stool in front of the bottling machine.

'Ambroggan House. A *private* Mental Hospital for Helen Riddel, if you please.'

'Whatever name it goes by, its purpose is the same,' God Knows snapped, nettled by the sarcasm in Lil's voice. He had never had very much meed for any of the Riddel breed – except Hugh Riddel's father – but he had even less for Lil Jarvis; always running himself and the other cattlemen off their feet with her perpetual cry of 'more milk for bottling'.

'And all kinds of queer going-ons in between,' God Knows continued, ignoring Lil, and deliberately turning his attention to the Plunger.

'Goings-on that you and me will never likely get to the bottom of,' he added regretfully, 'for God only knows *what* the world is coming to.'

God Knows had been speculating on what the world was coming to for the best part of sixty years. A narrow enough speculation, since it was simply the neighbouring parishes outwith Caldwell that gave him such cause for anxiety. Caldwell itself was the promised land; its inhabitants the chosen people, though just as wilful whiles as the Israelites themselves. Until now, that was, for the world still knew nothing of Caldwell's fall from grace.

'There was not a single word about it in any of the Sunday papers,' God Knows confirmed. 'Just the usual tell of a puckle queans in the South being followed, or offered lifts in cars, syne kicking up a terrible rumpus about it all afterwards.'

'*I* have never been followed in all my life,' Lil boasted from the bottling machine, as though this was some hard-won personal triumph. 'And I have walked about the earth for a good few years now. But I never ran into anything worse than myself on a dark night!'

It would have greatly surprised God Knows and the other dairy workers had Lil ever done so. Still, God Knows felt it more prudent to let her avowal go unchallenged.

'They must be a terrible lot, thae queans in the South,' was all he could think of saying in reply. 'They must just all go about asking for it!'

'It's my opinion' – Lil clamped her conclusion firmly down with the bang of her bottling lever – 'my honest opinion – that Hugh Riddel, to say nothing of yon stuck-up daughter of his, Helen, with all her fine college education, and her eyes looking at you over the top of yon specs she wears, as if you were some kind of thing she didn't see very often – it's my opinion that they just all got what they've been asking for, for a long, long time.'

'They say it's still just touch and go with the Riddel quean, though,' the Plunger ventured, reluctant to condemn one who might be at death's door.

'*She'll* survive,' Lil, plagued by no such ethics herself, assured the men. 'Yon wish washy molloching kind of creature always does. And as for yon Charlie Anson, he's been asking for a good hiding all his life. And deed, that was the only good thing in the whole sorry business. They say that Hugh Riddel made a bonnie mess out of him!'

'Deed aye.' Despite himself, God Knows found himself in complete agreement with Lil on this point. 'For I never yet looked on yon buck teeth of Anson's but they put me in mind of a rabbit sitting up on its hunkers and laughing at something or other. But Anson will laugh no more like yon, for they say that Hugh Riddel didna leave a tooth in his head.'

'There's *one* thing, though,' the Plunger straightened himself up from the tank to give his reflections full weight, 'and *it's* certain. Sue Tatt hasn't gone into mourning over Friday night's affair, for I saw her at the Grocer's van, just yestreen, as large as life yonder and twice as sinful, chewing the fat and skirling away like a sixteen-year-old, with the new vanman that's on the round.'

'I never could understand that Sue Tatt business at all,' God Knows pondered. 'It was just fair beyond my comprehension. You would have thought that a man like Hugh Riddel would have been a bit more choosy, Sue being such a byword in the Parish, like.'

'There's no mystery to that at all,' the Plunger said. 'You know what Burns had to say about it? I'll tone it down a bit – for Lil's sake, there. It wouldn't do to shock our Lil's maidenly modesty. A desperate man has no conscience, and a willing woman has no objection. That's what Burns said. In stronger language, though. But that, if you ask me, was all there was between Sue Tatt and Hugh Riddel.'

'Maybe that, then,' God Knows conceded, 'though I'll wager you that Hugh Riddel will give Sue the Soldier's farewell from now on.'

'He'll have no other option,' Lil concluded, 'for I can see Darklands showing Riddel down the road real smartlike for Friday night's work. For Darklands will not have very much option either, what with him being an Elder of the Kirk, forbye a County Councillor.'

'I wouldn't take a bet on it.' God Knows spoke out of authority of long acquaintance with Darklands – the farm, and the farmer. 'For I mind when I was fee'd to come home to Darklands here. And that wasn't yesterday. That was before Darklands' herd was built up, when he was just pleit-ering about with a bit of mixed farming and, say, a forty fifty stots; for even then, he had a kind of passion for kye. No T.T. Testing *then*, Plunger. You just had to take your chance with weedy milk and all the rest of It. And it was in the days when we were allowed to keep our own hens. In those days, Plunger, you could judge a farmer by his attitude to his cottars' hens. If he said, "No Hens", then you could be pretty certain that you had gone and bonded yourself not only to a suspicious man, but to a man as mean as cat's dirt as well. Anyhow, the first question Darklands asked me was if I kept hens of my own. "Aye," I admitted, "I've got a two three hennies." He pondered on that for a while syne. "Well, well," says he at last, "I'll tell you what I'll do. I'll allow you, along with your Fee, a pucklie oats for your two three hennies!" I was just about to thank him for the favour, but he wouldn't hear of it. "Not at all," he said. "I'll allow you the oats to save you the bother of getting out of your bed in the middle of the night, and slinking up to the barn to help yourself." So you *see*, you can never tell what airt the wind will blow with a man who reasons like that! And don't you forget this either,' God Knows continued, fired by his listeners' attention, 'don't you forget that it was Hugh Riddel's father who was Darklands' first cattleman when he started to build up his herd. They kind of built it up together. It was the only job that old Riddel had ever lasted in. He was never sent down the road on that job, for he was a grand cattleman. By God, he was that! It was never old Riddel's *work* that was wanting. He could tell when a cow was in heat, when the bull itself would still be standing wondering about it! And he could have clippit a cow blindfold, going over her flanks as surely as he could always find his way home on Term Nights, and him as full as a distiller's cask!'

'Get to hell out of it! Back to your byre.' Hugh Riddel's voice sent Lil's stool swivelling round in front of the bottling machine, and set the Plunger's back bending over the tank again. The lorry men sauntered in with the large deliberate assurance of men who had every right to be there anyhow.

'I said back to your byre,' Riddel repeated to God Knows, who, lacking his fellow-workers' speed of camouflage, still stood staring blankly.

'Aye, aye surely, Mr Riddel.' It was only when he reached his byre that God Knows reproved himself for not taking a firmer stand. 'There was me *Mistering* him!' he confided to the Third Cattleman. ' "Mr Riddel," says I, and the man accepted it, as if it was just his due as usual. You would think that Hugh Riddel would walk humbly enough now, after last Friday night's happenings.'

Last Friday night had started off like any other Friday night in Caldwell – furious with activity.

Up at Ambroggan House, the younger nurses coming off day duty made hasty applications for late-night passes, and sprawling on each others' beds indulged in sartorial barter. Not without reason were the nurses the best-dressed girls in all the parish. And, having acquired a Late Night for themselves, and finally decided Which of Whose to wear, were puzzled now by how to use both gains to best advantage: to the Half Crown Hop in Caldwell Hall, on the pillion of a Vespa with some male nurse as hard up as themselves; or to the Guinea Dinner Dance in the Town, in the front seat of a Consul, with some farmer's son who – sure as death –

would, at some time or another before the night was over, suggest, and even attempt, a bodily transference to the back seat of the car.

Their older colleagues, contemptuous now of such acrobatic feats, were just content to sink into easy chairs, slip off their shoes, and proffer their advice – rejected either way.

The nurses coming on Night Duty cast eyes half filled with sleep upon the world outside their bedroom windows, took yet another vow that never again would they skip morning sleep to have their hair done, not if they walked the world the rest of their days looking like Meg, the 'parish patient' who did the laundry. And yet one other vow they reinforced, as the isolated landmarks of Caldwell penetrated their half-awakened consciousness, to apply forthwith for a transfer to the Hospital's branch in the Town, for in all four years between taking her Prelims and sewing the strings of Charge Nurse on her cap, Caldwell was surely the most forsaken dump a girl could land herself in.

While all the afternoon the daft Dominie, their patient on parole, had sat on Soutar Hill, certain it was the mountain of Gilboah, with neither dew upon it, nor fields of offerings.

It was the night the Misses Lennox, and other like ladies of the parish, slipped from small houses with long names on their gates, armed with damp sandwiches, and clinging trails of jasmine, just in bloom. Then, drawing fur tippets firm around their necks, sniffed the night air and bowed their heads against the oncoming wind before stepping warily Kirkwards, decrying the noise and fumes of passing cars, hell bent for Dugald's Road-house, and all New Rich, and ostentatiousness in every form, as well as couples who boldly strode the road together, hand in hand, pausing to watch the lights go up in distant farmhouses, acclaiming each and recognising all. Then stopping to kiss each other under the moon, and in the sight of the Misses Lennox; laughing about

it to high Heaven, as if love itself were but a joke. For Miss
Lennox had never thought love so, while Miss Maud even
doubted whether it was love at all, or just one more manifes-
tation of why Caldwell had the highest illegitimacy rate in
all the County.

The Misses Lennox felt themselves to be the guardians of
Caldwell by right of birth. And yet – despite this accident,
and for all their years within Caldwell – could not have told
you from which direction the wind was rising now, nor in
which quarter the moon above them lay. They only recognised full moons, and rapturously acclaimed the huge red
harvest ones; could never discern quarters, nor yet appreciate
small blue elusive February moons like this, which seemed
to them but accident of light and cloud.

Their thoughts turned Kirkwards now, and to the men in
their own lives, the Minister, visiting missionaries home on
furlough – and God. Perhaps God most of all. Though He, of
course, was more than man, but yet fulfilling their emotional
needs, without man's nuisance value.

And thinking so, the Misses Lennox' remembrance fell,
while their wrath rose on one such man. It was just the man's
presumption roused their ire.

A farm-worker to be asked – far worse consent – to give
the speech, and toast 'The Immortal Memory', at the Burns'
Supper the other night, an honour usually reserved for
Colonels retired, or Ministers, active and passive. The insolence of the man, Head Dairyman at Darklands, Hugh Riddel
by name, to stand barefaced up and tell *them* that half the
people sitting there, listening to and praising Burns' songs
and poems, would have no more meed for Burns himself if
he were to settle down amongst them tomorrow, than the
'unco guid' had for him in Mauchline in his own day.

To dismiss the people of Caldwell like that was bad
enough, but the man had gone on to do something worse

than that: he had deprived them of the comfort of myth; had flung, as it were, all the little china statues of Highland Mary off their mantelpieces and left them lying in broken pieces.

Nor had he left them with their other substitute for comfort intact, their *Bonnie Jean*. In places like Mauchline and Caldwell, he had claimed, Burns would have been left with little choice but to marry Jean Armour – Oh, but aye! For any man could live after being worried, but no man could live after being disgraced. So, no particular credit to Burns for *that* marriage. And, having married him, Jean Armour would have had little choice but to put up with Burns. For, wasn't that just the way of it in country places? In all their years in Caldwell, now, had any one of them ever known of a farm-worker, or even a farmer for that of it, going and getting divorced? Nor was it their religion which imposed this attitude upon them, for there wasn't a Catholic within fifty miles of them.

There were, the man had said, plenty women of Jean Armour's sort who would have been willing enough to share Burns' name, his bed and his board, but he had needed something much more than that in a wife; he had needed the impossible. To have one foot on the front step of the castle, and the other trailing behind on the dunghill, and never both together, was just about the loneliest thing that could ever befall a man, and the woman wasn't born who could have bridged this gap with Burns. But, mind you, that had never prevented Burns from searching for her, and even glimpsing her fleeting reflection in the faces of all women; personifying her in the love songs he wrote to all the Peggys, Marys, Jeans and Nancys, for they but fuelled some flame already lit. And the self-same thing applied to all his nature lyrics. Had Burns never set eyes on the daisy, the briar, or the canna white ablown, he still would have sung for 'some wee sma' flower, whose seed was never sown', knowing that the herb which cannot be found will not bring relief.

Oh, but it had been galling to find Hugh Riddel's Immortal Memory printed in full in the national press. ONE PLOUGH-MAN SPEAKS OF ANOTHER – ROBERT BURNS, the heading had said, instead of as usual tucked away in a column of the local paper under CALDWELL EVENTS, where everybody who was anybody in Caldwell would have been certain of seeing their own names in print. But not one word about the Colonel who had piped the haggis in, nor the Dominie who had 'addressed' it, or the Minister who had said the Burns' Grace over it. Not a mention of 'The Ladies' – which had included the Misses Lennox – 'who had helped to make the event such an unqualified success, by working like Trojans behind the scenes', as their functions were normally described. Not even a mention of the 'fine rendering of *The Bonnie Lass O' Ballochmyle*, by Miss McCombie of The Whins'. Though quite unknown to the Misses Lennox, Hugh Riddel himself had observed on this to God Knows on their way home from the Burns Supper:

'Miss McCombie will now render *The Bonnie Lass O' Ballochmyle*, said the Chairman. And the Chairman was just about right at that. For yon bloody woman nearly tore The Bonnie Lass apart!'

Not a mention of anyone at all, except a local farm-worker whom nobody even knew, nor, as far as the Misses Lennox were concerned, wished to know either. It just went to show. You never could trust the uneducated. Take that miner turned lay preacher, who had addressed them up in the Kirk Hall last month, accusing *them* of being quite capable of crucifying Christ again because they lacked recognition. A recollection which rankled particularly with the Misses Lennox, for it was one of their great dreams and small hopes that, for His Second Coming, Christ would choose Caldwell, convinced that they would be the first to recognise Him, after a lifetime acquaintance with Holman Hunt's *Light of the World* in their front parlour.

And so they talked till other like ladies of the parish, who lurked in waiting, pounced out upon them from small side roads or clumps of whins, giggling together with feared surprise. Like ghosts of girls.

At this time, too, the farm-workers' wives were taking the opposite direction to the Women's 'Rural', their tongues as sharp, their thoughts as bright and bitter as the jars of marmalade clanking in their baskets. For this was Marmalade Competition Night; two classes – Rough and Fine. These were no guardians of Caldwell, but content merely as critics, an easier role, and altogether safer. Yet, not one amongst them but knew how mornings were, earlier than you have ever known them: how in such isolated hours the well-trod path towards their byres was like some track in an uncharted world; how when darkness fell, overtaking them on the road, a lamplit farmhouse five miles away was surer guide than bright Orion and all the mariners' stars. Small wonder, then, their tongues wagged wild, in general observation, for the small particular was ever without voice.

Now! What did this one make of Hugh Riddel's Immortal Memory, a week ago tonight, up in the Hall? They had not quite got beyond the fact that one of themselves had been allowed voice at last, and were inclined to warm themselves contentedly at the thought; till God Know's wife began to scatter straws of doubt within their minds. ''Twas just the kind of thing could make a man go all above himself,' she vowed, 'not, mind you, that Hugh Riddel had ever had other than a fine conceit of himself – and that kind needs just a little push to send them clean off their balance.'

'Take Charlie Anson now, and for example,' the Plunger's

wife remembered. 'Until yon creature was appointed Treasurer of the Farm-workers' Union, who would have ever given him a second thought? And now the man was taking himself seriously. Just you observe him. Speaking English! As if he had never learned a word of Scots, or else was shamed of it!'

'He has even given his bonnet the go-by,' Lil recalled, 'and taken to wearing a hat instead, lifting it to every conceivable woman he met on the road, just to prove that he knew what to do with a hat.'

'Though, God help us,' as the Plunger's wife pointed out, in an attempt to modify resentment, 'the creature looks just as like a weasel under the hat, as ever he looked under the bonnet! And, when he lifts his hat to *me*, I just look through it, and him too.'

'Oh, but Charlie Anson does worse than that,' as God Knows' wife reminded them. 'He not only speaks English, he's beginning to think he discovered Scots as well. Yon talk he gave at the Cultural Society – Words Your Heritage, he cried it, and didn't even know he was being insulting. As if it was *us* who had forsaken our Scots tongue, and not himself! I will say this much for Hugh Riddel; you may not like him, but you cannot despise him. And another thing, did you notice that when Hugh Riddel was saying *Holy Willie's Prayer* that night at the Burns' Supper, did you notice, he never once took his eyes off Charlie Anson?'

'God!' Lil remembered, 'I even began to feel sorry for Charlie Anson himself, sitting squirming yonder under Hugh Riddel's glower.'

'Yon was a sight pleased me right fine,' the Plunger's wife admitted. 'But I'll wager you this much, Hugh Riddel would have done a damned sight more than glower at Charlie Anson, if he'd had any inkling that Anson's taken up with his daughter. It's an odd thing, but I'll wager, too, Riddel will be the last man in Caldwell to hear anything about that.'

'You always are the last to hear anything about your own,' Lil pointed out. 'And I, for one, wouldn't take five pounds to be the first to tell Hugh Riddel about Anson and his daughter.'

'Nor me, either,' God Knows' wife agreed. 'But I would give ten pounds to be the first to see his face after somebody else has told him.'

'Even so,' the Plunger's wife felt that the issue was getting out of perspective, 'the pot can never call the kettle black. At least Hugh Riddel's daughter is single. She can please herself, as can Charlie Anson for that of it. Though the woman who would ever look twice at him must be pretty desperate.'

'But Helen Riddel *is* desperate,' was Lil's Opinion. 'for all her education, and all the speak of the brains she's gotten. She's a poor white shelpit creature. She takes after the mother in that respect.'

'I just wonder what Isa Riddel would have thought of her man's Immortal Memory, if she'd been there to hear it,' God Knows' wife pondered.

'All Hugh Riddel's women-folk were better away that night.' Lil's emphatic largess consigned a harem to him. 'Though I can tell you this much: if Sue Tatt had been yonder to hear him describe her like as "necessary" to Burns, she would have sent him away with a flea in his lug.'

'Still and on,' the Plunger's wife recalled, 'the way Hugh Riddel spoke that night, about Burns' farms at Lochlea and Ellisland, there was a while yonder I got the feeling that they were just two farms lying somewhere under Soutar Hill here. And that Hugh Riddel had ploughed every acre of them himself.'

'Come ony man at all
And tak me frae my faither'

164

Lil started to sing, desirous suddenly of freeing herself of her companions, and strode away down into the night on her own.

> 'For it's O dearie me!
> What shall I dae
> If I die an auld maid in a garret.'

'Wheesht, you now!' the Plunger's wife admonished, catching up on Lil. 'Look see!' she whispered mysteriously, grabbing Lil's arm and holding her firm captive till the others caught up with them before revealing the mystery. 'Look see! There's a light just gone up in Sue Tatt's bedroom. Business as usual there, on a Friday night!'

'Fiona!' Sue Tatt shouted upstairs in warning, to her eldest daughter. 'If you go mucking up all my new cleaned bedroom, I'll land you one. You'll go flying straight through the wall. And that's a promise!'

Having got this off her chest, Sue made her way back to the kitchen again, pausing in the doorway as though she were some complete stranger come to pay a visit to herself, and, standing there, took in every aspect of her newly turned-out room. Sue, a woman of many parts, was equal to many roles, and Fridays always brought out the house-proud in her.

True, her household would rough it contentedly enough all the rest of the week, when Sue would be absorbed in some other role, though she would always justify her muddle to anyone who crossed her threshold uninvited, with the dubious welcome, 'You're just about the last one I was looking for. But come on away inside. The clartier the cosier! Or so they say' – accompanied by a slap on the back that would have flung you flat on your face if you hadn't been expecting it. But, when the pendulum swung the *other* way, as now, a tiny speck of dust in any corner of her house was enough to send Sue up in smoke, and was more than a little unfair on her family, who could never quite adjust themselves to the suddenness of their mother's change of role. And doubly unfair tonight, when Sue was combining two roles.

She would let days pass on end, giving her face a lick and a promise, and her hair a rough redd through. But today a sudden beautifying spasm had seized her; a visit to the Town and Woolworth's had become a Must. Descending on the cosmetic counter, Sue had bought up everything that promised anything: a Face Pack which 'erased tell-tale wrinkles', a Highlight rinse which 'brought out hidden golden glints', a lipstick which 'carried a breath of Spring'. And, miser-like, Sue was now preparing to lock herself away in the bathroom, with all her little packages, and looking forward to lying, soaking herself leisurely, and reading the instructions on her Beauty Aids as lovingly as if they were the word of God – though with more faith.

'I'll be in the bathroom if I'm wanted,' she reminded Fiona. 'And don't any of you lot go mucking all my place up,' she warned again.

'Forget it, Mam,' Fiona advised casually from the bedroom. 'Don't let it go and get your wick.'

'I'll tell you what does get my wick' – Sue turned to survey her kitchen again – 'and that's just the sight of a pair of sharny boots lying on my new-brushed rug. You would think,' she added in pained protest, 'that we all lived in a pig-sty.'

'We do, too.' Young Beel dodged Sue's aim, but gave her the cue for another role.

'I work my fingers to the bone for you all,' she complained, 'slaving to bring you up, and that's all the thanks I get.' She made her way to the bathroom almost tearfully, remembering now that she was 'a widow woman, bringing up a young family, all on her own'.

And indeed it was a kind of truth. Though Sue did whiles confuse the names of the mythical husbands who had widowed her, certain it was that she worked with a fair degree of regularity to bring up her bairns. '*Drag* them up' was Caldwell's private interpretation of her efforts. But, then, Caldwell was seldom charitable towards its own. For though they accepted Sue as their own, they condoned neither Sue nor themselves for this acceptance.

The role of Self Supporting Widow was dear to Sue's heart. Mounting her bicycle two or three times a week to do the wash for surrounding farmers' wives, Sue was aware of the heightened interest she aroused both in them and in their daily helps, who were forever making some excuse to pop into the wash-house for a news with Sue. And the self-same thing with the farm-workers' wives. Sue Tatt was well aware that their attitude to herself veered between superiority and a kind of envy. And their approach towards her was transparency itself.

Meeting any one of them alone on the Ambroggan road it would simply be as housewife to housewife: newsing together of this and that; the cost of food, exchanging a recipe maybe, or a cleaning hint. In such moments, Sue would become so enthusiastic over the preserving qualities of bees' wax and turpentine, that she would deceive even herself and, mounting her bicycle, would take down the road a glow of goodness over her, and the assurance within her – I, Sue Tatt, am just an ordinary housewife after all. And what is more, I am accepted as such by the Plunger's wife.

When Sue Tatt ran into a group of farm-workers' wives, things took a different turn altogether.

'Aye! But it's another fine night, again,' the Plunger's wife would shoot out of the side of her mouth in hurried passing, the remembered mutual addiction to bees' wax and turpentine simply forcing the salutation out of her, while the other wives would just keep going, their gaze fixed steadily on the road ahead, their mouths clamped down in firm disapproval. Such an attitude always had the effect of bringing out the worst in Sue towards woman-kind – 'A drab-like lot! All gone to seed. Not one amongst them would have seen their feet if they hadn't been all gripped in with brassières and stays': while she, Sue Tatt, could stand, and sometimes did, as now, as firm mother-naked as other women in all their harness; and standing so, she would think, 'Oh, the pity of it! And the waste. To grow old. And there's the whole wide world. And all of them that's in it. And I have never seen the world. Nor half of them that's in it. And what is *more* the pity is that *they* have never seen *me* so!'

Sue would have stripped herself at any time, and just for that. The way a child might rush from school, its crayoned drawing held aloft, and shouting, 'Look what I've got. It's all my own!' . . . And, just as the praise of some loving observer would ring in its mind for a long time after, so would some lover's praise, when he himself and all his intimacy were long forgotten, bell in Sue's mind – 'God, Sue! But you're a bonnie woman right enough.'

It was when Sue Tatt ran into two wives on the road that she really came into her own, for they held the fallacy that two could keep a secret. And, having taken the risk of a friendly encounter with Sue Tatt, two wives would become bolder still, skipping hastily over the polite preliminaries like bairns, weather and neighbours, till at last they landed warily but with relief on basic ground; drawing gradually from the well of Sue's reputed experience . . . For men were just a perfect nuisance – wasn't that so, now? My goodness me! No wonder women always aged much quicker than their menfolk; considering all they had to put up with, one way or another. A man could go on being a man till he dropped into his grave; but a woman had to call a halt, sometime or other. 'Oh, it was all right when you were young and daft,' the Plunger's wife had once confessed. 'Though even then,' she had admitted, 'I got to just wanting my good night's sleep. And now, to tell the truth, it's gotten like a cup of cold water.'

Oh, but to tell truth was always so much easier than to *be* truth. At least, Sue Tatt had found that so; for she met so many sweet deceptions in herself, and each seemed genuine truth. As in times like that, when Sue would find herself in entire agreement with the wives; with, all the time, the other side of it badgering her inwardly for a hearing – 'But I never felt like that about a man, in all my born days. Well, maybe I did. But only once or twice. And even then, I always managed to put a face on it. For I could never let any man feel that he was other than the best man ever.' Sue knew instinctively that a man in bed was as vulnerable as his own nakedness, and that only by covering his failure for him, could she reveal her own completeness.

'There are some men, though,' she had once assured Lil and the Plunger's wife – only because she felt she owed them some little comfort and confidence for all that they had confided in her – 'There are some men, though,' Sue had informed them, 'and I have met one or two of them, that whiles feel the same way about it all as you and me. They go so off themselves when it's all over, that they could just cut their throats.'

Still and on, it was fine to be looked upon as something of a woman of the world, but overburdening whiles, and more like myth than truth; then it was finer to dissolve the burden in the wash-tub, for the sight of their washing blowing high and white along the lines seldom failed to produce the comment from the farmers' wives:

'Let Sue Tatt be what she likes. One thing is sure. She never fails to hang out a bonnie white washing!'

The same thing when they sent for her to help out with the spring cleaning.

'I never found anybody could get the grain of that wood as white as you can scrub it, Sue,' Kingorth's wife had confessed to her just the other week. And coming from Kingorth's wife that was praise, for she was a tight woman, and had she been a ghost, would have grudged giving you a fright.

Such praise was sweet to Sue, for she cared. At least, one of the many parts of her cared. So often Sue Tatt felt the conflicting burden of all her various potentialities bearing down on her. For Oh, but it was a terrible thing to have within you the power to be a plain woman or a beauty, a slut or house-proud, a respectable body or a light of love. All of which Sue had been at some time, and could be at another, for she always grasped the immediate potential.

'From now on,' she had vowed, under the impetus of Kingorth's wife's praise, 'from now on, I'm always going to clean my own little house as thoroughly as I clean other folks' big houses.' And she did – for nearly a week. A week in which she almost drove her family mad; confiding sadly to Fiona, when the cleaning mood had deserted her:

'Do you know something, Fiona? I could be one of the most house-proud women in all Caldwell, if I just wasn't *Me*!'

It was true too. And Fiona, although she was only fourteen, understood the truth of it. Fiona was the only one of her children that Sue Tatt really liked; and then simply as one human being likes another.

She had named her daughter, even before she was born, after the heroine of the serial she had been perusing – a favourite occupation of Sue in her carrying times.

'Fiona' – for that dark, willowy girl who strode the heathery hills of Scottish 'Family Fiction'. Tweed clad and wind-swept. Her head flung back. Her eyes always 'set wide apart and grey' – scanning the far horizons of loch and hill, against whose background stood the ancient but fast-decaying House of the noble but impoverished laird, loved by and at last won by Fiona, despite all the intrigues of that wealthy London blonde, who never really cared about each stick and stone of the Ancient House. Not as Fiona did, her eyes set wide apart and grey.

It was some flaw in Sue Tatt's nature, made her accept Fiona – a flaw she shared with many of her like. Even those in Caldwell who had never known their Scotland so, preferred their image of it thus – a fable-flowering land. But, even so, their need of the 'Rowan tree' was such, it could cause the antrin bush to bloom unpruned within their minds. Only an alien, and then perhaps out of a need as urgent as their own, had ever attempted to deprive them of their illusions.

Even God Knows himself could laugh about that, now. 'Yon Italian prisoner of war was one I'll never forget. For Oh, but he had a right ill will to Scotland. "Nothing for look," was always yon one's cry. "In Scotland. Nothing for look. Tatties, Turnips. Rain and Wind. And no Divertiment. In Italy now! Plenty for look. Plenty Sun. Plenty Diverti-ment. Plenty plenty sun." God Almighty. The way he spoke about that country of his was enough to set you thinking that the sun itself had a hard time of it getting around to get its blink in anywhere else on the face of the earth. According to yon one, it just bided in Italy. Aye, but he had a right sore grudge against Scotland. Still, like the Poles, he appar-ently found our women much to his liking. For I never saw a man so set on women. He had even gotten the length of teaching Sue Tatt Italian. And whatten a waste yon was. Sue could have understood what he was seeking in any tongue!

Still, if his taste in countries was anything like his taste in women, Scotland lost nothing at all through his opinion of it.'

But there had been those whose tastes had been worth taking all the care in the world for. Sue Tatt remembered that as she stood surveying the result of all her beautifying efforts in the bathroom mirror. It had taken a Second World War to bring Sue one tithe of the admiration which she had always felt was her due.

The curious thing about wars was that you were born in the remembrance of your parents' wars, and grew up within their constant recollections of an age, alluring as myth, 'Before the War', so that you got the feeling it were better never to have been born at all than to live in the dull eras 'After the War' when 'Times have changed', and always 'For the worst'.

Sue Tatt had reached her prime during the Second World War. She now knew why the period of one's life, lived through wartime, never became relegated to the past, and, though foreshadowing the future, stood in the present, like the Celtic Cross in front of Caldwell's Old Established Church, erected to 'The Memory of the Men of This Parish' who had fallen in battles as near in time and far in distance as the Dardanelles and Libya. Despite that, there still was room for the names of men who might fall in future battles, since war was never the countryman's first urgency nor last loyalty. A glance at the names on the Celtic Cross would have convinced you that, by and large, it was the country-side's artisans who 'fell' – its labourers and tradesmen, and sometimes farmers' only sons, not old enough for their first heritage, side by side with crofters' younger sons who had none, since the croft ever provided for but one heir.

Maybe the flatness of 'After the War' was but in natural contrast to its years of heightened tempo. Sue Tatt could see it all, as clear as yesterday, without today impinging. The first hot flush of patriotism. 'All in it Together.' China and Russia swinging into their orbit. Aid for them both. Knitting Bees, plain and purl; socks and balaclavas; picking up dropped stitches side by side with the Misses Lennox, and Miss McCombie of The Whins, while Colonel McCombie, resurrected from retirement, manoeuvred up on Soutar Hill with a platoon of Tractormen and Cattlemen who formed Home Guard. The sudden prestige of men in uniform, particularly their own regiment, the Gordon Highlanders. But, though you sang *Scots Wha Hae* and *Highland Laddie*, the paradox remained: the soldier, except in times of war, in moments of high sentimental fervour, in retrospect or in song, was regarded as the lowest form of life. 'Where's my Mam?' . . . 'She's run off with a Sodger!'

In peacetime, few girls kept company with soldiers. Sue Tatt herself had drawn the line at them, and had hitherto ignored all mating calls from kilties. This prejudice may have had its roots in 'old, unhappy far-off things', when paternity claims could be avoided by the simple expedient of enlisting. Certain it was that a strong prejudice against the soldier prevailed in country places; until wars came, of course. And then the girl not clinging to the arm of a soldier became an oddity, and an object of pity.

Sue Tatt herself had clung to not a few. The Fusiliers, when the boast on everyone's tongue was 'We're going to hang out the washing on the Siegfried Line'. The Tank Corps, when the prophecy was 'There'll be bluebirds over the white cliffs of Dover'. And when the war was in its closing stages, Sue had vowed to the music in the Sergeants' Mess 'This is my lovely day, this the day I will remember the day I am dying'.

When the first high tension of war had passed, Caldwell had settled down again to minding its own business. For its business was a total war effort – or so the Government ruled, by bringing out the Stand Still Order, which forbade all in reserved occupations to leave their jobs. But, since your born farmworker would never have dreamt of doing so anyhow, the Stand Still Order was not only superfluous, but unsettling! As the Plunger had observed at the time, 'It just never dawned on me before to leave Darklands. But then I suppose I always knew I could leave, if I so desired. And that's how it should be! I don't like the idea of this Stand Still Order. I don't like it at all.'

Men who had even less control of themselves, or more within themselves, saw in the Order something against which they could test their initiative, and left their jobs on the land for no other reason than to prove it could be done. But, by and large, Caldwell had settled down again, and subsidies began to roll in – subsidies for bull calves and potatoes. Farmworkers' wages began to rise, and with them their status. The two Term Days of the year became a thing of the past. No longer could the townsman, half affectionately, half contemptuously, instantly recognise the 'Country Geordie' walking his streets, for the farm-workers' uniform – navy blue suit and bonnet – began to disappear, too. Nor was such prosperity confined to farmers and their workers. Even the tinkers wandering the countryside began to benefit. For, though they had always sold their all, their all had now increased – clothing coupons, sweet coupons, food 'Points' – so that Caldwell itself was moved to protest. 'The World is coming to a pretty fine pass when you can no longer tell whether it's the farmers or the tinkers that are driving round the countryside in brakes.'

Sue Tatt had also shared in the rising prosperity, though, strangely enough, not in any material way. It had been sufficient for Sue to feel that she 'lived' at last. She began to roll distinguishing abbreviations off her tongue – R.S.M,

C.S.M, Q.M.S., Warrant Officer, Sarn't and simply Lance Jack – with an expertise which impressed before it shocked those in Caldwell whose acquaintance with the military within their gates remained long-distance and objective towards anyone under the rank of Lieutenant. Sue had moved from one intense emotional crisis to another with Lofty, Shorty, Nobby, Bootlace, Snudge, retaining her resilience, recovering from their Postings, and even surviving their Overseas Drafts.

There had been an element of competition in those war years which had presented a challenge to Sue Tatt, for, having no fellow-like in Caldwell, Sue had lived in a Crusoe kind of loneliness. But when the war came, it had revealed that all the surrounding parishes had, unknowingly, harboured at least one of Sue's kind; submerged for years, but rising to the surface, and suffering some great sea change at Bugle Call.

Sue could still remember the excitement of getting ready, and making up, with all her little clique, in this same bathroom, their children skirling in and out amongst their feet, small nightmares interrupting large dreams, and silenced only by a sixpence, or quietened with a curse.

None of the female friendships Sue had made in those years had lasted, of course. For, although all were of the pack, each had remained a lone wolf. Now and again Sue would run into one such crony from those years, submerged once more into respectability and beyond personal recognition, so that they would have less to say to each other than utter strangers, since some kinds of memories shared ever make for mutual silence.

Oh, but there had been no holding of them in those years. It was as if all the world had joined hands and were rushing together towards the end of the War, and nothing had mattered in between. The end of the War. The very phrase had conjured up within itself the magic and escape of some Open Sesame to a new and different world. But, anticipation, once so keen, had now dissolved itself, though, for some months after V-Day, Sue had still cast searching, disappointed eyes over Caldwell, seeking some kind of transformation, and finding it only as an exile, after long absence from his country, might find that the mountains of his memory were but hills.

Caldwell itself though, had gradually become aware of some change in Sue Tatt. She had become 'more choosy' after the War, 'more particular' – or so they said. And small wonder! For whatever else she had learned from the war years, Sue had learned comparison. While never being unaware of her own needs, nor contemptuous of the needs of men, she had simply discovered that there were ways and means of supplicating for them. It had been better to lie down on the windswept target range up at Balwhine, thinking it was for love, than to stand up against Kingorth's byre door, knowing it was simply out of good nature. Nothing put Sue so clean off now as Caldwell's matter-of-fact approach . . . 'Well, Sue. What about it then?'

There was the exception, though. And, once again, Sue had created it for herself, in her relationship with Hugh Riddel; for once deceiving herself only in small externals, knowing instinctively that any other woman could have served his purpose, though even then the relationship for Sue had to become one of acquisition, 'Anyone *could* have him. But it is I, Sue Tatt, who has gotten him.'

'You stink of stuff, Mam,' was all that young Beel could find to say, when Sue, her elaborate toilette completed, stood once again on the threshold of her kitchen, pausing this time for appreciative acclamation.

'You just stink of stuff.'

Coarse, that was what young Beel was! Just like the father

of him. Unlike mothers in wedlock, Sue Tatt seldom associated herself with her children at all, but had acquired a rare degree of parental objectivity. Coarse. It always came out.

'That lipstick doesn't look too bad on you, Mam,' Fiona conceded. 'Can I have it when you're done with it?'

'No. You can *not*.' Sue advanced into her kitchen, conflicting roles battling within her – Helen of Troy and Widow Woman Bringing up Young Family. 'What you *can* do,' she suggested, looking at Fiona as though seeing her for the first time, 'is to take that muck off your face, and give that neck of yours a right good scrub. The pores of your skin are going to all clog up for the want of plain soap and water.'

'Skip it, Mam,' Fiona shrugged, certain in the knowledge that she would fall heir to all the little pots of stuff anyhow, when her mother had got tired of them.

'What do you mean . . . *Skip it*?' Sue demanded ominously. There were moments when her comprehensive methods of rearing her family suddenly back-fired on herself. And this was blowing up into one of those moments. Sue felt an old inexplicable anger falling down over herself and her daughter, and cloaking them in awful proximity. Her eyes took in each detail of Fiona, with the cruel, confining clarity of temper. 'Dolling yourself up there in my best shoes! *And* my new bracelet. Eyebrow pencil too. And eyeshadow. You look' – it was either this, or slap the girl until all rage was eased out of herself – 'just like a little whore. That's what you look like.'

It was true too, Sue assured herself, her eyes still fixed on her daughter's face. But now, the concentrated image was diffusing. Sue turned her attention to the mantelpiece and started rearranging her ornaments. 'You can keep the bracelet if you like.' Her offer came rough and jerky, acquiring smoothness only in its enlargement. 'But those shoes of mine will ruin your feet. I was thinking of taking out another

Provident Check. You can have a pair of shoes for yourself off it.'

'What about *me*?' Young Beel had sniffed out the favourable drift of his mother's mood. 'I'm needing a new pair of trousers.'

'I'll get a Provident Check big enough for all of us. then,' Sue promised, suddenly feeling capable of bequeathing the moon in gratitude for the lightness within her.

'Got a fag on you, Mam?' Beel was taking every ounce out of the advantageous wind.

'Try my cardigan pocket,' Sue acquiesced, equably enough, 'but you'll have to run down to Davy for fags later on. And you can have the price of a packet for yourself.'

'Ta, Mam.' Beel's interpretation of the offer equalled his mother's casual bribery. 'I'll nip down for them when Hugh Riddel comes!'

The kitchen and its occupants now settled down into an intimacy of a kind which was rarely experienced in more orthodox homes.

'I saw Hugh Riddel this morning,' Fiona said, waving her newly acquired bracelet in front of the fire till it reflected its light.

'Oh, did you now? What time would that have been about?' Sue asked, as if the answer didn't concern her.

'I don't right remember what time it was.' Fiona felt stubborn. 'Early though,' she added for safety's sake, her eyes still fixed on the changing lights of her bracelet.

'What time's early?' Sue demanded, irritation creeping into her voice.

'First Bus.' Fiona, apprehensive of stretching her mother's patience too far, was yet reluctant to reveal too much, too soon. 'He had driven Isa Riddel down to catch it.'

'She must have been for the Town the day, then?'

'Must have,' Fiona agreed absently.

'*Was* she, or was she *not*?' Sue demanded impatiently. 'Surely you know what bus she got on to?'

'The Town bus, of course!'

'Well then! Couldn't you have said that in the first place? How did she look? Was she all dressed up for the Town?'

'No. The same old usual,' Fiona admitted at last.

'An awful-looking frump of a wifie yon,' young Beel said, getting the mood of the thing at last.

'Did Hugh Riddel himself seem in good bone?' Sue's interest almost defied discernment.

'Never him! He's a right dour dook yon. But he's coming here the night,' Fiona remembered. Her bracelet, reflected by the firelight, glowed like the jewels of story-book memory. 'He's definitely coming here the night.' Fiona handed her ace to her mother at last. 'I'm sure of that. I heard him telling Wylie the Blacksmith that he'd call in by for the bottling lever tonight, because he'd be passing this way anyhow.'

'That will just depend on the weather,' Sue said irrelevantly and, rising, made her way out to the gate to have a look at the weather.

'It's as bright as day, and as quiet's the grave.'

'Aye. It's going to be a right fine night. Mam,' Fiona assured her mother, finding her hand and squeezing it, the only demonstration of affection they ever allowed, or needed between them. 'It's going to be a fine night, Mam,' Fiona insisted, as they stood looking out on a night that their wish had willed.

You would never have thought that a moon on the wane like this would give such light. But with it was ground frost, and in your mind the promise of the lengthening nights. The quietness over it might well be known to the dead, where every sound was in itself an interruption, and lights snapped up like noise upon the landscape.

'I'd know the Plunger's wife's skirl anywhere.' Sue broke their own silence.

'It's all the Darklands' cottar wives making for the Rural,' Fiona said.

'So it is,' Sue remembered. 'God help us. They'll all be singing *And Did Those Feet* and *Land Of Our Birth* the night, then.'

'I know. Grown-up women seem terrible gowkit when they're all together,' Fiona reflected, as they laughed together in the darkness, adding for good measure, in the great good-will of their togetherness, 'But *you're* never like that, Mam.'

'Fiona!' The pressure of Sue's hand indicated the urgency of her question. 'The *truth*, now. Say you had never once set eyes on me or on Isa Riddel in all your life, and suddenly you met us both together on the road, which one of us would you say was the bonniest?'

'You, Mam.' The answer was unhesitating and sincere. 'You are far younger looking and bonnier than Isa Riddel.'

On this night too, Isa Riddel, by some mischance or vagary of mood, forsook the local bus and took instead the 'Scholars' train' home to Caldwell. On the Scholars' train travelled the youngsters of Caldwell, who were completing their education in the Town.

Not all were promising, though some could simply afford the fees. These wore the colours of the Town's Grammar Schools, elegantly, like casual afterthoughts, slung across their shoulders. The others, conscious that their places in the Secondary Schools were won in contest and held by merit, wore their school colours with little elegance, but with much bravado, as if to say, a thing not worth a damn, but all my own.

Yet each of them and all of them had this in common: Caldwell was home, and sounding ground; the place wherein they exercised their hard acquired, though never completely mastered, English accents, and gained a genuine – albeit grudging – admiration; the place where they could fall back into Scots, in moods and moments no other tongue could so convincingly convey, and all without any loss of face at all.

That once in all their lifetimes when separate worlds – the town and country – waited with patience, offering them choice of ultimate domicile. In this, their stateless time, they recognised no fellow-countrymen. And so it needed an adult without sensitivity, or with the heart of Bruce, to board the Scholars' train.

Isa Riddel was not without sensitivity. But neither was the Commercial Traveller, easing himself down into the seat across from her, without the heart of Bruce. She could have sworn that he winked to her, before pulling his hat down over his face and disappearing behind it, though what the joke was, she didn't rightly know.

She only knew a sense of isolation, as the Scholars' train pulled itself out of the station, and a growing feeling of non-existence as it gathered speed and shot past small suburban stations, ignoring all the waiting travellers in the world not destined for Caldwell Via Lendrum Junction.

Not even the Mother Tap of Soutar Hill seen from the new angle of a train eased Isa Riddel's feeling of outwithness, or lessened her wordless protestation, a captive there amongst the teenagers of Caldwell, yet knowing each of them inti-mately, though not personally. Their new accents rising up all round her, battling with their old idioms, were enough to make you laugh, had you not realised its seriousness to themselves.

Her daughter, Helen, used always to be on at her for her persistent use of old out-dated words and phrases. Words like 'forfochen' and 'blae' – though what others could so well describe in sound body's tiredness and weariness of spirit?

Speech was so important, Helen had always maintained: the first thing to betray you, and the last to stand by you. It had been a long time now, since Helen had bothered to correct her speech. To her own wonder, Isa Riddel admitted to herself that she had missed her daughter's corrections; she knew that one only stopped bothering about something when one had stopped caring about it.

'I know what the Latin words on your blazers mean,' she heard herself inform the faces round her. '*Ad Altiora Tendo* – We Aim For Higher Things. Though my Helen once told me that you all say it means "We'll have a shot at our Highers". Only in fun, and just amongst yourselves, of course,' she added, lest they might take offence. 'My Helen took her Highers.' Isa Riddel rushed on, afraid of the silence that had fallen over the compartment, but terrified to stop, lest she should fall into it. 'That was a while before your times, of course.'

The Vet's youngest daughter started to giggle in the corner, his eldest son put his head out of the carriage window and heaved silently.

'I was reading somewhere that they are thinking of making the Highers easier to take, now,' the Commercial Traveller said, suddenly appearing from behind his hat. 'Your daughter must have taken hers when they really *were* something to take.'

'Oh, but she did.' Isa Riddel felt that somehow he had the right to know. 'Helen got to the University on an Arts Bursary.'

'But I thought they all went,' the Commercial Traveller said. 'You know, with their bolls of meal, their barrels of

salt herring, then came out Doctors of Divinity at the end
of it all.'

'Oh, no.' She had a feeling that he was teasing her, but
perhaps not. 'It was the crofters' sons did that,' she assured
him seriously. There's a big difference between a cottar's
child and a crofter's child. You see' – she realised that he
was but a townsman after all – 'you see, a crofter works his
own little bit of land. A cottar works somebody else's big
bit of land.'

'I see. So there is a difference then?' The Commercial
Traveller sounded as if this was indeed news to him. 'And
didn't your daughter go to the University then?' he asked.

'Yes, and no.' Isa Riddel found herself having to explain,
again. 'She didn't go for her M.A. And do you know something? I always thought that M.A.'s were what the University
was really for. But Helen went to it for a Diploma in Social
Science.'

'It's the thing now,' the Commercial Traveller nodded his
approval. 'They're all going in for that.'

'Still and on,' Isa Riddel regarded him doubtfully, 'it
wasn't the thing *we* had set our hearts on for Helen. Her
father was even more put out about it than I was myself. He
said at the time Helen would have been as well leaving school
at fifteen, putting on one of yon Salvation Army bonnets
and selling the *War Cry* down in the pubs by the Docks, if
she wanted to put the world to rights as badly as all that.
Oh, but mind you, *I* was disappointed about it, too,' she
added urgently, emphatically, for she hadn't spoken so freely
to anyone in years – and the man a complete stranger to her
at that. The very realisation brought her to a sudden silence.
The wonder was the man was sitting there listening, as if all
she said was sensible enough, and even waiting for her to go
on.

But that was impossible. Isa Riddel had never – not even

for herself taken the reasons for her disappointment out and looked upon them fair and square. Vast indefinable disappointment was easier to accept than any of its small ridiculous manifestations.

. . . Helen gaining a Scholarship to a Secondary School. Her own rising prestige amongst her neighbour cottar wives. Nothing seemed so worth having from them, and there was nothing else she so needed from them. How well she had masked her pride, on the sunlit Thursday afternoon of that Summer, standing with them all at Ambroggan cross-roads waiting for the grocer's van.

'We see you've gotten Helen home for the summer again, then, Mrs Riddel,' Lil, the Bottler, had remarked.

'Aye,' she had replied. 'Just that.' And not one amongst them could ever have accused her of being big on it, in that testing moment. Though, inside herself, she had felt big enough to burst. But 'Aye,' she said, calmly enough, 'Helen's home for a while. Not for long though. She's going up to the University in October.'

Credit where credit was due, Isa Riddel had to admit that to herself. Only her own like could have equalled her in understatement. And Lil had done that, right enough. 'Oh, is she now?' Lil had replied, as casually as if Helen had just been going up to Soutar Hill to pick blaeberries. 'Well, the University will be a fine change for her.'

But, even so, Helen's glory had still reflected on her, through the University years, every Thursday at the grocer's van. Once her neighbours realised that it had given her no side at all, their interest became genuinely appreciative; while she herself managed to retain casualness. She could hear herself yet, in reply to Lil's enquiries –

'You're quite right there, Lil. Helen does just look forward to her week-ends at home here. What with all that studying, and all the different classes she's got to attend, and that Town lodgings of hers. For you know yourselves that the feeding's never the thing in the Town. And I can never get round her at all, to take back a bit of oatcake or fresh-baked scone. She says the students she shares with would never eat the like. As far as I can make out, they all seem to live on coffee and tinned beans.'

'I never could look at yon things myself,' Lil had condoled with her. 'The smell of them's enough for me. But never you mind, Mrs Riddel. Helen will be taking her M.A. And one of these days, off you'll be on the head of the road to see her Capped.'

And there Isa Riddel's difficulty had lain. How to explain to them all that Helen had no desire in the world for an M.A. It was hard to explain to others something you didn't understand yourself. A Diploma in Social Science just seemed a come-down from an M.A. So Isa Riddel had kept her silence on the subject, and held on to her glory for as long as it lasted.

It was Helen's father who had given words to it all, when she left the University to take up an appointment with a Youth Centre in the Town. Hugh Riddel always did have the release of words.

'Well, Helen! If your Youth Centre is anything like the set-up Charlie Anson has just started here in Caldwell, it's heaven preserve you! There he is yonder, clapping his hands as if he were the Almighty himself. Calling loons he has known from the cradle "Lads!" Lord, but I can mind when he drove third pair at Ardgour. I was third Cattleman there at the time. And Anson was sent down the road for taking advantage of yon poor silly bitch, Bess Ainslie, that washed the cans in Ardgour's dairy. He never could get a woman, unless she was some poor natural like Bess, with only her body normal in its function. And you needna put that superior face on either, Helen. There's nothing sorer needed than a bonnie, whole man. But yon's not one! Though, there he is, trying to worm his way into the County Council by taking up Voluntary Youth Work. You'd want to throw your porridge up, running into his like first thing in a morning. If *your* Youth folk turn out to be anything like Charlie Anson, it's God help you, lassie.'

There never had been a great deal of communication between Helen and her father. There was less after that. Helen had put on the defence of an even deeper reserve. Her man's bitter dislike of Charlie Anson still puzzled Isa Riddel, for Anson aroused no such feelings in herself. On the contrary, he was always civil enough when he stepped across her door. Though what put Anson in her favour above all else was that he was the one person who could take Helen out of herself: for they spoke the same tongue, using the same kind of words. Oh, but Helen always had the best of it in the talking. All the words were really hers; though Charlie Anson would catch them as they fell, and be right and properly grateful for them. 'You are right there, Miss Riddel. Quite right. For that is just how I am finding things myself. Only in a small way of course. For I would never compare my own small organisation here with the work you are doing there in the Town. Still, it's expanding. Oh aye, it's expanding. The Minister is beginning to sit up and take notice. But what I really want is to catch the eye of the Rural Council!'

In times like these, Isa Riddel felt almost happy. Getting the tea ready, listening, but never adding a word, to the great talk going on around her. Yet feeling part of it, and quietly convinced that every word being uttered was correct, until Riddel himself came blustering in, confusing them all; for he had a way of sounding right by proving other people to be wrong.

Darkness was beginning to close in on the countryside

now. And though officially it was spring, the train rushed through a land that still lay lurking in its winter. For spring was that green something which took the southern places by surprise, but left this northern land unmoved; holding itself in grim reserve for summer's fullness, and autumn's onslaught. And when you were aware of spring at all, it was in some sudden thaw and in your hearing; when hillside burns broke off from mother peaks, and, in an anger of anonymity, roared down to swell the River Ruar, and share its name. So. In this sudden water rush of movement, the land itself would sometimes stir a little, but then sink back – as though even time itself had sounded false alarm, leaving you but the sky to measure seasons. And in the gradual, lengthening light, you would know that it was spring. Such a thaw had not yet broken the winter's fastness. Not even here at Lendrum Junction, where all things happened earlier than in Caldwell.

'Change here for Lendrum.'

The porter's cry roused the Commercial Traveller, and set him into the reluctant and contemptuous motions of one who had not yet resigned himself to representing his firm in an area which seemed to include all the 'Change here for' Junctions in the world.

Oh, but *there* was a man knew how to face the world, Isa Riddel thought admiringly, as she watched him elbow the Lendrum scholars aside, while he took his suitcase down off the rack, dusted his hat, opened the window and peered out of it, as if querying the porter's claim that this was Lendrum Junction at all.

'It's a nice little place is Lendrum,' Isa Riddel assured his back, wondering why she did so. She herself had never set foot in Lendrum, for all her years beside it. And yet she knew that had she ever found herself at the world's end, and met there one from Lendrum, although a stranger, she would

acclaim him like some long-lost friend of the heart. For
Lendrum was a sound as familiar to her as far-off Borneo,
whose Wild Man threatened all of child-hood's misdemeanours.

'Lendrum's just about five miles to the other side of Soutar
Hill,' she added, realising that this was all she really knew
of Lendrum.

'Thanks.' The Commercial Traveller smiled quickly
towards her and leapt on to the platform. She kept him still
within her sight as the train drew out, brushing his hat against
his trouser leg, peering from side to side in search of the
Way Out. It just showed you. There was a man you could
have sworn was certain of his way about the world. Yet there
he was, standing lost like in a little place like Lendrum
Junction. The image bucked Isa Riddel somewhat. The train
speeding under Soutar Hill was making good time. She would
be home a good hour earlier than Helen.

There was still an hour to go according to the clock in the
cafeteria. Helen Riddel sat trying to discover its hands going
round. Usually her glances clockwards were furtive, for
sometimes she felt that no one on the staff of St Andrew's
Young Communal Centre ever watched the clock at all,
except herself. There was a feeling of letting down the side
about such an attitude to time, in such a vocation. For it
was a vocation, as even a stranger would have immediately
gathered from the conversation rising up from the staff tables.

'We cannot always *like* the teenagers we deal with,' Miss
Booth, the Warden of the Centre was impressing upon Miss
Rennie, the newest recruit to the staff.

A lifetime's acquaintance with her own creed had familiar-
ised it into meaninglessness for Helen Riddel. 'I believe in
God the Father. Jesus Christ his only begotten son. The
Holy Ghost. The Holy Catholic Church. The Communion

of Saints. The forgiveness of sins. The resurrection of the body and the life everlasting.' So it was small wonder that the words rising up around her in the cafeteria hit her awareness, like drops against a window-pane in a day of unceasing rain.

'But we must always *love* them,' the Warden was insisting.

Helen Riddel didn't even need her eyes to observe Miss Rennie's reaction to this edict. Her own remembrance could do that for her – could recall the pondering assimilation, the sudden excited recognition.

'I see what you mean, Miss Booth! I think I always realised that myself. But I just never managed to *pin it down* so *exactly*.'

Miss Booth was right too. Helen Riddel was in entire agreement with Miss Rennie on this point. But then, Miss Booth always did sound right the first time she expressed a sentiment. It was simply repetition that robbed her words of original force.

'Did you read that article in yesterday's *Telegraph*, Miss Booth?' The conversation was becoming more general now, its topics flung from table to table, the way the teenagers would fling empty orange squash cartons at each other later on. 'That article about the Espresso Bar society?'

'I'm afraid not. I never find time to read.'

Pride, not apology, sound our confessions. Those bold confessions which defy anybody to think less of you. – 'I've got a shocking temper when I'm roused.' 'I say exactly what I think.' 'I've got no time at all for sentiment. *Practical* – That's *Me*!' – Those bold confessions; seldom their shabby weak antitheses. For self keeps silence and its secrets still, lending its other images and imitations voice.

'I just happened to glance at the article in the train.' – Lack of time for reading, it now transpired, was general, and had assumed a kind of virtue.

'It is simply that they don't *Know*,' Mr Fleming of Senior Lads' Group was emphasising to his assistant, 'and that is where *we* take over. If we take it from there, Melville. From *zero*.'

Mr Fleming had suddenly discovered a new application for an old word, all by himself, and one to his liking. But soon it too would become current: soon it would punctuate all their speeches, just as 'Good Show', 'Will Do' and 'Fantastic' had done.

Helen Riddel grinned wryly to herself. How down she used to be on the Doric tongue of her own people! And what a long, long time it had been since she had admitted to herself that they were her own people. And how contemptuous always of the outlandish words and phrases her mother had used! They had become more than balm to her hearing now; they could sound her soul so that it leapt to the recognition of meaning again.

'So you've won home again, Helen?' That was exactly how her mother would greet her tonight – the welcome extended when she had returned as a child from school; one which would remain unchanged, were she to return an old woman from a far country. You 'won home' either way: Won . . . Gained. Merited. Attained. On her people's tongue the very sound of the verb 'won' implicitly acknowledged all the distractions, hazards and mischances you might well have to overcome, whether on the road home from school in the foolishness of childhood, or on the road across the world in the wisdom of age.

'Good evening, Miss Riddel.' Helen Riddel's eyes followed a large expanse of fawn and brown checks, to land on Miss Booth's face beaming on top of them. 'This is your weekend off, isn't it? Miss Riddel is fortunate in having her home in the country,' Miss Booth turned to explain to the newest recruit. 'A country house,' she repeated, laughing to emphasise that she was really joking, and having revealed her human potentialities, briskened up into being the Warden of the Centre again. 'Let me see, now.' Miss Booth shot her arm out in front of her face, pulled it sharply back till her hand almost caught her nose, and studied her wrist-watch before turning an accusing eye towards the cafeteria clock. 'Is your clock at the correct time, Mrs Lovat?' she demanded of the cafeteria lady, so importantly that the staff broke off their conversation and turned all their eyes and all their attention upon the cafeteria clock.

'It wasn't right according to the Wireless,' the cafeteria lady grumbled. 'I went and missed the six o'clock News through that clock.' Her tone rejected suggested ownership of it. 'And it wasn't *me* that touched it. I've got enough to get through here in an evening, without going and messing about with other folks' clocks.'

'Of course it wasn't *you*, Mrs Lovat,' Miss Booth hastened to reassure the cafeteria lady. 'You wouldn't dream of doing such a thing.'

'It could have been one of the lads,' Mr Fleming ventured. 'They get up to all sorts, trying to wangle an extra ten minutes at table tennis.'

'*Robert*!' Miss Booth turned her back on both Mr Fleming and his opinions, and shouted again for the Patrol Boy. '*Robert*! Where *has* Robert got to?' No one moved to search for Robert, but all seemed to be poised at the starting tape. '*Ah*! *There* you are, Robert,' Miss Booth acclaimed him gladly, the way an amateur conjuror might acclaim the rabbit he hadn't really expected inside his hat. 'NOW.' Miss Booth's enunciation of that simple word adjured all to listen carefully, although Robert, slightly overwhelmed by the prominence in which he found himself, was the one to whom she spoke. 'Now Robert. As you well know, I like this Centre efficiently run.'

I know it all, Helen Riddel thought wearily, letting the rest of Miss Booth's words slip away from her. I could say it for her, word for word; or rather for the benefit of the newest recruit. Indeed it was for the newest recruit's benefit that the Warden was repeating her edicts to a patrol boy who was familiar with them.

'She's such a personality, isn't she?' The newest recruit sat herself down beside Helen Riddel in a fervour of admiration for the Warden. 'She mixes so well. It must be very difficult to get close to that type of teenager, and that's half the battle, Miss Booth assures me. How do *you* manage it, Miss Riddel? I believe you've worked here for quite a time.'

'For eight years,' Helen Riddel said, 'and I've never managed it.' It didn't matter now; you could admit to murder when it no longer mattered to you. And you'll never manage it either, Helen Riddel thought, smiling at the shocked blankness of the newest recruit's expression. 'You see,' she added, kindly enough, 'knowing the way and being capable of walking straight along it are two different things. In theory I know the way, and it sounds simple enough. It just means keeping in mind that, in our Welfare State, the only difference between these teenagers and ourselves is that we have lived that little bit longer, and so should have more experience of life.'

'Of course you are right, Miss Riddel, you are quite right.'

'No.' Helen Riddel shook her head. 'That's the theory, but it just doesn't always work out like that.'

'But we must keep it in mind just the same,' the newest recruit insisted.

You're shaping all right, Helen Riddel thought, rising and collecting her registers; you have already got the most essential thing, the team spirit (for she had observed the instinctive natural use of the collective pronoun 'we'). Perhaps your face will fit better than mine ever did. My personal distaste for teetering, high-heeled children, rescued from all-night cafés, was cancelled out by the knowledge that even the sluttiest of them had more experience of the basics of life in one wet night than I had in twenty-five years.

She could cope much better now, Helen Riddel realised ironically. But now was too late.

The bus for Caldwell was already standing in Glebe Street when Helen Riddel took up her place at the end of the queue, though this by no means signified its departure on time.

'God Almighty, Jean, where are you off to now?' Beel Grieve, the crofter, grumbled after the disappearing figure of the conductress. 'When that red-headed one's on the conducting,' he informed the rest of the queue, 'she's just like a hen on a hot girdle.'

'She's a lot more obliging than the wee dark creature that was on the conducting before her,' the Joiner's wife defended. 'There's nothing Jean won't bring you back from the Town, if you ask her nice like. And she's away the now for rings for poor Bert Wheeler's pigeons.'

'Is yon mannie taken to rearing pigeons, then?' Beel Grieve's irritation was momentarily overcome by his contemplation. 'He was awful set on ferrets at the back end of the year.'

'He's on the pigeons now then,' the Joiner's wife snapped, turning her attention on the bus driver, who was struggling to put a crate of day-old chicks up on the rack. 'Turn that box over on its other side, Davie,' she advised him. 'You'll have the chickens standing on their heads that way. What are they, anyhow, day-olds?'

'God knows what they are,' the driver grumbled, pausing to examine the label on the crate. 'Day-old pullets for Balwhine.'

'You would think,' the Joiner's wife reflected, 'that Balwhine would just set a clocking hen and let her do the rest of it for him; for she's a lot better at it than all yon scuttering about with oil stoves.'

'There's not a sign of that conductress quean coming back yet.' Beel Grieve was becoming irritable again. 'And I've got a Union Meeting in Caldwell the night at eight o'clock.'

'Jean will be holding on for the Late Final Editions,' the driver explained, 'and the lassie canna get them till they come out.'

'But I tell you, Davie, I've got a Meeting at eight o'clock,' Beel Grieve insisted again.

'Excuse me,' a voice behind him interrupted, 'but I understood that this bus was scheduled to leave Glebe Street at seven o'clock.'

'You understood right, Mistress.' The driver surveyed the newcomer severely. 'But this bus takes fits and starts. It's the last bus to Caldwell the night. And I'm not budging an inch from here till my regulars turn up.'

'But don't you realise,' the woman protested, 'I am due to judge a Competition in Caldwell at eight o'clock.'

'Good God!' – the Joiner's wife nudged Beel Grieve – 'that must be the Marmalade Competition wifie. It serves them all right, too, if she never turns up,' she added resentfully, 'for they say she's a first cousin of the Dominie's wife; and she's got a good sweep of her, when you take a right look. We should always have complete outsiders to judge our competitions. It's a lot fairer that way.'

'Rob Finney's pulled a muscle and will be out of the Cup Final the morn,' the conductress shouted from the other side of the street, a bundle of Late Finals slung in one hand, and her own free copy waving in the other. 'That's the Town's chances of the Northern League up in the air. And your coupon gone for a Burton, Davie. Look see.' She thrust the paper under the driver's nose, and they relayed the headlines together. 'Voodoo Hits The Dons. What Price Pittodrie Tomorrow?'

'Dundee United will just murder them the morn, then,' the driver prophesied, handing the paper back to Jean. 'And that reminds me. Did you call in by Bruntslands to collect yon wrench for Wylie the blacksmith? He says Hugh Riddel will lay hands on him if it doesn't turn up this week.'

'God, Davie,' the conductress gaped, crestfallen. 'I clean forgot all about that wrench. But it won't take me two minutes to nip back to Bruntslands for it.'

'You may just as well all get inside the bus, then,' the driver advised, as the conductress shot off out of view again, 'and get yourselves settled down in comfort till Jean gets back.'

'But it isn't good enough,' the Marmalade Competition lady protested, struggling through the queue, and making her way first into the bus, as if this was but her natural right.

'It's *my* bus, Mistress,' the driver reminded her.

'It isn't good enough,' she repeated. 'I haven't got all the time in the world.'

'But Caldwell has,' Helen Riddel thought smilingly, before putting on the white, serious mask of Miss Riddel again, and getting into the bus.

'It's you, is't then, Miss Riddel?' The Joiner's wife swung round in her seat. 'I didna notice you in the queue.'

'I was at the back of it.'

'Excuse me,' the Marmalade Competition lady hovered above Helen Riddel. 'Do you mind if I share this seat with you? I usually prefer a back seat, but there's a crate of chickens in the rack above my head.'

'And a great pity they didna file on her hat,' the Joiner's wife whispered, as the Marmalade Competition lady struggled to put her belongings up on the rack before easing herself down beside Helen Riddel.

'Ridiculous things, these country buses,' she confided, when she got settled. 'And, do you know, although my work takes me all over the countryside – Domestic Science, you know – this bus is just about the last word.'

Helen Riddel turned her face aside to the window.

She didn't want to be involved in conversation. She wanted to be left to herself, and to her own thoughts.

'Miss Riddel? I thought it was you, hiding yourself away in the corner there.' The Vet's wife was now leaning over the Marmalade Competition lady's knees. 'I was speaking about you just the other day, with Mr Anson. We both thought it would be an excellent idea if we could persuade you to give a talk to our Churchwomen's Guild on Present-Day Teenagers and Their Needs.'

'So you got the wrench then, Jean?' The driver popped his head through the small window, and to her gratitude prevented Helen Riddel, from committing herself. 'Right then. So we're all set, are we?' the driver asked, his foot on the accelerator.

'No, Davie. Good God, not yet.' The conductress stopped him. 'Donald Craig's just on his road here for the bus. I got a glimpse of him making his way down the Kirkgate.'

'It's just not good enough,' the Marmalade Competition lady protested again.

'Pitmedden Lodge. Stott's Smiddy. Hill of Inish. Tyrebagger Corner.' The conductress did not indicate a route, but pinpointed a whole countryside. No bus in all the world was so uncomfortably personal in its function. 'Kingorth Crossroads! That's your stop, Donald. Donald's stop,' she shouted, rapping on the driver's window.

'But I'm not wanting off here, Jean,' Donald Craig observed, equably enough. 'You might just put me down a bittie further on, at Geordie Scobie's place.'

'But this is your stop, Donald.' The conductress was inexorable. 'You bide at Kingorth Crossroads.'

'I bide at Kingorth, lassie.' Donald's equanimity was beginning to desert him. 'I was born at Kingorth, and like as not I'll die there. But for all that, I just want to be put down at Geordie Scobie's place the night. Is there any law against that? Tell me.'

'Further on, Davie. Geordie Scobie's place.' The conductress rapped on the driver's window before casting a beseeching glance towards her passengers, which implied that any man who refused to be set down on the doorstep of his own home must be clean out of his mind.

'Lendrum Village.' No London conductor could have announced 'Trafalgar Square' with more aplomb, nor could his bus have entered it with such an anticipation of Occasion.

'Well, we may as well get out and stretch our legs for a bit,' Beel Grieve suggested, making his way out of the bus as the conductress disappeared to deliver the Late Finals to the shop, while the driver followed her, laden with personal errands he had undertaken to deliver from the Town.

'This is one place my work has never taken me to.' The Marmalade Competition lady leaned across Helen Riddel to peer out of the window.

'You havena missed very much then,' the Joiner's wife assured her. 'For it's a dead and alive hole of a place, is Lendrum. That's so, isn't it, Miss Riddel?'

'I couldn't say.' Helen Riddel kept her face averted and her eyes fixed on the darkness.

Edinburgh. Glasgow. Aberdeen. Dundee. How small Scotland sounded, summed up by its four main cities, but what a width of world its little villages stravaiged.

'I've always just passed through Lendrum in the bus,' Helen Riddel explained, 'so I've never really seen it.' But then she recollected to herself:

I've never been to Mamble
That lies above the Tame.
So I wonder who's in Mamble . . .

'What a stramash there was in the sawmill in Lendrum the night,' the conductress burst into the bus, brimful of the news garnered from the shop. 'It appears Robb's got one of thae misplaced Hungarians working for him at the sawmill; and the night, when the men were getting their wages, two women turned up and claimed the Hungarian and his wages. They both said they were his wife.'

'Lord. *That* had put Robb the Sawmill in a right lather,' Beel Grieve said, 'for Robb was aye awful feared of women folk.'

'Poor Robb just didna know what to do about it,' the conductress agreed. 'According to Bell in the shop, he just did nothing. Nor did the Hungarian. It was the two women that fought it out amongst themselves.'

'None of the local women, surely, Jean?' the Vet's wife demanded, aghast.

'No. Of course not!' The conductress felt contemptuous of such stupidity. 'Just two Town women. Apparently the Hungarian goes off to the Town and gets mixed up with the women every other weekend.'

'And Robb the Sawmill would *not* have approved of that,' the Vet's wife concluded decisively.

'Robb wasna muckle concerned over that part of it, one way or the other,' the conductress contradicted aloofly, as one in first possession of all the facts. 'It seems the Hungarian's willing and a worker; and Robb doesna want to lose him. So long as he keeps the women from the Town from popping up and creating at the sawmill!'

'Next Stop, Caldwell,' the conductress announced, in the

wearied tone of one who, having more than fulfilled her
duties to her fellow-men, has tired of the species at last; and
slumping herself down into the seat vacated by Donald Craig,
kicked off her shoes, took a Late Final out of one pocket,
an apple out of the other, and withdrew herself.

'And George, of course,' the Vet's wife began to inform
loudly, 'is always the same. I *was* annoyed when the Garage
said they couldn't possibly have the car overhauled by
Monday.'

'We know fine she's got a car,' the Joiner's wife turned
round to whisper, 'so she needn't go on about it like that.
We know fine she doesn't usually go by bus like other seven-
day folk.'

'But George simply refused to let me have the brake,' the
Vet's wife went on, 'although I told him I had to take the
chair up in the School Hall tonight.'

'Michty! We forgot all about George's brake.' The Joiner's
wife swung confidentially round in her seat again. 'Aye, aye.
Of course George has got a brake. *Two* cars. Well, well! We
really have got it right this time!'

The bus was skirting round beneath Soutar Hill. Caldwell,
spread out before it, was anonymous to all except its own,
who could interpret its far-flung flickering lights.

'What's the School Hall all lit up for?' the Joiner's wife
demanded suddenly, in the incredulous tone of one who had
neither been consulted nor informed.

'God, I forgot.' For she had now remembered. 'Charlie
Anson is holding what he calls an Open Night, up yonder
at his Youth Club. But of course you'll know all about that,
Miss Riddel?'

For an instant Helen Riddel was not quite sure whether
she had been stung into replying aloud.

'Yes. Of course. I know all about that. But do you know

something else? I'm going to marry Charlie Anson. I'm going
to accept when he proposes tonight.'

She couldn't have spoken aloud though. The Joiner's wife
was now peering out of the window at the other side of the
bus, debating over what was going on up in the Church Hall.
It was her inner intention, Helen Riddel realised, that had
sounded loud to her own ears, so that she herself could no
longer ignore it.

I'm going to say Yes, she reassured herself. I only wish I
had said it long ago, when there was no compulsion on me
to do so; before my instincts revealed themselves and
shocked me. Not so much for what I did, but for the way I
did it. No, not even for that. Just that Charlie Anson or any
man at all should discover my need in the moment I was
discovering it for myself. I didn't know I was like that till
then.

'*Well!* That just about takes the cake.' The Joiner's wife
demanded their attention again. 'I did hear tell that Jeems
Leslie stood with his hands under his hens' dowps just waiting for their eggs to drop into them, but I never did hear tell
that he stood in his parks watching for his corn to appear,
the minute it was sown. For I'll swear that's Jeems. There,
see! Down in his nether park yonder. He aye did claim he
could see in the dark.'

And you could, Helen Riddel knew, staring out of the
window. Form and shape had loomed up into their own,
with trees but images of themselves carved out in wood, and
Soutar Hill more mountainous than in memory, so that were
I but child or stranger I could be guided by the hand and so
exhorted 'See afar, Mount Everest rise. See it tilt to strike
the skies!' Even thinking otherwise, I would believe.

On nights like this a man could stand stride-legged
between the furrows he himself had ploughed, and yet feel
alien. On nights like this you could defy yourself, your small

mortality, your monstrous isolation. And meeting one of your own like, lie down together in a nakedness of need. Thinking that darkness hid you from yourselves and from each other; and hoping it might turn out to be the perpetual night of all the world. And half believing that should the daylight ever dawn again, the memory of what you did would fade with darkness.

'One flesh.' How exact that was. The fusion of bodies. So that I can never tell whether it's you caressing me, or I you. Nor does it matter. Nor do I care. One flesh. What does matter is my own knowing that the flesh could have belonged to any man.

Her father would be beyond himself when he knew. But, at this moment, Helen Riddel felt all the thoughts with which to combat his contempt rise up within her.

It was easier for her father and his like. For all the male in him got out, gleamed in his leggings and glinted on the hairs of his hands; strode in his walk, and snapped in his voice. It was inside of him and it was outside of him.

But it was only inside herself. Sometimes, when she caught her father looking at her, she could feel him wonder how a man such as himself ever came to father such a daughter, though, had her outward looks but half the colour of her inner feelings, she could have had a choice of men.

As it was, she had been grateful enough for Charlie Anson. A woman could create her own image of a man, but first she had to find him. And she had found him. Never the 'bonnie whole man' her father was always on about. But was there anyone at all bonnie and whole? Was anyone at all completely so?

Maybe, maybe if one was not begotten, but fell out of the sky, a second old, to land on Soutar Hill maybe. Maybe then one might grow up – bonnie and whole, knowing the fundamentals as time went by: hunger and thirst and cold the way the sheep now wintering up on Soutar Hill might come to know them. And loneliness surely! For, though the sheep seek solitude only in the oncoming intuition of birth and death, their bleating through the darkness would make of the world a waste, and of Soutar Hill, a mountain not removed, yet wholly lost.

James Aiken, the Minister of Caldwell, was approaching Ambroggan Croft with some misgiving. Crofts always did have this effect on him – 'the first and last adventures of the land'. And since risk lies at the heart of all adventure, this was undoubtedly true of the crofts. He remembered the parish of his Induction of forty years ago: a West Island parish, consisting solely of crofting townships, bold white-washed houses, their windows searching the ocean, like their inhabitants, with an eye always on the sea; being dependent on both the land and the fishing had rendered them curiously independent of either. Nor were their crofts ever crowded out, diminished or put to shame by large, contrasting farms, unlike Caldwell, whose crofts forced themselves up out of the earth in small defiant protest.

The Minister always felt at a disadvantage in a crofter's house, and always vaguely resentful of the man who could put him in such an uncomfortable position. A farm-worker was an easier proposition 'Well, Beel,' he could say with easy familiarity, 'I see that the weather kept up till you got in the harvest.' And to his wife, 'Just a cup of tea, then, Mrs Petrie, thank you. No Not a thing to eat, though I must say that the look of your scones tempts me sorely.' For it was the tenant farmers' privilege to bestow supper upon him; a privilege shared by the Misses Lennox, and like ladies of small independent means and large Good Works. Dinner was the prerogative of the gentlemen farmers, the Doctor, and the Vet, and his approach to them all – 'The ninety and nine that

safely lay in the shelter of the fold', albeit in separate pens –
was graded accordingly. But there was no grading of the
crofter, no easy overtures, since the crofters were dependent
not only on the weather, but on the help of their fellow-
crofters to take in the harvest, and no light refusal. 'You'll
just pull your chair in about then, Reverend, and take a bite
with us,' with all the complete assumption of the landowner.

In all his years of rural Ministry, the Reverend James
Aiken had never quite comprehended how thirty acres of
land could compensate a man for such a slavery. Unless,
unless it was just that – the freedom of equality that the croft
bequeathed. Sometimes, though, he thought he had caught
the reflection of his own question in the momentarily
unguarded eyes of the crofter's wife; but her guard would
slip down again, and answer, when it came, was echo: 'Yes.
Just you sit yourself down, Mr Aiken, and I'll be with you
the minute I've taken this mash over to the cow.'

The crofts in Caldwell sometimes troubled the Minister's
spirit, but Ambroggan Croft always offended his mind. It
had lost the dignity of and claim to the title of croft, with
the death of Charlie Anson's parents. Even the two or three
lean stirks scratching their flanks against the rotting paling
posts were not his own, for his grazing was now let out to
more enterprising crofters. The wooden water-butt, long
since unnecessary, still stood dark and stagnant outside his
porch door, side by side with a discarded butter churn;
forgetful now of its original purpose, it stood in abject hit-
or-miss capacity under the overflow of the water-butt.

'Step inside, Mr Aiken. I wasn't expecting you, but it's a
real pleasure. Just you step this way, now.'

The Minister's resentment increased. He suddenly felt that
he was no longer paying a call out of his own volition, but
was being drawn inside the house by some grinning suction.

'I've just put the kettle on. A man on his own, you know,

it's always the brew. Always the brew. You'll drink a cup of tea, Mr Aiken?'

The Minister raised his hand to emphasise his refusal, but felt his vocal cords refuse to co-ordinate with his movements.

'There's always room for the cuppa, Mr Aiken,' Charlie Anson insisted, scurrying round his kitchen, opening all his cupboards at once, and flinging their contents down on the table. The Minister watched with increasing distaste; for Anson had none of the confirmed bachelor's swift bare utility of movement, but all the finickiness and frippery of a woman, without any of her tidiness.

'Apricot jam? Or strawberry jam? Let me see, now.' He dived under the sink and scrabbled amongst the contents of a cardboard box. 'Ah. Apricot.' Holding the jar against the light, he studied it in the manner of Miss Perks, judging preserves at the Summer Show. 'Nice,' he pronounced, clamping it down on the table. 'Just nice. A little walnut cake, Mr Aiken? Or you'll try a little bit of blue cheese, maybe?'

The Minister would not have been surprised if Anson had suddenly offered him 'a finger-length of sherry; and one of these sweet wholemeal biscuits to which you are so partial, Mr Aiken', in the voice of Miss Lennox. But no, he was still urging the blue cheese. 'Good stuff. I get it sent out regularly from Coll and MacGillvary, you know.'

Coll and MacGillvary. The By Appointment Purveyors to the Royal Family when in residence; and to the professional people of Caldwell the rest of the year round. The Minister felt his gorge rise up inexplicably but definitely.

'It was the Vet recommended them to me.' Charlie Anson's hand brushed the crumbs of cheese off the table on to the floor. 'Aye.' He looked up at the Minister, trying to interpret his silence. 'So you're admiring my desk, I see. It's a good bit of work that.'

'It looks familiar,' the Minister admitted.

'It would at that,' Anson agreed. 'It's identical to the one Kingorth's got. As a matter of fact I had it made by the same cabinet maker.'

The house, like its owner, had taken its shape from others, the Minister realised, and so had lost original design.

'What with the Youth Club and all my Committee Work,' Anson explained, 'I got to needing somewhere to put all my papers. It's just amazing how they all accumulate.'

'Ah. That reminds me.' Grateful of the reminder, the Minister straightened himself up. 'I'm on my way over to see Mr Gordon of Darklands. He had a word with me the other day. He is most anxious that the farm-workers should be represented on the Rural Council, and I myself share his conviction. Most strongly,' he emphasised, to reassure himself. 'He is intending to propose his Head Dairyman, Hugh Riddel, for election. He will have to be seconded, though, by a member of the Council outwith the Committee. I was wondering whether you, with all your – ' the Minister halted, searching for words.

'You want me to second Hugh Riddel, like?' Charlie Anson himself filled in the blanks for the Minister.

'Yes. I thought perhaps – '

'Just so. Just that.' Anson again concluded for him, turning to concentrate on the teapot, and measuring out the tea with the concentration of an alchemist sifting gold.

'He was a great lad, was old Riddel, Hugh's father,' Anson observed at last, straightening himself up and planking the teapot on the table. 'A great lad. Not that I really knew the man myself. Just what you hear tell, of course. Aye! He's a byword in the parish, old Riddel.' He laughed, dismissing the parish. 'As it comes, Mr Aiken?' he asked, lifting the teapot.

'As it comes, thank you.'

'A rabid Socialist.' Anson stirred his tea and gazed beyond

the Minister. 'Always agitating about one thing or other. Or so they say. But then, of course, as you know fine, Mr Aiken, they say everything hereabouts except their prayers.' His joke fell flat on the Minister's ears, but Anson continued: 'Aye. And he could take off his dram, too, could old Riddel. They still tell of how he could drink his cronies under the table.'

'But about Hugh Riddel himself?' the Minister prompted. 'It's with him we are really concerned.'

'Aye. Aye, of course. Hugh Riddel. You'll try a slice of the walnut cake, Mr Aiken? Just a corner of it, then. A real chip off the old block is Hugh. But you would have gathered that yourself from his Immortal Memory at the Burns' Supper last week. Too forthright was the opinion I gathered from some quarter of the parish. Mind you, there's just no pleasing in some folk. Still and on, I thought he went pretty near the bone myself.'

A sentiment with which the Minister was in silent agree-ment. '*He dearly lo'ed the lasses O*' – a permissible statement about the poet; but there was no need at all to detail the form that such loving took. None.

'But then, of course,' Charlie Anson was saying, 'the speak is that Hugh Riddel has no little experience in that airt himself. Now, Mr Aiken, you'll just let me fill your cup up again.'

That was that, Charlie Anson reflected, as he stood watching the Minister's car make its way over to Darklands. With just the right touch too. Planting the seed; but so lightly that the soil itself would not begin to feel it till it had taken root.

It was each man for himself in Caldwell. Nobody was more aware of that than Charlie Anson. Yet it only needed face all round. Friendly to farm-workers; not too familiar, though. They would take instant advantage of that, himself being one of them so short ago, and slap him on the back, as if he were one of themselves again; and him of independent means, with twenty grazing acres rented out, breeding Cairn Terriers, and always the odd bit job of carpentry turning up.

The face he turned to farmers, that was more subtle altogether. A casual word about their crops. An opinion tentatively offered on local affairs and fervently beseeched on world affairs. Charlie Anson had long since discovered that his strength lay in gauging his fellow-men's weaknesses. Sharing the saloon end of the bar with them on market days, and now and then a bawdy story, for nothing bound man to man as close as dirt did.

Not quite accepted yet, though, at their front doors as guest or friend. Still, that would come through time. Oh, but you could be the biggest rogue walking Caldwell, and if 'twas so your Great Grandfather had farmed its acres, *that* would be remembered in your favour, and much of fault forgiven you for it; or if you were a scholar, for nothing won such respect as a hantle of letters behind your name.

There was a third way, though, and Anson was taking the right and canny road in its direction. A foot in here, a foot in there; Secretary of this Committee, Treasurer of that. Unpaid, of course, but zealous. Zealous!

It hadn't been easy. In retrospect, it hadn't been easy. But he would show Caldwell yet. Oh, he would show them all. He had no illusions about the attitude of its Upper Ten towards himself – a bare tolerance, and a shrewd usage. He had even fewer illusions about the scorn in which its lower orders held him. They never made the slightest attempt to conceal it. Riff Raff! Always resentful of any of their own kind with the ambition to get on. Resentment being overloaded though, and aimed at the particular, was something he had managed to dodge by the ready laugh; the pretence of no offence intended, so none taken. But contempt, a more elusive weapon altogether, was deadlier, and always accurate: aimed at the whole man, it left no part of him unscathed or undiscovered. And none had more contempt than Hugh Riddel.

The grinning mask of habit dropped from Anson's face. Hugh Riddel would learn yet, the bonnie mannie. For Anson, now as always, tackled his enemies only in their absence. 'You'll learn yet that I was at least man enough to take your daughter on the slopes of Soutar Hill. And virgin. And since then, as many times as I've got fingers on my hands. And if she isn't filled by this time, it's not my fault.' And now, as always, the blow struck by the imagination left him the victor.

Strange thing, he reflected, as he set out to meet Helen Riddel off the bus; given even a small choice, she never would have been that choice. But, given no other, and all things considered, he hadn't done too badly for himself. Not too badly at all. She was educated for one thing. A great thing the education! She would be able to fill in the blanks for him in his Youth work. Behind the scenes though! For Charlie Anson's obsession with women never extended to a recognition of their equality. Under a man always, as nature intended. Remembering all the slights and snubs he had ingratiatingly laughed off from their sex, the only warmth he could ever feel for them was the heat of rising lust.

Sue Tatt's uncurtained window cast a pool of light across the road, setting her house apart in an instant isolation. That was another of the injustices of life, Charlie Anson thought, as he drove towards it from Ambroggan cross-roads. He knew a farmer – aye, he knew two or three – could draw up at Sue's door in broad daylight, as large as life, with a sack of tatties or new-killed cockerel as offering, and bide within her walls far longer than the civilities required. The neighbours, ever watchful, might speak about it afterwards, but that was all. Though, Lord, if it was *him*, there would be such a speak all round the country; he would get shrift that was short enough. The character of a Coming Man must hold no blemish, but once you had arrived you'd get more scope. All the burdens of responsibility before the pleasures of its privileges. Still!

'A fine night again, but cold, Sue.' Charlie Anson slowed down and drew up at Sue Tatt's gate. 'Did you happen to notice if the last bus from the Town was on time?'

'It was about half an hour late,' Sue Tatt answered without turning to look at him.

'It was easy half an hour late,' Fiona enlarged on her mother's brevity.

'Late or no, I still seem to have missed it. I don't suppose you noticed if Miss Riddel got off it?' Anson asked.

'*Helen* Riddel' – Sue emphasised the Christian name – 'got off the bus and got a lift home in Darklands' milk lorry.'

'I've missed her too, then. My bad luck again, Sue?' His question was double-edged. But Sue's reply was single and to the point.

'Your bad luck again, Charlie. I wouldn't,' she confided to Fiona, as they watched Anson's car disappear round Ambroggan cross-roads, 'let that creature put hands on me. Not for a hundred pounds.'

It was from the moment he reached the dairy to supervise the first loading of the milk lorry, that last Friday started to swerve off its course for Hugh Riddel. Darklands himself stood in the small office off the bottling shed, fiddling about with the loading orders.

'There's a double load, a double run the night, Hugh,' he

said, looking up from the orders. 'But I see you've already noted it down.'

'Aye.' The real reason for the farmer's rare appearance at this time of night puzzled Hugh Riddel. 'You sent the memo in about the extra run yesterday morning,' he reminded Darklands.

'Of course. So I did. But there was something else – Oh, aye! About the General Meeting of the Rural Council the night, Hugh – it's off. Only postponed, like. Mr Aiken, the Minister, has just had a word with me about it.' Darklands pushed the orders aside and came to the point. 'Do you know anybody in Caldwell, Hugh, that would like to cut your throat?'

'There's a two three might like a try,' Hugh Riddel admitted, smiling, 'though I doubt if they would ever just go that length.'

'Not even Charlie Anson? Whiles I think that if the Minister had four feet, he would put them all into it. He asked Anson to second my proposal for your election.'

'Anson! But I'd refuse to stand at all with yon mannie as my seconder.'

'But that's just it, Hugh. Anson's not going to second you.'

'You mean – he refused?'

'Not exactly. He felt – '

'Of course not. Anson never did anything exactly in his life. He never supped the brose for that.'

'It's only a matter of time, Hugh,' Darklands was saying. 'Dave Morrison, the crofter, Wylie, the blacksmith, either of them will second you. It's just a matter of time.'

'Aye. Just that.' Hugh Riddel dismissed the subject and reached for the file that held the next week's orders. A matter of time. And time has come.

'You've just missed Helen,' Isa Riddel informed him when

he reached the house. 'Charlie Anson was in by and took her up to see some Do that's on in his Youth Club the night. Oh, and there was a man in the train the night,' she gabbled, knowing that anything she said would be wrong, but always hoping to find something that would be right.

'Was there now?' Hugh Riddel spoke without looking at her. 'Men are still allowed to travel by train. Or so I understand.'

'But this was the Scholars' train,' she explained.

'Oh! That's different, then. That would just have been about your mark, wouldn't it?' He looked at his wife now; her hands, without immediate task upon them, fumbled forlornly with the strings of her apron, and he felt his anger increasing. 'Had the man gotten one eye then? Or three legs? Or a wooden cock, maybe? What to hell was so special about him?'

'Nothing.'

'Nothing be it then. If there was nothing, let's just say nothing.'

Isa Riddel watched him go into the scullery and pull his shirt over his head; he slung the towel across his bare shoulders and, turning on the tap, bent over the sink, and stood unaware of the running water. All his attitude and actions that of a man who was isolated within himself. An isolation as complete as her own.

Isa Mavor. Isa Mavor . . . she began, repeating her maiden name to herself. But it made no impact on her recognition. The sound of her own born name never did manage to re-establish her. When that did happen, and it was a rare enough occurrence, it was almost accidental; like the impulse that whiles forced her to let the cows find their own way back to the byre, when May filled Ambroggan Wood with fat clumps of wild primroses; her hands that stuffed them into a jam jar, and set them on the ledge of the porch window, had some ancient surety of touch. Whiles, too, when she took off her stockings, kilted up her skirt, and got down to scrubbing the stone flags of the scullery floor, her bare knees accepting almost eagerly their cold rough pressure, criss-crossed and red and young, in a pattern of some old famili-arity. She never saw herself in times like these; but had she found a mirror then, Isa Riddel might for an instant have looked on Isa Mavor.

'Surely to God you've seen a man out of his shirt before!' Hugh Riddel swung into her vision again. 'So stop glowering there, and lay out my best shirt.'

'You'll not be needing it for the Election, anyway,' Isa Riddel surprised herself, 'for God Knows' wife was telling me that it's been cancelled.'

'That's true enough,' Hugh Riddel agreed. 'But then I neither proposed myself for election, nor made up my mind to stand for it if I was proposed.'

'No?' Isa Riddel's brief question was without satire. She knew it was in her man's nature to reject anything that hinted of patronage. Burns' Suppers were far more in his line, she reflected bitterly, remembering the Press's reaction to his Immortal Memory. 'But no doubt it was the free whisky and coarse songs that was bait enough to lure you to the Burns' Supper.'

'Well, no. It wasn't now. It wasn't that at all.' Hugh Riddel moved towards her, towelling himself dry. 'That surprises you, doesn't it? But if I hadn't accepted, Charlie Anson would have jumped at the chance. I thought that Burns would be a lot safer on my tongue that ever he would be on Anson's tongue. For yon's the damnedest apology for a man that ever I cast eyes on. Though yon one's reckoning's coming.'

'He's got a clean tongue in his head at least,' Isa Riddel

defended, knowing she was trapped, and yet unable to resist closing the trap in on herself.

'He's got all that.' Hugh Riddel agreed so quietly that his outburst, when it came, was unexpected. 'He's the kind of creature whose eyes are never off the little lassies. Nor his hands either, when he gets but half a chance, patting them where they're rounding, father-like. But if a woman, full grown and stark naked, was to offer him herself, then yon's the creature would go flying for his life. The dirt inside him is all bottled up.'

'And it comes out of you. You're always there, or thereabout.'

Were he to lay hands on Isa Riddel now, he knew that he might kill her. Though that, he also knew, would be self murder.

'*You* have nothing to complain of on that score, for I've got better places for it!'

The anger within Hugh Riddel had broken up, so that by the time he had reached Dave Morrison's croft, it was outwith him, touching him only at points and in particulars.

'Well. What do you think the weather's going to do, Hugh?' the crofter asked him, searching the sky for the answer to his own question. 'It's cold enough for a fall of snow,' he said when he had found it, 'but tight enough for the thaw to burst.'

'You could be right,' Hugh Riddel agreed. The acknowledgment easing him. 'You've just got down from the hill then, Dave?'

'And not a bite on it,' the crofter complained. 'I'm thinking of moving the ewes down the morn; they're too near their time for a thaw to panic them, or a storm to bury them.'

'Unchancy creatures sheep, Dave.' The smile glimmered in Hugh Riddel's eyes. 'If they're not riving themselves naked on old whin bushes, they're getting blind drunk on the young broom bushes. And if they don't panic in the thaw, they bury themselves in the snow. And if it isn't that, they go falling on their backs and die with their legs in the air, because the creatures haven't got the balance to get themselves up again. What you should have had, Dave,' he suggested, his smile sounding in his suggestion, 'is just a two three Highland stirks wintering away fine up on Soutar Hill yonder. Apprehensive enough creatures by nature, I'll grant you that. But sober in habit and, most important of all, Dave' – his smile widened into a grin – 'with all yon fine bonnie hair happing their eyes, they see damn all to panic for. It must be a good thing whiles, just to be a Highland stirk.'

'You can keep your two three Highland stirks. You're welcome to them,' the crofter snapped, treating the suggestion with the contempt that Hugh Riddel had deliberately teased out of him.

A true sheep-man, Dave. Just as Hugh Riddel's father had been a true cattleman. Each guarding his own particular knowledge and contemptuous of the other's skill, though never of the man who plied them. When shepherd and cattleman agreed on anything at all, it was but on the elements, and on the aspects of the soil that reared their products.

'If I didn't know Kingorth had been at the spreading the day,' the crofter turned his attention to the steam still rising from the newly spread dung on Kingorth's upper park, 'I'd swear that they were at the burning of the whins, yonder.'

'Aye. The whin burning used to be a great ploy with us as loons, before April went out,' Hugh Riddel remembered, minding not so much on the flame-licked dusks of his boyhood, and racing against the wind in an elemental conflict that always ended in a personal battle; nor on the startled moments when bird and boy met face to face in a flutter of fear, nor even on the lie that echoed round the hill till it sounded true – 'The Pict's Horse is on Fire! As sure as God.'

It was the width of feeling that was over him then, Hugh Riddel most remembered now, when Soutar Hill stood in eternal time, a keep from whose spyholes he'd looked down on all the world, knowing fine that he could run its length and breadth before his legs gave out, and certain then that the boy he was would grow much greater than the man he had become.

'You'll step in by for a minute, Hugh?' The crofter's invitation broke into his thoughts.

'Thanks. But no, Dave. I've got a thing or two to attend till the night. A bottling lever to collect, for one thing. And you know what Wylie the Blacksmith is, for another thing; it's just catch him as can on a Friday night.'

'Maybe we'll see you a bit later on, then, down in the Hotel?' the crofter suggested. 'Some of the Union boys are to be there the night, giving tomorrow's Agenda big licks and short shrift amongst themselves. They say Charlie Anson is resigning as Treasurer. But of course he's got bigger fish to fry now, what with his Youth Club and District Council. But he'll be there just the same, with yon long lugs of his flapping on the ground, sniffing out the airt of public opinion.'

'You think so, Dave?'

'I'm certain of it.'

'Well. That being so, maybe I will see you later on in the night at the hotel.'

'There was a minute the night, yonder,' the crofter confided to his wife later, 'when I thought that Hugh Riddel must have gotten sime wind of Charlie Anson and his daughter, Helen.'

'I wouldn't be in either of their shoes when he does get wind of that,' his wife commented doucely enough, but reflectively. For her own passion, though brief-lived, laboured-out and all but forgotten now, still made that of any other person intriguing. 'The thing is,' she jerked herself out of contemplation, 'the thing is this Hugh Riddel has little room to condemn his own, for he has shown them but little example. And it's ten to one that he himself was on his road to see Sue Tatt when you ran into him.'

'It's Hugh Riddel.' Fiona nudged her mother excitedly. 'I told you that he was coming here the night. He's walking. That's why he's so late.'

'My eyes are in my head, not in my backside,' Sue snapped. 'And I must say you've taken your time on it,' she greeted Hugh Riddel when he reached the gate. 'And you,' she turned to Fiona again, 'can just make yourself scarce. Take a turn down to the cross-roads for my cigarettes, and take young Beel with you.'

'There's no need for that the night, Sue,' Hugh Riddel interrupted. 'I'm not biding. I've got other business on hand the night.'

'Surely your business can keep till you've had a drink of tea,' Sue protested, beginning to unlatch the gate. 'But just you please yourself, of course.'

'Are you still wanting cigarettes, then, Mam?' Fiona broke into Hugh Riddel's hesitation. 'Because I can easy run down for them.'

'There's no need,' Hugh Riddel answered, turning to her mother for confirmation. 'That is, of course, unless you really want cigarettes.'

'I don't want cigarettes.' Sue began to lead the way into the house. 'To hear you all going on like that, you would think that I had nothing else in my head except cigarettes. I don't care if I never set eyes on another cigarette till my dying day. Now! Does that please you all.'

Following in the flare of her protestations, they reached the kitchen wordless. Its sudden cleanness again took Sue by surprise.

'Sit yourself down, then, now that you are here,' she urged Hugh Riddel when the possibilities of the situation had struck her. For never before had he seen her isolated from the darkness of the upstairs bedroom. And all at once she was glad and grateful that herself and her house were both so right for this first objective examination.

The Woman Who Would Have Made A Good Wife For Some Lucky Man. The role presented itself as sudden as that, and began to enlarge in Sue's mind. Not only a Good Wife, but A Well Preserved Woman For Her Years into the bargain.

Setting the table, she began to combine the roles, and with all the concentration of a small girl playing a game of Statues, each gesture became a deliberate demand for attention, and each question a secret provocation.

'Cream? Say when?' *Who am I now, then?* 'Sugar? Two spoons or three?' *I've got no real name at all.* 'Strong? Weak? Or as it comes?' *Unless you look up at me now and bequeath one on me.*

'Just as it comes,' Hugh Riddel answered without lifting his gaze from the floor. 'And stop hovering, woman! For the love of God sit down on your backside and drink up your tea.'

'You haven't even poured out your own tea yet, Mam.' Fiona jumped up out of the silence that had fallen on the room. 'Sit down, and I'll pour it out for you.'

'I'm quite capable of pouring out my own tea, thank you.' Sue interpreted both the amusement in Fiona's eyes and the pity in her voice. And it was the pity angered her. It wasn't fair. No two people should ever have such an intimate uncomfortable knowing of each other. It wasn't fair to either of them, though it was the unfairness to herself that struck Sue first.

'What you *can* do,' she stood searching her mind for the worst thing to be done, 'is to take that white blouse of mine off your back, and give your black neck that's under it a right good scrub.'

Half her life, Sue thought resentfully when Fiona had gone, was spent in taking it out of her daughter, and the other half in atoning for that.

Had you at any other time tried to explain to Sue Tatt that, far from dividing her life, this relationship was one which gave it wholeness, she would have rejected you. But not now, not at this particular moment, when she was dimly perceiving that for herself.

I can easily put myself right off him. Her anger transferred itself to Hugh Riddel. And, true enough, Sue had hitherto always managed to get a man out of her system by concentrating on his worst physical defects. Pot bellies and bad teeth had been godsends to Sue at such times. But not this time. She knew that, absorbing Hugh Riddel with her eyes and remembering him with her body; for he would never have a pot belly – not if he lived to be a hundred.

'Your bonnet,' she bent in a pain of pride to lift his bonnet from the floor beside his feet.

'Aye.' Accepting the time-honoured symbol of dismissal, he rose awkwardly, taken aback by its suddenness.

'You've got *other* business the night,' she reminded him, leading the way to the door.

'Aye,' he said again, pausing in the doorway, for some explanation of his other business offered him a more dignified form of exit. 'I don't suppose you saw anything of Charlie Anson the night. I'm anxious to have a word with him.'

So there was no fault in herself. His explanation vindicated

Sue's pride, and the relief of it almost overcame her vanity, though not her curiosity.

'I was wondering when you'd get around to hearing about that little shennanygin,' she reflected. 'Though it would never have passed my lips first. I've got enough to do to keep my own doorstep clean.'

A Woman of Comparative Virtue – a part such as had never been landed on Sue Tatt before and never would be again, so not to be resisted.

'It's been the speak of Caldwell for weeks,' she assured him. 'And, as it happens, I did see Charlie Anson the night, but only in the passing. For yon's a one never managed to win round me. I just happen to be that bit particular, even if I havena gotten a college education. What they're all beginning to wonder now,' she went on, undeterred by the look that had come over Hugh Riddel's face, 'is whether Anson has any intention of marrying Helen or not.'

Helen Riddel herself was beginning to wonder.

'Doesn't that beat everything?' was all that Charlie Anson had found to say when she told him that her suspicion of pregnancy had been confirmed.

'Doesn't it just take the cake.' As if it were some achievement on his part, but of less importance than the other triumph that was uppermost in his mind.

'The County Youth Organiser has promised to take a look in by at the meeting the night. A great pity,' he added regretfully, 'just a great pity that I didn't know that in time to put it down in black and white on the Invites. But then, of course, Mollison's a busy man, and couldn't tell till the last minute whether he could fit me in with all his other commitments. Still,' he reflected, cheering up, 'it's a start. Once you get the interest stirring at the top, it's a start. And at least,' he observed, as they slowed down at the School Hall, 'the folkies are all beginning to drift in.'

They were, although apprehensively enough, seeking each other out and clustering together in small embarrassed groups, for this particular function had not yet received the seal of Caldwell's official approval – that seal which could ensure a packed attendance even when it was only old Ag and Fish, the Hen Wife, lecturing on Rhode Island Reds. But then, of course, her presence was always sanctified by the imposing notice that preceded her. Under the Auspices of the Ministry of Agriculture and Fisheries.

Still, as Anson had observed, they were beginning to drift in, and in numbers small enough for him to assess them and to conclude that, so far, not one amongst them was important enough locally for him to welcome in his official capacity. A vague general acknowledgement of their presence – 'So you all managed up then?' – would just have to suffice until worthier words of welcome were warranted.

'And of course,' as he confided to Helen Riddel on their way through the hall, 'I just cannot make a move till the Vet's wife shows up. She promised to take the Chair for me, though she should have been here by this time,' he protested, examining his watch with an anxiety that informed the observant company he was now a man at the mercy of time and beset by its vagaries. 'She should have been here long since, to sort out the exhibits of the youngsters' handiwork.'

'She might have had to wait for George's brake,' Helen Riddel remembered. 'She was going on about it in the bus. But I can easily sort out the exhibits for you.

'All properly named, mind, then.' Anson accepted her offer dubiously. 'And set out in their correct age-group cat-egories. The Vet's wife knows all about them.'

'So do I,' she reminded him sharply. 'At least I know the work of the different age-groups.'

The truth of her claim surprised herself. The small raffia calendars were the work of girls, fourteen-year-olds; they always did tackle something the end of which they could see from the beginning. But, she remembered, fingering the small plastic ladybirds that adorned the calendars, only so that they can have all the time in the world to experiment with their final decorations.

The cane waste-paper baskets were the work of boys in the same age-group. Her hands began to recognise the basket they held, as if they had woven it. The fine close-knit start made by the teacher; the tightening tension of a determined effort to follow the start exactly; the gradual slackening off to the widening gaps which marked that midway moment when boy and basket fell out of mood with each other and the end seemed as far away as the beginning; the teacher's even work again, bridging the moment; the last wild spurt to the am's edge, and the careful finish applied to all con-clusions.

The nightdress was the work of a much older member. Old enough to be engaged, Helen Riddel knew, examining its care and detail. The work of some girl who had simply come here to learn to sew. She would be the first to arrive in the Dressmaking group, and the last to fold away her work. She would join in no other activity, so officially she would be defined as a poor Youth Club Member, and described as one who took everything and gave nothing. 'But she'll never forget how, as long as she lives,' Helen Riddel reflected, smoothing the folds of the nightdress; 'though I doubt whether any of the small boys will ever again tackle a waste-paper basket.'

'But surely that isn't the important thing.'

For a moment she felt as if Mr Fleming, of Senior Lads' Group from her own Centre, had taken her up on her con-clusion. But no, it was Anson who had spoken. He had not

yet got the rote of it, but she could feel the principle struggling within his comprehension.

'It is only . . .'

'Only incidental to the purpose behind the work.' She
supplied him with the words he was searching for, and so
coveted. That was one thing she could bring to him in marriage, she thought, watching him assimilate her words and
tuck them away in his memory. A lifetime of foolproof
phrases.

'But it's perfectly true,' Anson claimed, 'and not to be
smiled at' – for the irony had reached her mouth. 'Surely
you're not trying to make out that there's no real purpose
behind the work?'

'Purpose in plenty,' she assured him, still smiling. 'So much
purpose that sometimes I feel it's like the reams and reams
of wrapping paper that conceal the smallness of a gift. The
giver has to make it look good, for his own sake at least.
And purpose, I suppose, is as good a way as any.'

'But there's results,' Anson protested, beginning to claim
them. 'Even here, in my own small way, I'm beginning to
get them. Just you take a look at this.' He lifted a canvas
that leant against the table and held it up for her inspection.
'Now this is the exhibit that me and the Vet's wife have
decided on as the show-piece of the exhibition.'

They were painted from memory, Helen Riddel knew,
staring at the flowers on the canvas. She knew that suddenly,
but just as surely as she knew the origin of the memory.
Searching for specimens up in the Free Kirk Wood. Tracing
them in dark blue jotters. Pressing them in dark green ones.
Suspended between wood and classroom, and concentrating
in a dimness with the sunlight flickering in the back of your
mind, so that when you wrote 'Dog Violet' more carefully
than you would ever write again, and closed your jotter,
memory itself would ettle to straighten out the crumpled

purple petals so that the mind's eye could see again the splash
of yellow hidden in the corner of the flower. The painter
too had remembered. The flowers on her canvas revealed all
that their natural origins had tried to conceal.

'Take a right good look at it, now,' Anson urged, 'for the
girl who did it never painted before in her life, till Dr Finlay's
son – the one that's the Art Teacher in the Town – dropped
in on us one night, to see how we were getting on, and just
as a kind of experiment like, set them all to trying their hands
at a painting. Here, as you can see, is the result.'

'It deserves,' Helen Riddel agreed simply, 'to be the show-
piece of the exhibition.'

'So you cannot deny that I'm getting results, then?' Her
humble admission increased Anson's arrogance. 'And that,
mark you, without any of your Social Science Diplomas or
Government Grants either.'

It was his arrogance, rather than his slighting allusions to
her own qualifications and Centre, that stung her into truth.
'She'll never paint another. Not unless Keith Finlay, or one
of his calibre, continues to draw it from her. And that's
unlikely – people like him have wider worlds to work in.
You see, he didn't discover a potential artist; he created the
potentiality. Not that it matters,' she added despite herself,
and for herself; 'if it happens only once, it's enough.'

'I'm sorry I'm late. I had an awful job to persuade George
to let me have the brake.' The Vet's wife's apologies reached
them before herself. 'Ah, but I see you've had expert help.'
Bright with acknowledgement, her eyes smiled down on
Helen Riddel, and her hands began to rearrange the exhibits.

'I couldn't label them for you.' Helen Riddel moved aside
to let her take over. 'I didn't know their owners. Except *in
absentia.*' The phrase came to her suddenly, out of summers
and summers ago, when she had rheumatic fever and couldn't

come up here to the school on Prize Day to get her medal. But all her disappointment had been atoned for on the day the local paper reported the prize-giving. *Dux Medallist, Helen Riddel. In absentia. In absentia.* Seen in print, the words had added extra to her name. Spoken aloud, they had sounded her somebody special.

The teenagers, crowding round the table now, laid claim to their own work by loud rejections of it. You didn't need to know their names. Their likeness to each other was such that, if you knew one, you knew them all. And certainly they never wanted to know your name, for their curiosity seldom extended to anyone beyond themselves, so that you became but someone odd, old as Methuselah, to be absorbed from top to toe in a glancing instant, and then ejected in a second's cool conclusion. Helen Riddel knew that, now that she was outwith them. For still and only *in absentia* was she endowed.

It was then that she found herself searching their bodies and not their faces, as if her own body, groping out for reassurance, searched for one in like condition. Her very hands could have questioned such a body, her urgency to know was such. Did it feel trapped by its conception, subjected, in anger with itself, and so repulsed?

The chatter round her began to quieten down as Anson mounted the platform to open the meeting. Gripping the back of the seat in front of her, she tried to break the trend of her thoughts by concentrating on his speech. His words ventriloquised but touched her hearing, keeping her eyes fixed on their source. A man and a woman should sleep together completely naked, she thought, staring, so that when next they look upon each other fully clothed, the metamorphosis is so absolute that neither can the imagination distort nor speculation intrude.

The laughter round her was subsiding, and she knew she must have missed the point of some joke.

'Thank you, Ladies and Gentlemen,' Anson was saying. 'Thank you. But to conclude on a more serious note. Although I would be the very last to claim perfection for the samples of work you have seen here tonight, I would be the very first to claim that if perfection happens only once, it's enough.' He raised his hand to acknowledge the appreciative applause. 'At the same time,' he continued when it had subsided, 'at the same time, all that you have seen here tonight is but incidental; but incidental to the real purpose behind the work.'

How naked you felt when the mask slipped from your face, leaving your eyes out of focus, your mouth trembling, and yourself wondering where the mechanism which had always controlled them had gone to.

Outside the hall, Helen Riddel waited for the sickness within her to settle down. Only once before had she been so conscious of her body's separate entity. That was in the summer of her rheumatic fever, when she discovered that once she could will herself to accept her pain's severest spasms, the lesser ones seemed respites, but long enough for acquiescent wonder. This is how it feels to be free of pain. Illusory enough to raise false hope. Maybe I'm better now.

Or like the way we used to work it with the wind, she remembered, its sharpness against her face stirring the recollection. When the wind was in our faces, we'd just turn our backs on it and go racing in its own direction.

But now she knew that, were she to live to be a hundred and feel the first winds of more than seventy springs sharp on her face, never again would they rise from a landscape where every landmark led to some long innocence.

'It all went off very well, I thought.' Anson was as full of his own importance on the road back as he had been on the way going. 'I got a few points home the night. You could tell by the way Mollison held back at the end and stood yonder asking about this and that. Well, didn't you think so?'

Helen Riddel's lack of response gratified him. He simply put it down to professional jealousy – an interpretation that suited his mood of general triumph. His mind now touched on the particular triumph. He was going to marry her all right. That had always been the intention. In his own time though, and on his own terms; for a lifetime of snubs and slights from her father demanded an eradication as slow and deliberate as their accumulation had been. Not that they ever could be completely eradicated. Anson himself was aware of this. You could overcome one of your own like – that was simply a test of strength; but you could not wipe out your antithesis – that opposite aspect of yourself which had first revealed itself years and years ago. A small enough revelation at the time, but still the embryo of an antipathy that was to grow to its full height.

It was on the day Hugh Riddel had left school. The kind of day the younger boys dreaded, when all the long-breeked scholars who were leaving set about them, sighting them. Whether by accident or design, Anson had been Hugh Riddel's victim; and Riddel's finding had rang out through the Free Kirk Wood. 'Anson's got nothing. Charlie Anson's got damn all!' And, although the other young victims had got very little either, their persecutors had simply accepted the fact as but one more proof of their own approaching manhood. But not Hugh Riddel. Never Hugh Riddel. It seemed to Charlie Anson that, ever since, Hugh Riddel had gone on discovering him, had kept on proclaiming that he had got damn all.

But at last, and for all that, he *had* got something – nothing less than Hugh Riddel's daughter.

'Well then, Helen,' he remembered, slowing down and drawing the car in to the edge of Soutar Hill, 'so that's how things are with you? God, but you must have clicked very easily.'

The numbness began to gather on her mind and left her body to its own devices. Surely, to prove its independence, it began to lead the way to the clumps of bracken in search of the hollow to lay itself down in.

'You might be the better of my coat under you,' Anson suggested, disconcerted by her waiting body, 'the bracken's damp.'

'No.' She shook her head and, freeing her face from the pressure of his own, lay looking up into the nothingness of the night.

'Come on now, quean. You can do a lot better than this. What ails you?'

His urgency reached her mind from a long way off; but her body, exercising its independence still, responded to the clawing of his hands.

'That's better. That's more like it. We can go the whole hog the night, seeing you're filled.'

It was her father's hands were round his throat; her father's voice that rose to blaspheme; his body that took over from her own and set her free. But neither for her, nor for her sake. She stood in envy and in need of every blow her father struck at Anson. Thrusting herself forward she was at last observed by him. But not in possessive anger, nor outraged shame, nor even with the saving grace of sorrow's self, but just with pity. That wondering brand of it, and brief, which casts its glance on the misfortunes of some utter stranger, then passes on.

'You poor bitch. Was *this* the best that you could do for yourself?'

'But she must have seen the brake coming,' the Vet's wife was insisting when Hugh Riddel reached the crowd that had gathered at the cross-roads. 'She must have seen it, for I saw her clear enough. She just stepped out from the side of Soutar Hill, and walked right in front of me.'

'They took her to Ambroggan House, Hugh,' Wylie the Blacksmith was saying. 'Only because it happens to be the nearest hospital,' he insisted. 'For I'm sure that it was an accident. I'm sure Helen never saw the brake till it was on her. I'm damned sure of that, Hugh,' he urged, thinking it mattered.

Last as usual, God Knows clattered up into the dairy, rattling his milking machines.

'There's no need for you to sound so bloody busy all of a sudden. It's only me that's here. Darklands hasn't arrived yet.'

Hugh Riddel's voice snapped through the empty dim-lit dairy, and God Knows shot up like some soundless shadow.

'If your hands had been half as ready at the milking as your tongue's been at the gossiping,' Hugh Riddel said when he himself found voice again, 'that lot of milk could have been through the cooler, bottled and off with the first load.'

'So you've gotten the first load off on the road then, Hugh?' Darklands, as always, entered his own dairy with the courteous curiosity of a visitor who doesn't know the answers, yet asks all the right questions.

'How's Andromeda's yield after calving this time, Andrew?' He turned his attention to God Knows, who, surprised by the privilege, began to fuss and fluster.

'She's up, Mr Gordon. She's well up on her last calf. Look see,' he urged, 'just you have a look for yourself.'

A dark face within Hugh Riddel watched God Knows tugging and riving to get the lid off his milking machine. Poor fumbling bugger – fear still made his fingers thumbs; and though there was no need at all for it now, it was a fear God Knows had grown too old within to ever outgrow.

'Let me see the damned thing,' Hugh Riddel suggested at last. 'It's just as I thought,' he said when he had unscrewed the top; 'it's that machine me and the Plunger got jammed the other day, and hell and all to manipulate since.'

'But you were right, Andrew,' Darklands agreed when the machine was opened, 'you were quite right. She's well up on her last yield. I could near swear she's doubled it.'

'Any more news of Helen?' Darklands withheld the question until God Knows had disappeared down into his byre again.

'Not so far,' Hugh Riddel said. 'They're going to ring through next door when there's any change.'

'I've been wondering, Hugh,' and because he still wondered, Darklands didn't find the right words easily, 'I've been thinking, maybe, that when all this blows by, you might feel the better of a bit change. I've got a brother down in the Mearns yonder, who has been thinking this while back of changing over to dairying. And I know for a fact he wouldn't refuse the chance of a good Head Dairyman.'

Hugh Riddel shook his head, refusal reaching him faster than his reasons for it.

'It was Mistress Riddel I was thinking mainly on,' Darklands went on as if he hadn't noticed. 'They say that this kind of thing hits women folk the hardest. And it could just be that she's feeling a change might help. A fresh start like, Hugh.'

Hugh Riddel shook his head again. East or west, north or

south, a mile near or a hundred miles away, the only fresh start a farm-worker ever knew was within the space and in the time it took him to get from the old farm to the new. He had long since found that out from the frequent flits of his boyhood. Only when the horse and cart, with themselves and all their worldly gear piled high on top of it, turned out of sight of the farm they were leaving, had his mother stopped worrying whether she had scrubbed the cottar house they had left behind clean enough for the new folk. And it wasn't until they came in sight of the new farm, that she started worrying about the dirt she was sure she would find in the cottar house they were going to take over. But, in between, they had travelled in some high, far-seeing anonymity that liberated them from every place and every person they passed on the road, and bound them all together in a rare happiness with each other. Much as his mother had always grumbled about all the shifts they made from farm to farm, it was only then, with the past behind them and in the hope it would not precede them, that his mother had taken on some strange new quality.

Gay she had been at such times, he remembered, defining her mood. That was how she must have looked before she ever came to be with his father and himself. The glint of her gaiety caught at his remembrance, but it was wonder held him as he began to recognise the face of a girl he had never set eyes on.

'It would be a fresh start for you all,' Darklands was urging still, misinterpreting his silence.

'No.' Hugh Riddel had found his reason for refusal this time. 'There's no such thing as a fresh start. Only the belief in it, somewhere on the road between the old farm and the new.'

'But at least you'll speak it over with the mistress,' Darklands coaxed. 'Do you know something, Hugh?' he confided, thinking it was his own secret, 'I never yet fee'd a man to work for me without first trying to win over his wife. It's the only way I know to ensure a contented worker. And if I hadn't given in to your mother, years and years ago, your father would never have stayed on to build up the herd with me. That was a precedent, mind you. But I hadn't very much option. It was your father smuggled the two three bantam hens into the farm, but it was your mother insisted holding on to them, once she found out that they were there.'

And although that was something Hugh Riddel hadn't known till now, it was a lesser wonder. But still . . . 'I'll talk it over with the wife,' he promised. 'I'll speak to her about it tonight.'

'Darklands has just been having a word with me.' Now that there was no need of thrust and parry, and words were no longer weapons, Hugh Riddle used them awkwardly. 'He was thinking that maybe you'd like a change of district.'

Her face averted, Isa Riddel stood by the kitchen window, her hands plucking at the curtains; and her silence, as habitual as her attitude, was not to be misinterpreted.

'Well, what do you think? Will we give the south a try?'

She shook her head, and it was but the answer he had expected.

'No,' she repeated aloud, and it was her emphasis that disturbed him.

'So you've been considering it, then?'

'No.'

'You didn't?'

'No.'

'No?'

'No. No, I didn't consider it.'

'So you didn't consider it. But you did think about it, like. Was that the way of it?'

231

'That was the way of it.'

The swiftness of her submission took him unawares and left him at a momentary loss, for the value of her admissions lay only in their extraction.

'What was it made you think of it, then?'

'It was the neighbours suggested a change.'

'I see. I might have known that much.'

Nothing, he remembered, ever came out of herself, except her protestations, and these were but contradictions of his own opinions.

'And I can well imagine the reasons the neighbours gave you. Were you in agreement with them?'

She shook her head again, truth needing no utterance.

'So you didn't agree. My, but wasn't that a wonder now?'

'Was it?' She spoke before he could invade her silence, though she no longer needed its protection: grief afforded more, since grief demanded you, and forcing you beneath its dark and heavy self prevented thing or person from taking your attention off it. Depriving you of tears, it yet intensified your need of them, and threatening you, it vowed that never more would your eyes light on other than itself, or smile again. And grief had guile. Clasping you closely to it, it lent you voice for everything except itself, so that you could utter still, without once lifting eye or mind from grief's own face.

'They were wrong in one of their reasons.' Her small immobility setting up its own defence began to thwart him. 'They were wrong if their reason was Sue Tatt!' He flung the name that had never been spoken between them, to sound her silence, and waited for the ripples to rise to the surface.

'It was one of their reasons,' she said at last. For it had been. But she had long since come to know that, if by a thousandth chance, they shifted to some parish that had no Sue Tatt, the need of her would still be there. You could take the bull to the Castle door but it would still sniff out the byre. 'Though it just wasn't reason enough,' she admitted, as if to something far away and unimportant. 'Though,' she remembered, 'they were only trying to be kind.'

'Kind, is it?'

The fluttering fragility of her statement impelled its own capture and destruction. She had always tried to protect herself by stating the obvious, under some old illusion that its small surface truths could guard her. To her, it would 'turn out a fine day now', when the sun gleamed for an instant in a sky that was overcast for the rest of the day.

'Kind, is it? Oh, but of course, I've noticed their "kindness" these past days, I've noticed the way they've all been in and out of the house here, clutching their offerings of oatcakes, and their tastes of jam, their eyes skinning the road between here and the dairy to see whether I'm coming or going, and, thinking the way clear, scuttling inside to see what's to be seen and hear what's to be heard. The damned curiosity of them! Is that what you call kindness?'

'It isn't like that,' she defended. 'It isn't like that at all.'

'Isn't it though? All right, then! All right, I'll tell you what it *is* like.'

She was listening now; he could tell by the sudden stiffening of her back, for the preliminaries of their communication mattered only in that they led to its conclusion, to that moment of giving and receiving – that instant of fusion when hostility, finding itself at last, dissolves within itself.

'This is what it was like.' He restrained the rush and flow of his words, for, loving them, he was loath to let them go. 'It was like that day the Angus bull gored Betsy Ann the tinker, in the Nether Park. But you'll mind on yon day fine. Surely you'll mind on't. For were you not yourself but one of them went running in and out of Lil's house where they took her, with your bits of sheets for bandages, and your pannikins of hot water. Kind folk right enough, from the tractor-men who carried her in, to their wives who clucked round her. I wasn't there. But I know as much about Betsy Ann now as them that were there. And that's but damned little. Though it must have struck the rest of you as hellish important. What is it that any one of you mind on now, or speak about at all, when you catch sight of Betsy Ann making her way up the road? Damn all! Except that she wears her man's combinations, and that they're coal black. What a comfort it must have been to all the wives to discover that what Betsy Ann had gotten under her skirts was dirtier than their own. And what a consolation to their men folk for finding that out too. A fair enough exchange for all their "Kindness".'

'It wasn't like that.' She turned to look on him now, her eyes refusing to be trapped by any particular part of him, such as his hands that grasped the back of the chair till his knuckle bones shone white.

'And it isn't like that now,' she repeated, staring at the whole man. 'If Betsy Ann had died on the day the bull gored her, not a one would even have noticed what she wore. Not a one would have spoken of it afterwards. All they would remember was just that Betsy Ann had died.'

'I've just heard about Helen,' God Knows said when Hugh Riddel caught him up on the road to the dairy.

'I've just heard it myself.' Hugh Riddel neither slackened his stride nor made room for God Knows to fall in beside him, so that now as always they walked in single file along the track: though a brave new road had been built for them years ago, the windows of the farmhouse stared down its length and breadth, and so they still preferred this old dark devious route that covered both their comings and their goings.

'There was no need for you to worry about the last loading

the night,' God Knows protested behind him, 'there was no need for that at all. Me and the Plunger would have managed perfectly for once.'

'There's nothing I can do the night that won't keep till the morning.' Hugh Riddel's matter of factness surprised itself no less than it puzzled God Knows. Though, come to think of it, man, being animal, was subject to the habit of his body from the moment of its possession. Even the foal that died within an hour of being born could in its final death throe still lash out and image for an instant some long-legged lifetime.

They halted now that they had reached the dairy; for though they walked their world from point to point, their eyes upon the ground, they never once went in out of its night without straightening up for that last look in which to prophesy tomorrow's weather.

Time out of mind, God Knows remembered, had he stood just so, with Hugh Riddel's father, in a silence the one had defied the other to break.

'I'm sorry about Helen.' God Knows broke it now. 'I'm real sorry.'

'Aye.' Hugh Riddel's acceptance was as brief as God Knows expected it to be. There were no words for death itself, only for its justification. God Knows stood listening for them now, although he knew their every qualifying adjective by heart – the very old who were 'better away from it all'; the very young, 'happier out of it'; the middle-aged who rarely died, but when they did were apt to 'slip away', taking their secret word 'incurable' with them. Even so, they were the kind of words which had to be uttered by the one and heard by the other. You accepted death, but found the reason for it before burying the body.

'Still, when you consider how things were – '

'Just so.' God Knows implicitly confirmed Hugh Riddel's

reflection. Words which he had heard from the beginning of time, when it was only the brute beasts that died and man was immortal; and, though time in its passing proved that man died too, the words kept their truth: never completed, yet needing no expansion.

It could have been Hugh Riddel's father who had uttered them just now, as so often he had done, when the 'sharger', the 'runt', the freak calf, had to be put down. Not simply because as cattleman he recognised it could not add to the strain of the herd, but because its own species, recognising that too, would have less mercy.

'Just so,' God Knows assured the father, and waited for his son to speak.

'It looks as though Dave the shepherd was right,' Hugh Riddel remembered, for the wind that had been threatening to work itself up into a gale all week had succeeded at last. A fresh gale at that. Soutar Hill was beginning to crackle under it already. By this time tomorrow the thaw would have set in, and hill and element would come racing down together to water the world. But hill would win. Its swift escaping burns, tumbling without restraint, would land as always first at Caldwell's feet.

'Dave was quite right,' Hugh Riddel conceded as they began to move towards the dairy; 'it looks as though he just managed to get yon ewes of his down off Soutar Hill in time.'

ANOTHER TIME, ANOTHER PLACE

To Avril and Ken

THERE would be no gathering in of the corn today. The rain that had swept across Inveraig blotted out the firth itself. The corn that had stood just yesterday, high and ripe and ready to fall to the binder, bent earthwards now, beneath the driving lash of the wind.

She could, the young woman thought, be standing high in some inland country, not in a sea-girt place at all. But then, she had not yet become accustomed to this alien place in which she now had her being.

'You'll not be needing the bag apron the day, mistress. I'm saying, Mistress Ainslie.' She turned to find the shepherd at her shoulder. 'I was saying, mistress': it still took her unaware to be addressed by her recently acquired married title, still took her time to respond to it, as if those who uttered it spoke to another person, a different person from the one she knew herself to be.

> If no one ever marries me
> And I don't see why they should

They say that I'm not pretty
And I'm very seldom good

But someone *had* married her, though she hadn't got used to that either. 'If this wind keeps on rising,' the shepherd prophesied, scanning the sky for a break in the hill-locked clouds, 'it might just manage to dry up the corn.'

'Little chance of that.' Finlay, the farm foreman, ambled towards them, his scythe sheltering under the sacking that should have protected his shoulders. 'If my scythe cannot get at the inroads then it's God help the binder. You'll be a wee thing short in your pay poke,' he warned the young woman, 'if the rain keeps dinging like this. *And* you, Kirsty,' he shouted across the dyke to her neighbour. 'Still. That'll give you both time to catch up with your washing.'

'In weather like this,' Kirsty snapped, rising as always to Finlay's bait, 'there's no drying in it, man.'

'Maybe no then, Kirsty,' Finlay conceded, grinning, 'maybe no. By the by,' he turned again to the young woman, 'you're going to have neighbours next door. *That'll* suit you, that'll keep you from getting lonesome.'

'Neighbours,' Kirsty protested, 'that bothy next door's not fit for neighbours. There's been nobody inside it since we stopped breeding pigs, and the boss sent the pigman packing.'

'It's not the pigman this time', Finlay assured her. 'It's Italians. Three of them. Prisoners-of-war.'

'*Italians!*' Kirsty gasped. 'Foreigners. Prisoners-of-war.'

Prisoners-of-war, heroic men from far-flung places: the young woman felt a small surge of anticipation rising up within her at the prospect of the widening of her narrow insular world as a farm-worker's wife, almost untouched by the world war that raged around her. She always felt she was missing out on some tremendous event, never more so than when she caught a glimpse of girls of her own age, resplendent in uniform, setting out for places she would never set eyes on. Or when she caught their laughter-filled whispers of a whirling social life, the like of which she had never known.

'Does that mean, does that mean, Finlay, that you'll not be needing us for stooking the sheaves?' She could interpret the anxiety in Kirsty's voice. True enough the women would have preferred minding their homes to the darg in the fields. But, as Finlay was always pointing out, 'Tenpence an hour is not to be sneezed at.'

'Devil the bit of it, Kirsty. From what I hear tell of the Italians, they're none too keen when it comes to bending their backs, and you'd better get the scrubbing brush going,' Finlay advised the young woman, 'and get that bothy cleaned up for the Italians. It will help to make up for the loss of your wages. Kirsty there can give you a hand if she likes,' he suggested, as he turned to go.

'Not *me*,' Kirsty shouted after his disappearing back. 'I've got better things to do than wait hand and foot on a bunch of foreigners.'

Slamming her door behind her, Kirsty took her resentment inside the house, and immediately thrust it out again with her bairns. Bundling them threateningly through the door, 'Late for school again,' she warned them, '*another* morning.'

Scarfed, hooded, and belted, the bairns stood on the doorstep, momentarily unsure of their bearings, until Alick, spying the snail, shot forward to pounce on it.

'Snail Snail
Put out your horn'

he chanted to the small captive, imprisoned in his hand.

Mornings like this the young woman remembered from her own not-so-distant childhood, always lured the snails from the safety of their hiding places, to creep along the highways of danger.

> 'And I will give you
> A barley corn'

she sang across to the bairns, concluding their chant for them. Too grown-up now, though, to intrude on the small miracle that she knew was happening before their eyes, the tremulous appearance of the snail's tiny horns, at the first touch of a human hand.

'Are you lot *still* there?' Kirsty demanded from her door-step, dissolving the spell, and sending the bairns plunging up through the bracken.

'God knows what *she'll* think of the Italians.' Taking her attention off the bairns, Kirsty directed it now to Elspeth, making her way down the hill from her croft at Achullen.

Of all their small community, Elspeth was the only one involved in and affected by the war. Engaged to Callum, a Scots-Canadian, to be married when the war was over, to go to Canada, to live forever. A fine place for Scots to settle in, Elspeth had always maintained. For, as she had often pointed out to the young woman, 'You could work your fingers to the bone, on a small croft like Achullen, and not earn enough to buy the six foot of earth to bury yourself in, when it was all over and done with. But in *Canada* now . . .'

It was after Callum was reported missing at Monte Cassino in Italy that Elspeth had stopped speaking about Canada; and the young woman had never since mentioned Canada to Elspeth. It was as if a whole continent had suddenly disappeared out of their ken.

She missed the 'speaks' though. The fine long 'speaks'

herself and Elspeth had shared, when Canada existed. Not
that the young woman herself had been able to add much to
Elspeth's knowledge of it. Remembering only how one of
the boys in the orphanage where she had been brought up
went to Canada to work on a farm . . . 'He had a new tin
trunk, Elspeth, we all envied him. Going way on a ship, I
mean. He was so excited. We envied that too. Then, on the
morning he left, he started to cry. I couldn't understand the
reason for such tears. Not until the day I left the orphanage
myself. Not even then. For I cried too, and I didn't know
what I was crying for . . .'

Elspeth's excitement had also affected the young woman.
'O, Elspeth. You *are* lucky . . .' Her envy had been heart-
felt.

'You'll come and see me,' Elspeth had suggested. Half-
teasing, half-serious. 'When your boat comes in . . .'

But she herself knew that she would never see Canada.
'Nor anywhere else, Elspeth. Just Scotland . . .'

'Nonsense,' Elspeth had reproved her. 'Stuff and nonsense.
You're but young yet, lassie. You've got the whole world in
front of you yet . . .'

She had thought that too. Before she was married. She had
thought she could go anywhere. Go everywhere, do anything. Do everything . . . 'Not now though Elspeth,' she had
confided. 'It's all different now. Being married, I mean . . .'

'You've *got* to laugh,' Kirsty said, as they watched Elspeth,
her old waterproof coat flapping wide in the wind, striding
down the hill towards them. The staff she always carried for
the steep climb back lashing out at the bracken, clearing the
way for the imperious passage of a queen. Boadicea, from
remembered history lessons, taking on flesh at last.

'You've got to laugh,' Kirsty insisted. 'Rain or shine. The

same old waterproof. And rain or shine. She never bothers to button it up. You've got to laugh . . .'

Kirsty, almost devoid of laughter herself, was always urging it on to the young woman. Leaving her puzzled, in serious search of laughter's source. There was nothing funny in the aura of dignity that Elspeth always carried within herself. An independence lacking in the young woman and her neighbouring cottar wives. But then there *was* a fundamental difference between them. Elspeth worked her *own* small acres of land, although whiles having to eke out her livelihood by helping with the seasonal jobs on the farmer's large acres of land.

Elspeth, as she often claimed, could 'pick and choose', could remain unmoved by Finlay's moods and demands, and be unafraid of telling him 'exactly where *he* gets off'. The young woman envied Elspeth's liberty of choice, her freedom of utterance.

'You're redding up,' Elspeth stared round the bare, dust-filled bothy. 'The pigman's bothy, you're redding it up.'

'For prisoners-of-war,' the young woman said.

'For *Italians*,' Kirsty contradicted. 'Foreigners. Did you ever hear the like?' she demanded.

'Italians,' Elspeth echoed, turning to the young woman. 'And *you* are redding up the bothy for *them*. For Italians.'

'*I* refused,' Kirsty claimed. 'When Finlay asked me, I just refused. Point blank.'

'Just odd jobs, Elspeth.' Aware now of some inexplicable need to apologise, the young woman heard herself plunging deeper into explanation, felt herself falling deeper into disfavour. 'Little jobs just, getting the grocer's van, a bit of washing sometimes, things like that.'

'Ah well.' Taking a last look round the bothy, Elspeth

turned on her heel to go. '*That*'ll be worth a bob or two in your pocket.'

'It's only because I live next door,' the young woman pleaded to Elspeth's retreating back. 'That's all, Elspeth, only because I live next door.'

'Elspeth gave you short shrift,' Kirsty remarked, as they watched her making her way back up the hill. 'Not that you can blame her,' she reflected, 'with her Callum missing in Italy. Enough to put you off Italians for life. And *another* thing . . .'

Stifling an impulse to rush up the hill after Elspeth, the young woman let Kirsty's tirade flow over and round her. She hadn't found it easy to comfort Elspeth on the day that Callum was reported missing. Her attempts at consolation had sounded too facile to be true. Even to her own ears. 'But Callum's not dead yet, Elspeth. He's not dead . . .' Words out of context. Running away with her. 'Callum could still be found. He could still turn up. That sometimes happens. I read about that once. In a book . . .'

How much more difficult it would be to find words for an offence that had neither been committed, nor specifically defined.

She would miss Elspeth's friendship. Elspeth who had tried to initiate her into the strange ways of this new life. Who had taught her to bake. Conjuring up a living entity out of a raw ingredient. 'Lightly now – *lightly*. That scones will never rise. Thumping away at the dough like that. Leave it now. Let it alone. For the love of goodness. Give the dough a chance to *breathe* . . .'

'What,' Kirsty began to wonder, as the young woman's husband dipped down into view from the high ridge and led the horse and cart into the turnip field, 'what will *he* have to say about the Italians?' Kirsty knew what *her* man would say about that, she claimed. Only she hadn't given him a chance.

The day that had started out this morning on its everyday course was beginning to take on some new and threatening dimension in the young woman's mind. Leaving her without concrete reply to Kirsty's half-articulated reflections.

Her man, she knew, wouldn't have very much to say about the Italians. Not in words. Always on his own, as a cattle-man, and working apart from his fellow farm-workers, he had got out of the way of using words. Sometimes, some-times she felt he had grown out of the need of words at all. She was learning though to interpret by look and mood. The way her man, himself, could interpret each need and nuance of the dumb beasts he worked amongst.

Watching him from a distance, as he topped and tailed the turnips, bending down and straightening up, he seemed to the young woman like a man performing some simple exercise to an easeful rhythm of his own composing. Unlike winter, she remembered, when an agonised tussle, an eternal tug-of-war, waged between himself and a reluctant crop held fast to earth. But the frost had not yet fixed its grip on the days, nor on the crop. Nor on the image of his deftly moving hands.

'I'll get you a turnip for the pot,' she said at last, in reply to Kirsty. 'I'll get it when Alick comes down with his load. Before the frost gets at them.'

'Prisoners-of-war. Italians.' Her man stood on the doorstep of the bothy, digesting her information. 'But I thought they were going to bide in the camp over, and just coming here to work – day-to-day.'

'Not this three. They're going to bide in the bothy.'

'And *you're* going to look after them, like?'

'No.' She shook her head, uncertain herself of the demands of her rôle as 'next door neighbour'. 'I'm just redding up the bothy for them.'

'But why you? What about Kirsty and Meg? Have *they* refused?'

'Kirsty and Meg have got bairns,' she pointed out. The look, tightening up her man's face, setting her off on the wheedle, hating herself for the use of it, and momentarily hating the man, who was the instrument of its use. 'According to Finlay, it's something or nothing. Scrubbing out the bothy, once in a while. Getting the odd bit message off the grocer's van. Just things like that. It'll mean a bit extra for us,' she persuaded, 'to save in the tea caddy. A bit to put by. *That'll* please you.' She could hear the resentment beginning to sound in her voice. 'You're always on about "something to put by".'

'Your man didn't seem sore pleased with your news,' Kirsty shouted across from her doorstep. 'No more would mine. If it was *me*.'

'*My* man,' she retaliated, her resentment blowing up into positive anger, '*my* man wouldn't mind if I got down on my knees and cleaned up horses' dung. Not if it would give him "something to put by".'

And that was true, she assured herself, slamming the bothy door behind her, in confirmation of a fact.

Certain facts though, she realised, even before she reached her own door, certain facts were out of context. And not for utterance. Shamed by the realisation, and aware of Kirsty's shocked silence, she turned back with her offering. 'Here's a neep for your broth, Kirsty. The frost hasn't got at it yet.'

Kirsty's wordless acceptance reaffirmed an opinion gathered from experience. Peace offerings by themselves were never enough. Explanation was always an essential accompaniment. 'My man isn't really like that, Kirsty, it's me. It's just me.'

Me.

Her image, reflected in the looking-glass above the sink, gazed back at her. Assessing each other, before breaking into a wide smile of recognition. Absolved by confession, sudden lightness of heart overtook her.

> 'One morning I rose
> And looked in the glass'

she sang to the smiling reflection, that mouthed along with her.

> 'Said I to myself
> I'm a handsome young lass
> I've plenty of money
> To dress me so braw . . .'

'They're here,' Meg shouted, as herself and Kirsty flashed past the window. 'Your new neighbours. The Italians.'

They stood, the prisoners, as she had seen the bairns stand this very morning, as if struck to stone by the sudden strangeness of their situation.

'This is Mistress Ainslie,' Finlay elbowed her towards them. 'Your neighbour, next door.' Rapping on her door in an attempt at interpretation. 'She'll keep an eye. Rat-tat-tat. Grocer. Food. Eat. Knock wall. Rat-tat-tat.'

It was hard to tell whether the Italians understood Finlay's frantic miming, or whether they were simply reluctant to bring such a fascinating performance to a close.

Kirsty did that for them. 'Good God, Finlay,' she shouted

from the gale end of the row. 'Good God, man, but you should have been on the stage.'

The laughter of the watching farm-hands swirled up and round, leaving the young woman standing beside the Italians within the circumference of their own unease, for what the Italians *had* understood was that she had been thrust upon them. And was in some way involved. Neither acceptance nor rejection revealed itself in the blank eyes of their appraisal. Leaving her with the urgent need to appraise herself. And, in the doing, she became suddenly conscious of her mud-splattered wellingtons, of the bag apron that gave no hint of the small waist hidden within it. Sharply aware that she stood neuter and sexless. Clad in the garments of renunciation.

The young woman stood envying Kirsty's busyness, the cluck of her hens and the clatter of her pails. The normality of it. She would be glad when the weather settled down into its own season again. When each day had its yoking beginning. And its lowsing ending.

'You'd be better uprooting that muckle clump of rhubarb,' advised Meg, leaning over the gate of Kirsty's yard. 'Spreading all over the place like that. Once it gets inside the ree, it will poison all your hens.'

The moment for advice of any kind was inopportune. And Kirsty rejected it. She would, she declared, as soon dig up her grandmother as uproot the clump of rhubarb.

There was no real acrimony in the exchange between her two neighbours. It was part of a pattern they wove together to relieve the tensions of their long years of proximity.

She, the young woman realised, had become part of the pattern too, leaving her neighbours puzzled by, and pondering upon, a shape and colour that had appeared, as if by accident, amongst them, and was not of their design.

The texture of her own life now seemed to hang suspended

by the uncertainty of her new, undefined responsibilities. Shy of intruding on the Italians next door, anxious lest she should miss out on a knock on her wall, yet apprehensive of responding to it, since that first time it happened.

'*Buona sera, signora,*' Luigi, alone in the bothy, had greeted her. '*Buona sera.*'

'Hello.' She smiled, recognising the sound of salutation.

'*Parla italiano?*' She shook her head. '*No parla italiano.*'

'French,' she heard herself claiming, starting to dredge words up out of schoolday memory. '*Je parle la langue française.*'

'*Français.* Similar *italiano.*' Luigi flung his arm round her shoulder. 'Similar! Posseeble speak.' But not possible to communicate, she realised, her thoughts lingering on half-forgotten irregular verbs . . . *Je suis. Vous êtes. Nous sommes.*

The transformation the Italians had worked on the bothy took her mind off the frustrations of communication.

'*Madonna!*' Luigi said, following her gaze, fixed on the blue poster above his iron bed. Bowing, crossing himself as he moved forward to lay personal claim on the Mother and Child that gazed down on them both. '*Madonna Mia . . .*'

His apartness, excluding her from some mystery, allowed her time to resort to fantasy . . . 'That's the *Madonna,*' she would point out to Kirsty and Meg, when she invited them in for a quick look-see at the bothy, which had once belonged to the pigman. 'The Madonna,' she would emphasise, knowing that Kirsty would just think it was the Virgin Mary. She too would bow and cross herself, her explanation of such a performance would be as casual as tongue could sound it. 'That's what Catholics do, Kirsty. That's what she's there for . . .'

'*Mama Mia.* You like?'

None of the quick words of appreciation – true or false –

but always necessary in such circumstances, came to her aid. 'You like? *Mama Mia?*'

'Yes.' She nodded. 'Yes.'

'*Yes.*' Luigi lunged at the word. 'Yes! *Si! Si!* Yes!'

'*Si.*' She had uttered her first word of Italian. 'Posseeble?' His grip tightened on her shoulder, as if all obstacles to communication had been swept away. 'Posseeble you like the jiggy-jig?'

She had never before heard the word jiggy-jig. But instantly understood it. But it was the lack of outrage, of affront, which she had felt such a stark suggestion should have aroused within her, that surprised herself.

'No posseeble me like.' A tone of apology sounding in her voice, as if she had simply rejected an invitation to supper.

'*PERCHE* no posseeble? *Perche* no posseeble you, the jiggy-jig?'

'Husband me.' She explained. Twirling the wedding ring around her finger to prove it. 'Married me.'

She was relieved when the door of the bothy swung open. Grateful for the arrival of Paolo and Umberto. Yet suddenly guilty in their presence. A guilt they themselves seemed to fling over her, as they flung their raincapes over the chairs. Their wordlessness sounding their suspicions.

'You've got an odd lot in there,' Meg greeted her, when she closed the bothy door behind her. 'Not one word of Scots between them.'

'Nor English,' she agreed, turning to stare across the firth. The wind was beginning to blow itself out. The fields on the other side of the water were thrusting themselves into view again. Tomorrow, maybe, they might make a start to the stooking.

'And not before time,' Meg grumbled. *Nothing,* she claimed, got herself so down in the mouth as rain. 'Dinging on and on like this.'

She was right, was Meg. Weather, the young woman was beginning to learn, was never an event. It was always an emotion.

'What *are* they seeking now?' her man demanded. For the knocks from the bothy were becoming more frequent, and had begun to irritate him.

'Maybe it's their tilley lamp again. They haven't got the knack of it yet.'

'It's high time they did, then,' her man said. For he'd never seen anybody so slow to pick up the knack of things as the Italians.

They had other 'knacks' though, the young woman had discovered. Paolo, carving wood that was dead into shapes that became alive under the flick of his knife and the curve of his fine brown fingers. Umberto, teaching children in a small village school. The tremendous respect the farm-workers had for teachers was never reflected on Umberto.

Luigi. O, Luigi. A barrow-boy from the streets of Naples. She knew instinctively from memories of her own early street-spent, barefoot childhood, how it was for Luigi. Cocking a snook at the whole wide world.

Sometimes, sometimes she wished that a magic carpet would whisk all the farm-workers away to Italy, and set *them* down in an alien place. They wouldn't have the 'knack' of it either!

Even Finlay, her man was saying, was beginning to lose patience with them. The little patience he *did* have. For he never had very much of it. He'd set them in the morning to patch up the old sacks for oats. And had come back after dinner to find they'd glued all the sacks together! The language that was on Finlay when he found out was something terrible, just! The memory of Finlay when 'the language was on him' filled the young woman with laughter.

'It was yalla and purple
And violet and blue'

she sang, grabbing her man to dance him round the kitchen.

'Neath the boughs of a rowan tree shady'

'You'd better see what they're seeking next door,' he warned her, disengaging himself, 'or they'll be knocking on that wall all night. One of these days,' he prophesied, 'they'll pump that tilley lamp up so hard they'll blow themselves and all the rest of the world up with it. Though they shouldn't be needing the lamp, it's not nearly lighting up time yet.'

Neither it was, she agreed, when she got out into the night. For they had not yet finished stooking the sheaves. But then the harvest was late this year. The wild ducks were already beginning to take their leave of the land. Soon, the wild geese would go honking through the night. *That,* she remembered, was a sound for a real dark night. Dropping invisible down upon you. Turning in at the bothy, a rabbit started up at her feet, as silently as if one of the little shadows on the road had suddenly picked itself up, and flitted away.

Luigi and Paolo were crouched on opposite sides of the fireplace when she reached the bothy.

'Come!' Luigi commanded. 'You hear? *TIC-A-TIC-A-TIC-A. Che cosa? Che cosa? TIC-A-TIC!*'

'It's only your clock, Luigi,' she laughed, pointing to the alarm clock on the mantelpiece, 'only your clock.'

'No *clock!*' Grabbing the clock to himself, Luigi scurried to the other end of the bothy. 'No clock!' he insisted. 'You hear now?'

'A beetle, Luigi,' she assured him, straightening up from the wall. 'Just a beetle. Lives inside wood in wall. A death watch beetle,' she added, as if some extension of her words would help comprehension. '*Morte*', she remembered a word that might be universal.

'*Morte! Che? Che morte? Che . . .* ?' The alarm in Luigi's face confirmed her feeling that death, like jiggy-jig, could be understood in any tongue.

'Nobody *morte*, Luigi, nobody. Just name we speak.'

It was nothing, she told her man. 'I could have got a rabbit for the pot,' she remembered, smiling. 'If only I could have catched it.'

The stubble fields crackled like spun glass beneath their feet as they made their way to the gate. The field stood stooked. Golden tents in a serried array.

'That's that, then,' Kirsty said, 'for another year.'

The contentment in her voice reached out to touch the others. As if she had handed each of them a gift of unlimited leisure.

There was nothing, the young woman realised, as they leant over the gate, reviewing the scene of their ended labour, nothing in all the world that could ease your own tiredness like watching others still at work.

'You would think Finlay hadn't another minute to live! The way he's hounding the Italians,' Kirsty didn't blame him for *that*. For they had no idea, she claimed. None at all. 'Look see,' she commanded, 'they're missing the stack every time. The sheaves are slipping off their forks before they reach the stack.'

'Ah, well then.' There was a hint of satisfaction in Meg's voice as they turned to go. '*That'll* give Finlay a few grey hairs. That'll teach him who his real workers are.'

Turning now on the young woman who was lagging

behind, Kirsty demanded to know what ailed her, that she had so little say for herself the night. If it was the stooking that had knackered her, then God help her at the lifting of the tatties, Kirsty prophesied. She'd know *then* what tiredness was, walking around for days with a broken back.

It was the thistles, the young woman said, they had started to scratch her all over. There was, Meg agreed, more thistles than corn this year. But it was no wonder the young woman was scratched all over. *Anybody* would be scratched, Kirsty pointed out, if they were daft enough to go to the stooking in a short-sleeved blouse. And a skirt up to their knees. Kirsty had never, she claimed, 'seen the like'. But, by God, the young woman would know all about it when she got into bed the night. The heat of the blankets would see to *that*.

They were right, Kirsty and Meg, and that was the trouble, they were right about everything. And the righter they were the more resentful the young woman became. Their cottar houses, 'tied cottages', only partially described their way of life. They were 'tied' to each other. Dependent on each other, in the very isolation of their habitation.

The change that had come over the young woman since the arrival of the Italians might have escaped their microscopic eyes, if it had been gradual. But it hadn't been gradual. It had overwhelmed her, taking herself by surprise. A key which had opened a door that had never been unlocked. And herself becoming the prisoner, stumbling blind, into the light of a new awareness, bursting out of her body in response to Luigi's admiration, shouted in the fields, whispered in the bothy . . . *Bella. Bella. Bella ragazza* . . .

It wasn't for Luigi that she had donned her short-sleeved blouse, or kilted her skirt up to her knees. And Paolo hadn't noticed. She could have been Kirsty or Meg, concealed within their woollen greys.

She ran, now, where once she would have walked, leaving them behind to their own middle-aged pace, ignoring their tight-lipped comments. 'For she could,' they observed, 'fairly shift when the Italians were around. Flaunting her bare legs in front of them. Showing off, just.'

They were right about that too, about 'showing off. It was just that she had never before been aware of all the things she had to 'show off'. . .

'God almighty, Beel,' Kirsty protested as the tractor roared round the corner sending them scurrying against the dyke. 'You damned nearly had the lot of us head first into the ditch!'

'You wouldn't have drowned,' Beel assured her. 'We drained the ditch the other day.'

'If *Finlay* caught you taking round the corner at a lick like that, burning up the tyres . . .' The threat implied in Kirsty's voice took the grin off Beel's face, reminding him of more serious matters.

'Finlay,' he remembered, shouting down from the tractor, 'Finlay says if you see Elspeth at the grocer's van, you might tell her he's expecting her to lowse to the threshing mill, first thing Tuesday morning.'

'Finlay's got a hope,' Kirsty snapped. 'Some nerve.' Elspeth, she reminded him, had refused to set foot in a field with the Italians, and she for one didn't blame Elspeth for *that*. She would have felt the same herself if her Alick had been missing in Italy.

'Better dead than missing,' Meg concluded. 'You know where you are when you're dead.'

'The seaplanes! The seaplanes!'

The bairns, shouting in the distance, quickened their pace.

Either they were late, or the bairns had got out of school early.

'The seaplanes! The seaplanes!'

'That damned thing's on the go again.' Meg brushed all interest in the weapons of a world war aside, turning to admonish the excited children. 'Never mind the seaplanes. Get yourselves in amongst the stubble there. And gather up some corn for the hens.'

They were flying low, the seaplanes, skimming huge and heavy across the firth. So heavy, the young woman stood wondering how they could ever raise themselves up into the sky.

'You're just as bad as the bairns,' Kirsty admonished her, standing there gooking. As if *your* man wasn't expecting his supper the night.'

Out now from the hard brightness, into the dead dimness of her kitchen, the contrast caught at the young woman's throat. And stuck there, tangible. A lump, preventing words from coming out. If words could be found, for the worst thing about working in the fields was getting geared up again, to tackle the work lying undone in the house.

> 'Moonlight becomes you
> It goes with your hair'

the singer assured her when she turned on the wireless,

> 'You certainly know
> The right things to wear.'

She did too, but only in her imagination, and in an absorbed study of Kirsty's mail-order catalogue. But two shillings a week – the limit of the instalments she could afford defied imagination, and whittled choice down to bare essentials, working boots for her man, wellingtons for herself.

> 'If I say I love you
> I want you to know
> It isn't because it's moonlight
> Although . . .
> Moonlight becomes you so . . .

'You're early, surely.' The unexpected arrival of her man set her off on the attack. 'I'm just this minute in. And the supper's not on yet.'

'A cup of tea will suit me fine.'

His mild acceptance increased her resentment. It was not a fitting apology for an intrusion into her rare moments of privacy. Intrusions that seemed to surround, and close in on her – Kirsty, Meg, Beel, Finlay, the lee-long day. Himself, the long night.

'The heifer's at the drop of calving,' he said, easing himself down on the settle. 'Her udder's swollen. Gey and big, we could be in for a night of it. It being her first calf, you might take a turn up to the byre later on. I'll maybe need a hand.'

'Aye. All right,' she agreed, wondering where her resentment had disappeared to, and why it had ever been there in the first place.

'You'd be better of the lantern,' he suggested, as he rose to go back to the byre. 'I'll away and fill it up for you.'

She had no need of the lantern. Real darkness never fell down out of the night. It was when it rose up out of the ground that you could lose your bearings, and yourself.

Besides, she liked walking in the dark. There was something nocturnal in her. Atavistic. Something that had never had a chance.

The reflection of Meg's fire flickered against the window.

Enough edge to the nights now for a fire. The time of fires, she remembered, stopping to watch the flames rising up from the burning of the whins, that snapped and crackled in protest to the night.

Unprepared for the voice whispering behind her. '*Cara . . . cara mia . . .*' She turned to confront Luigi. Grasping her by the shoulders, he pulled her against himself. 'Posseeble . . . posseeble . . . one time posseeble . . .' Taken by surprise, anger lent harshness to her voice. '*No* possible. *No* time possible . . .

'*Scusi, Signora. Scusi, scusi, mi scusi.*'

The supplication in Luigi's voice, his instant humble acceptance of rejection dissolved her anger. Fear had done that to Luigi. She knew that, as she watched him clinging to the fence, fumbling his way back to the bothy. Fear always had the power to humiliate.

'I thought I smelt burning.' Flinging open her door, Meg crouched within it, her head thrust forward, peering accusingly out into the night. 'I could swear I smelt burning.'

'Wrong spy, Meg.' The young woman's laughter relieved her tension. 'You're right about *one* thing, though,' she conceded. 'Your nose would be worth five pounds in a pointer pup! They've made a start to burning the whins up at Achullen.'

She arrived at the byre in the nick of time. One of the older calves, overcome by curiosity, had got out of its loose box, hell-bent on making the acquaintance of its newly born kinsman, to the fury of the cow, butting and lashing out at friend, foe, and all inanimate things alike.

'Hold on to the daft devil,' her man commanded, 'till I get the cow settled.'

A safe place the byre, lacking the competitiveness of all other areas of farm work. No 'knacks' – implying that there were several methods – needed here. There was only one way to milk a cow. And the young woman had mastered it. Only one way to calve a cow, and her man was familiar with it.

A fine place to be born in the byre. Sweetened by the cows' breaths, and the tang of newly sliced turnips. The relationship between her man and the brute beasts he worked amongst becoming intimate, at times like these. A warm 'mash' for the cow, a gift for her motherhood with a touch of black treacle added as a treat 'for a good lass'.

The newly born calf was beginning to find its balance. Staggering to grope under the cow in search of its udder. Licking her calf from end to end, almost knocking it over in an excess of maternal devotion. A pity, the young woman thought, watching her man guiding the calf to its urgent objective, a pity. It was to be a sucker calf, a pity it was a bull calf. Not well enough bred to enjoy a lifetime of lascivious freedom. 'You're a fine calfie,' she assured it, stroking its damp head. 'A fine calfie.' Pity to end up a stirk, for prime beef. But she didn't mention that to the newly born calf.

'It's lucky in a way though,' she reflected, as herself and her man made their way home from the byre. 'It will be left with its mother. Sucking for a long time.'

'But God help us the day it stops sucking.'

Her man was right, she remembered. The crying of the cow when its calf was weaned would make of the byre a place of lamentation. For endless days.

She had spent the whole of yesterday evening on her knees in her yard, untangling her sweet peas. Persuading them to climb up the tiers of twine she had woven between the posts, in an attempt to give them individuality, to discover this morning that they had defied her efforts, scrambling through each other, their tendrils in a twist, clutching at each other's hair, as if they couldn't bear to grow up apart.

She would, Kirsty suggested, peering over the fence, have been a lot better with a bit of netting wire. For Kirsty 'hoped to God' that the young woman wasn't expecting to win a prize at the flower show in the village 'with rogue sweet peas. Running riot all over the place'.

She had no intention, the young woman snapped, offended by such unwanted criticism, no intention in the world, of setting foot within a mile of the flower show. Nor of 'exhibiting' sweet peas.

She *must* go, Kirsty insisted. They *always* went. It was expected. They all went together. The young woman would *have* to put in an appearance. Maybe, maybe she only imagined a tone of desperation in Kirsty's voice. A plea for reinforcement.

It hadn't been imagination. The young woman realised that the moment she stepped inside the marquee. For, although the village lay little more than a mile away from them, the cottar wives had no real part in its integral life. They could have 'dropped in' from another planet, to find themselves invisible, in a marquee. Huddling closely together, they began to wander round the different 'sections', their voices rising loud in praise of each and every exhibit on show. As if the sound of themselves could merge within that of the folk who surrounded them.

'Miss McCarthel, from Burnside, for her foreign mission,' Kirsty whispered as a woman homed towards them, rattling a collection tin. 'She gives herself to the poor.'

She would never, the young woman reflected, confronted by a large, weather-beaten woman, brown from her felt hat down to her brogues, be asked to give herself to the rich.

'Come *on!*' Kirsty nudged the young woman. Elbowing her towards the home baking section. 'Come on and see how Elspeth got on this year.'

'If she entered, that is,' Meg qualified. 'If she had the heart. Considering . . .'

Elspeth had the heart, and hadn't lost the 'knack'. Two yellow tickets and a red. A first prize and two second prizes adorned Elspeth's entries. Setting their seal on her proficiency as a baker of scones, oatcakes and pancakes.

Elspeth, herself, seen now in a dimension beyond her croft at Achullen, belonging to the parish, accepted by the village. Her five acres of land entitling her to that privilege.

They made no attempt to join Elspeth, chatting easily with a group of her own kind. 'We'll see her the morn. At the butcher's van,' Meg said as they turned away towards the cut flower section. There was a time and place . . . Meg had the sensitivity to recognise both.

'You see what I mean,' Kirsty reminded the young woman as they stood admiring the sweet-pea display. 'Yon things of yours would never have stood a chance!'

But the young woman's mind lingered on *other* folk's sweet peas. As she stood, eavesdropping on the tale of a miracle, that would, for her, always retain its mystery.

'Madam Beaver isn't *always* reliable,' a lady was assuring a man with a first prize red ticket in his hand. 'Not always, true to colour. But *congratulations*! She came true for *you*.'

Kirsty's mail order catalogue had taken on a new dimension from the moment Finlay had offered the young woman 'a week's lowsing at the threshing mill. Providing the weather keeps up. Seeing as Elspeth – a contramashious bitch at the best of time – she decided against.'

She had never before lowsed at the threshing mill. An admission that Finlay had swept aside, assuring her that there was nothing to prevent her from trying. Not at the going rate of tenpence an hour. 'And *that*,' he had reminded her, 'was not to be sneezed at.'

Neither it was, the young woman conceded, as she sat studying the pages of the catalogue, which had now assumed its true function. A purveyor of goods, luring a customer, who now had a prospect of purchasing away and beyond the section marked 'footwear'.

Always she had been aware of her potential as a female, given the essential transformation.

> And you shall walk in silk attire
> A chain of gold you shall not lack . . .

'But why *you*? You've never lowsed at the threshing mill before.'

Her man's reaction to her good news was only to be expected. But never quite condoned. If there was a crock of gold lying ready to be lifted on the other side of Achullen Burn he would 'have his doubts' about reaching it because the burn was in spate.

'What about Kirsty and Meg?' he demanded. 'They've got experience . . .'

So much experience, the young woman discovered, that they had both rejected Finlay's tenpence an hour. All hell, Kirsty recollected, was let loose at the threshing mill. You could neither see yourself, nor anybody else, for that of it, with the chaff flying all over the place. Into your eyes. And blinding the young woman. You thought the thistles was bad enough, she reminded you. But wait you. Just wait you, till the yavins got at you. You'd be scratching yourself to the bone.

It was her back that lowsing always went for, Meg remembered. She could hardly straighten herself up, after a day at the threshing mill. The hardest tenpence an hour she had ever earned, and never wanted to earn another the like!

Her neither, Kirsty confirmed. Finlay knew better than to seek her! And as for old Randy Rob, him that owned the threshing mill. Eighty, if he was a day. And only two things on his mind in eighty years. And one of them was the threshing mill . . .

'All hell', as Kirsty had described it, was let loose as the traction engine, reeking with smoke, shuddered its way into the corn yard. The threshing mill, rattling and swaying behind it, seemed in a mood to part company with the engine, dragging it unwillingly along, piloted by 'the devil himself'. The young woman's first glimpse of Randy Rob completed Kirsty's impression of hell, as black as his own engine. His curses rose darkly up with the smoke.

'Watch out for Randy Rob there,' Beel advised her, as he rushed past, shouldering the forks. 'He'll have his hand up your skirt the minute you turn your back.'

'Fine lot of micies nesting in the sheaves,' Alick warned her as he passed, bending beneath a burden of empty sacks. 'They'll run as far up your legs as possible!'

'You'd better keep an eye on Possible,' the casual workers suggested, choking on their own laughter.

Only the Italians, isolated by their idleness from the frenzied busyness of all the other workers, seemed to share her bewilderment at the chaos in front of them.

'*Che? Che cosa . . . ?*'

She could find no answer to Luigi's query. No word of reply to the questions asked by his gesticulating hands.

Advice began to pour thick and fast from all airts of the corn yard.

'Back her up, man! Round with her. Round a bit yet! Too far. Too far. Back a bit. Forward!'

Unnerved at last by the contradictions surrounding him, the 'devil' leapt out of the traction engine.

'Where the hell do you want the bloody thing?'

'I could tell you,' Finlay snapped. 'But I'll keep that bit pleasure till next year, when we get our combine harvester.'

'*Non capisco*,' Luigi confided, sidling towards her. 'Me *non capisco* . . .'

'Me neither,' she assured Luigi, 'me neither.'

The strap that held the knife for cutting the 'bands' that tied the sheaves together had begun to cut into her wrist. It had to be tight, Finlay explained, when he fastened it on to her wrist. 'Else, slack, it will fly off and cut all our throats. It's as sharp as that.'

It needed to be sharp to cut the strong straw 'bands' fast enough to satisfy the 'devil' who fed them into the gaping maw of the threshing mill. Its haste and appetite inexorable. A malevolent creature. Crying out for corn. Its cry changing to a whine the moment she slackened pace, to straighten her back.

'Come on. Come on. Move yourself, quine. Move yourself,' the 'devil' bawled in her ear. 'Keep her going. Keep her going.'

'Fling a stone in her, quine!' Beel shouted from the top of the corn stalk. 'That will slow the bugger down. That will give us a breather.'

Leaping up and out from his mill hole, the 'devil' spurted across to the edge of the mill. 'Try that!' he snarled to Beel. 'Just you try that, my mannie, and you'll blow the whole caboodle up. Yourself along with it!'

The forkers, beginning to tire now, were flinging the sheaves across to her at random, their sharpness catching at and cutting her face. Half-blinded with the yavins attacking her from all directions, her rising anger became the only proof of her humanity. Alive only in the mechanical way the threshing mill itself was alive.

'Keep it clear! Keep it clear!' she could hear Finlay urging on the Italians, stumbling blindly around, struggling to clear the wind-blown chaff.

'Keep it clear, lads. Keep it clear!'

The pity she was beginning to feel for herself extended to, and encompassed, the Italians, setting her apart with them, from all the other workers, who seemed to be so lucky. Moving and living and having their being in a way of life that was familiar to them.

'You didn't come home for your dinner, then?' her man greeted her, when she got in from the threshing mill.

'I couldn't, I couldn't move to go anywhere. I just sat at the bottom of a corn stack, hoping to God I'd manage to rise up when the mill started again.'

That, her man pointed out, was just because it was her first time at the threshing mill. She would, he prophesied, find it easier the morn.

Times like these, she couldn't trust her own voice. Obscenities, known and unknown, would have risen up from their deep dark places to blacken out the world. Times like these, fantasy would come to her aid.

> Fish of the sea
> Come listen to me
> For I would beg a boon of thee.

Gold?

Aye. All the gold in the world.

Quiet, she would be, when she scattered all the gold in the world at her man's feet.

Here it is. Gold. All the gold in the world. You never need be anxious about money again . . .

'You'd be the better of a cup of tea,' he suggested. 'I'll put the kettle on. There's no need,' he turned at the scullery door, hesitant, as if in search of words that could penetrate the armour of her silence, 'there's no need to go back to the threshing mill the morn, if you're not feeling up to It. We'll manage. We'll manage fine.'

'It wasn't too bad,' she heard herself assuring him. Disarmed. Pleased and surprised by his rejection of all the gold in the world. 'Finlay was pleased with me. He said I'd the makings of a good lowser. Nearly as good as Elspeth,' she added, as an afterthought. That wasn't quite true, but she would have liked it to have been true.

Released at last from the pains and perils of the threshing mill, the young woman squeezed herself onto the wooden form, in a state of expectant euphoria.

'Ladies and gentlemen! Order please!'

Beel, in his new rôle as master of ceremonies, stood stiff in his Sunday suit with its white starched 'dickey', attempting to bring to heel the workers wandering around, criticising or condoning – according to their frame of mind – the transformation that had changed the familiar barn into the venue for the annual harvest home.

'If *that's* the band,' Kirsty said, drawing their attention to the fiddler and accordionist hovering together by the barn door, 'it's some *band!* You would have thought they could have risen to a piano.'

The entrance of the farmer with his own personal guests lagging behind him brought an order to the barn that Beel, unaided, hadn't managed to achieve.

'Take your partners!' he commanded, with the confidence

of one who now had authority behind him. 'Take your partners for the Grand March and Circassian Circle.'

'We'll never hear the end of *that!*' Kirsty hissed as the farmer, stepping forward, offered his arm to Finlay's wife to lead off in the Grand March. 'She'll be bragging about that for months,' Kirsty concluded.

'It's the custom,' Meg pointed out. 'She's the foreman's wife. He leads her off every year.'

'Custom or no custom,' Kirsty insisted, 'she's never got over it. She'll be on and on about it till next year.'

> 'March! March!
> Ettrick and Teviotdale
> Why my lads dinna ye
> March forward in order
> March! March!
> Eskdale and Liddesdale . . .'

The martial music, and the marchers, stumping around the barn stirred the young woman into action. 'Come on, Kirsty,' she pleaded. 'You and me. Come on. Let's get ourselves in amongst them.'

The young woman, Kirsty declared, declining the proposed partnership, could make a fool of herself if she like. That was up to *her*. But she, Kirsty, had no intention of doing likewise, not with 'everybody looking'.

Nobody was 'looking'. They should have gone through life invisible, Kirsty and Meg, their fear of attracting attention to themselves was so deeply rooted.

Even on social occasions like this, neither frill nor ribbon put forth a frivolous claim, no innocent coquetries, no small vanities. It was as if the whole chapter of their youth had been torn from their book, and they had turned the page from childhood to middle age.

Even so, the young woman was beginning to feel that maybe she *was* over-conspicuous in what had been her choice from Kirsty's catalogue, described as 'a frock in which to go forward into autumn. In a shade that blends with this most colourful season'.

The marchers, having finished applauding themselves, now scrambled around trying to reclaim their former places on the forms. For it was by no means certain that having given up your place you could claim it again. Which was why, Meg pointed out, as they listened to territorial disputes rising up around them, *they* had been wise to have simply sat on their backsides, and held on to their places.

'To give you all a chance to get your wind back,' Beel announced, 'I will now call for a song. On our good neighbour, Mistress Fraser. A song, Kirsty. If *you* please!'

' "The Barley Riggs", Kirsty,' the workers urged. 'Come on, Kirsty. Give us "The Barley Riggs" ' – starting up the chorus themselves, to encourage the song of their choice.

'One singer, one song,' Beel reminded them sharply, turning towards Kirsty. 'Right then, Kirsty. Is't to be "The Barley Riggs"?'

' "The Rowan Tree"!' Rising to her feet, Meg made Kirsty's mind up for her, momentarily depriving Beel of ceremonial authority. 'Kirsty, Mistress Fraser, will render "The Rowan Tree"!'

> 'Thy leaves were aye the first o' spring
> Thy flooers the summer's pride
> There wasna sic a bonnie tree
> In a' the countryside . . .'

Strange, now that everybody was looking, Kirsty seemed unaware. Maybe you could face the whole world, and its stares, when you could do something to perfection. The young woman hadn't known that Kirsty could sing. Not as she was singing now. Her voice, clear and sweet, rising up through the stillness that had come over the barn. If Kirsty and me could just sing to each other, she thought. Instead of speaking. We'd never contradict each other again.

> 'So fair wert thou in summer time
> Wi' a' thy clusters white
> How rich wert thou . . .'

There had been a rowan tree at the gale of her grandmother's house. And a bourtree at the back of it. As a city child, come to visit, she couldn't tell the difference between the two trees, in summer, their white flowering time. But to Grandmother, the rowan tree had been 'special', guarding the house within it from evil.

Strange, that Grandmother, who said prayers every night, and believed in them, had just as much faith in the rowan tree, at the gale end of her house. Maybe not so strange after all. The shadow of paganism. And its substance. Grandmother, suspended between heaven and earth, had been making sure of both worlds . . .

> 'How rich wert thou in autumn dress
> Wi' berries red and bright . . .'

'She used to sing all by herself in the kirk,' Meg whispered, as Kirsty made her way back to them. 'She did that. My, but Kirsty could sing.'

' "Corn Riggs and Barley Riggs"'!' Dave Smollet shouted, crashing through the blank that Kirsty's song had left behind. 'No excuses now. You all know the words.'

'Corn riggs and barley riggs
  And corn riggs are bonnie'

Swaying together along the forms, stamping their feet, they sang as if in a sudden burst of release.

'I have been blithe wi' comrades dear
I have been merry drinking
I have been joyful gathering gear
I have been happy thinking

'But of a' the pleasures e'er I kent
Tho' three times doubled fairly
That happy nicht was worth them a'
Amang the riggs wi' Annie

'Corn riggs and barley riggs
Corn riggs are bonnie . . .'

'Now that *that* lot are making themselves scarce,' Meg confided, as the farmer and his guests turned at the barn door, raising their arms in a wordless gesture that could have been one of benediction, or farewell, 'we'll see some fun! The flasks will be whipped from the men's hip pockets. And Beel will be legless before the night's out.'

'On your feet!' Finlay had now stepped swiftly into the role of mine host and master of ceremonies. 'Take your partners for an eightsome reel. You too, Meg! And you, Looeeshee! You can give Meg a birl or two . . .' For the first time the young woman became aware of Luigi, hovering on the threshold of the barn, as if unsure of his reception. As a fellow-worker, or as a prisoner-of-war.

She would dance now, despite Meg, despite Kirsty. With her man. But she would dance. For the joy of displaying her new frock. For the pride of 'showing off' her 'steps'. For the appreciation of Paolo.

'The cheek of Finlay,' Meg was protesting. 'Thinking *I* would dance with the Italian, and the cheek of the Looeeshee one. Forcing himself *here* in the first place. I'll say that for the other two Italians. They *know* their place.'

Strange, for once, and suddenly, she felt in agreement with Meg. A feeling of dislike for Luigi, standing grinning in the doorway, took hold of her. He wasn't Paolo.

'Come on, quine. On your feet. *We'll* show them.' Mellowed by the contents of the flask in his hip pocket, Finlay advanced towards her, 'We'll show them, quine!'

'And you showed them right enough,' Kirsty accused, as the three of them walked back together to the Cottar Row. 'Your petticoat flying above your head, flinging yourself about the barn like yon.'

'It was Finlay's fault. You saw that for yourselves. He was trying to birl me off my feet.'

'He wouldn't have danced with one of *us*,' Kirsty pointed out, 'if he hadn't had a good dram inside of him.'

She *should* have said it, she reminded herself, as she watched Kirsty and Meg disappear round the gale end. She had meant to say it, wanted to say it . . . O Kirsty, but you sang right bonnie the nicht.

> Wi' a' thy clusters white
> How rich wert thou
> In autumn dress

The sound of laughter drifted across from the bothy. Bicycles, slanted against its walls, proved that Paolo and Umberto were celebrating the end of harvest in their own

way, with their own kind from the main camp. Stiffening
at the sound of approaching footsteps, the young woman,
preparing to confront and dismiss Luigi, turned at the sound
of her man's voice . . .

'That was a real good night. Finlay and Beel were in fine
form.'

'Aye,' she agreed, making no mention of the fact that
Paolo hadn't set eyes on a frock that 'vied with the colours
of autumn'.

'That's that, then. For another year.' The finality of Kirsty's
observation held within it a tone of regret, as they stood
together, watching the men clearing out the barn after the
harvest home. Sounding to the young woman as if the whole
of their year could be concentrated into the essence of a
single day.

'There's Christmas,' she ventured, in an effort to salvage
something out of the bleak prospect.

But Christmas, as Meg pointed out, wasn't the same.
Except for the bairns.

'Hogmanay, then.'

'You can keep your Hogmanay,' Kirsty snapped, rejecting
Hogmanay as if the young woman herself had invented that
festival. As far as Kirsty was concerned, Hogmanay 'just
makes work for the wives. And beasts of the men'.

'Sing horse. And you'll get corn,' Meg advised Finlay as
he came into sight. Weaving from one side of the grass verge
to the other, examining pot-holes in the road that led to the
loft.

'That damned lorries again!' he grumbled,, turning into
the field. 'They'll have no bloody road left!

That, as Kirsty explained, was 'the bee in Finlay's bonnet'.
For a constant war waged between Finlay and the lorry
drivers from the town. No quarter given, no battle either

won or lost. The weight of the lorries, and the speed of their drivers churning up the stones and howking great holes in the road, leaving the task of filling them up again to the men on the farm. A task never to their liking. And one they considered, and rightly in *Kirsty's* opinion, outwith their particular territory. There would, she prophesied, 'be hell to pay now that the lorries would be coming with winter feed for the cattle. And here comes the *first* of them!'

'You stupid-looking bugger!' Finlay shouted, waving his fist under the nose of the driver whose lorry slanted precariously between the ditch and the bend of the road, I've gotten a mind to put my foot up your backside and getting *you* down into filling up this road. My men have better things to do than kirn about with holes in the road. They're not bloody navvies. You stupid . . .'

'Bugger! *Stupido* . . .' Darting out from amongst the men, Luigi had come to Finlay's support. 'Bugger! *Stupido!*'

'That's *it*, Looeeshee. Go on. *You* tell them.'

'Bloody wop!' Stung into retaliation by the intervention of Luigi, the driver leapt down from his cab. 'Italian bastard!'

'Put a finger on that man,' Finlay warned the driver. 'Just one finger and you can say fareweel to that damned lorry of your. For it's an *ambulance* you'll be needing, my mannie.'

There would be no lifting of the tatties today, nor the morn, not if the rain kept dinging on like this. But the real storm, the furious conflict between the wind and the rain was being waged high over the firth. For the earth itself never put up a fight against the vagary of such weather, but laid itself down, flat and desolate, in submission.

It had upset Kirsty, her bairns 'let off' school to help with the 'lifting' . . . 'In and out amongst her feet'.

'Keep away from that bothy!' Her voice rose in warning

to the bairns. 'I've told you before. And will not be telling you again. Keep away from the *Italians*!'

Bird-like, the bairns seemed to the young woman. Hopping cautiously but curiously up to peep through the bothy window. Fluttering away in a startled group as their mother's threats became louder.

'This weather,' Kirsty confided to the young woman, 'will suit the Italians. Nothing to do but sit on their backsides in the bothy. It will fair suit them.'

It suited the terns, taking up its challenge, scudding high across the firth, wheeling defiantly round in the teeth of the wind, filling them out with white pride, like pictures the young woman had seen of sailing ships in olden times. Hard to tell whether the crying of the terns sounded distress or delight. Delight, she liked to think, as she watched them zooming down and rising high. Like fighter planes, across the firth.

'Nothing for look,' Luigi lamented, when she went into the bothy with their milk, where he stood gazing out of the window to the rain-blurred hill. 'In Scotland, nothing for look. Tatties and turnips. Wind and rain. Wind. The bloody wind.'

They said that pigs could see the wind. Whiles, the young woman had the feeling that Luigi could 'see' the wind, the feud between himself and the wind becoming almost personal. This she could understand. Time and again the wind had sent herself and Kirsty and Meg on a futile search for the towels and pillow-slips it had filched from their washing lines. To be found again, an autumn away, hidden and discoloured beneath the bramble bushes. You must never, she remembered, pick the brambles when the Devil spits upon them ...

But it was the grapes that Luigi was crying out for now.

Mourning their loss . . . 'No one get grapes for *Mama mia*. No *vino*. No sun. No *divertimento*. Plenty grapes, Napoli. Molto, molto. Plenty sun. Plenty *vino*. Plenty, plenty, Napoli.'

She was almost tempted to let her mind linger in his sunlit wine-drenched land, but her voice rose in defence of her own countryside. 'Not *always* wind, Scotland, Luigi. Not always rain. You *wait*!' she urged. 'You *see*! You look on hill when heather comes. September . . .'

She had not yet learned to avoid the pit-falls that could send Luigi pacing the floor in a gloom of anger, had not yet learned to avoid pin-pointing time, bringing its passing to his attention.

'*Settembre. Quando? Quando? Quando? Quando finita la guerra? Quando? Quando? Mama Mia!*'

She could sense the wordless reproach of the others. The rustling of the pages of Umberto's book. Paolo's renewed attack on his blocks of wood.

'You make, Paolo. You finish?' Moving towards him, she stretched to touch the wooden figure in his hands. The way she might reach out at passing jetsam, after a shipwreck. 'You make, Paolo. Beautiful . . .'

'Paolo *stupido*,' Luigi accused, diverting his anger. '*Molto stupido*. Make for *bambini*. Not for sell. Friends camp. Giovanni. Giuseppe. Plenty make. The rings. Brooches. For sell. For money, for play cards. For cigarettes. Paolo? No. No sell. *Stupido* . . .'

The weather had settled itself at last. Dry with a touch of frost. Promising fine for the tattie howking. Another landscape lost, the young woman realised, staring down on a field of withered tattie shaws. Her eyes had become accustomed to the purple blaze and yellow bloom of the tattie field in flower. She would miss that.

'Tatties,' she shouted to Luigi, as he trundled past in the

bogie. 'Tatties for ever!' It was one of their jokes, bridging the difference between their staple diets. God alone knew how the Italians could stomach macaroni, Meg always declared. Since she herself 'couldn't stomach the stuff!' An avowal that puzzled the young woman, since Meg frankly boasted of never having tasted it.

Maybe God *did* have something to do with it, she remembered, the memory smiling her. They liked cheese, the Italians, but not calfie's cheese, the cheese she herself made from the first yield of the cow's milk after calving. '*Che cosa? Che?*' Luigi would query, gazing down in bewilderment on her blood-red offering. Crossing himself as he gazed. A ritual that seemed to her not only a recognition of the presence of God, but a protection against potential Evil.

Kirsty and Meg, shaking the mats outside their doors, emptying their ash around the shrubs in their yards, were not yet ready to set off for the tattie field. The unreadiness of reluctance to leave their homes and housework behind.

Their bairns were on their way, though. Banging on their pails as they raced past her door. Grabbing up her own pail, the young woman ran to catch up with them.

> O we can play on the big bass drum
> And this is the way we do it!
> Bang! Bang! Bang!
> On the big bass drum
> And this is the music to it!

She would have little breath for singing, Kirsty informed the young woman when herself and Meg got down to the field. Aye, would she. By the time this day was done. *They* had better things to do, herself and Meg, than caper around with the bairns. *Or* to fash, putting curlers in their hair for tattie howking. She couldn't even *sleep* in the things, Meg declared, she just turned and tossed all night. Still, Kirsty concluded ominously, they knew what all the palaver was in aid of. They weren't born yesterday.

So. They *knew*. They had noticed. Strange that the young woman could still delude herself, that the changes coming over her had not been apparent to others.

'*Bella*,' Luigi greeted her, as she walked towards the tattie pit. '*Bella. Bella.*

Paolo, squatting on his upturned pail, was oblivious to her presence. All her preparation, her keen anticipation of the early morning, fell away from her. Appreciation, like the rising wind, was coming from the wrong direction.

Reeshling through the tattie shaws to the pit, Kirsty and Meg now arrived at the point of debate. The sight of the Italians sitting at ease sent them straight into the attack.

The riddling of the small tatties for next year's seed had hitherto been Elspeth's job. Now that there was no Elspeth on the 'squad', it was but *right* that it should fall to one of themselves, since it was, after all, 'a *woman's* job'.

'Or a bairn's,' Beel reminded them, backing his tractor away from the pit.

There were times, right enough, when Beel got all above himself. This was threatening to be one of them. They would, Kirsty reminded him, 'see what *Finlay* had to say about that. Him being the boss.'

His authority confirmed, Finlay put it to immediate purpose.

The best thing, he suggested, the squad could do was just to get hold of their pails. And get themselves to the top of the drills. As fast as maybe.

'When the digger's ready,' Kirsty pointed out with some degree of satisfaction. 'By the looks of it, it will never be ready.' An observation which passed unchallenged. For it was true. And it was familiar. No matter, no matter how much time and work was spent in getting the mechanical machinery 'right and ready' for their seasonal tasks, they seemed to rear themselves up in objection the moment they were confronted by their tasks.

They could, the women agreed regretfully, as they eased themselves down amongst the straw, prepared for a long wait, have had their washing out on the line, on a good day like this. Not much drying in it. But the wind was still rising, with that touch of frost in it that always seemed to whiten the sheets.

'That'll be my new catalogue,' Kirsty claimed, when they spied Postie leaning her bicycle up against the dyke. 'You can save Postie's legs for her,' she shouted to the bairns, brandishing the withered shaws as they chased each other round the pit. 'You can get my catalogue.'

'Posseeble *me!*' Luigi had leapt to his feet, stumbling through the tattie shaws. 'Posseeble *lettera* ME. Posseeble . . .'

Never expectant of letters herself, the young woman had taken no notice of the coming of the mail, until the Italians came, finding herself now looking for letters, through *their* eyes.

'Domani, Luigi,' she would try to console in the long, letterless days. 'Letter *domani*. Maybe letter *domani*.'

'*Domani. Domani. Sempre domani!*' He was right about that, her habit of holding out a vague promise of tomorrow, for the certain disappointment of today.

'No lettera. No *lettera Mama Mia*. One month, two month, *five* month. No *lettera*. Maybe *morte*. *Mama Mia* . . .' Directing his emotion from herself to the Madonna on the wall, a source of more powerful consolation, with a greater capacity to bear the brunt of the blame.

'Nobody get *vino* for *Mama Mia*. No for *mangiare*.

Nobody for work for *Mama Mia* . . .*Quando, QUANDO finita la guerra?* . . .'

Times like these, Paolo huddled on his stool, Umberto hidden behind a book, it seemed as if Luigi had deprived them of all *their* emotion, had grabbed it to himself, and shook it fist-high in the face of Heaven and of the Madonna.

The digger in working order at last, Finlay loped towards them, where they stood determined at the tattie pit. What ailed them all then, what was the trouble now, he demanded. 'The riddling,' Meg said. 'A woman's job. Not right that the Italians should have it.'

'The Italians,' Finlay assured her, 'don't want your bloody jobs. The Italians, poor buggers, couldn't tell the difference between a tattie shaw and a tattie tuber, never mind wanting to riddle the rooshac tatties.' The Italians would do just as they were told, Finlay confirmed, his patience beginning to desert him. And so would the women, he prophesied, if they wanted to keep their jobs, that was. And lucky to have jobs at all, with land girls springing up all over the place, just waiting for the chance to jump into their shoes.

'That'll be right,' Kirsty muttered, as they scrambled to collect their pails. 'No land girl on this earth would work under Finlay.' And if she *did*, Kirsty concluded, she would be as daft as they themselves were.

> 'Bless them all
> Bless them all
> The long and the short
> And the tall'

'I hope you've lifted that drill clean,' Finlay shouted, as the young woman sang past him, on the way to the top of the field to start on a new rigg.

'Clean as a whistle, Finlay,' she assured him.

'Just you get yourself back here,' Finlay commanded, 'and give Meg and Kirsty a hand to finish *their* drills.'

She had forgotten. In the release of spirit that had over-taken her, she had forgotten the unwritten rule, made by themselves, for themselves, to help each other to keep up the same working pace. A mutual insurance against days when they 'didn't feel up to it', against the threat of old age, and the ailments it brought in its wake. She had forgotten. Old age seemed so far away from herself. And tiredness was still something outwith her ken.

'We'll manage, Finlay,' Meg shouted from her drill. 'We've managed before by ourselves. We'll manage again.'

It always took a little time to work your way back into the fold, to get on friendly terms with Meg and Kirsty again. Sometimes, sometimes the young woman felt that she had to humour the whole wide world. Her man. Kirsty and Meg. The Italians. Delving within herself for words that might atone for her breach of the Rule, she could feel the loss of her own identity.

'*They* didn't break their backs the day,' she said, as Paolo and Umberto mounted their bicycles, and went freewheeling past them down the road.

'Whiles,' Meg reflected, as they watched the Italians dis-appear, 'whiles, I feel it's me, myself, that's the prisoner. Hardly ever getting away from the place. The Italians, now, they're always on top of the road. Always going somewhere. If it's not off to Mass, as they call it, it's up and away to confession. But, no doubt, they've got plenty to confess.'

'*You* should become a Catholic then, Meg,' the young woman suggested teasingly. 'Then *you* could be up and off.'

If, Meg said, firmly rejecting the suggestion, *if* she ever had anything to confess, her tone implying that was highly unlikely, she would go straight to her Maker to do so. Not to some Popish priest who was only a man, after all.

'It's not dinner time yet,' the young woman warned, as Luigi huddled past her door. 'It's not nine o'clock yet.' Another 'off day' for Luigi.

She was beginning to read the signals that brought them on. Mist as thick as a wall had closed itself around the farm, which took its mood from the weather, just as it took its colour from the passing seasons. The fog had kept the sun from setting, and the moon from rising, holding it, white and startled, suspended in the sky. Only the dull and distant hammering of the men repairing the fences gave witness to a world that was still inhabited. An 'odd job' day. Neither here nor there. With neither positive beginning nor satisfying ending.

'Me sick. *Soffrire* me,' Luigi mumbled over his shoulder. Turning at the bothy door to assure her that he had Finlay's permission to get off work, his state of mind sounding in the defiance of his voice. A defiance that found its echo in the anger beginning to rise up in herself, as she waited for the knock that was sure to come.

'Though I speak with the tongues of men and of angels', she remembered. For she had always liked to hear the minister expounding on that, though all she wanted now was a down-to-earth working knowledge of Italian, so that she could berate Luigi in his own tongue: 'You are cunning. You get off work to get at me alone. You think I am vulnerable, sorry because you didn't get a letter. You are cunning . . .'

She didn't know the word for sly or cunning, when the knock came. 'No possible' was all that she could find to say. All that Luigi could understand . . .

'No possible.'

'Me sick. Me *soffrire*. Too much *soffrire* me. *One* time.
One time posseeble?'

'No possible, Luigi. No one time possible.'

'*Paolo* posseeble! Posseeble Paolo. Paolo you like.' Left
without words in any language at all, she realised that her
feeling for Paolo was transparent.

'What about the Italians' milk?' her man was asking. 'Are
you not taking it in to them then?'

'In a minute. They can wait. Surely to God they can wait
a *minute*!'

Her outburst was not against her man, taken unaware, but
a protest against fear. A fear that was almost physical. Like
a thin, yellow worm, beginning to crawl around inside her.
Her own man, her own kitchen, had taken on a sudden
safety that she felt reluctant to leave.

Luigi's 'off day' had infected the bothy, as she knew it would.

'Too much *sick* Luigi.' Vehemence, rare in Paolo, took her
by surprise, although not directed at herself but intended for
Luigi. 'Me sick,' he claimed. 'Umberto sick. Everybody sick.
Me work. Umberto work. Sick similar.'

His resentment would never reach Luigi, would never
penetrate. Despair had taken on the tangible form of a man
lying face downwards on a bed, hidden by blankets.

'*Domani* Luigi work. *Domani* Luigi joke. Plenty joke.
Domani,' Paolo informed Umberto as they went to the table.
'Today. *No* joke. No work.' Two prisoners sat down
together at the table. They had eliminated the third.

A lack of mutual compassion was an aspect that was new
to the young woman struggling to find words to overcome
it. She knew them all right. Surely. *Surely* since you are all
in the same boat. Surely . . .

But she hadn't forgotten the Italian for that.

'*Domani*. Luigi OK today. No like. *Me* no like. *Umberto* no like. *Soffrire* similar . . .'

Shoving his plate away from him, and clattering his knife and fork on the table, Paolo leapt to his feet, and retreated to his stool by the fire, cupping his down-bent head in his hands. 'Me too. Me *soffrire*.'

'Eat, Paolo.' She tried to persuade him. '*Mange*. Eat, Paolo.'

Maybe, maybe compassion had another side to itself. Not just an understanding of suffering, but an involvement with it.

Luigi had gone beyond captivity. Umberto, eating calmly at the table, held himself aloof from it. There were only two prisoners in the bothy now.

But she wasn't a prisoner, not a *real* one. All *she* had to do was just turn around and walk out. It was her legs that refused to take her to freedom. She needed the password for that. She hadn't got it, but knew it was necessary. The knock on the bothy wall ended her search. 'Husband,' she said. 'Married me. Knocking for me.'

'There should never be three,' she reflected when she got back to the safety of her kitchen. 'Never three.'

'Three what?' her man asked, puzzled.

'Three prisoners. Three of anything.'

Nobody knew that better than herself – the whole cottar world knew that – they always disliked to find themselves in a cottar row of three houses. For there was always one left out . . .

Come to think of it though, where would Meg and Kirsty be in those times when they 'fell out' with each other if they hadn't got herself as the go-between. The recipient of their 'honest opinions' of each other. The ultimate bearer of the olive branch, which both wanted to extend but for which each claimed that she had 'too much pride'. Maybe, maybe three in such confined, close-knit circumstances was essential after all. A buffer was needed. She was beginning to recognise Umberto, the school-teacher's rôle.

Now is the hour
That we collect our pay

The young woman sang out as herself and Kirsty waited for Meg, kirning about amongst the shrubs at her door. Meg was always like that, Kirsty complained, always pretending that she was in no hurry for her wages. All put on, just. Pretending that she wasn't as hard up as the rest of them.

If she had *one* regret, Meg confided, when they got to her door, it was this jasmine bush. Always in leaf. Never in flower. Her one wish, that she should have remembered to take the jasmine from her last cottar house. She had grown it herself, from a cutting no bigger than her finger. But then, you knew yourselves what 'flitting' was like. By the time she'd got her bit sticks furniture loaded up on the cart, the mare was fit to bolt with all the clang and clatter going on around her. That was her one wish. For she never had jasmine that bloomed like yon. Never before, nor since.

Too small a wish for such a long regret. You needed magic for the granting of a *real* wish. For the gaining of something outwith the bounds of probability. The young woman was almost tempted to reveal the heart and matter of a *real* wish . . .

One week. Just one. Out of all my life. To spend with Paolo. Then I could live fine for the rest of my life with my own man.

'Canada,' she told them. 'That's *my* one wish. I'd like to see Canada.' And near enough true, it was distance that made a lie of it. Canada was a long way from a village near Rome.

Instantly regretting, not the lie, but the utterance of it. For it brought Elspeth immediately to mind. It wasn't likely that Elspeth would set foot in Canada now, Kirsty remembered. Nor that she would set foot in the farm again, not with the Italians around.

'It wasn't the Italians' fault,' the young woman ventured. 'Not *our* Italians. They weren't even *at* Monte Cassino.'

'*Our* Italians.' Kirsty, considering the claim, sniffed in rejection.

'They're Italians all the same,' Meg snapped, remembering Abyssinia. Minding it, she said, as clear as anything. Because the minister had got so worked up about it in his sermon, 'he nearly flung himself out of the pulpit. With the rage that was on him.'

The young woman, ignorant of what had happened in Abyssinia, let her thoughts touch warily down on the here and now. On that other difficulty that had pushed itself into her days, the meetings with Elspeth when the vans came round. Grocer. Butcher. Baker. Dreaded days of the week. Not that Elspeth ever uttered. It was her silence that hurt.

They must have come into a fortune, Finlay deduced, as he handed them their wages. For they had been in no hurry to collect them. Still. If *they* didn't want *their* money, that was all right by him. He could do fine with it. Himself, apparently, not being endowed with *their* worldly wealth. His one fear *was*, now that they'd got their hand on it, they would make straight for The Tappit Hen, and get drunk.

Finlay would have his little joke, they agreed, as they made their way back to the cottar row. For none of them had ever set foot in a pub. They left that to the women of the town. Still, they concluded, Finlay wasn't all that bad. Not when you got to the bottom of him. He hadn't even kept that hour off her, Meg remembered. That time she had to wait in for the doctor for Jamie's shingles. She had worked for a foreman once who kept ten minutes off your pay if you didn't turn up 'on the dot'!

Although they had never tasted drink, itself, the wage packets, tucked deep down inside their coat pockets, always had an intoxicating effect on them. Their *own* money. Earned by *themselves*. Giving them the illusion of independence. To be spent, in illusory moments like these, on themselves. In a conspiracy of spirit.

> 'From the bonnie bells of heather
> We brewed ale in auld lang syne'

The young woman started to sing in an uprush of feeling that had come over them. Each for the other.

> 'It was sweeter far than honey
> It was stronger far than wine . . .'

They hadn't really seen the heather this year, Meg reminded them, tugging them to a standstill, to reflect on the enormity of such a loss. They'd just never got the length of the hill. Time had flown by so fast. And they had no idea where it had gone. There would be other times though. The hill would always be there. At least they had managed to pick the blackberries. A lesser pleasure, the young woman remembered. Riving and tugging amongst the thorny bushes, to emerge as fretful as porcupines. Linking arms together again, they set off for the Cottar Row.

> It was sweeter far than honey
> It was stronger far than wine.

The young woman was, on this night, the most affluent wife

in the Cottar Row, with silver in the tea caddy. And paper money under the mattress.

Snecking her door, she drew her curtains to shut out the inquisitive eye of the night before she settled down at the kitchen table to help her man with the count. They knew to a sixpence how much the tea caddy contained. And to a pound how much lay under the mattress. But this was the night of the grand total, with its addition of harvest money. Mill money. And tattie money . . . 'All the gold in the world', she remembered. Here it was, spread out in front of them. It had taken on a different dimension from past nights of reckoning though, and become a kind of atonement for the guilt she felt for the betrayal of her feelings towards her man. If he had been a bad man, she thought as she watched him, quiet and serious, smoothing out the crumpled bank notes, or if only he had been her father, or even her brother . . . Jumping up from the table, she could hear herself beginning to gabble. She had worked hard at the threshing mill, hadn't she now? Even Finlay admitted that. She would work there again. It was well worth it. Wasn't it? Kirsty and Meg didn't have as much money as *she* had the night. But they, they hadn't worked as hard as her. Wasn't that right?

'Aye,' her man agreed. That was right, that was right enough. Advising her to 'settle yourself down now. Or you'll put me clean off the count.' The real joy of the count lay in the spending of the total.

'Curtains,' she suggested. 'New curtains. Like the ones Kirsty got out of her catalogue.'

There was nothing wrong with the curtains they had, her man pointed out. They were more in need of new planks to shore up the old hen house.

'Cockerels, then. Six-week-old cockerels, for fattening up. To sell to the butcher's van at Christmas.'

'Some late for that,' her man reminded her, 'with Christmas only weeks away.'

'What about bikes, then? Two second-hand bikes.'

He saw no need for bikes either. 'Not when the milk lorry runs us into town. On our day off.'

That was only once a month, she protested. There were other times. Other places to see.

Never as far as Napoli, though. Never as far as Roma.

Extra money never bought 'extra' things, she realised, as she let the coins trickle through her fingers, having lost interest in their purchasing power. It came down to essentials after all.

'Even the prisoners have bikes,' she reflected, as the sounds of laughter reached them from the bothy next door.

'They have that,' her man agreed. 'But then, *they* didn't have to pay for them.'

Kirsty and Meg had already perched themselves up in the dyke. On the look out for the grocer's van. And Elspeth had begun to make her way down the hill from Achullen. Poised uncertainly on her doorstep, the young woman decided to join the other wives before Elspeth reached them. She found it easier to stand quiet, within the silence that Elspeth's presence always brought with it now, than to go crashing through, and into the middle of it.

Strange how herself and Elspeth, who had always had so much to speak about, now seemed to communicate through the voices of Meg and Kirsty.

'Grocer. *Quando*?' Luigi's voice rang across from the steps of the bothy. '*Quando*? Grocer.' Unwilling to respond, the young woman squeezed herself further into the circle of her silent neighbours.

'Your Italian friend is crying on you,' Kirsty nudged her, breaking the silence, turning away to confide in Elspeth.

'Little did I think. Little did I dream that a day would come, when we'd have to share the grocer's van with prisoners-of-war.'

'Italians at that,' Elspeth said. For *their* men, she concluded, *their* prisoners-of-war in Germany wouldn't get such liberties. *Their* men wouldn't have a copper in their pockets to lash out on anything they fancied.

'It's only pocket money,' the young woman protested. 'Only for little extras. Shaving soap. Things like that.'

'Shaving soap!' The very idea of it, Kirsty claimed, took her breath away. Though it seemed to leave her with enough breath to belittle the commodity, claiming that a bit of carbolic, 'worked up into a lather', was good enough for *her* man. An ounce of bogie a week. A pint of ale on a Saturday. That was the extent of Kirsty's man's 'extras'.

There was, the young woman thought, something in Kirsty's condemnation. *Her* man had said the selfsame thing about the second-hand bikes. Extras were rare in their own lives, hard to come by.

'*Quando? Quando* come grocer?'

'For the love of goodness,' Meg advised the young woman, 'have a word with that Italian of yours, or he'll stand bawling there all night.'

'*Pronto!*' she shouted across to Luigi. 'Grocer *pronto*.' The anger she heard rising up in her voice was inexplicably directed against him.

'She can even *speak* Italian now,' Elspeth said, turning to the other wives.

They rightly referred to the grocer's van, rather than to the grocer himself. Peering down on them from between its shelves, his bulk prevented them from having a real good look at his wares, as if he, himself, were reluctant to reveal them. What was it that 'the Eyetie' wanted, he demanded, in a tone that implied whatever it was, he might not be of a mind to supply it.

'Pig. Pig me like. *Prego.*'

Flummoxed by Luigi's request, the grocer's van threw it to the waiting wives for their consideration. ''Pig,' he says. Well, well then, so he would like pig.'

'It's bacon he wants.' The young woman stepped forward. '*Bacon.* That's what he wants.'

He would need coupons for that, the grocer's van snapped. And as far as *he* knew, prisoners didn't have coupons.

That was right, the young woman conceded. Their coupons were held in the camp. He could, she offered, have some of hers, since there was no law against that! There was no virtue in her offer. It was just that bacon – a luxury at *any* time – was seldom on her own list.

Herself and Meg, Kirsty offered, would see Elspeth up the length of the hill. For it was just the night for a walk. It was, the young woman remembered, watching them set off together, the kind of night she liked in the days when she accompanied Elspeth. The frost sealed the world to itself. It held the earth, as the moon took to the sky. It would already have begun to weave its fine silver webs on every whin bush from here up to Achullen. She could never resist drawing her fingers through those fine silver webs. A compulsion, for touch's sake. To see if they felt as cold as they looked. Strange, that she should remember such a small pleasure with such regret.

'You no walk? No walk with friends?' Luigi put his arm across her shoulder.

'No. Too cold for me. Too much cold.'

'Sileence!' Luigi shot up his arm in command, when she opened the door of the bothy. 'Sileence. Umberto write. *Lettera* for me. *Mama Mia.*'

Paolo, on his stool by the fire, sat entwining his rosary

beads around his fingers. The way that Elspeth used to wind her wool on winter nights. 'Scusi,' Paolo greeted her, starting to rise up from the stool. 'No, Paolo,' easing him down, she shook her head. 'YOU *scusi*. You *scusi* ME.'

Luigi, crouched over Umberto's shoulder, as if such close physical contact could instil Umberto with words, the words that Luigi himself struggled to find, was beginning to batter against the barrier of Umberto's objections and rejections.

It wasn't possible, Umberto insisted. 'Imposseeble' for Luigi to mention in a letter that some friends from Napoli had arrived at the main camp. Censorship, Umberto pointed out, would never pass that. Censorship, it appeared, would never pass any of the things Luigi wanted to write.

'*Perche*? *Perche*? *Perche* imposseeble? *PERCHE*?'

Perche. Luigi's anguished whys began to pervade the bothy, countered by the calm, sharp logic of the ex-school-teacher, until it seemed that nothing worth communicating could ever be penned.

Tearing the letter from Umberto's hands, to utter the half-truths it contained – Health good . . . plenty rain . . . time soon pass . . . food OK . . .

'*Clock*,' she said, minding on her mission and moving towards the mantelpiece to reset their alarm clock. 'Tomorrow, one hour early. Tomorrow, winter come.'

A cold snap had set in. On a morning like this, you'd want to crack the frost-bound world wide open. The men were already setting out to do so. Armed with forks to crash through the ice on the cattle troughs. The others armed with billhooks on their way to the turnip field, on an even more arctic expedition.

'It's neeps or forks,' Finlay was bawling at Luigi. It was always the same when the men were divided into two squads. It always set Luigi dithering, wondering which job would be the easier. Even now with the bogies starting to move off, he darted between one and the other, holding everything and everybody up.

'The one's as bad as the other,' Finlay roared. 'You can either break your back pulling neeps. Or dislocate your shoulder cracking ice. And I don't give a bugger *what* you do, so long as you get a move on and *do* it!'

'Gloves no good,' the young woman tried to persuade Luigi, as he hunched himself round to the back of the turnip bogie. Muffled from head to foot in his balaclava and top coat. Looking for all the world like a picture she had once seen of Scott of the Antarctic. A different kind of explorer, Luigi, but still an explorer adrift in an alien world of turnip shaws and cattle troughs.

'Gloves no good for turnips,' she assured him. 'Gloves get wet. Fingers get frozen.'

> 'O come all ye faithful
> Joyful and triumphant . . .'

she could hear Kirsty carolling more clearly than she could see her. A dim figure, sweeping her doorstep against the snow whirling down around her. A waste of energy, but not of spirit. Simply a bursting free from the ice-bound days.

'Thank God the snow's come at last!' Kirsty shouted across to her. 'It'll take the bite out of the air.'

Even so, Kirsty's largess of spirit didn't extend to accepting the young woman's invitation to accompany her to Achullen Wood, in search of holly. Although there were holly trees in Achullen Wood, not a one of them, Kirsty claimed, had ever borne a berry. Not in all her years of knowing them.

But then, they were wary, Kirsty and Meg, of the wild abundance that flourished outside their own small, cultivated yards. And the wildness had long since gone out of the flowers they grew and cherished. Flowers with heart-remembered names. Snow in Summer. Lad's Love. Dusty Miller. Heart's Ease.

How horrified Kirsty had been last spring when the young woman had gathered hawthorn blossom and set it in a jar on her windowsill. Kirsty's mother would never allow her to bring hawthorn blossoms into the house, certain that trouble or death would follow in its wake.

She hadn't believed that of course. But the idea of it had darkened the white cloud of flowers, had dulled her pleasure in them. Sown by a word, superstition's omen became accepted.

Achullen Wood stood white and sculptured in the precision of its winter, defying an intruder to leave a footmark that would break into the delicately traced signatures of its own inhabitants. Defying an intruder to sound out against its silence, the snap of the holly branches shouting sacrilege in her ears.

She had warned her well, Kirsty said, staring on the berryless bounty the young woman had lugged back to the Cottar Row. For Kirsty knew fine there would be not a berry on the holly. It would, she pointed out regretfully, have been far better to have collected fir cones in the autumn, and painted them all over with yon silver stuff, the way that wife had shown them at the WRI. Still, Kirsty conceded, they'd had more on their minds than silver cones in the autumn. Forbye, it was a real 'scutter' of a job. If you hadn't 'got the hands' for it. But surely, surely, the young woman wasn't going to kirn up her kitchen with that berryless stuff.

It was really for the Italians, the young woman explained. They set such store by Christmas.

It was to be *hoped*, Kirsty protested, that they wouldn't be kicking up a din, like they always did, with the comings and goings from the camp of strange Italians that you'd never set eyes on. And all the singing that was on them all, into all hours of the night.

She had set the holly in a jar on the windowsill of the bothy. Three Christmas cards on their mantelpiece. And put the box of dates she had wheedled from the grocer's van on the table.

'*Buona Natale*,' she greeted the Italians. '*Buona Natale*.'

The singing that had rung out from the bothy last night left no echo behind itself this morning. If I could paint, she thought, staring round the bothy, I couldn't capture Christmas. Only a jumbled image of letterless days. Selected by time. Pounced upon. Held high in time's hands for microscopic examination.

'*Buona Natale*, she said again to the silent figures on the frieze of her perception. '*Buona Natale*.'

'Christmas ITALIA!' mumbled Luigi from beneath the blankets.

'*Natale* here too, Luigi.'

'ITALIA *Natale*.'

'*Natale* everywhere.'

'*Prego. Molto gentile*.' Paolo's voice reached her as she made for the door. '*Grazie*.'

Maybe Christmas *could* only happen in Italy, she thought, gazing across on the turnip field where the men were already at work. There was no sign of it on the farm.

'We're in for it now, then,' her man prophesied, as the bicycles rang past their door. 'That'll be some of them over from the camp. We'll be in for a night of it.'

Maybe the Mass the Italians had attended in the morning had worked some Christmas wonder – beyond the power of holly, and three Christmas cards.

'We were *invited*,' she reminded her man. 'You too.' *She* could please herself. But not *him*. He would never, he claimed, understand a word they were saying.

She didn't understand many of the words either, but she could sometimes interpret the sound of them . . .

The whole of Italia seemed to be crowded inside the bothy. The emotionalism of the relationship between the prisoners something beyond her ken. A physical embrace between men, something she had never seen before. They were sparing of loving words and gestures, the men on the farm. If ever she were to set eyes on Finlay clasping Beel in his arms she would have thought they had lost their wits in a world that had come to an end.

'*Buona Natale, signorina.*' One of the visiting Italians stepped forward to greet her.

'*Buona Natale,* ' she responded, smiling because she knew she had got the accent right.

'*Parla italiano. Lei parla italiano.*' He swung round to inform the company. '*Allora! Lei parla . . .*'

His reaction overwhelmed her, forcing her into truth. '*Poco italiano. Poco poco . . .*'

'*Poco. Poco!*' They began to surround her. Grinning in appreciation. '*Bene. Bene.*'

'Dance me.' Elbowing his way through them, Luigi laid claim on her. 'Dance. Me.'

'*Che bella cosa,*' he sang, his head thrown back, his eyes closed as they circled as if in a trance.

'*Che bella cosa,*' the others took up the song, serenading her within a circle of music.

'*Che bella cosa . . .*'

Never before had she felt so desirable. Knowing in that moment how Eve must have felt, waking up from the trance of her creation, to look into the dark, appreciative eyes of Adam.

Coyness, which until now, she hadn't known she possessed, took over. Brought to the surface by her awareness of Paolo's presence. Surely he would see her *now*, reflected in the admiration of other men's eyes.

Tomorrow, she would feel ashamed of her posturing, of her emphasis on her physical attributes. So blatantly displayed, an offering to Paolo.

It could never be Paolo. She realised that, catching a glimpse of him, seated on the windowsill, absorbed in conversation with a friend from the camp, unaware of her existence, apart from the circle of celebration.

The dream that had so often kept her awake at night would have to be put by, laid away, maybe forgotten in time. The desert island her imagination had created for herself and Paolo, flora'd and fauna'd for their sole benefit and appreciation, that island would sink down and disappear into a sea for which she had not yet conjured up a name. That had distressed her: a dream, to be whole in substance, demanded perfection in the smallest of its parts.

'One time posseeble,' Luigi whispered, as he saw her to the door when the evening ended. 'One time posseeble jiggy-jig. For *Natale*.'

For the first time, for seconds as long as centuries, she hesitated, trapped within her thoughts. She would lie quiet at nights now, by the side of her man, bereft of the ecstasy of her wakeful dreams, bereft of the possibility of Paolo.

'No time possible,' she said at last. 'Maybe,' she heard herself promise, aware of the anticipation that had come over Luigi. She owed him that much for her hesitation. 'Maybe . . . some day. One day.'

'That looks like the minister.' Kirsty stopped in her tracks to rap on the young woman's window. 'I could swear it's him, on one of his visitations.'

The sight of anybody, far down on the main road, always demanded their attention. Crusoe, catching his first glimpse of Man Friday. Sometimes, sometimes, the young woman had a great urge to cup her hands against her mouth and shout across the distance to any passerby. 'Look up. I'm here. Look up. And give me identity.' Prisoners though the Italians were, they would one day be free of this isolation. She envied them that.

When she was a child, on her rare jaunts to the country, she had thought that the fields and woods and all of the land belonged to everybody. To each and all. Took the brown furrowed fields for granted, the way she accepted the wild hyacinths growing in the woods. She hadn't realised that every acre of that wide, childhood land belonged to an individual, was the property of. And, for that property, other men worked the miracle of a precise and patterned earth, ploughing it, dragging it, rolling it to change its patterns to green shining corn.

Even now, grown up, the illusion would return, when she walked down to the village and turned to look back on the uplands she had left behind, seeing it the way a townsman might see it. The tractor quiet in the distance, purring across the fields. Beel and Finlay forking the hay for cattle fodder. Picturesque men. Silhouetted against the rick, a leisurely image. Unhurried, seen from a distance.

She knew now, though, that such images not only deceived the eye, they cheated the mind, for the tractorman was no leisurely tin toy figure, but a man who whiles needed the precision of a mathematician, or a lifetime's experience, to manoeuvre his machine through its different tasks and different gradients.

Screwing her eyes tightly together, she could see that the corn had already begun to bree, covering the fields with a fine green mist. Hard to believe that such fragility had survived the heavy roller that had gone over it yesterday, hard to believe it survived such an onslaught in its small, shimmering, elasticity.

'Lift up sacks. Lift up tatties. Lift up shit.' Luigi grumbled as he came towards them at the end of a day spent in carrying sacks of potatoes to the lorry, for sale in the town. He hadn't yet learned that the only way to carry a heavy sack was to hoist it high on his shoulders. His inability to do so had not only irritated the men who knew how, but had impeded their own bent and burdened approach to the lorry, and had aroused Finlay's anger.

'Finlay speak me lazy,' he mourned. '*Everybody* speak me lazy. Plenty work me, Napoli. Plenty work . . .'

'Plenty skive here,' Kirsty muttered. 'You're not in Napoli now.'

Strange to hear the sound of Luigi's city echoed by Kirsty. As if Napoli was a place with which she was familiar, and one that was not up to much in her opinion. Kirsty had no intimacy with cities. Even the knowledge of her market town was proscribed to High Street, MacInley's Tearoom, and the bus terminal. For the young woman – with half her childhood spent in the streets – Luigi's Napoli merged easily into her own remembrance. Not even ignorance of its language could have made of her an exile from *Sturm und Drang*. Thrust and parry. Pitting of wits. And sleight of hand

'I believe him,' she said. 'Nobody's lazy when they're doing the thing they like to do.'

'*You* didn't like the threshing mill,' Kirsty pointed out. You said that *yourself*. On and on about it for days, but *you* did it. That's the difference. You *did* it.'

'Milk!' Luigi shouted from the door of the bothy. 'Milk for supper, me.'

'You'd better see to that one's milk,' Kirsty advised, turning to go. 'Or he'll stand bawling there all night. And *you*,' she reminded Luigi, in the passing, 'you had to wait till you was *born*.'

'Luigi can wait,' the young woman decided, catching up with Kirsty. 'He can just wait till the other Italians come.'

Time, since the Italians' Christmas party, had taken on a quality of nightmare in the young woman's mind, had turned into a game of hide-and-seek, where the cry of 'I spy' became translated, on Luigi's tongue, to the persistent reminder, 'You promise. One day. You promise . . .'

Sometimes, the young woman remembered, sometimes in the lost days of childhood, the hiding place could become more fearful than discovery itself. She had felt safer when Paolo haunted her waking dreams than she felt now, confronted by the full-blooded reality of Luigi.

'I would have thought he would have keep it to the hill,' Kirsty said when the shepherd swung down into view. 'Lambing being just on top of him,' she concluded, straddling the seasons.

A man apart, the shepherd. Solitary, working only with other men at the shearing and dipping, even his cottage was outdistanced from the Cottar Row. The young woman liked the shepherd, and the fine 'speaks' they had on their rare encounters. The things she had learned from them. Snow, warm enough to kill, if you sheltered within it and fell asleep in its warmth. Sheep that whiles got drunk, gorging themselves on the young broom. The broom was as potent as that when young and new. The ewe, with the mischance to fall on her back, that would be dead within the hour. The creature, unable to raise herself up again, because she was not 'born balanced'. And hoodie crows, 'the carrion brutes', diving always to peck the eyes of the stillborn lambs.

She would like fine to work with the shepherd. There seemed to be no monotony to his days, unlike the other

men, making their way home from the tattie shed. She had
seldom seen them quicken their pace. They would walk in
their downbent gait to their graves. It was monotony that
was beginning to make herself feel old. Or maybe it was
marriage that had shut a door, the door that led to romance
and adventure, one that she had never given herself time to
unlock.

'There's something amiss,' Kirsty said, as they watched
the shepherd signalling to the men. 'Something gone wrong.'

'Combustion,' muttered Finlay, as he went past. 'Shepherd
saw it steaming up as he happened by.' They'd gone, he
roared in accusation to the men, and built the damned stack
with stuff that was wersh. Too green. Too raw. And the best
thing they could do now was to get themselves up to the
barn for ladders, and move themselves down to the haystack.

Strange, the young woman thought, staring at the stack in
the distance, standing as it had always stood. Nature secretly,
stealthily, committing arson. Fire without flame.

There would be flame right enough, Kirsty assured her, if
the stack was left to itself. They would soon see the flames
rising when the men took the thatch from the top of the
stack.

Green and growing taller the corn now. Out now in the field
the cattle nosed the grass, sniffing out their old smells again.
The farm-workers pausing to catch their breath between the
urgency of seasonal demand. 'Time now to straighten my
back and light up my pipe,' as Beel expressed it. And he
surely needed that, was Kirsty's dry observation, for she
wondered why Beel ever bothered to smoke a pipe at all,
since he never seemed to get the damned thing to draw.

But if the pace of the farm had slowed down, work in the
cottages in the row was beginning to speed up, was taking
on frenzied proportions, Kirsty whitewashing the sills of her

windows. And Meg, beating the life out of her 'clootie' rugs, gazing askance as the young woman swept past them, bound for Achullen Wood.

'The weather,' Kirsty warned, 'could break any minute now.' The tattie planting would soon be on top of them, Meg reminded her. And by the looks of it, the summer would be gone before the young woman made a start to her spring-cleaning.

'The cleaning will keep,' she shouted back, when she had got beyond reach of their reproaches. 'The wild hyacinths won't.'

The mass of them cast a blue bloom across the wood itself. Forcing themselves up into the consciousness of the trees. The only wood flowers that had the power to impose such colour. The early snowdrops couldn't do that, she remembered, standing knee-high amongst the strong flowers. Nor the aconites. She had never been tempted to uproot the snowdrops, to take them away from the small, close intimacy of their groups. Meg and Kirsty always boasted that they loved flowers enough to let them grow. Maybe they had the right way of it. Maybe her love was too possessive. Too destructive.

Plunging her face down into their dew-drenched mass, her senses aching at the intensity of their scent . . .

> Shade-loving hyacinth
> Thou comest again
> And thy rich odour seems to swell the flow
> Of the lark's song
> The redbreast's lonely strain . . .

They *were* right, Kirsty and Meg. She had to admit that. For the wild hyacinths began to droop in her arms, limp from the moment she had uprooted them from the wood. Protesting as she did so with their broken, squelching cry.

'You go wood,' darting out of the bothy, Luigi looked accusingly down on the hyacinths. 'You no speak me you go wood. *Perche*? *Perche* you no speak wood? Me posseeble wood. You. You promise one day . . .'

All the water in the world could not revive the hyacinths. But she would never be guilty of such an offence against them again, for the wood had become proscribed territory. Luigi had unwittingly ensured that.

> We'll go no more aroving
> In the middle of the night
> Tho' the heart be ne'er so loving
> And the moon be ne'er so bright . . .

'I'll never look a tattie in the face again,' Kirsty vowed, straightening herself up from the drill she was planting. It was enough to put you off tatties for life, Meg agreed, reminding them there was still the Kerr's Pinks to be planted yet. Her reminder causing them to stand in depressed contemplation of the work that still had to be done.

'What's all this then?' Beel shouted from his tractor. 'The Mothers' Meeting?'

'Fathers not invited.' The young woman's attempt at levity sounded flat to her own ears.

'You want to get your backside up off that tractor,' Kirsty advised him, 'and get *your* back bent over the tattie drills.'

'No chance,' Beel laughed. 'I wouldn't want to do you all out of your jobs.'

'Cut the claik,' Finlay roared, taking a flying leap over the dyke, and landing himself amongst them in the tattie field. 'Just you keep your mind on your tractor,' he warned Beel.

'You're cutting the corners some fine. You'll have the whole bloody caboodle coupit in amongst the drills.'

It served Beel right, they agreed, as they stood uncertain whether to get on with their planting again, or to wait in hope of a full scale 'row' blowing up between Finlay and Beel, giving them a legitimate excuse for a breathing space. It was Kirsty who came to the conclusion that they would be well advised to get on with the planting. 'With Finlay in a mood like that. It's well seen that he'd got out of bed wrong side this morning.'

'Where to hell are the Italians?' Finlay demanded. 'I gave orders for every man jack of you to be at the tatties.'

The Italians, Beel reminded Finlay, were across there in the Nether Park, gathering stones and rooting up thistles as Finlay himself had ordered them.

'*Christ*!' Finlay's expletive brought Beel's tractor to a bumping halt, and riveted all attention on the field where the Italians were working. 'You've gone,' he accused Beel, 'you've gone and given the buggers billhooks. They'll have the legs cut off beneath each other.'

'Want to see the Italians come at the double?' the young woman whispered to Kirsty. 'Watch this, then.' Running to the dyke, she shouted across to the Nether Park, '*Bull*. Quick. *Run* Luigi. Bull come. Bull come quick.'

'You stupid-looking bitch,' Finlay thundered, as the Italians sent the billhooks flying and scrambled over the dyke to safety. 'You'll try that trick once too often.'

Lacking in appreciation. That was Finlay's trouble. The young woman felt resentful. At least she had managed to get the Italians on to the tattie field 'at the double'.

'You would think,' Kirsty commented, 'that the Italians would know the difference between a bull and a cow by this time.'

'It's all that tits,' Beel informed her, doubling up with

laughter over his steering wheel. 'That's what gets the Italians muddled up. All that tits.'

It was Beel's 'pea-sized brain' that got Beel 'all muddled up', Finlay snapped, and the sooner he took himself out of Finlay's sight, the better.

The bad start to the morning set the 'mood' of the tattie planters for the rest of the day. The squad spirit had gone, with the Italians huddling dourly together and Finlay and Beel stumping around the field, ignoring each other.

The young woman would never, not if she lived to be a hundred, get used to the sudden changes of mood that could come over the workers. You would think a field too wide for offence to close over it. The sky too high for offence to thrive beneath it.

The mood was infectious though. It was beginning to affect herself. She would never, she vowed, as she stumbled over the clods lying unbroken in the drill, she would never sing, laugh, dance, or try to cheer them up again.

Time itself began to be measured out in inches. Distance defined by the planting of a potato. Twelve inches one foot. One foot. One potato.

'Another rotten tattie,' Kirsty shouted over to Finlay, straightening herself up to wonder who on earth had he gotten to 'sort this lot out. Enough to put you clean off your supper,' she confided to the young woman since Finlay had taken no notice of her complaint. The young woman ignored it also . . . 'I have piped unto you. And you have not danced. I have mourned with you. And you have not wept.' She would do neither. Never again, renewing her vow as she hopped over to the dyke to free her wellingtons from the clods that encrusted them. No wonder the townsfolk nick-named them clod-hoppers. No amount of harrowing, rolling, raking or gathering would ever free their earth of fast-cleaving clods . . .

'I'm just helping myself to a two three wee tatties for my hennies,' Kirsty was confessing to Finlay. 'Is that all right with you?'

'You can help yourself to the whole bloody field,' Finlay barked, loping past them to guide Beel and the tractor through the narrow field. Desperate now for one civil word out of anybody at all in the whole wide world, Kirsty turned to the young woman as a last resort. 'What about *your* hens? Are you not taking back a tattie or two for *your* hens?'

'*My* hens,' the young woman informed her, as she swayed to find her balance after a day rocking around in the tattie drills, '*my* hens wouldn't look at rotten tatties.'

She was daft, they assured the young woman, as they stood waiting for the butcher's van. For they concluded that the hen she was holding preparatory to barter was 'worth a damned sight more than anything the butcher would give her in exchange'.

That wasn't important, it was just that the young woman couldn't face the thought of eating a hen that she had become acquainted with, had reared from a chicken. The farmer's wife, she pointed out, with all that sheep and pigs and cattle she owned, would never have thought of eating the creatures. There was no difference, in *that* respect, between herself and the farmer's wife.

There was, Kirsty insisted, all the difference in the world. 'The law' didn't allow the farmer to kill his own beasts. *Hens* were a different thing. You could please yourself what you did with your own hens. You had the choice. 'And that hen,' Kirsty concluded, eyeing it regretfully, 'would have made a fine pot of cock-a-leekie broth, enough to last two days.'

'And second day's broth's aye best,' Postie sang out, as she creaked past them on her bicycle towards the hill.

'You've got a letter for Elspeth then?' Meg ventured to ask.

'Official,' Postie said, in her post woman's voice. 'Official.'

She never did give much away, did Postie, but, as Meg assured them, they would know the 'news' soon enough, when Elspeth made her way down to the van.

'No sign of that butcher yet?' Kirsty's man shouted from the tractor shed. The only thing the men folk could think of was their bellies, Kirsty snorted, ignoring her man's query. For Kirsty and Meg disliked weekends. It upset their routine, with the bairns out of school, in and out amongst their feet all the time. *She* should consider herself lucky, Kirsty turned in attack now on the young woman, what with her man being a cattleman, with no weekends off, and no bairns to drag around her tail all the time.

It depended, of course, on what Kirsty meant by 'luck'. That time, the young woman remembered, that time when the sick and squeamishness wouldn't leave her, and she had gone to the doctor. Pregnant he thought, insisting that she return with a sample of urine. She couldn't be pregnant, she had insisted, rejecting both his diagnosis and his sample bottle. Why not, he had demanded. Pointing out that she was young, strong and married. Because. She had tried to explain it to him . . . Because . . . You must know. When something important like that is happening. You must know. You must feel something. I never feel anything. That, he had assured her, was by no means uncommon. But it should be. She remained convinced of that, not to feel anything should be the most uncommon thing ever.

Did Kirsty or Meg know, or feel? She had never been able to ask them. If Elspeth had been married, and if Elspeth and herself were still friends, she might have asked Elspeth.

'Down in the valley
Where nobody knows
Stands a young lady
Without any clothes'

The bairns, circling around in front of the Row giggled themselves to a standstill. 'God alone knows where the bairns pick up dirt like that,' Meg said. At the school, Kirsty thought. Where else, she demanded. They themselves had learned more than lessons, after they went to school.

'She sang and she sang
And she sang so sweet
She sang Alick Corbie
Off his feet'

'Keep your noise down,' Kirsty admonished, when they caught sight of Elspeth making her way down the hill, 'and run off and play yourselves somewhere else.'

It was as if they suddenly needed both space and quietness to observe Elspeth's approach, to read from her lineaments, the contents of the letter marked 'official'. *Her* secret still. Her gait, stately, deliberate as always, revealing nothing. Even the men, pausing to watch, were aware of the dignity with which Elspeth surrounded herself, although it proved no armour against the crude familiarities they voiced behind her back. 'I wouldn't touch Elspeth with *your* cock,' Beel boasted, laughing to Kirsty's man.

'*You'll* never get that chance,' the young woman assured them, quick with contempt. 'Elspeth happens to be particular.'

'I'm sorry, Elspeth,' Kirsty was saying.

'Me too,' Meg echoed.

'And me, Elspeth.' Compelled into utterance, the young

woman spoke, knowing her words would be received in silence. 'I am sorry too.'

For it was, as Postie had described it, 'official'. Elspeth's Callum, no longer missing, had been discovered, identified and dead. A confirmation leaving no loophole for hope. All their condolences combined seemed to bring no consolation. Had it been some calamity that had befallen *themselves* now or in the past, they could have keened together in lament. But their men were safe, in reserved occupations. The realisation made the young woman feel uncomfortable, as if their immunity might be offensive to Elspeth.

'I'm the King of the Castle'

Kirsty's small son declaimed from his stance on top of the dyke,

'Get down you dirty rascal.'

'Don't you *dare*,' his mother warned him, 'don't you dare *jump*.' He would go head-first into the ditch if he did, Meg remarked objectively, 'good trousers and all.'

'Jamie has found a puddock,' the small girls screamed, as they scrambled up out of the ditch, their coloured knickers bobbing up amongst the bracken like wild convolvulus flowers. 'He's found a puddock. He's away for a reed to blow it up.'

Swerving to catch him as he rushed past her, the young woman grabbed Jamie by the shoulders, shaking him to a standstill. 'If you blow up that puddock,' she warned him, 'I'll *kill* you.'

Gathering up the small frog that sat stunned at her feet, she carried it back to the bank and set it down amongst the bracken. The force of her anger surprised herself, as she stood waiting for the trembling that had come over her to die down. It, she realised, had been no idle threat, but uttered in a moment when she felt capable of, and inclined to, murder.

'I was just saying to Meg,' Kirsty informed her when she rejoined them, 'I was just saying we never go down to the rocks to gather winkles now.'

'We always used to,' Meg remembered, 'when the tide went out.'

They had spoken. The young woman had the feeling that they might never utter again. Elspeth never would. She accepted that. But at least she would not have to walk in perpetual silence through the high places of this upland country.

It was not until Elspeth had gone, that they got down to the heart of the matter. There would be neither widow nor war pension for Elspeth, her not being married, like. You had to be legally married to get a widow's pension, or badly wounded to get a war pension.

Still, they concluded, having pondered it over, it could have been worse. Elspeth could have been left with fatherless bairns to bring up. Though that would have been unlikely in *her* case, for she was well into her forties was Elspeth, and bound to be 'past it' by now. Come to think of it, when you really got down to it, if it had been one of *their* men that had been killed in the war, their loss would have been far greater than Elspeth's. That stood to reason . . .

Dear God *forgive* me. The young woman was appalled by the thought that had sprung so sudden and unbidden into her mind. If *her* man had gone to the war and been killed, she would have had a second chance. Another time to start a new life, to be up and away from the ingrowing, incestuous way of the farm, in search of something that had eluded her. Often, in the evenings, when she stood watching the flow of traffic far down on the main road and the smoke rising up from trains rushing past on the other side of the firth it seemed as if a whole vista of escape unfolded itself before her eyes . . .

> So many roads lead outwards
> There's one that leads to London
> And one that leads to Rome
> Some lead to the mountains
> Others to the plain
> But every road that's taken
> Must lead you back again

Dear God. Forgive me . . . Forgiveness, though, she had discovered from the Italians, was never automatically granted, but paid for by penance, which she attempted now, dedicating this fine spring day to dirt, scouring her kitchen from top to bottom.

'My! But you've been hard at it the day.' Her man's appreciation of the bright kitchen moved her by its innocence. Sometimes, now and again, she would have liked to have been blind, so that the small externals that always seemed to surround him could never disarm her – hacked hands, threadbare shirts.

'You've cut yourself with the neep hasher,' she said, covering his hand with her own. Her frock, she remembered, was almost paid up, in Kirsty's catalogue. She could put a new order in now. 'A couple of working shirts,' she suggested, as they sat down to their supper. 'You're in need of them.'

'What about *you*. Is there nothing you're needing for yourself?'

'Nothing,' she assured him, 'I'm fine.' The truth of her statement took herself by surprise.

Meg had 'gone clean off Kirsty'. The young woman now found herself in the circumference of their triangle. 'A certain party', according to Meg, had 'let the cat out of the bag'.

'*A certain party*', always unidentified, always malevolent, who drifted invisible in and out of the perimeter of cottar life, causing havoc whenever she appeared, intrigued the young woman. This time, the nameless one threatened to disrupt the old order of turnip hoeing.

According to Meg, Kirsty and her family had decided to take on piece work at the hoeing this year. And you knew what piece work was, paid by the length of the work done. Couldn't you just see Kirsty and her brood taking down the neep drills like the hammers of hell. Anything for an extra bob or two. Leaving them, the ordinary workers, all behind like cows' tails. And paid by the hour. Showing *them* up. That, Meg emphasised, was what 'got her goat, a showing up'. She didn't, she assured the young woman, mind the fat wage packets that Kirsty and her family would collect, for, strictly between herself and the young woman, Kirsty needed every extra penny she could get, to keep up with the payments of all the stuff she was forever ordering out of that catalogue of hers.

There might, the young woman suggested, be no need of piece work, now that they'd got the Italians. 'The Italians', Meg reminded her, made a right soss up of thinning the kale. Riving everything that grew right up out of the drills, driving Finlay demented. God help the crop if the Italians were let loose with the hoe, amongst small finicky things like young neeps. But the young woman, Meg conceded, pausing in her tirade, to make the allowance, the young woman could please herself about taking on the hoeing. As for Meg, she was by no means sure if she 'would be in the mind to put in an appearance' at the turnip field.

The soil was in fine tilth for hoeing, softened by last night's rain, so that everybody on the farm – including Meg – had turned up to get the hoeing over and done with, while earth and weather were in such fine fettle. Even Else, the servant girl from the farm, had joined them in their task.

Meg was right. Hoeing was proving competitive. The blisters were already beginning to rise on the young woman's hands. Tomorrow, Meg pointed out, the blisters would break and then the *real* agony would begin. But by the end of the week, her hands would become as hard as the handle of the hoe itself. She just wasn't holding her hoe at the right slant, Meg said, holding out her own unblistered hands for inspection.

Times like these, the young woman felt imprisoned within the circumference of a field. Trapped by the monotony of work that wearied the body and dulled the mind. Rome had been taken. The Allies had landed in Normandy, she'd heard that on the wireless. 'News' that had caused great excitement in the bothy, crowded with friends, gesticulating in wild debate. Loud voices in dispute. Names falling casually from their tongues, out of books from her school-room days. The Alban Hills. The Tibrus . . . 'O Tibrus. Father Tibrus. To whom the Romans pray . . .' Even in her school days, those names had sounded unreal. Outdistanced by centuries, from another time. Another place. The workers in the fields made no mention of such happenings. All their urgency was concentrated on reaching the end riggs at the top of the field. The long line of army jeeps roaring down along the main road provided nothing more than a moment for straightening their backs, never impinging on the consciousness of the turnip field.

'*Che?*' . . . tugging at her shoulder, Luigi gesticulated towards Else. '*Ragazza . . . Che?*'

'Servant,' she told him. 'Works for boss's wife.'

'*Bella . . . Bella ragazza . . .*' She could hear Luigi shouting.

She could have misheard of course, she was so used to Luigi applying the words to herself.

'She's a daft bitch, *that*.' Meg drew their attention to Else, as they stopped for a moment, before starting up on a new rigg. 'Skirling round the field there, with that Italian panting at her tails.' It was easily seen that Finlay wasn't around. He'd soon put the clampers down on a carry on like that.

'You're supposed to start a new rigg when you're done with the old one,' Kirsty shouted in warning to Luigi, 'so you'd better get a move on.'

'*Non capisco* me,' Luigi grinned as Else dodged giggling past them. 'Me no understand.'

'Me no understand,' Kirsty mimicked, turning aside to the others. 'He can understand fine when there's a bit of skirt around. And that Else is just as bad,' she concluded. 'Anything in trousers.'

Ragazza. Ragazza. The words stuck in her mind, and depressed the young woman as they made their way home from the turnip field. *Ragazza.* A title to which she felt she was losing her claim.

She hadn't got much to say for herself tonight, Kirsty commented. If it was the blisters on her hands that was bothering her, she would get used to that, all she had to do was to steep them in water as hot as she could thole, with a good fistful of coarse salt thrown in. It would nip right enough, Kirsty assured her, but, by faith you, it would fairly harden up the skin on her hands.

It was jealousy that ailed the young woman. Not of Else, herself, but of the single freedom Else enjoyed. Older than the young woman, Else was still '*ragazza*'.

I'm here for ever, she thought, staring round the dim kitchen, before bracing herself to tackle its demands.

The bourtrees, in full blossom, arched themselves across

the track that led to the main road, breaking up the vista of the world beyond the farm. The young woman could no longer nip round the side of the house to gaze on the traffic far down the road, could no longer imagine that time when she would slip quiet down the track into the wide world. She had always imagined that moment, but had kept postponing it . . . Tomorrow. Next Friday. This time next week. Still holding on to its bright secret possibility. Some day. One day . . .

> With the bright pennies cold on my eyes
> I shall fly up to the warm sun
> And leave my shift where it lies . . .

The bairns had already plundered the blossoms of the bourtrees, leaving them strewn across the track, froths of cream-coloured lace. Soon their berries would hang down in long purple chaplets, safe from the bairns. Warned off by their mothers' cries of 'poison!'. Or near enough safe, for danger itself was a compulsion to taste. And bitter to the tongue. Eyeing each other with apprehension, in anticipation of one or other, or all, dropping dead on the spot.

She came upon them congregated round the Italians, squatting on the steps of the bothy, shirtless in the sun. Their attention concentrated on the toy bogie which Paolo was hammering out for Kirsty's son.

> 'Who's the lucky boy
> That's going your way'

the singer on the wireless enquired through the open windows, to send the young woman waltzing down the length of the Cottar Row in accompaniment.

> 'To kiss you good night

In the doorway?'

'Finlay wouldn't like *that*,' Kirsty proclaimed, bursting out from her hens' ree and breaking up both the solo performance, and the carefree mood of the sunlit day, commanding their attention to Beel's tractor, which stood facing up to Achullen. That tractor, she informed them, would never start off first go – not facing up the hill like that. Still, she admitted, before disappearing back into the hens' ree, that was *Beel*'s concern, and she, Kirsty, 'washed her hands of the whole affair'.

Kirsty's knowledge of the tractor, and of the demerits of Beel who worked it, always impressed the young woman. She always seemed to know when Beel had 'cleaned' the plugs, and, even more frequently, when he had 'forgotten' to clean them.

'It was just,' Meg said, sidling across from her doorstep to confide in the young woman, it was just that Kirsty's man was fed to the back teeth working the old Davy Brown tractor, and was ettling to get his hands on Beel's International. That, Meg concluded, was all there was to it.

Who was of a mind to go for firewood then, Finlay, stumping round the corner, demanded to know. For although it was still summer, they were already getting ready for winter, all set to cut down the old trees for cottars' firewood.

They could all freeze to death if they liked then, Finlay threatened, confronted by their lack of response, but, by God, he vowed, if he were to set eyes on a one of them, crawling round the steading in search of paling posts when winter did come ... There was nothing, he informed them, that he himself liked better on a winter's night, than just to fling a leg up on each side of the mantelpiece, and spit into a good roaring fire. But it was up to them, he admitted, for Finlay realised that the cutting down of old trees was voluntary. Free firewood for those who took the trouble to cut it down for themselves.

'Wood. Come wood. Today posseeble.' The young woman turned to find Luigi at her shoulder. 'You promise. You promise one day. Today. Posseeble.'

For the first time, for a long time, armoured by truth, she could look Luigi in the face. 'Today no possible. No possible wood. Me byre. Cows. Milk.'

'No posseeble. No posseeble. *Sempre* no posseeble, no posseeble, no posseeble, NO POSSEEBLE . . .' The anger rising in Luigi's voice had reached the others, quiet and speculative, as, turning on his heel, Luigi rejoined them at the bothy door.

'What's *she* seeking now?' Meg broke through the silence as Else, like some runner from a battlefield, crashed in amongst them. Their relationship with the farmer's wife's servant was cautious. Wary. Something in domestic service seemed to eat up character, to form the spy, the gossip, the snob and the hypocrite, seeing always the underside of their employers' lives. Sometimes though, on occasions like this, Else had her uses, warning them now that 'the mistress is on the road. Collecting for the foreign missions, making her way up to the shepherd's house at this very minute.'

There was no call to warn *her*, Kirsty claimed. The Queen herself, if so be she'd a mind, was welcome to come into Kirsty's house without warning. Not so, the young woman, the sun had infiltered itself between her and her morning chores, and the farmer's wife would be more interested in the state of her husband's cottar house, than in far-flung foreign missions.

'Wood,' Luigi was urging Else. 'Everybody go wood. *You* like? You like go wood?'

He had no need to take that one the length of the wood, Meg observed, as they watched the giggling tug-of-war that waged in front of them. No need to go further than the barn door with that one. That, Meg impressed on her avid listeners, was why the last servant was sent packing. Bag and baggage down the road. It was Meg's own man that had 'catched them at it'. With a lorry driver. Up against the barn door. He'd gotten a right fleg, had Jamie. All he could see was big bare thighs. 'Disgusting, just.'

'Big bare thighs'. The image haunted the young woman, all the way to the byre. Usually she liked the byre. She was good at milking the cows. At ease and at one with the job in hand. Her face pressed against the cow's warm flank, sensing the intimacy between them. A need on the cow's part to give. And on her own to receive.

'Yield' – they used the right word for it, country folk. For although the cow could be serenaded, or talked into yielding her milk freely, she could never be forced. But the young woman was in no mood to apply such persuasion. 'Big bare thighs'. She should, she knew, share Kirsty's disgust at such an image, but found herself instead, resentful of Else, in envy of her.

'She's slow in letting her milk down.' Her man, puzzled, hovering by the side of the stall. 'She shouldn't be going dry yet. She's not that long calved. I'm saying . . .' His words lost impact within the vision of Luigi, squatting brown and shirtless in the sun. 'I'm saying she shouldn't be going dry yet.' The sharp and sudden outbursts of anger that had of late begun to possess her at inexplicable times, were threatening now. She recognised that by the trembling that had come over her body, by the word of accusation, fighting within her. Pounding to get out . . . 'It's not fair. You *had* your life. You had time . . .'

The trembling was easing down now and she hadn't

uttered. The relief of that poured out from her in a sweat that was cold, but set her on her normal course again. Grasping the cow's teats firmly within her hands, she drew them down, until the beat of milk falling into her pail kept rhythm with the song rising in her throat

> Will you gang to Kelvin Grove
> Through its birches let us rove
> Will you gang to Kelvin Grove
> Bonnie lassie O . . .

If the wild hyacinths couldn't endure being plucked from their wood in full bloom, they might, the young woman thought, as she planted out the bulbs she had uprooted, accept and survive transfer to her own yard. That such tiny bulbs could produce such a profusion of blossom intrigued her. The improbable becoming possible. Their tiny comet tails curling round the bulbs, transforming legend into a truth. Sudden and clear, she remembered, the wild hyacinths were, she had learned at school, Persephone's favourite flower, and had followed her deep and down and half-way to Hades. Hades. The word, shooting up out of memory, pleased her. She must, she thought, smiling, use it for the confusion of Kirsty . . . It isn't hell, Kirsty. It's Hades, that's what the Greeks called it . . .

'*Perche*? *PERCHE*?' Getting to her feet she confronted Luigi. '*Perche*? You no come bothy. *Perche*?'

'Because . . .' Answers in their multitudes swirled in her head, too elusive to be caught, to be worked in concrete. 'Because. Me busy. Work outside. Finish . . .' It wasn't explanation enough. She knew that by the rigid disbelief on Luigi's face. Turning away, she was unable to look on him in the clear light of day, for she had raped his privacy, had conjured up his every intimacy in fantasies covered by the night. She

319

felt the shame of it, tangible, porous, oozing out to settle on her face.

'Come,' Luigi loosened his grip on her shoulder. 'Come. Speak bothy. One *minuto*. Paolo. Umberto gone camp. Come.'

The drought had settled itself down to stay. The cows, huddling together in splatches of shade under the trees, shifting as the shade shifted. The last of the summer's flowers drooping in the yards. The hot iron that was earth pinching away at their roots. Only the corn throve and rejoiced in the thick blanket of heat that had flung itself across the land, but then corn always grew harsh and strong. With neither flower nor fragrance. For utility's . . . 'If only the rain would come,' Kirsty lamented, 'it would wash away all the dust.' There seemed little sign of that. The mist was rising up across the firth, eliminating the sea itself . . .

'Mist from the sea brings honey to the bee,' the young woman reminded her.

'You wouldn't think,' Kirsty commented, as the Italians drooped past them, 'that the heat would affect *them* like that, coming from a hot place like Italy.' At least, she remembered, they'd always had the manners to give you 'Fine morning' in passing. 'It must be this heat affecting them.'

It was neither the heat, nor lack of manners, that had set the seal of silence on the Italians. The young woman sensed that. It was a subtle change that had come over their relationship with herself, and with each other. She had sensed it since the day she had accepted Luigi's invitation to the bothy.

Her waking dreams of the night taking on confused dimensions. Her body that had taken her unaware, asserting a life of its own, clamouring for its needs, lay quiet now, cold with apprehension. While her mind whirred blind and batlike, seeking for escape. Her thinking taking on a quality of nightmare. Naked. She would go into the bothy, offering herself to Paolo and Umberto. So that by this act of giving herself in bribery, they would feel no resentment. Sometimes, her thinking extended to include all the friends of the Italians. She was sure that she had seen speculation in their eyes, and had heard the sound of knowingness in their salutations.

'You no speak. No speak Paolo. No speak Umberto,' she would urge Luigi, when the need for his reassurance overwhelmed her. 'No speak no person.'

'No speak me. Me no speak *persone*. One time. One more time. Posseeble. Me no speak.'

She would like to believe that, despite the hint of black-mail, she would like to believe it. Sometimes, times like now, she could will herself into belief. Standing safe, flanked between Kirsty and Meg, as if time itself had moments of compassion. Willing to turn back on itself and allow her a momentary illusion of security in familiar things. Although she was discovering familiar things could no longer be taken for granted, but commanded an absolute concentration on themselves . . . 'That's that then. For another day . . .' Even her man's nightly greeting, when he got in at night from the byre, although never varying and heard a hundred times, took on a new significance. Another day 'got through'. Brought without mishap to a satisfactory close. Ordinary things, enclosing her briefly within their own assurance.

'It's come round again,' Kirsty was saying, as they gazed down on the grain-ranked fields. For, it seemed to Kirsty, 'like yesterday, since we were at the stooking last year'.

'O it is but a week the morn'

The young woman sang. In sudden remembrance.

'Since I was weel and hairstin corn
But something in my head gaed wrang . . .'

An old song that, Meg said, older than themselves. A long time since they'd heard it. 'The Dying Ploughboy', Kirsty informed them, taking up the words herself.

> Farewell my nags my bonnie pair
> For you I'll yoke and lowse nae mair
> Farewell my maister . . .

God but they were in good voice the day, Finlay commented, on his way to the tractor shed. 'The Glasgow Orpheus Choir will have to look out for itself.'

At least, they consoled themselves, when Finlay had passed out of hearing, *they* didn't need 'The Barley Bree' to put *them* in good voice.

They should have said *that* to Finlay. An odd thing that, they agreed, contemplating its oddness. You always knew the right thing to say, when the chance to say it had gone.

The binder had broken down. Now that the damned thing was at a standstill, Finlay informed the women, there was no need for them to stand around claiking. One of them, he suggested, might just take a turn up to Achullen, to see if Elspeth was of a mind to give a hand to the stooking. Now that they had lost the Italians . . . Lost the Italians. The phrase took the young woman by surprise. The unexpected kindness of it. She would go, she volunteered. She was used to the climb. More than that, she needed to go. Needed to know that if Elspeth decided to work with them again, whether it could be if not in friendship, at least in tolerance. Not in a silence that would straddle itself across the seasons of their lives on the land.

It would have been easier to take the track through the heather, but she was not ready to take that track again. In years to come maybe, in another time, she might return to the place. But the climb released something within herself. Straightening up to stand high and knee-deep amongst the russet bracken crackling round her legs, the sun, it seemed, had never set with such fire and flame as it was setting now, a hill-crest fire, she remembered. Far beneath her the Cottar Row took on a new perspective, dwindling, huddling within the farm-steading, as if seeking for anonymity. Only yesterday, it had been the pivot around which the whole world revolved, before it had whirled and shuddered to a stop.

'No more corn. No more hayeerst. No more tatties,' Luigi had proclaimed, as he rushed past her window, dodging the bikes of prisoners from the camp, and shouting through the clamour of their bells. 'Tomorrow. Go home. Italia. Home Napoli.'

Again, the young woman had the feeling that the whole of Italia was squeezed into the narrow length and breadth of the Cottar Row, even Kirsty startled by the sudden din, disapproving of the uninhibited displays of emotion taking place in front of her eyes, laughter and tears no longer rational, no longer manifestations which separated joy from sorrow. Even Kirsty was disarmed, as Luigi swept her off her doorstep, whirling her along the length of the Cottar Row . . .

> O are you sure the news is true
> And are you sure he's weel
> Come Jade put on your Sunday frock
> Good wife put by your wheel . . .

Relief, in one great gush, was the young woman's first reaction to the news. Like one who has been granted a last minute reprieve. 'One time,' Luigi was whispering. 'Today. One time. For last . . .'

323

She would truly never know whether she had yielded to the instinct of her body or to a sense of long loss that the word 'last' had evoked within her. 'The dream,' both the Bible of her childhood and those who read from it, had tried to din into her, 'the dream' could only come true 'through a multitude of busyness'. The 'busyness' was now all that remained.

'One last time,' she said to Luigi.

They had taken separate tracks up through the heather, herself and Luigi, apprehension increasing as she watched him come towards her.

> Come to the stolen water
> Come leap the guarded pale
> Come pluck the flower in season
> Before desire shall fail

Her apprehension was justified. A subtle change had come over their relationship, as if their rôles had been reversed.

The man who stood before her was no longer a prisoner. No longer a servant of circumstances, as she herself remained. Tomorrow he would be free to return to a world in which she would have neither part nor power. The triumph of this glistened on Luigi's face, glinted in his eyes, as he leant forward to embrace her . . . 'Napoli. *Pronto*. Napoli.' The words, gasped in her ear, were not intended for her hearing, but words of affirmation. Of confirmation for himself. She was aware of that, as he eased her down into the heather.

In her fantasies of the night, consummation had been a perfect thing, requiring no comment. Needing none of the reassurance she heard herself beseeching now, 'ME *amo*, Luigi? ME *amo* . . . ?'

'*Si, si. Ti amo.*'

'*Sempre*, Luigi. *Sempre.*'

'*Sempre. Si.*'

It was to the sky above that Luigi spoke, staring up at it as he lay, his hands clasped beneath his head. Staring as if Napoli itself was reflected within it. Raising herself slow and clumsy up from the heather, she had stood wondering how she could get her feet to carry herself, and the corpse of illusion within her, down from the hill with some small remnant of dignity.

The eyes of the workers gathered round Kirsty's door seemed to measure each step of her approach to the Cottar Row. The silence that had come over them when she turned the gate of her cottage, exploded the instant she reached them. Where had *she* been then, they demanded in chorus, as if she had forgone the privilege of being witness to great events.

For Else, taking the short cut through Achullen Wood, on her afternoon off, had been jumped on. Assaulted. Near enough ravished. If it hadn't been for Beel there, taking a turn through the wood. He'd heard the skirls of her in the nick of time. One of the Italians. Though which one, Beel wasn't rightly sure. For the man had taken to his heels, and Beel only got a glimpse of his back.

That could well be, they agreed, with all the Italians that were around the day. And the height they were at. Forbye, Kirsty's Alick remembered, Else was very thick with the Looeeshee one. They'd all noticed that. So thick, Kirsty remarked, that he'd have no need to ravish her.

It wasn't Luigi. It couldn't have been Luigi, the protest forced itself up in the young woman's mind, but stuck, somewhere down in her throat. What was more, Jeems reminded them, there was neither hair nor hide of the Looeeshee one. The other two Italians were in by the bothy, it seemed like there was nothing on *their* conscience.

Don't let Luigi come in sight . . . The young woman's prayer rose up in panic . . . Make him take the back way. Dear God, don't let them see him coming down the hill. . .

If it was the Looeeshee one, Meg prophesied, there would be no Italy for him. No Napoli, that place he was always on about. As if it was the only place on the face of this earth.

It could have been any of the Italians, the young woman found her voice at last. There was a crowd of them here the day. They'd all know soon enough, Alick promised. According to Beel, they were taking the prisoners back to the camp to interrogate them, Else and all, to identify. As for himself, Alick declared, there was no doubt in *his* mind. No doubt at all, for there was still no sign of the Loogee one. And that, surely, spoke for itself.

Only she could speak for Luigi. Something she felt compelled to do. But in the doing she was aware that her world as she now knew it would change, that the relationships she had begun to form would alter. She herself might survive the condemnation of the Cottar Row. It was the burden of shame within herself, and which would be extended to, and cast over her man, that was beyond enduring.

They could go away though, to another farm. They would easily get a job. They were good workers. A clean breast. A new start. The prospect beginning to light up in her mind, was snuffed out by the sudden remembrance of the Stand Still Order, that prevented farm-workers from leaving the land. There would be no other farm, no hiding place. No Roma. No Napoli.

So this was what it was like to be a prisoner. Small wonder that her attempts to console the Italians had been futile. Unable to interpret their language, which might have given more shape, more meaning to their experience.

Nothing for look . . . She remembered in a sudden despairing survey of the landscape in front of her . . . In Scotland.

Nothing for look ... She *knew* now, how it must have seemed to Luigi.

'It wasn't Luigi.' She heard herself telling the officer. 'It couldn't have been Luigi.'

Father forgive me for I have sinned ...

That, she realised, must be the easiest part of the confessional. The sinfulness announced, but the sin not yet defined. The officer's eyebrows rising up in perplexity, demanded definition.

'Luigi was with me. Up in the heather. When ... that happened to Else.'

'I see.' He didn't, not clearly. His hands scrabbled amongst the papers on his desk as if proof of her statement could be found there. Or maybe, maybe she thought, he was searching for words that could afford her a loophole.

'The time?' he asked. The precise time she had spent with Luigi, could she remember that?

'No.' She couldn't remember that. 'Not precisely.' Time out of bounds, time out of mind, time of that kind defied precision.

Her relationship with the Italian, was it of 'an intimate nature'? Yes, she had known the nature of the barrow-boy from the slums of Naples, had instantly recognised it, and had deeply understood it. But she knew that was not what the officer meant by 'intimacy' – knowing. Abraham and Sarah, she remembered, recalling long sermons in the kirk other girlhood, shortened by her avid researches through the Old Testament. Knowing and begetting.

'Yes,' she said to the officer.

'A prisoner and a civilian, *any* civilian,' the officer was emphasising, 'in such circumstances ... You understand?' His words fading in horror of the realisation that engulfed her. The conviction against Luigi would stand, confirmed by *her* compulsive confession. Else, by admitting that she could not 'identify', had spared him that.

Twice she had lost the rudiments of dignity, that outward physical dignity that held the visible self together. Once in the heather with Luigi, and now on leaving the officer's room. Strange, that on both occasions it was the landscape, the land's life, against which she had protested strongly, that came to her temporary release, diminishing horror.

Losing herself in the absorption of the solitude of the dark mountain peaks on the other side of the water. Dissolving with herself in their indifference to pain, blame or shame.

'That's that then,' Finlay said as they straightened themselves up from the stooking to wave goodbye to the jeeps crammed with Italian prisoners on their way to home and freedom. 'The Looeeshee one will not see that Napoli of his in a hurry. Poor bugger.'

'Poor bugger right enough,' Beel agreed. 'For there's damn all wrong with Else. A bit tousled and scrattit, but as right as rain now that she's gotten over her the skirling and blubbering. Beginning to brag about it now. And no more ravished than Kirsty standing there was ravished.'

She herself, Kirsty admitted, had never had much time for the Looeeshee one. Too cocksure of himself. But for all that, knowing Else, no man body needed to go the length of rape with that one, not even Looeeshee.

That was as maybe, Finlay pointed out, grabbing the sheaves to set their minds, by his own example, back to the stooking again. 'One of you,' he suggested, 'might just take a turn up to Achullen to see if Elspeth's of a mind to give us a hand now that we've lost the Italians.'

Elspeth, on her knees, was uprooting the withered nasturtium leaves that drooped amongst the whitewashed stones around her door.

'Finlay says,' the young woman addressed Elspeth's back, rigid and bent, 'Finlay was wondering, Elspeth . . .'

'So. Finlay was wondering, was he?' Elspeth spoke without raising her eyes from the ground.

'Elspeth,' the young woman knelt by the bent figure, to make sure that Elspeth would hear. 'They've gone. The Italians. They've gone, Elspeth.'

'You was saying about Finlay?' Heaving herself to her feet Elspeth flung the withered nasturtium leaves over the fence, keeping a firm grip on the trowel in her hand, as if one wrong word would set it and herself down in attack among the stones again. 'Finlay. You was saying about Finlay . . .'

'The Italians, Elspeth, they've gone.'

'I see.' Elspeth stood considering what she saw. Her own pain or a reflection of pain that betrayed the young woman by rising sudden up out of its secrecy to look out of her eyes.

'You'd better come in.' Scraping her trowel careful and clean on the grindstone by the door, she repeated the invitation. 'You'd better come on inside.'

Only the empty bookshelves in Umberto's corner and the cigarette stubs lying in the grate remained as proof that the bothy had recently been inhabited. Staring around it, the young woman's eyes came to rest on the poster of the Madonna still hanging on the wall. Askew now, as if her usefulness was over. She'd had a hard time, this Scottish Madonna, miracles demanded daily, blame and praise in equal measure.

It was when she was turning to go that the young woman noticed the ship inside a bottle lying on the table. She had caught brief glimpses of it in Paolo's furtive hands, but now it lay revealed in completion. Lifting it to examine it she saw the note hidden beneath it . . .

Dina
Con amore e molta felicità
Paolo   Umberto   Luigi

They had never known her real name, she remembered. And had bequeathed her with a name of their own choice.

'Wifie', the general title of the Cottar Row touched both her mind and her mouth with irony. Wifie. Luigi would never have never found the Italian word for that in his dictionary. Wifie, the title that had made her feel old before her time. Quine. Lass. That was different now, but used rarely, and only by men.

'How did they get that ship into the bottle?' the bairns demanded, crowding round the bothy door. 'How did they get it inside?'

She didn't know either, it would remain a marvel and a mystery. But she knew what *'con amore'* meant, that was what she did know.

WHERE THE APPLE RIPENS

For Sharon, Melanie and Joanne
Dear Grandchildren

WHERE THE APPLE RIPENS

Never pry
Lest we lose our Eden
Adam – and I –

'ON 29 August, 1932. Helen. Aged eighteen years . . .'
Her mother's voice drifted to a halt. And Isabel knew
it was true. Everything became true when it was read out
loud, from the morning paper.

'The funeral's the day, then,' her mother remembered,
letting the paper drop from her hands. *That* had been confirmed by the big, black-edged card in the shoemaker's
window.

All Friends Respectfully Invited

'I keep forgetting about the funeral,' her mother admitted,
gazing out of the window. 'But then, of course, it's been
such fine weather. Such fine shimmering days. And I suppose
you've forgotten all about school!' Her mother whirled

round on Isabel, now. 'Your last day at school at that! You can just run up the stairs and look out your father's shirt. His funeral shirt. Bottom drawer down. And bring Davy's Sunday shirt when you're at it. He'll have to go to the funeral. He came up through the school with Helen Mavor.'

Isabel, herself, had shared the same class-room as Helen Mavor. But, being three years younger, and in a junior form, the boundary between them had been unsurpassable. On the rare occasions when it was bridged, the embarrassment of such a unique situation diminished the pleasure of it. She could have died with hot thumping pride when any of the big girls took her hand. Or even said hello! And, if they ever called her by her name, she was so surprised they knew her at all, she couldn't look at them the whole of the day for shyness. Except in peeps. They *know* me, she would think, gripping herself with excitement. I'm *Isabel!* I *am* Isabel. Most of the time she thought everybody else thought she wasn't anybody at all.

Helen Mavor had never spoken to her. Nor she to Helen Mavor. Yet, she remembered her voice. Better than she remembered Else Finlay's voice. And Else, her best friend.

'*Pan loaf,*' everybody said Helen spoke. Because her parents wouldn't allow her to speak Scots. Not even outside school.

'Scots is good enough for everybody else!' they all protested.

'But Helen Mavor is *English*!' Isabel's mother had pointed out. 'At least the mother of her is English!'

That was it, then. Maybe that was why Isabel had always secretly admired Helen Mavor's voice. It spoke the language of the poems she liked to hear. She would write out her transcription as fast as she could, then curl herself round her book, and listen to the top classes saying their poetry.

Where Alph the sacred river ran
Through caverns measureless to man
Down to a sunless sea

But, when Helen Mavor spoke, she would listen harder than
ever. Knowing there was a different language, somewhere.
And Helen knew it. Another country. And Helen came from
it.

It was an Abyssinian maid
And on her dulcimer she played
Singing of Mount Aborrah

'You might bring down that skirt of mine!' Her mother's
voice rose from the bottom of the stairs. 'It's on top of your
trunk. I'm in the middle of making it down for you.'

That was another thing. Helen Mavor's skirts had always
fitted her properly. They were her *own*. Not her mother's
made-down.

And Helen wore *shoes* to school. Not just to the kirk, on
Sundays. And yet ... maybe ... Helen Mavor had never
known the challenge of lacing up a pair of boots so tightly,
that they looked almost as neat as shoes. She had never
known the excitement of announcing with truth ... 'My
boots are needing toecaps again. I'll have to wear my Sunday
shoes to school!' And, most of all, had never known the
heart-shattering gladness of your mother's small concessions,
her brief, unguarded admissions.

'I suppose you can wear your shoes for one day. But I'll
never know what you've got against your boots! You've got
such trim ankles.'

Had Helen Mavor ever flown down the road, neat and
nimble? Knowing from a source that was infallible that she

had 'such trim ankles' – worthy of the silver stud sparked splendour with which they were shod.

The colour of her mother's skirt wasn't too bad. But, fingering it, Isabel knew from experience that the 'making down' would be a process that would continue as long as the skirt itself would last. 'A tuck in here. A dart out there!' A conclusion that was a curious mixture of triumph and defeat. 'It's a bit on the wide side for you. But that's a good fault. You're still filling-out.'

Her uniforms lying inside her trunk, ready for the tremendous prospect of 'going out into the world', were a different thing altogether. Unworn by anybody else in all the world. The blue cotton dresses and grey serge aprons 'for the rough work in the mornings'. She buried her nose in the strong, drapery smell that testified to their newness. But best of all, she liked her 'afternoon uniform'. The black dress that wasn't real silk. But looked and felt just like it. Her small lace-trimmed caps for showing in the visitors.

Good afternoon, Madam. What name shall I announce, please?

Lady –

Lady? *Lady?*

> The Lady of the Lea
> The Lea
> The Lady of the Lea
> The Lea
> Was beautiful exceedingly
> Exceedingly

Strange how small sudden fantasies could take such hold of her. Whirling her round in their own tempo, before releasing her into a kind of emptiness again.

Exceeding

      ceeding

           ly

She didn't mind so much now, about having to go into domestic service. Though it seemed such a short time ago when her future seemed to be simply a matter of chance, like their skipping game.

> Whom shall I marry
> Tell me true
> A handsome young man
> With eyes of blue
> Rich Man!
> Poor Man!
> Beggar Man!
> *Thief!*

Of all the futures Isabel had visualised for herself – and they had been many and various! – domestic service had never come into her reckoning. At least, not until she was old enough to hang around Barclay's Brig, with the girls, home, on 'their day off', from service in the town. They brought traces of its grandeur back with them. In the form of their mistress's cast-off fox furs.

Slung with casual pride across their shoulders. Hand-me-downs that were different, somehow. Signifying a good relationship with their employers. Not one of necessity, like her mother's skirt.

'My *word*!!' her mother had taken to saying lately, 'Jean Craig must be doing *well*! Her mistress is very good to her,' in a tone which implied that she, Isabel, would never do as 'well' as Jean Craig. Not if she lived to be a hundred.

Their world had widened too, for the girls in service in

the town. They now knew people Isabel didn't know. The milk boy. The butcher's boy. The grocer's boy. And most fascinating of all, the tram conductors.

. . . They're a right lot, aren't they, Jean? Mind the time my heel got caught in the platform? And yon conductor! The cheek of him! I thought we'd die laughing . . .

Isabel had never set eyes on a tram conductor. But lately, she had an awful longing for a tram conductor to set eyes on her!

Ting-a-ling-a-ling. Laughter you could die of. High-heeled shoes for evermore. Fairy-footed and fox-furred. And glass eyes glistening red across your shoulder.

Their repertoire had expanded too. It was no longer one they shared with her. But something smiling and secret between themselves. Encircling her with rings of sound, but no longer including her.

> Blue heaven
> Just you and I
> When first we kissed
> Neath a moonlit sky

If only they had sung it often enough for her to get the tune, for she could always make up her own words. How she would have blue heavened it, in the school porch on a rainy day, to a captive audience, mystified and admiring.

> Blue heaven
> Just you and me
> Ta rum da dee
> Ta rum da dee

Still. Very soon, now, she would learn all the words, and catch all the tunes. Casting aside the other words, the other melodies, that had notched up the seasons of her childhood to its sum total. Yet, still uncertain. Checking and re-checking. Carrying over old enchantments, not quite erased.

> How sweet the lily grows
> How sweet the breath
> Beneath the hill
> Of Sharon's dewy rose

'Haven't you found your father's shirt, yet?' her mother shouted. 'You're going to be late for school. On your last day, too!'

Although school, itself, had never been very important in her mother's eyes, it was important not to be late for it. Her brother Davy's certificates, nailed up on the walls of his bedroom, testified to years of punctuality and regular attendance. Isabel had never bothered to nail hers up on the wall. Except her *real* certificate for excellence in English. The words were written in gold letters. You could see they were gold, if you looked closely. And, sometimes, depending the way the sun was, you could still see they were written in gold, even from a distance.

> . . . dependent on Thy bounteous breath
> We seek Thy grace alone
> In childhood manhood age
>   and death

'You certainly took your time!' Kate Emslie grumbled. 'And that's not your father's funeral shirt! Your mind's always on everything. Except the job in hand! I would have thought there was precious little to sing about on a day like this! There's such a thing as respect!'

'But it's a *hymn*!' Isabel protested. 'That was the hymn we sang for Helen's memorial in the kirk on Sunday.'

That was another thing. They would sing 'By Cool Siloam' for you when you were born. Or if you died young. But just 'The Sands of Time', if you died when you were old. That, itself, might almost be worth dying for, Isabel concluded, having thought it over. All the folk standing up in the kirk, singing just for you. And thinking about you all the time they were singing. The way you, yourself, had thought about Helen Mavor. Remembering things you hadn't even known were memories. Like the watch Helen had been given on her birthday. The older girls surrounding her admiringly. Yourself, and the other younger ones staring at a respectful distance, in the semi-official capacity allowed on birthdays. It was the first time that anyone had ever worn a watch to school. And, although you hadn't been close enough to set eyes on the watch, you had relayed detailed confirmation of its existence to the other small outsiders.

It's real *gold!* And it's got Roman numbers!

A memory of a memory, maybe. Your mother's watch, locked away in a drawer in the dresser. Signifying the twenty-first year of her life. But isolating it, as if nothing worth confirming had happened to her since. Maybe, maybe the *important* things that happened to folk fell out of time altogether. And flowered into space.

That Sunday in the kirk. They had just finished singing 'Summer Suns Are Glowing'. The day was right for the hymn. And the hymn was right for the day. With the sun streaming in through the stained-glass windows, so that Isabel could have stretched up her arms and pulled down the thick, coloured rays of dust that had gathered above her head. The heat had dragged out the strong sweet smell of the Himalayan cowslips in front of the pulpit, sending it surging towards her. So near a smell, till she remembered that the cowslips were Himalayan. Far off and foreign. The thought of that had excited her. Something realised only by herself. And secret to herself. She had sat down gripping the secrecy, squeezing it within her. Hard and hot and physical, till it exploded. Her body had shuddered under its force, before it trembled down into a release it had never before known.

'I think I have started to have my periods,' she had whispered to Else Finlay, the moment they got out of the kirk. 'Is there a stain on my frock?' Else's furtive examination had revealed nothing. So it was something different after all. A glory. And ordinary people like Else could find no trace of it.

'You're a woman, now,' her mother had said, without looking at her. 'You know what *that* means.' It was a statement, not a question.

'Aye,' Isabel had answered hurriedly, positively. 'Aye. I know.'

Freed from the threat of personal embarrassment, her mother had relaxed.

'I'll get some material for your towels, next time I'm in the town. I'll show you how to make them up and sew them. You'll see to the washing of them yourself. And keep them away in your chest of drawers. Out of sight of Davy and your father.' For a second in time, they had become women together. Bound by a conspiracy of sanitary towels. But Isabel kept the secret of the Himalayan cowslips to herself.

'Seeing,' Kate Emslie announced, 'as there will not be a hand's turn done in this house till Isabel clears off to school

341

and you two clear out for the funeral, Davy might as well saw up a log or two for the fire.'

'*Me?*' Davy asked, incredulous.

'Aye. You.'

'A *fire?*'

'A fire.'

'*At this time of year?*'

'A fire at this time of year.' Each word Kate Emslie uttered struck at protest, till you thought protest could never recover and rise up again.

'You'd be just as well sawing up a log or two.' Her voice felt its way through the silence. Reaching out for, and trying to touch Davy, again.

'If you ask *me!*' Dod Emslie said, finding his voice again.

'Nobody asked you!' Kate Emslie snapped. 'I was speaking to *Davy!*' she emphasised, believing it herself. For Davy could have disappeared clean off the face of the earth, for all the notice they were taking of him. Yet if Davy ever *did* disappear, Isabel at least, would know where a memorial to him was to be found. Scratched out on the walls of the blacksmith's smiddy.

DAVY LOVES CHRIS B

'*Do* you, Davy?' Isabel had once asked him. 'Do you love Chris B?'

'*Her!*' Davy had scoffed. 'Yon muckle fat thing?'

'But, DO you, Davy? Not counting she's fat.'

'NO!'

'Not once Davy? Not *ever?*'

'Not once! Not *ever!*'

Sometimes, sometimes when they got speaking close like that, herself and Davy, Isabel had a right wish to say to him. *Davy.* Davy, if you wasn't my brother, and pretend you hadn't set eyes on me in your life, and you looked up one Sunday in the kirk, and saw me sitting there in my Sunday frock. My blue frock with the white collar. Pretend you hadn't seen it before, either! Would *you* have me? For your 'lass', I mean.

But she had never put that question to Davy. He might laugh at her for one thing. Worse still, he might even ask her the same question. And she could never have said Yes. Even if Davy had not been her brother, she could never have felt heart high for him.

She could never have said No, either, though. She knew that well enough. She would just have patted him on the shoulder, and run away. Like she always ran away when she patted him. Pretending it was nothing. Or just something that had happened in the passing.

> Davy E
> Doesn't love Chris B
> Not once
> Nor forever more!

'Keep your eyes on the clock!' her mother warned, 'instead of wheebering away to yourself there! You're going to be late for school. And this is your last day!'

'You promised you wouldn't wear your coat, today. If it was fine!' Else Finlay accused, when Isabel caught up with her at the crossroads.

'You promised! And it's going to be a scorcher!'

'I know,' Isabel submitted humbly. 'But I forgot. I just clean forgot.' She emphasised the lie. It wasn't that she had forgotten, it was just that her mother had remembered.

'Here's your coat!' her mother had shouted, a minute before Isabel had got out of sight of the house. 'Fine day or no fine day,' she had insisted, stifling Isabel's rising protests. '*You* are wearing your coat! Else Finlay can run around the countryside exposing herself if she likes! But *you* are going to wear your coat!'

Not once. Not ever. Had Isabel been allowed to walk the world the way she wanted to walk it . . . Wear your cardigan! It's no day for thin shoes! Get your hair back into its plaits again! Flying all round your face like that! Gathering up the dirt . . .

Nobody in all the world knew the *real* Isabel. The Isabel that lurked somewhere within the long coat, tacketty boots and tight plaits. The only thing that made the world's ignorance tolerable was the secret surprise Isabel had in store for it!

'You're laughing at something!' Else accused her. 'Anyhow!' she boasted, as if she were a different species altogether, 'I'd just *melt* if I'd to wear a coat on a day like this. It's going to be a sizzler!'

It would and all. For Ben Achie lay light and near in the sun. Full of fields that danced and ran as fast as herself and Else, with the sun dancing along them. But you could lose your way to Ben Achie, Isabel remembered, when the sun was off. And twenty miles wouldn't bring you up to it.

The women waiting for the bus at the crossroads were full of the funeral. And of the pity of it. Helen Mavor had been young, they said. And strong. She had survived the birth. But would neither eat. Nor try to eat. You could die of course, of a broken heart. Or of shame, itself, just.

'And it could just as easily have happened to *you*!' The joiner's wife predicted, suddenly aware of Isabel. 'So you can wipe that grin off your face. And just you mind on that, my lady!'

0, for the bravery that Isabel regretted she was too young

to possess. Except, of course, the kind of bravery that spurred her imagination, at the oddest times, and in the strangest places. Taking the illicit short cut through the barley field, with the wind in her face, fighting against her, and the bearded barley conspiring against her, and closing in on her, stinging her cheeks, and her mind, into some recollected spirit of defiance.

> I wad hae made a wudden horse
> Oot o ilk aiken tree
> And slashed the rowans intae spears
> For sake o chivalrie

You are, her mind attacked the joiner's wife, just a nasty old bitch! You'd like fine for such a bad thing to happen to me, because you don't like us. Not since my mother had bravery, and told you what to do with your planks that got all warped and ruined our hen-house. You was just too greedy to wait till the wood got ripe and could shrink no more. And!!!

I *will* have The Garden *of Allah!* Her mind flew forward to some possible future attack on Miss Merit, the mobile library lady. I'm not too young. I know what I want to read. I have read *Masterman Ready*. Ages ago. And I just hated it! So thank you, Miss Merit. But I'll just hold on to *The Garden of Allah*, if you don't mind!

'So you're going away to service in the town, Isabel!' Kate Riddrie said. Launching the others into a concentrated attack.

She'd have to *work,* they said. By God, she would! No more time to sit and scratch herself. For they knew what was what! Once the young ones got to the town, they went all to hell, just! And, if they didn't do *that,* they got too big for their boots altogether!

Take Jean Selby. Her that got married on to a bricklayer, last month. The bragging and boasting that was on *her* had to be heard to be believed! No more paraffin lamps for yon one. GAS! If you please. No more running outside to the water closet. Emptying pails, and all that soss! She'd just to pull a chain, now! To hear *her* speak; you would have thought she'd got married to Sir Robert McAlpine himself! Not just one of his bricklayers.

You couldn't blame them altogether, Nell Phillips ventured. Not for wanting things a bit easier, like. Although, it was a queer thing, in spite of the gas, and the inside lavatory, the town way of life could never have been the way for Nell Phillips, herself. Wasn't that the queer thing?

It could never have been the way for her mother, either, Isabel knew, as the small images of her mother's life fluttered to the surface of her mind.

The surprised triumph in her voice on churning days when she'd call out, 'The butter's come! It's come at last.' As if, after all the years, she hadn't expected it to 'come' at all. The absorbed precision with which she patterned the butter into small intricate whirls and twirls, that none but her family would ever admire.

The careful concentration with which she'd bend over the lamp. Trimming it down to a minute perfection, as if aware that the giving of light lay within her hands.

They had it too easy altogether, Lil Eadie concluded. Those that went to the town. Take Helen Mavor, now. Though one should not speak ill of the dead. And her not buried yet. *She* had paid in full for what she'd done. Poor thing! She'd always had everything that money could buy. No wonder she got into trouble. If it had been some poor farm-kitchen girl, you could have understood it, poor bitches! A bit of toss and tumble was all *they* had to look forward to! And, even then, the way they carried on up in the farms was a perfect disgrace, just!

'Lil Eadie was quite right!' Else panted, as they ran towards the school. 'Our servant's just like that. Always skirling with the horsemen up in the dark in the loft. And you know fine what they're up to!'

Isabel *did* 'know fine'. But, another knowing, and one outwith her experience, seized sudden hold, carrying her body up into some dark hay-loft, and placing it under, not one horseman, but all the horsemen that ever was. She could have deserted Else there and then, and gone flying up to Corbie's Wood, to ease the agony that her mind's unexpected vision had thrust upon her unsuspecting body.

'They must be a *terrible* lot, then,' she agreed with Else. Glad that the trembling hadn't reached her voice. 'They must all be disgusting, just!'

'But the Egyptians overtook them encamping by the sea beside Pi-hahiroth before Baal-zephon. And the pillar of cloud went from before their face and stood behind them.'

The dominie slammed the Bible shut, and leaning on his elbows on the high lectern, cupped his face in his hands, and surveyed the class in silence.

'Watch *out*!' Isabel whispered in warning to Else. 'He's got on his black suit!'

'Not the mark of Cain!' The dominie's voice cracked through the silence. 'Though there is no doubt in my mind, that a few of you will end on the gallows! But the stoop of the farm labourer is early upon you. Square up your shoulders, men!'

'I *told* you,' Isabel confirmed, bolting upright in her form. 'He's always in a bad mood when he's in his black suit.'

'The inspector must be coming the day,' Else whispered.

'When I – sa – bella Emslie condescends,' the dominie broke into Else's speculation, 'to give us her *undivided* attention . . .'

A bad start to her last day at school. A day on which some quarter was usually allowed. A day when small, personal compulsions had to be acted out and inanimate things took their ultimate revenge. Desks, walls, and stones touched in wordless gestures of farewell.

'You will have an extra hour at dinnertime,' the dominie said. 'Do any of you possess a time-piece?'

'It's not the *inspector*, Else!' Isabel remembered. 'It's the funeral. He'll be going to Helen Mavor's funeral. I forgot all about that.'

'Do *you* possess a time-piece, I—sa—bella? I thought not,' the dominie said, answering his own question. 'The acres at Slack-o-Linn, all eighty of them, would not rise to a time-piece.'

Cowards! All of them! Giggling audibly under the dominie's protection. The way Isabel, herself, became a coward, when the dominie made a joke about somebody else. The force of her rising anger confirmed her faith in her own strength to fell them *all*, the moment they got outside. One by one. Or all together if need be!

'Silver or gold have I none,' the dominie said, his watch glinting and jangling in front of her eyes. 'But this time-piece is above price. I leave it in *your* custody, I—sa—bella . . . I—sa—bella!'

'Isabel's got the dominie's watch!' the cry rose in the playground.

> 'The dominie's watch!
> The dominie's watch!
> Isabel's got the dominie's watch
> On a cold and frosty morning.'

The Loch Wood had always been the older girls' favourite hiding place. The privacy they scrambled towards, now enclosed them. Here, they could see yet not be seen. Utter, yet not be condemned out of their own mouths. The 'extra hour' began to draw them into its passing minutes, the way the funeral was beginning to draw the mourners far down the Loch Road.

'Helen Mavor's baby is going to be baptised at the funeral service,' Liz Aiken said. 'At the head of Helen's coffin.'

'It's a lie!' Isabel protested, bursting out from the bewildered silence. Birth and death were such opposite things. You couldn't fuse them together and make them into one! 'By Cool Siloam' was for *birth*. 'The Sands of Time' was for *death*. You couldn't harmonise such divided melodies. 'We sang 'By Cool Siloam' for Helen's *death*,' she reminded them, trying to formulate it. 'They can't sing it for the baby's *birth*,' she added, as if the baby had missed out on something.

Never had Isabel ran so fast up through the Loch Wood, nor stumbled so often in the bracken, nor picked herself up so soon. Never had she climbed the tree so high, nor swung so sure and careless along its branches. 'By Cool Siloam' singing inside her head, and she couldn't get it out of her head, nor could she slow her body's movements down into its rhythm, but speeded up the lament it was, till it became a paeon of praise for being alive itself.

'Jump! Isabel!' The girls' voices rose up to her in warning. 'It's the dominie! He'll see you swinging up there. He's on his road to the funeral.'

She could see the dominie now. Striding far down the Loch Road, in his long, black elder's hat and long-tailed coat. A sight familiar enough in the kirk on Sunday, but alien and out of context on a bright week-day of harvest-time. A *special* occasion this, though. And, maybe, she thought, one worth dying for too. The dominie walking the long road to her funeral. Announcing from his high lectern: Owing to the sudden and tragic death of *I—sa—bella Emslie*. At an age when she was about to cross the threshold of womanhood. It was not to be. *Thy* will, not *ours*, be done. The school will be closed. Let us pray.

I spy! The impulse to shout, and startle the dominie below, almost overcame Isabel. 'I spy,' she said, but in a whisper that couldn't stir the wood into some ghostly echo.

'It was some man in the town, that got Helen Mavor into trouble!' Jean Begg was saying, when Isabel got down to the others again. 'A *married* man at that, my mother said,' she emphasised. Her voice containing all her mother's condemnation.

'My mother *saw* him, once,' Meg Allan remembered. 'At the bus stop at Mealmarket Street,' she added, placing the villain of the piece in a landmark that was familiar to them all, and giving him immediate, horrific reality. 'He'd got a black moustache, and a pair of yon brown suede shoes.'

'Our Davy had a pair of them, once,' Isabel volunteered. Knowing nothing about the man, but something about suede shoes. ' "Never again" my mother told Davy. The toes got all shiny and scuffed.'

Aware that her contribution, wordlessly received, had added nothing to the intriguing topic, she began to expound with a vehemence that she knew would 'get' them!

'And anyhow! I'd never have a man with a black moustache. Nor brown suede shoes either! Never!'

'What kind of man would *you* have, Isabel?' They asked, beginning to crowd round her. 'Tell us, Isabel,' they pleaded. 'Go on! Do tell !'

'Tall. Dark. And handsome!' Meg Allan prompted.

Too vague a description altogether. And one that never came to life in Isabel's mind. Not the way a boy might smile. Sharp and sudden in the passing. Or his hair quiff up. Leaving her mind and body quivering with the small surprise of it.

Or like times when the tenor, standing opposite her in the kirk choir, sang

> That to perfection's sacred height
> We nearer still may rise

She could have transported him clean away, to some dark, warm isolation. Certain of finding with him, the perfection his voice had promised.

'It's Alan Soutar!' Else prompted. 'Isn't it, Isabel? You love Alan Soutar!'

Not now. Not any more. Though time was when the briefest physical contact with Alan Soutar, like handing him a book, or skirting against him in the passing could induce a fork flashed flame of mind and body, in confirmation of which, was there for all the world to see, scrawled across the lavatory wall:

IE LOVES AS

It was on that day when a note from him, passed from desk to desk, unread by the couriers, with that integrity which governed such rituals, exhorted her to 'Give me a ride in Corbie's Wood', that revulsion had overcome her. Inexplicable revulsion. She, who would willingly have lain down in the dark, with a thousand horsemen! Maybe. Maybe it was just the wording of the request that had repelled her, and sent her flying to the girls' lavatory, to erase all trace of the fact that IE had once loved AS.

'She doesn't *know*!' Meg Allan said. 'She doesn't know the kind of man she would have!' But, she was beginning to grope for his identity in her mind. And the quest for him had already begun; a silent sharp scrutiny of the few boys and men, within her limited knowing.

351

Oh I'd know my love
By his way of walking

'She doesn't *know!*' Meg Allan insisted, as they began to scramble down the slopes of the Loch Wood. 'She doesn't even know, *herself*!'

And I'd know my love
By his way of talking

The heat had gone out of the day. The sun was going down slowly, and only slowly was the day going down after it. Ben Achie that had looked so near, and within hand's touch, in the morning, was blue now, and far. And twenty miles wouldn't bring you up to it. Yet, Isabel remembered, her mother had said when *she* was young, and went to be a servant in the south, Ben Achie had walked with her, all the way to the Pentland Hills.

'See you on Monday morning!' Else said, when they reached the crossroads. 'If it's hot like today,' she reminded Isabel. 'Don't wear your coat. And I won't wear mine.' Her instructions carried themselves across the barley field. For they had always kept up a running conversation, till they lost sight of each other.

'Promise!' Else's voice echoed on the air.

'Promise!' Isabel echoed in reply.

It was only when she turned up her own road that Isabel remembered she wouldn't see Else on Monday. Or on any other morning. The ritual of last day at school, which gave it implicit finality, had been submerged. Cancelled out by Helen Mavor's funeral.

On Monday morning, the dominie would stand behind his lectern, telling how the Israelites had managed to cross the Red Sea. They would cross it all right, Isabel knew. God and the dominie would see to that! They had always been on the Israelites' side. But Isabel would not be there to witness and confirm the achievement, and so the Israelites would be doomed to wander forever through her mind, in a pillar of cloud. Somewhere between Pi-hahiroth and Baal-zephon.

The feeling of anti-climax that had overtaken Isabel increased when she reached the house, to find Davy, still in his funeral suit, pumping up his bike.

'You're *going* some place, tonight, Davy,' she accused. 'Some place special. You've still got on your best suit!'

'I *could* be,' Davy admitted, grinning. 'I could be that!'

'*Where*, Davy?' She pleaded. '*Do* tell!'

'If I told *you*.' The grin spread itself across Davy's face, convincing her it was some place *good*. 'If I told you, you would be as wise as *me*, then. Wouldn't you, now?'

'*Where*, then, Davy?' she insisted. Hating the urgency of having to know, and the envy she heard in her own voice. For Davy was allowed to walk a wider world than herself. Down to the blacksmith's forge on a Saturday night. Off to the town with their father, now and again, to sell a bull calf, or buy a heifer calf. Away some nights free-wheeling down the brae on his bike. 'After some lass or other' as their father put it. Davy had never to create another world for himself. Had never lain beneath the blankets, awestruck in Xanadu. Or trembled in the ice-cold immensity of a cavern 'measureless to man'.

'I don't care anyhow!' Isabel assured him, shrugging, and beginning to pass on. 'I don't care *where* you're going tonight. Because I'm going away *myself* soon. Not just for an hour or two. Or half a day! But for a long time. And further than *you've* ever been!'

Lord I'm one
Lord I'm two
Lord I'm three
Lord I'm four
Lord I'm *five hundred* miles
From
      my
        home

'Beldie!'

'What is it, now?' Isabel turned, stiffening with suspicion. For Davy only called her by her family 'pet name' when he wanted something. 'What do you want *this* time!'

'Beldie. Will you deliver the blacksmith's milk, for me the night? You're always shouting to go other nights,' he reminded her.

True enough. Isabel had always loved an 'official' visit to the blacksmith's smiddy. To discover who now LOVED whom, from the names that flickered across its firelit walls.

'But you never let me go *other* nights!' she remembered. Past injustices rankling within her.

'Because you're too *young* other nights!' Davy pointed out. Logic and patience beginning to desert him. 'You know fine what I mean, Beldie!' he said, when the laughter had left her.

'On one condition, then!' she stipulated, restored to good humour again. 'If you tell me where you're going tonight.'

'To a ball,' Davy admitted. 'To the Harvest Home Ball.'

'Did Mother say you could?' Isabel asked. Hoping somewhere, that Mother had said *no*!

'Not yet,' Davy confessed. 'I'm waiting for the right time to ask her.

'I'd dive *right in*, Davy!' Isabel advised. 'I'd dive right in and ask, if I was you!'

'I might. In a wee while,' Davy agreed.

'I wouldn't even wait a wee while!' Isabel urged out of past experience. She herself had stood so often within that precarious moment of time. Before *no* was irrevocably uttered. And *yes* was still an entrancing possibility. '*I* could ask for you,' she suggested, willingly enough. It had always been easier to ask favours for other folk. Besides, it always put them in your debt.

'Some hope,' Davy said. His voice holding none. 'You know *fine* what she'll say to that!'

'Has Davy not got a tongue in his own head?' Isabel remembered, putting on her mother's voice.

'Do you know something?' Davy asked, staring at her, as if he bad just discovered something himself. 'You looked just like Mother for a minute, there!'

'I'm like Father!' Isabel protested. 'Everybody says! Has he got back from the funeral, yet?' she asked, remembering.

'Not yet,' Davy said. 'He went back to the vet's house for a funeral drink.'

'That's your chance, then, Davy!' Isabel urged. 'You should ask Mother about the ball, now! When she's on her own. Before Father gets in to side-up with her!'

'I can't,' Davy said. 'Mother isn't in, either!'

'The Rhode Islands are laying away from home,' the note under the milk jug told Isabel. 'Have gone up to Crombie's Wood to look-see. If your father gets home before me start getting the supper have finished your skirt try it on with the house all to yourself.'

Isabel's skirt lay on the floor, as if her mother had flung it from her, in her haste to be gone. Her unwashed cup and saucer were still on the table, and the teapot still felt warm. Although it was empty, the kitchen had a spell of livingness over it. The way the three bears' cottage might have seemed to Goldilocks, when she stood on its threshold, aware of her own intrusion.

'Where on *earth* has your mother got to, then?' Her father's voice behind her, echoed Isabel's own resentment, his gaze searching the kitchen, as if his wife might be hiding somewhere within it.

'To Corbie's Wood,' Isabel told him.

'To Corbie's Wood? At this time of day? Away up to Corbie's Wood!'

Her father's bewilderment lent distance to the journey. And cast remoteness over the traveller

> . . . faithless is she
> She left lonely forever
> The kings of the sea

'Has *Davy* gotten back yet, then?' her father asked, as if Davy, too, might have disappeared.

'He's round at the back,' she told him, 'pumping up his bike.'

'Still kirning away with that bike of his, then?' her father grumbled. 'I would have thought he might have made a start to scything the inroads. Seeing the weather's holding up like this!'

Davy would never get to the Harvest Home Ball, now. Isabel knew. Her father would never let such fine harvest weather go wasted by.

'Aye. But the weather's holding up just grand!' her father confirmed. 'Look-see, Beldie!' he urged. 'Just you take a look over at Ben Achie, there! Not a speck of mist on it. I've never seen the Mother Top so clear as 'tis the night!'

> Ye mountains of Gilboah

Always Isabel had loved the proud, implacable sound of those words that evoked a vision of some bearded patriarch, bowing to the mountain. Honouring it. But yet commanding it

> Let there be no rain
> Neither let there be dew

'Well then! Beldie lass!' Sudden and jovial, her father whirled round on her, rubbing his hands in anticipation. 'What's about some supper, then? You'd better be getting your hand in, eh? Going away to the town, to service, and all! Next week, is't? Next week, sometime?'

'On Monday!' Isabel reminded him. Resentful that he had forgotten. 'This first Monday.'

'You'd better give Davy a cry,' he said, turning to look out of the window again. 'We'll need to make a sharp start, if we want to get through with the cutting of that corn. Aye, will we. Me and Davy.

'You've got to get ready for your supper!' She shouted to Davy, waiting till he reached the door; to hiss with a vindictiveness that took herself by surprise. 'And you'll never get to the Harvest Home ball, tonight! I know that much!'

'Have you not got a start to your suppers, then?' The attack in Kate Emslie's voice took them by surprise, and disarmed them.

'Where did you get to, then?' Dod Emslie asked. But he had already lost the first round.

'You know fine where I was!' Kate Emslie snapped, clamping the basket of eggs down on the table. 'I left a note. I was away to Corbie's Wood.'

To Faery Lands Forlorn, Isabel knew, struck by the bright expectancy of her mother's look, searching the kitchen, as if she hoped for some transformation. Her hair, in some wild escape from the bun that usually held it tight with such severity, ruffled in curls round her forehead. She must have been pretty once! Isabel realised with small, pleased surprise. Maybe Davy was right, after all! Maybe she *did* look a bit like Mother.

'Was it worth it, then?' Father asked. 'This trek away up to Corbie's Wood?'

'Well worth it!' Kate Emslie confirmed. 'I *knew* the hens were laying away. I found nine eggs up there. And all sound. At least sound enough for baking with,' she qualified. 'I see you haven't changed out of your best suit, Davy!' Her vision had dimmed down to the level of the kitchen again, and she was noticing at last.

'The sooner he does *that,* the better!' Dod Emslie agreed with her. 'We'd maybe get a start to some work, then!'

Speak, Davy. Speak now. Isabel exhorted him silently. Or *forever* hold your peace.

'I was going out, the night,' Davy said, as if in answer to her wordless plea.

'Out?' Dod Emslie spoke as if Out was a place beyond their ken. And Kate Emslie's voice an echo from its farness. '*Out?*'

'To the Harvest Home Ball,' Isabel blurted. Lest Davy would never find the words for himself.

The reaction began to whirl round the kitchen in dark circles of sound. A Harvest Home Ball on a night like this! And a funeral day at that! For, who on *earth* had disrespect enough to hold a ball at such a time? It showed you just what folk were coming to. Though they themselves, had not yet come to that. Nor would they ever countenance the like! If Davy thought, that for a single minute, they would allow … 'then Davy better have *another* think!' Kate Emslie warned, halting the tempo.

'I didn't mean to tell, Davy.' Isabel's voice broke through an appalled and quivering silence.

'You blabbering bitch!' Davy said, without looking at her. 'You big mouthed mare!'

'Language!!' their father warned him. 'Just you guard your tongue, my Mannie!'

'I didn't mean to, Davy,' Isabel pleaded. 'It just came out!'

'You never *mean* to do anything!' Davy said, grabbing the saw from the porch shelf, and turning to look on her before he slammed the door behind him. 'But you go and do *everything* just the same!'

'Everything,' her mother added. 'Except make a start to getting the supper!'

'Aye,' her father sided with her mother, 'Beldie's whiles some quick with that tongue of hers.'

The treacherous, wayward tide of family opinion had begun to turn against her.

'I didn't *mean* to, Davy!' she shouted against the high scream of the saw. 'Davy!' she urged. 'Do you *know* something. Davy? I got the dominie's watch the day! It was *gold*, Davy. Real gold.'

'That's nothing!' Davy said, moved into speech at last. 'That's nothing, just. The dominie was always giving his watch to some lass or other.

'*I* never saw him do it before!' Isabel protested.

'You wouldn't see everything!' Davy assured her, calmly, bending to pick up the sharpening stone.

'I *would* have seen that!' Isabel insisted, in a desperate awareness, that some important part was falling out of her day. 'I *would* have seen that. And remembered.'

Maybe, maybe she didn't see everything! Come to think of it, she had never really known Davy 'young'. Strange to think that Davy's boyhood was held within the dominie's memory.

'Your brother!' he had once chided her. 'Your brother could have given me that square root, in the time that you are fickering about there, sharpening that pencil! I doubt, though,' he had qualified, 'if David ever truly comprehended that splendour

> that falls
> On castle walls
> And snowy Summits.

But the thing she had just seen, too elusive for words, clamped her mind down in a small tight vice of pain. The way Davy had gripped the back of the chair, till his knuckle bones showed white. His wrists were awful thin, she had realised. Davy's wrists are awful thin, she had thought, staring.

'I just *hate* the sound that sharpening stone makes!' Isabel burst out, at last. 'It cuts me all up into little bits!'

'A pity, that!' Davy said, the grin beginning to spread across his face. 'A pity it didn't cut your tongue into little bits as well!'

> You're *right,* my boy!
> Hold up your head.
> And look like a gentle man, Sir!
> Now tell me who King Davy was
> Now tell me if you *can,* Sir!

'You'll get your legs cut off and all!' Davy warned her, 'if you keep dancing round the saw, like some daft thing!'

> King Davy was a mighty man!
> The King of the Cannibal Islands
> He ate his only daughter Jean
> And was banished to the Highlands!

Now that her father and Davy had left for the fields, Isabel had a large, but illusory sense of freedom.

'You can get on with the pressing of your skirt, now,' her mother suggested, 'seeing as we've got the house to ourselves for a while.'

But I would rather wear a skirt of flannel. Red and wide. And a petticoat, white and frilled, flouncing beneath it. And I would run barefoot from Slack-o-Linn to Corbie's Wood. Past the smiddy. And past the kirk. Casting my eyes on none! But, knowing all had cast their eyes on *me*. And *blinded* for it! Until Cophetua broke the spell. And rang the silence with a remembered vow

This Beggar Maid
Shall be my QUEEN!

'You'd make a far better job of that skirt,' her mother advised, 'if you'd press it on the wrong side. The seams won't show up, that way,' she added, shattering the crystal ball, with an instinct that was almost unerring. 'It doesn't look too bad, now that you've pressed it,' she conceded, allowing neither time nor desire to gather the shattered fragments together again. 'I think I've got a blouse upstairs somewhere, that might go well with it. Pick up the blue check in it, like. The thing is . . .' Her mother paused and surveyed Isabel with a curiosity that began to embarrass them both. 'The thing is,' she repeated, turning away to take the kettle off the hob. 'You're a lot fuller in the bosom than I am. Or ever I was.'

Isabel had never dreamt of 'undressing' her mother, before. Being fine pleased to think that there was nothing at all under her mother's tweed skirt and cotton overall – *other* people's mothers were different, of course, as she had discovered from Else, on one unforgotten day.

'I know fine when they're doing it in bed at night,' Else had confided. 'I can hear them starting to grunt.'

'Mine don't!' Isabel had protested. Shocked beyond all reasonableness. That her parents 'did it' at all, was something that had to be accepted. But never quite condoned. 'They don't grunt though!' she had insisted. 'They just don't *ever* grunt!'

'Keep your hair on!' Else had advised. 'I never said they did. But *everybody* does something. Our servant told me she keeps her eyes shut. Because she doesn't like to look!'

'Dear God,' Isabel had prayed. 'Please help me when the time comes. Because I won't know whether to keep my eyes open or shut.'

'Anybody home?' Lil Eady shouted, pressing her face against the kitchen window.

'For God's sake, Beldie!' her mother urged, 'get that ironing board out of sight. We don't want *that one* carrying our business all round the countryside.'

'That's surely the skirt of your best costume!' Lil Eady accused, pouncing on the skirt. 'Lord, Kate, you're not going to start showing your knees!'

'I'm making it down for Beldie – ' Kate Emslie snapped, retrieving the skirt. 'It's on the tight side for me now. And Beldie's filling out.'

'It's to be hoped that she's not filling out like some I could mention in this parish.'

'It's to be hoped not, Lil,' Kate Emslie said.

'Unless, of course,' Lil repeated, settling herself back, and spreading herself out into an ease that betokened a lengthy stay, 'unless, of course, *she* is beginning to fill out, like *some* I could name, in the Parish.'

'It is to be hoped not, Lil.' The chill in her mother's voice would have frozen anybody else into silence, Isabel knew. Except Lil.

'Others have hoped that!' Lil pointed out, warming to her subject. 'I bet you the vet's wife hoped the self same thing! And look you what happened to her Helen! Not, mind you, she emphasised, 'but what yon lass of hers just *asked* for trouble. With yon high heeled shoes she always wore. The wonder to me was she never broke her neck in yon things. And stockings so thin, you could almost see the hairs on her legs through them!'

'Helen Mavor is dead!' Kate Emslie said. 'And buried now,' she added, reminding herself of something she should not have forgotten.

It was just that. Just being buried, that made death so ominous to Isabel. If one could lie, like Sleeping Beauty, encased in glass, and visible, for a hundred years, death might just about be acceptable. For one could look upon you then. And speak to you. And keep you in mind. Could even resurrect you. It was the end of *being* that was outwith her comprehension – if death *was* universal, that was! – Isabel had a feeling it might not be! Death couldn't remember everybody in the world. Surely one or two *might* escape, forgotten, from its clutches. O King Live Forever. She had a feeling, that *she* might just be lucky enough to be one of those whom death forgot.

'The mother of her was in a terrible state,' Lil Eadie was saying. 'Terrible, just. I heard tell of it from big Bill Mackie. You mind on him, Kate? He retired from the police. O, a good five years ago it would be, now. And he's never missed a funeral since! They say he dives for the local paper first thing every morning, to see if he can find some funeral or other to go to.'

'Seeing us all under, like?' Kate Emslie commented.

He had nothing better to do! Lil supposed. All irony lost on her. 'But, the thing is,' she continued, 'he was telling me Helen Mavor's mother was in a right state, the day! The pall bearers could hardly get her off the coffin. They thought she would never allow them to take it out of the house!'

'I can understand *that*,' Kate Emslie said. 'I can *well* understand it.'

Her mother's emphatic confession, surprised Isabel. She would hold me back from *death*, Isabel realised, with dawning wonder. For her mother had never kissed her. Not within her memory. 'That's a *good* Beldie!' she would sometimes say, when she was pleased, or '*Fine* lad, Davie!' But the most tangible expression of her affection was a hurried pat in passing. A trait Isabel had acquired from her. A poor and furtive symbol of things deeply felt. Sometimes, an impulse to kiss Davy overcame Isabel. She would grasp him round the neck, and take him by surprise. "*That's* how Chris B. kisses you, isn't it Davy?' she'd tease him. Pretending it was a kiss from Chris B. And not from herself, at all. It had taken only a kiss to waken Sleeping Beauty up after a hundred years. Isabel's mother might never kiss her into life. But she would hold her back from death itself!

HOLY MOSES!
I am dying

'God, Beldie!' her father's voice warned. 'You nearly had me flat on my face, there! Can you not look where you're going!'

'She takes daft turns like that, whiles,' Davy sniggered. 'Racing about like a mad thing.'

'Beldie!' her father's voice reached her at the byre door. 'What was that gossiping bitch Lil Eadie seeking? She's just taken herself out by the back door!'

Just a Word
Before I go

Bury ME
In silk and satins

The lamp had just been lit in the kitchen. It threw a sudden patch of light across the garden.

I am a stranger. Isabel gathered together the threads of an old, and favourite game. I have lost my way. The wind is beginning to rise. Soon it will be dark. And I must find a bed for the night. *That* looks a friendly house. Any minute now, any minute now, she would race all the way from the byre, and burst into the kitchen, in anticipation of the light and warmth that would rush towards her. And the sound of known voices that would envelop her in their safety.

'Shut that door behind you, Beldie!' her mother warned. 'There's an edge to the nights, now. We don't want to perish!'

But then, Isabel realised, focusing on her family, rooted in their familiar places, they were not strangers. Come in out of the night. They couldn't know how brightly the lamp gleamed. Nor how fiercely the fire burned. They could never catch the cadences of comfort after that wordless lament of the wind along the telegraph wires.

'What was that gossiping bitch Lil Eadie seeking then?' Her father asked.

'O nothing very much,' her mother said, knowing it was just one of the casual observations that gathered the day to an end, and drew in the night. 'She was just on about the funeral. And, speaking about the funeral, was there a big turn out there, the day?'

'Big Bill Mackie was there!' Isabel remembered. 'Lil Eadie said.' She urged the topic on, in the safety of the kitchen. For her mind had skirted round the funeral all day. Approaching it fearfully. Touching it lightly. Retreating from it swiftly, lest it should capture herself within the isolated circle that contained it. Petrifying her in its granite memorial.

'A fair turnout,' her father admitted. 'Considering the fine harvest weather.' *His* mind walking through the safety of his fields at Slack-o-Linn. 'George Kerr was saying he's got all his crop, home. But then,' her father reflected, his fields lie on the sheltered side of Ben Achie. The hill keeps the sun off mine.'

'Surely!' her mother contradicted. 'The sun must get round to *your* fields, *whiles*, Father! *It's* no respecter of persons!'

It seemed another time since Isabel had lain with Else among the gorse in the Loch Wood, sheltered from the sun. Yet it was only today. Fear no more the heat o' the sun, she had remembered, as they scrambled for a hiding place in the shade. How her mind had been trapped, whirling in search of the rest of the words, that had eluded it until she found some of her own. Nor its embroiling ray. The sun, she knew, in a moment of small, distinct, living clarity, would never reach its zenith, in time and place again, without the bitter burning smell of gorse.

'I suppose Alick Mearns was at the funeral, the day?' Her mother was saying. 'All togged up, as usual?'

'Somebody's making their way, here!' Davy announced, flinging his burden of logs down on the hearth. 'I saw the light of a bike turning down our road.'

'Who can it be at this hour of night?' Kate Emslie's dislike of unbidden guests found curious outlet in hasty resentful preparation for them.

'Draw your long legs in about to yourself, Davy. Other folk would like a glimpse of the fire! And you can just put on your wellingtons again, Father! Lolling about in your sweaty socks. As for you, Beldie! Sitting cocked on top of the fire, there. Small wonder you're always complaining about your chilblains. It's high time *you* was making tracks for your bed!'

Her commands flew thick and fast. Directed at all. And galvanising each into life.

'It's been a long day,' she reflected, by way of apology, surveying her family sitting upright in formal discomfort. 'A long day for all of us. You too Beldie,' she added, with dawning remembrance. 'Your last day at school. That must have been some day for you!'

And everybody had forgotten about it. Isabel was curiously grateful for the world's forgetfulness. One finger probed through the tenuous fabric of the day and it would disintegrate completely. For it was not yet shaped and concrete in her mind. Liquid and elusive, it trickled through her fingers the way the rain from the roan pipe always eluded capture on its way down to the water butt.

'Did they all give you your "Bumps" the day, then, Beldie?' Father asked, jovial, as if the answer really mattered to him.

'I suppose,' her mother ventured, 'that the dominie had a last word with you. Told you to behave yourself, did he! And work your work in the world well?'

'Aye,' father remembered. 'When the dominie had his last word with you, you would have thought you were going away to the end of the earth! For all that most of us never ventured more than a mile or two away from the school in our lives.'

'But the *dominie*'s time with us had ended,' Kate Emslie pointed out. 'And that was what counted with him!'

'They FORGOT!' Davy said suddenly, triumphantly, getting his own back. 'They all got off early for the funeral. And they forgot all about her last day. Serves her right!'

The loud knock at the back door sent Kate Emslie scurrying to peer out of the scullery window.

'We are not bedded yet.' The wariness of her greeting

reached them in the kitchen. 'But we are just thinking about it,' she prophesied ominously.

'It's yourself, is it, Alex?' Father shouted genially, forestalling his wife's reluctance. 'Come away in. Come on in and sit yourself down man!'

Her blood stirred in recognition. The thousand anonymous horsemen Isabel had longed to lie under in the dark hay-lofts began to merge into, and take on the identity of the guest by the fire from the gleam of his leggings to the hairs curling red on his hands. And memory completed the picture for her. Until the death of Helen Mavor had ousted him, Alex Ewan had been the object of eternal curiosity and speculation. It was high time he took a wife, some said. He had no need for one, others remembered. You never bought the cow when you got the milk for nothing. And the way the young girls were so willing to open their legs to him he could have fathered the population all on his own. Her mother's bitter denunciation rose to mind.

'Poor bits of lassies, just! *That's* who Alex Ewan takes for his housekeepers. Out of the workhouse with their unfathered bairns. Thankful to take on any job at all to get out of the workhouse. And himself just ready to father another bairn on them! Striding about yonder. Togged up to the nines, always!'

'He's a man that takes a proper pride in himself!' Her father had always defended. 'As well he might. For he's a fine set-up man.'

... The Wild Man Of Borneo who had threatened all of childhood's misdemeanours. Feared, but fascinating. Unseen, but always imminent. The word becoming flesh.

'I see they're after going and cancelling the Harvest Home dance,' he was saying. 'Owing to the funeral, I suppose.'

The criticism in his voice stung Kate Emslie into remembered resentment. 'And rightly so!' she snapped. 'It would be a sore pity if the living couldn't catch its breath to have a thought for the dead.'

'That doesn't bring them back, mistress,' Alex Ewan pointed out.

'No! But it shows some respect!'

As usual, Isabel remembered, her mother had got the last word. Alpha and Omega. As the minister always prophesied threateningly when he snapped the big Bible shut. 'The Beginning and the End!'

'In *my* opinion,' her mother's tone left no room for the opinions of others, 'half the trouble in the parish starts off with those dances. Poor Helen Mavor, herself, started her dancing days too young. Too soon.'

That was the thing that was worth dying for! Isabel had discovered it at last. If I could go once. Just *once* to a dance. I'd never ask for another thing in all my life again. That would be enough for me . . . They wore dresses of blue and pink and green. They shimmered in the light, and trailed on the floor. Their shoes were silver.

'And they are beautiful! I've seen them!' she heard herself announcing suddenly. 'In the Milne Hall. On my way home from the Bible class,' she explained, aware of the stiffening up of the kitchen.

'So that's why you're always so late home from the Bible class on a Friday night,' her father reflected. 'I always wondered about that!'

'Everybody *else* goes to the dancing!' she defended. 'Except *me!* I've always got to go to the Bible class.'

'Poor minister.' Her father condoled. 'He must have a very small Bible class, then. Just yourself, is it Beldie?'

'Anyhow! I can please myself where I go after next week!' The insolence that came rarely to Isabel was torn from her now as a protection against ridicule. And instantly regretted . . . *You* can just go straight up to your bed! . . . her mother

369

would command. And the night that had been proud and expanding, with its portents of approaching womanhood, would humble and close over a small girl sent to bed in disgrace.

'Next week is another matter,' her mother said casually, surprisingly evading such a catastrophe. 'What *does* matter, Beldie,' she emphasised, in the way she sometimes did, when they were alone together, 'is that a thing is either true or it's a lie. And whiles, Beldie, whiles,' she paused, speculative and puzzled, '*you* are very guilty of getting them mixed up, I know *this* much! You never set foot in the Milne Hall in your life! It's just not in your nature to push yourself.'

But she *had* heard the music of the dancing. Sounding through the quiet village, following her all the way to Corbie's Wood, and echoing through her mind long after she had reached home. Dispelling sleep itself.

> And you shall drink freely
> The dews of Glensheerlie
> That stream in the starlight
> When Kings dinna ken
> And deep be your meed
> Of the wine that is red

One day. Some day. *She* would dance to the music. She had never danced with a partner. But she had often danced by herself. A dance in which movement was never confined to setts and reels and ritual patterns, but to the interpretation of the moods of a moment. The 'dews of Glensheerlie' had not got the monopoly. She, herself, could . . . 'stream in the starlight' . . . When Kings dinna ken. How she would dance when the time came. How motionless the other dancers would be, mesmerised into immobility by the grace and sweep of her movements . . .

> On either side the river lie
> Long fields of barley and of rye

On and on. Round and round. Till she dropped exhausted from dancing. And the lament rising up around her, loud enough to assail her into consciousness again.

> Dear God! she hath a lovely face

'I said we're losing you, Isabel!' Alex Ewan was saying. 'They tell me you're going away to service in the town.'

'Aye,' her father agreed. 'We are that! Her mother's kind of anxious about it though. Her going so far away from home, like.'

'We've all got to stretch our wings,' Alex Ewan said. 'Some time or other. She'll be fine, though,' he assured them jovially. 'Isabel will be just fine! Won't you, lass? I warrant *you'll* set all the lads by the ears when you get to the town. With a bonnie head of hair on you like that!'

It had always needed the recognition of others to confirm her own secret potentials. Like the 'trim ankles' her mother had bestowed upon her. Now she had been bequeathed a 'bonnie head of hair'. She could have sung aloud for such emerging talismans. Protections against the Wild Man Of Borneo. Growing spells to cast over a fine set-up man with shining leggings and hairs that glinted red on his hands.

'It is to be *hoped*,' her mother said, 'that Isabel will keep her mind on her *work!* And have more sense than bother herself about the lads in the town!'

'You cannot put old heads on young shoulders, mistress,' Alex Ewan advised, as he rose to go, aware that he had outstayed his cool welcome. It was when he reached the door that he remembered the purpose of his visit.

'That cow of mine has gone clean dry,' he explained. 'She's

just at the drop of calving. I was wondering if you might manage to hold me in milk, for the next day or so. And I'll see till't, mistress,' he promised, 'that you'll get her first yield after calving, to make yourself a fine bit of calfie's cheese.'

'We're not all that partial to calfie's cheese.' Kate Emslie rejected the offer. 'We prefer a bit of plain Crowdie.'

'*Surely*, Alex!' Her father lurched up out of his chair. The geniality in his voice consoled Isabel, and atoned for her mother's rudeness. 'Surely we'll hold you in milk! I'll walk you as far as the end of the road. And I'll send Isabel over to your place,' he promised. 'First thing in the morning.'

Davy and her father were already at work. She could hear the reaper whirring across the Low Field. Her father perched on top of it, disembodied in the rising mist, as he skimmed along the edges of the uncut corn. Davy bobbing up and down behind him gathering the swathes as they fell.

'A thin crop the year,' her father had grumbled. 'More thistles than corn.' As the day warmed, and the pace quickened, Davy would grow careless, grasping wildly at the swathes till his hands 'stooned' all over with thistle stobs. Thistledown puffed along on the breeze would get into his eyes and soon he would start to pray for the reaper to break down. Just for a minute. Just to let him get his back straightened. It was the greatest blessing in all the world, Isabel realised, straightening herself up at the window, not to have a 'crick' in your back.

Down in the hens'ree the Rhode Island Reds clamoured greedily around her mother's feet. 'Hens always died in debt,' her mother would grumble in one breath, confessing in the next that she would be 'fair lost without them'.

The limitations that landmarked her mother's life increased Isabel's growing sense of freedom. When the red flowering currant, barren in its old age, hadn't come into bloom her mother's lament had echoed its regret all through the spring. 'I should have taken a cutting or two when that bush was young. I just never seemed to get the time.' Mourning was contagious, though. The bush, that could no longer flower, had forced itself into leaf. Crumbling the leaves between her fingers, and sniffing them, casually, absentmindedly, one day, with no thought of grief, the limitations had closed in on Isabel too. Spring would never be spring until the flowering currant came into bloom.

'Get a move on, Beldie!' her mother shouted up at the window. 'You should have been on your road with Alex Ewan's milk long since!'

Far into the night, she had heard her mother nagging away at her father. 'Whatever possessed you to suggest that *Beldie* should go *near* Alex Ewan's place!' had been her refrain. 'You know *fine* what that man is!'

'Who else could I send, but Beldie?' her father had defended. 'I can't spare *Davy!* We're making a start to the Low Field. First thing in the morning. Me and Davy!'

Davy would always be captive, within the landmarks. Isabel's pity for him was tinged with some vague sense of regret for herself. Her excitement over her own unknown future, diminished a little by a reluctant envy of Davy's safety in the familiar.

> . . . we ken a Place
> where the trout leaps *great*
> me – and Davy

Always, Isabel felt an intruder in the kitchen in the early mornings. Cool and dim and aloof, it seemed to hold itself in reserve for the heat and busyness of her *mother's* day. The stone flags her mother had just scrubbed were still damp to the touch of Isabel's bare feet. Their high wet shine had not yet dried up into sand streaked greyness.

'*You* slept your head into train oil, this morning!' her mother grumbled, clattering down the hens' pail and shattering the silence of the kitchen. 'You've got a long travel in front of you!' she reminded. 'Alex Ewan's place is away at the back of beyond!'

'I was brushing my hair,' Isabel said. Suddenly remembering the thought that leapt up in her mind on wakening . . . He said I'd bonnie hair . . .

'You have more need to get something on your *feet!*' her mother advised. 'Padding about the damp floor! You may have *brushed* your hair,' her mother added, surveying Isabel dubiously, 'But I see you haven't tied it *back!* You know fine how I feel about your hair flying all round your face!'

'Else Finlay has *ringlets!*' Isabel remembered. '*Her* mother puts them in for Else, every night. With papers!'

'More fool her *mother!* That's all *I* can say!' Kate Emslie banged the hens' pail down on the kitchen floor. And silenced the counsel for the defence.

But *she* had 'bonnie hair'. The knowing sang in Isabel's mind all the way down Slack-o-Linn road. At the end of it, the world widened, and the day began to widen with it, in growing confliction. This time next week she would be walking along a new road. Through a strange country. Landmarks that were rooted in her first consciousness became distorted. She had the curious feeling that she walked suspended through a world at once timeless and unreal. Poised on the stile that led into Corbie's Wood, she stirred herself, and thought. Yesterday, when I crossed this stile, I was on my way to School. I'll never cross the stile to go *that* way, again.

'*You're* out of your road this morning, Isabel!' the wives waiting for the bus greeted her, when she got to the crossroads. 'Surely you should be giving your mother a hand on a Saturday!'

'I'm away over to Alex Ewan's place with some milk,' she told them. 'His cow has gone clean dry!'

'*Himself* hasn't!' the joiner's wife said drily.

'More's the pity!' Lil Eadie agreed.

'You want to watch yourself with that one!' they all advised. 'It's a while since he's had one young enough to have all her own teeth.'

Their laughter rose in spasms around her.

'Time, somebody gave him a damned good bite!' the joiner's wife egged their laughter on.

Time Isabel was away to service in the town. Away from the coarseness that lurked around the bus stop, ready to spring up, and trap her in embarrassment.

Time to be glad her mother was her mother! For *she* would never stand skirling daft, at the cross roads. Would never never kilt her skirt high above her knees, as Lil Eadie was doing now. Prancing around, exhorting the other wives to admire her 'Long John Toms'. Her 'passion killers'.

Time coming soon, now, when Isabel would escape from all! Dark and mysterious she would be, the next time she passed that lot! 'Good afternoon,' she would say. Cool. Without pausing. Taking her dark, mysterious self past the bus stop, intact.

'Surely that was *Kate Emslie's* lass!' they would speculate, mystified, when she passed them.

'Her that went away to service in the town!'

The village before her lay misted and relaxed under its Saturday morning idleness. The women, their cottages 'thoroughed out' before they went to bed on Friday night, stood at their ease on their cardinal red doorsteps calling across to each other without urgency. The way the wood pigeons had cooed and coodled all the length of Corbie's Wood. And just as the crackle of a twig had silenced the wood pigeons, so the hen man's van, roaring its way through the village, now silenced the women into critical contemplation of the dust it raised up behind it.

Walking in the wake of the van, Isabel was aware of the attention instantly transferred on herself. She was too old now to escape it by kicking out at any stone that barred her way and scudding defiantly past the watchful wives.

'That hen van's a perfect menace,' the shoemaker's wife informed the others.

'One of these fine *days!*' the beadle's wife prophesied.

'So *you've* come to see the flowers too, then, Isabel!'

They swirled round on her, as if they had spotted her in unison with those eyes they always claimed they had in the back of their heads.

'All that *way* from Slack-o-Linn!'

'Mind *you!* They're well worth seeing!' Teen Ross assured them from her stance by the pump. 'There's a small *fortune* on that grave. And *no* mistake!'

'I don't hold with it, for all *that!*' the shoemaker's wife said. 'I'm one who likes flowers well enough to let them grow!' she boasted, hemmed neatly in by her hedge of box-wood. Spiked and enclosed by all her zinnias. The loss of *one* would have outflanked her.

'Come and see the flowers, Isabel,' Else Finlay invited when she reached the kirk gate.

'They're all white!' Jean Mavor said.

'White everywhere!' her sister agreed.

'Come on, Isabel!' Else urged, aware of her hesitation, for a barrier, subtle, but stronger than the kirk gate had arisen to separate Isabel from Else, and all her erstwhile classmates, kneeling on the grass, examining the cards on the high bank of wreaths. Although she had left school only yesterday, it was long enough to exile her from their inner circle.

'Have you lot read *this* one?' Ann Mavor demanded. '"Safe On His Gentle Breast",' she interpreted in a reading-aloud voice. '"With Love Always.".'

'Mimmy was Helen Mavor's grandmother,' Isabel said. And the barrier became tangible, as the others rose up off their knees and dumbly appraised her from the other side of the gate.

'It's an old Scottish word for grandmother.' She rushed into, and through the silence.

'We all know that!' Jean Mavor said.

'We know that, fine!' her sister echoed.

'*Anyhow!*' Isabel shrugged, for the moment had come to turn and go. 'Anyhow. I haven't got *time* to see the flowers. I've got to go over to Alex Ewan's place,' she added, infusing her mission with distance and importance. 'He's got to get milk. His cow's gone dry.'

No statement, she discovered to her own surprise, could have so effectively and firmly established her growing adult awareness.

'Alex EWAN's place!' they chorused, crowding round the gate, admiringly and apprehensively.

'*He's* just sent his latest housekeeper down the road!' Else confided. 'Sacked her on the spot. Our servant met her at the bus stop. Pram. Bairn. And all!'

'He'll be all by *himself*, then, Isabel!' Jean Mavor warned. 'Are you not feared to go there on your *own*?'

'Not . . . feared,' she admitted at last. And in the wake of her considered admission, realisation overtook her. She *wanted* to go. She wanted to go, more than anything else in all the world. '*Never* feared!' She threw back her head and laughed at the bewildered expressions on their faces. And for the relief of a truth acknowledged.

'Come on in, Isabel. Come on and see the flowers,' Else urged, and holding the gate open, stepped aside to let a grown-up acquaintance enter through.

She could never have gone to see the flowers. She knew that with every step that led her away from the kirkyard. She would have wanted to toss away the flowers. To see beneath and beyond them. To claw through the grave with her bare hands and penetrate the mystery of death itself.

O, she knew well enough what happened to the *ancient* dead. When the small graveyard was full the gravedigger just dug up some of the old graves and shovelled the contents over the dyke to make room for the newcomers. And that seemed fair enough. For they were old. Older than anybody's memory of them. As remote and far sounding as the inscriptions that struggled brokenly through the moss, encrusted on their slanting tombstones ... Until the Day Breaks and the Shadows Flee Away.

Five short days ago Helen Mavor had been alive.

'Here today. Gone tomorrow,' her mother remarked, as she washed the eggs. Counting them in the same breath. Certain that *she* would be there to sell them to the hen man tomorrow.

We'll all go to our long home *some* day. The congregation had reminded each other, as they clustered round the kirk gate after the memorial service. Casually, as if there was no hurry at all for *them* to go to *their* long home.

That bourne from which no traveller ever returns. The minister had forecast, with gloomy conviction. That had not convinced Isabel.

Lay hold on
   LIFE
     And it
       Shall BE

Thy joy and Crown

Ee
   ter
    NALLY

How often had they sung that in the kirk. And how she had hugged its sentiment to herself, in an embrace wide enough to hold the years to come and all that they might bring. And the years that had gone and all that they had brought.

Helen Mavor could never have let go of life so soon. Could never be as dead as that so suddenly. Lying under her bank of white flowers so near to the kirk door, memory must surely still hold good! She would know when it was spring.

They would all be singing.

> There is a green hill far away
> Without a city wall

And summer. She would remember it when they sang

> For the beauty of the earth
> For the beauty of the skies
> For the love which from our birth

And autumn. She would remember it, too, from the nearby singing sounds

> Earth seems to squander her plenty on the sheaf

But Helen Mavor had at least seen a bit of this autumn, she remembered, gazing across the landscape. The thought halted her and fixed her to the spot. I'm seeing it for Helen, she realised. Watchful. Expectant of some subtle change. From now on, she promised, I'll look at things for her. She won't miss so much, that way.

Clambering over the dyke, she raced down Teuchat's Hill towards the river. The rattle of her milk can scattering the grazing ewes and their half grown lambs. There had been no 'lambie's storm' in the spring, to her father's relief, so it was some of his lambs that stared after her, scandalised, from beneath the fleecy safety of their mothers' flanks.

'You're *our* lambs!' she shouted back, reminding them. 'So you can put *that* in your pipes and smoke it!'

'You'd better go by the road,' her mother had advised, when she set out in the morning. 'For, if you take the short cut by the river, knowing *you* you'll just plooter about there, all day!'

But she hadn't plootered about the river. And there were some things her mother didn't know about her. She could leave things behind fine! It was just that things would never let her go! And so the river ran on behind her, tugging away at mind and memory. The dark murky hiding places of the tiddlers in the deep water at its edge. The forget-me-nots that skimmed along its banks, rooted down in the water itself.

Frail life-lines you'd clutch at laughingly, to land. The stones that rose at random to form their own peculiar pattern for stepping over. The wild raspberries, their brief enticement broken by a more potent siren sound.

'Last across the stepping stones is a *hairy worm*!'

The roofs of the Smiddy Crofts swayed redly towards her through the blue haze. 'Half-way to the back of beyond,' her mother described the Crofts. 'And we'll get there by and by.' The shadows of the trees began to lattice the road into great squares of sunlight.

Iggledy Piggledy
ONE!
TWO!
THREE!
I love my
LOVE
And my Love
Loves
ME!!

'They must have money to burn on shoe leather at Slack-o-Linn!'

The unbeliever's wife stood in the dimness, half folded over the gate of her cottage.

'I've got a stone in my shoe.' She hopped to a halt, reddening under her instant lie.

'A queer way to get rid of a stone in your shoe.' The unbeliever's wife looked over and past her to the wood beyond. 'Leaping about the road like that!'

But then, the unbeliever's wife knew nothing about stones in shoes, she reassured herself, remembering to hirple lamely till she was out of sight. There was luxury in the pain of a stone in your shoe. And a feeling of power. You could end it instantly. Or endure it forever. The longer you held on to the pain, the sweeter the ease. She would never know such ease, the unbeliever's wife, for she would never endure such agony.

'The fear of the Lord is the beginning of wisdom,' her mother always quoted, when there was an argument at home over the unbeliever.

'He's a brave man. For all that he doesn't hold with the kirk,' her father would insist. 'Awarded medals to prove it! Not that he took them, mind you! For he's a man who knows his own mind. A man that went all through the blood bath of the Somme.'

Her father's highly coloured, far sounding vindications of the unbeliever never narrowed down to match the reality of the small, whey-faced man himself. As shadowy and with-drawn as his cottage that huddled amongst the trees. When Isabel came across him at all, it was accidental, with the wordlessness of unexpected impact. If words could have been uttered, they would have been words of apology for some inexplicable intrusion.

The unbeliever only came to life in her mind on Armistice Sundays. And then by his absence. When medals for bravery glinted and jingled on other men's breasts. And his voice never rose to swell the triumphant volume of

> When Zion's bondage God turned back
> As men that dreamed were *we*
> Then filled with laughter were our souls
> Our tongues with melody

'Where's the fire, then, Isabel?' The blacksmith's apprentice grinned from the door of the forge. 'You're fair out of puff.'

'That's because I ran all the way from the river with Alex Ewan's milk.'

'It'll be into butter by now, then!'

'Or buttermilk!' she suggested, as they laughed at the ridiculous idea, pleased with each other's wit. She hadn't laughed so much for such a long time, over such a little thing.

'I could swing this milk can right round my head. And I wouldn't spill a drop,' she claimed, nudging the tears of laughter from her cheeks.

'I bet you could too!' the blacksmith's apprentice said. 'It's the speed that does it,' he explained. 'It doesn't give the milk time to fall out.'

'Is *that* what it is?' she asked, her attention straying to the hair on his chest. Matted with sweat, it streaked down to his navel in a long black line.

A hairy man's a happy man, her father always said, lathering himself above the sink. But a hairy wife's a witch! Yet, it was important for a woman to be hairy, according to Else.

'I'll show you if you show me!' Else had once challenged. She hadn't accepted the challenge. Else only ever dared anything, when she was sure she would win.

She wouldn't let herself look at *his* navel, either! 'Belly button' her mother called it, that shut you in and held you together. You'd just pop out and spill all over, if it wasn't there.

'A shame the dance was cancelled on Friday,' the blacksmith's apprentice said, as if it was a regret they both should share.

'Wasn't it just!' The brightness that flashed up inside her sharpened her voice. She could feel it flooding her face and thrusting itself out from behind her eyes. That was what her hair loose, and her Sunday shoes did for her! She always knew they'd do that. Make her worthy enough to go to a dance. Even if she would never have been allowed to go in the first place!

'Maybe it will be on next Friday, though,' he suggested.

'Maybe.'

'Maybe we'll see you there, then?'

'Maybe.'

'Next Friday then!'

'Next Friday!' she confirmed, shouting back, as she ran forward in some bright, expectant certainty.

If she'd had whooping cough it would have been cured the instant she turned round into the Lecht Road. The fumes rose hotly from its newly tarred surface. Best cure in the

383

world for whooping cough, her mother always said. In the days when folk had big families and no money to throw away on doctors. She'd never tried it herself, mind you! But she'd heard tell of many an infant snatched from death's door by a sniff of the tar. Nonsense! Her father had contared. For he had no faith in miracles. Pure nonsense just! You went when your time came. Tar or no tar.

It was the kind of road that lured her into navigating it blind. When all sense of direction lay in the sensitivity of her feet. Veering sideways across the softness of the grass verge, teetering cautiously over the gritty gravel, shoe bound at last on the soft sticky tar.

'A menace to other folk. As well as to yourself!' Postie shouted. His bike grinding to a halt on the gravel. 'It's a blind corner that. And bloody dangerous!'

But then, she was a blind person! Though Postie would never believe that, she realised, staring startled up at him.

'I could have gone arse over heels!' he claimed. 'With you stuck on the road. Like a damned idiot!'

There was something odd about Postie, himself, she remembered. Searching his face to find it.

'You'll surely know me the next time you see me!' he snarled, remounting his bike. 'Stupid little bitch! You haven't even got the sense you was born with.'

Her mother had never been able to put her finger on what was odd about Postie. Though any man on the wrong side of forty with a secure job like his and a fine pension at the end of it, still stuck to his mother's apron strings must be an odd bod, right enough!

Not everybody was in such a rush to get the marriage banns cried out in the kirk as she herself had been, Father had always defended. *Some* folk likit to hold to their bit of freedom. Though few enough got the chance to do it. Poor buggers!

Maybe so. Her mother had snapped. But it always took two! And there was no call for language! Though *some* mothers had a lot to account for! If it was Davy now! She, herself, would only be too pleased to see *him* settled down with a nice sensible lass.

'If it was *me*,' Davy had boasted, perking up under the unexpected attention, 'and I had *Postie*'s mother, I'd take the King's Shilling!'

Wondrous shilling. Splendid shilling. Sounding always as if it was an honour conferred upon His Majesty. Sire, I will *accept* your shilling. Silver talisman that opened for Davy all avenues of escape. Gaining currency and glimmer on dark frostbitten mornings in winter, when she'd pass Davy on her road to school, howking turnips out of the stone hard earth in the Low Park. Hardly a copper to call his own, he'd confide, whacking his arms across his chest to get the blood going in his fingers again. His bed and his bite, just. And a bare bob or two in his pocket to tide him over a Friday night. For pure slavery. He'd be far better off with the King's Shilling. Other things he'd confide too, on such mornings. Things only half comprehended, as she stood absorbed in her breath, that abstract thing they said you could die for the want of, becoming tangible at last, rising white in the darkness. He'd hardly get anybody *better* than Chris B. Her not being all that particular. And, God knows, he didn't want the likes of *her!* Not with the one suit he'd had for three years. And it away above his ankles now. Near enough to make him a laughing-stock in the countryside. Though she didn't care! Not listening to a word he was telling her!

'But Mother,' she had remembered, keeping her eyes fixed on the breath that was drifting away from her, 'gets the Co-op van. Even if it *is* dearer than the other vans. Just so that she can get our clothes off the Divi. It's the only way she can save.'

'How many pounds of sugar do you think it takes, Beldie, to get enough Divis for one serge suit?' Davy had asked, in the voice the dominie always used when he knew she would never find the answer. Never. In a million years.

If a tank containing eighty-five gallons of water leaked at the rate of . . .

At least, she didn't have to worry herself about tanks that leaked any more. And for Davy there was always the King's Shilling.

Yet not, not in *all* its glory, did the King's Shilling have the high allure of that *other* enlistment fee her mother sometimes sang of, bent over the washing-board in the tub, on high wind-blown mornings.

> For my lad
> Would list
> When the Duchess
> Kissed
> He forgot
> All the vows
> He made
> He turned
> And he took
> But one last long
> Look
> When
> 'The Cock O' the North'
> Was
> Played

The hard surface of Leuchar's Road rang out under her feet. How Alan Soutar would have struck the blue sparks out of the stones, on a road like this, with the heel-rings of his boots! She had never mastered the knack. It was the twist of

the heel that did it, he'd always boasted. Making a fine thing
out of it. Not that she had cared. He could only make the
sparks, it was herself, racing on behind him, who saw them
all rising up.

> He forgot
> All the vows
> He made
> He turned
> And he took
> But one last long
> Look

'Sing in the morning. Cry before night,' the Howdie Wife
prophesied, peering above her byre door.

'Isabel, is it?' Shading her eyes against the sun, she began
to piece her together, bit by bit. 'Isabel, surely! Isabel. Isabel
Emslie! Though you'll not be minding on *me!*' The old
woman thrust her face forward, anxious for recognition.

The Howdie Wife everybody called her. Everybody except
Isabel's mother. Anybody. She said. Who brought you naked
into the world. And spruced you up to go out of it, deserved
the respect of their proper name. For they were in at the
beginning of life. And at its end. And that, surely, was a
something!

The first person to set eyes on her. Isabel tried to infuse
the thought with awe. Stark naked at that! Her body felt no
embarrassment, having outgrown the Howdie Wife's
memory. The first person to touch her. The old woman's
hands, scratching away at the nape of her neck, had outgrown
that memory too. Hard to tell whether the old woman
approved of her handiwork, hard to get out from, or under,
that silent appraisal.

'Rob Emslie will never die! As long as *you* live. You carry him in your face!'

Triumph rang out of the old woman's voice. 'You're small bookit, though,' she considered critically. 'Like your mother. But fleet of foot like herself. Fleet of foot.'

The sudden flash of memory increased the old woman in stature, and stabbed Isabel with envy.

Tell me. Tell me again. Tell me about the days when *you* was young.

How insistently she had deaved her mother for the stories of *her* young days. Stories that were never allowed to deviate in detail. To add to themselves. Or to take away. So that the young girl who became her mother ran forever through cone strewn fir woods, clothed eternally in a grey frock with blue braiding at the neck, a blue calico pinny with two pockets and black boots that buttoned right up to her knees. She always felt very close to that young girl. As if they could have been friends together. Best friends. The way herself and Else was. Sometimes, she ran ghost-like through the fir woods of her mother's stories, singing along with her.

> Poor old Robinson Crusoe
> I wonder how he could do so!
> He made him a coat
> Of an old nanny goat
> Poor old Robinson Crusoe

'The thing is.' The Howdie Wife thrust her face forward, till it almost touched her own. 'The thing is. She could never give you the breast.'

'I've got to go, Mistress Mutch. I've got to be back before dinner-time.'

'Either *that!*' The Howdie Wife said. 'Or her milk didn't lie on your stomach.'

'I've got to go, Mistress Mutch.' Instantly. Urgently out of the cone strewn fire woods of memory, before the ghostly girls who sang their way through them took on the burdens of their flesh.

'I'm TELLING you!'

The old woman's voice halted her in her tracks. 'There was only one cow the country round whose milk you'd suckle. Only *one*. The wee blue at Broadbec Inn. A wild Inn, yon. Still is on a Friday night. Still is. Oh, I could tell you a thing or two.'

Withdrawing her face, the old woman withdrew the things she could tell. Holding them all to herself, in the far away reflection of her eyes. Isabel knew the look. She'd sometimes seen it on her mother's face. Staring out of the window, yet not seeing what was beyond it. She never told what she had seen either!

'A wild Inn I was saying.'

The old woman's voice rose shrill behind her. Desperate at having let her captive audience go.

'A wild Inn. And WANTON!'

The white gates at the level crossing snapped shut to let the train go by. Its warning bell rang high up in the signal box. But they could sometimes hear the train coming long before the bell told of it. Herself and Else. Flinging themselves down on the grassy embankment, listening with their ears against the ground. Giggling together at the helpless anger of the signal man, shaking his fist at his high window. Racing like the wind the moment the train passed and set the signal man free. Racing against the train itself to reach the bridge before it thundered beneath it. Standing high and bereft on the bridge, holding on to the train till the last wisp of steam curling round and below, disappeared at Ben Achie.

Further down the line, Postie trundled his bike across the

sleepers, raising his hand to the signal man in acknowledgement of such a privilege. He never allowed anybody else to break the rules, did Postie. Wouldn't take an unstamped letter from her mother. Not even with the tuppence to buy the stamp. 'Against government rules, Mistress Emslie,' he'd insist. 'More than my job's worth!' A man who wouldn't even give you the dirt from between his toes, her father always said. Though why anyone should ever want that puzzled Isabel. And there he was, breaking the rules himself, taking the short cut that would have taken a mile off her own journey. It might be good to be old. You could break all the rules then. She, herself, might have taken the risk, if the signal man's eye wasn't fixed upon her. She might *still* have taken it if Else had been there to run it with her. Laughing in the wind, and in the face of the signal man. She missed Else.

LNER. The yellow letters flashed out and by on the green engine. And the train took on a personal identity. *Her* train. The train she herself would be sitting in on Monday morning. She'd watch out for the signal box. And for the bridge. She might even wave to the signal man, grinning at her right to do so. She'd remember Else. And maybe, maybe she'd find out at last if the steam really *did* disappear forever, when the train went round and under Ben Achie.

From *this* side of the bridge Ben Achie should have been transformed. Should have put on another face and laughed and rejoiced, the way the psalms and the paraphrases urged in the kirk on Sunday mornings.

It should have lifted up its voice and sung in the accents of all the people who lived and worked below it, who had died in its shadow, who had never even set eyes on it. For this was the 'back' of Ben Achie. Landmarked in the imagination, rooted in nostalgic memory. Pondering in the shimmering heat, it looked as if it might just make up its mind to rise up and do all, or any of those things, till the eye settled on the stocks circled beneath it. Only the men turning the stocks had motion. Only the dogs worrying at them, had voice.

'A penny for them, Isabel.' Alick Mearns grinned across at her, from the other side of the fence.

'Would tuppence buy them, maybe?'

She shook her head.

'I canna afford to bid higher,' the crofter sighed. 'Some lad or other?' he suggested.

'It's Ben Achie,' she said. 'I thought it would look different from the back.'

'You did, did you?' Turning to face the hill, the crofter joined in her silent search for the difference.

'Do you know something, Isabel?' he said, sharing the secrecy of his discovery at last. 'There's no back to Ben Achie. No back to it at all. But that's between you and me, of course. Ourselves two. And the both of us! It's like this,' he explained, and she knew from the twinkle in his eyes that he was laughing at her. 'It's like this. When I look at Ben Achie from my Park here, that's the *front* of it for me, but if I was to take a dander over the bridge and across the river to your place at Slack-o-Linn, that would be the back of it for me! Have you got that *clear,* now?'

'Aye.' She nodded to confirm it. For it seemed important to him that she'd 'got it' clear.

A well doing man, Alick Mearns, was her family's verdict on the crofter. Even if he *was* old and never took a wife, and lived by himself. They never saw anything odd about him. But then, as her father often pointed out, Alick Mearns had never neglected himself. Taking a turn over, every now and again, to see Nell Simmers. To see to her *henhouses!* Her mother would snap, for no apparent reason. Her being a widow woman and all.

Then there was that time in Canada her father sometimes

spoke of. Just after the war, when lots of the crofter's sons emigrated, to wait for the deaths of their fathers, to inherit the crofts.

Alick Mearns had been one of them. But he had always leapt long-legged out of anonymity. According to her father, he had chased all over Canada. After a lass. Her father's voice had always held the pride of Marathon, in the telling of it. And Canada, she remembered, had ever after seemed more familiar than all the other far away countries in the geography lessons. Losing all the immensity the dominie lent it, in a small, intimate picture of Alick Mearns chasing all over it. After a lass.

Strange, that the image of him in Canada had more reality than the man stood in front of her had in the flesh.

Coming to kirk only on Communion Sundays. Absolved by her *mother* for his rare attendances. A man on his own with both croft and house to mind. It would be a crying shame if the kirk session deprived him of his Communion token. You'd got to make allowances. The kirk, above all!

An elusive man, Alick Mearns. Hovering dimly on the outskirts of the parish. 'I gave Alick Mearns a wave,' her father would mention when he came home from the Mart. 'Alick Mearns gave me a nod,' he'd remember when he came home from a roup. 'I caught a glimpse of him in the distance.'

A far away man. He gave you a nod. You gave him a wave. Symbols becoming tangible. Kindly things handed out to each other. Across the distances.

'So you *see*, Isabel,' he was urging, 'Nobody can ever rightly say they've seen the *back* o' Ben Achie. But the thing is. The thing is,' he assured her twinkling, 'you and me have seen Ben Achie itself!'

Where the Gadie rins
Where the Gadie rins

O gin I were
Where Gadie rins
At the back
O Ben Achie

I never had
But twa right lads
But twa right lads
But twa right lads
I never had
But twa right lads
At the back
O Ben Achie

And ane was killed
At Louden Fair
At Louden Fair
And ane was killed
At Louden Fair
And the other
Was drowned

This was the first time she had ever been to Alex Ewan's croft. The track that led to it turned off the main road so suddenly that she almost ran on past it. The sign identifying it slanted inwards, as if outsiders were unwelcome, and those who belonged would never lose their way, anyhow.

Red Hill, the signpost claimed. The croft that held the chosen man. The sight of it disappointed her. It lacked the mystery of the furtive whispers at the bus stop and the school playground. It had none of the high gleam and glitter its owner had kindled in her mind's eye. It could have been Slack-o-Linn, her own home, lying grey and low. Half hidden in the tall barley.

The thing about a house without a woman, her mother often said, was just that it lacked a woman's touch. Always emphasising her *own* touch. Holding the jam she had just made admiringly up against the light. Whisking the invisible dust off her highly polished dresser.

'You found your road, then!' He came towards her. Smaller than he had appeared in her vision in the night. Those secretive nights, when, neither asleep nor awake, she'd lie in a world populated only by herself, but wide enough to hold any partner of her choosing. Narrow enough to isolate them both, beneath the darkness of the blankets. Fragile world. Shattered on the instant of her mother's footsteps sounding lightly on the stairs. Not to be rebuilt till her mother shut the bedroom door behind her for the night. Tortuous re-erection. Never to be rushed. Needing such perfection, in such a small thing as a name. Like nights when she rejected the partnership of the tenor in the kirk choir. Alan Soutar. And the young minister who always took over when the old one went to the General Assembly. Nights when she even handed Rochester back to Jane Eyre. And Heathcliff to Catherine Earnshaw. Building up for herself an image of some new, unknown partner. Sometimes falling asleep before she could find the right name for him. For he could never come into existence until he had a name. Often lying awake in an agony of frustration. Because the name wouldn't come.

'Do *you* ever dream, Else?' she had once asked. In the hope that she might not be alone in such shameful delight and painful frustration.

'*Do* you, Else?' knowing she would never get the true answer because she hadn't asked the true question.

'Sometimes,' Else had said. 'But my mother says you only dream if you lie on your back.'

She had never dreamed lying on her back.

'I was beginning to think that maybe you'd got lost,' he was saying.

'No.' She shook her head, bending to clap the old moth-eaten collie at his side. Burying her face in the hairy foostiness of the dog's neck.

'He's an old fool!' Alex Ewan said. 'He'll take any amount of that!'

'Our Nell does too! My father says she'll never make a good sheep dog.' She rushed on. Surprised herself, by her sudden volubility. 'Because she's just everybody's dog. He says a good sheep dog has only one master. Nell *will* come to you when you shout 'HEEL!' But she just sits looking at you, with her paw up, begging, when you tell her to go "Way WIDE!" My father says she's a young fool!'

'I'll take the can off you,' he said, lifting the sneck of the door. I've got the kettle on the boil. You'll be the better of a cup of tea. After your long travel.'

'I've got to get back!' The urgency of truth rang out in her own ears. 'I haven't got time!'

'Time to hold on, surely, till I empty the can for you!'

'There's no hurry for the milk can,' she assured him. 'Mother said Davy can collect the can at night.' Just you hand it in to Alex Ewan, her mother had insisted. And be on your way, again!

'Oh she *did*, did she?' Alex Ewan clattered the can down on the porch floor. 'But she *would*, of course. I've got something better than a cup of tea for you,' he said, straightening up, and speaking to her again. 'And you'll never guess what it *is*, Isabel! It's the new calfie! Born less than an hour since. I'll wager you've never set eyes on a calfie as newly born as *this* chappie!'

'Just one kiss, Isabel. A wee kiss. *That'll* not harm you.

Crushed against the cow's stall in the sweating dimness of

the byre, with the sharn, sharp and strong rising up and nipping her eyes, and the smell of tobacco on his breath, mingling with her own, the dark hay-lofts of her heated imagination had become real, at last.

'It's all right, Isabel. It's all right, lass. I'm not going to hurt you.'

Easing her down into the straw and stroking her hair, he whispered its bonnieness into her ears. 'Easy, lass. Easy now. Easy.'

'*Never* feared!' she had boasted to the girls, in a moment of bravado. Only feared now, because her boast was coming true. Feared that he would discover the shamelessness of her urgent need. Rigid and disciplined under the touch of his hand groping under the elastic of her knickers. Terrified lest she should urge him on in tongues. In words unknown. And still unheard of.

O Isabel. Isabel. Pettie. My Pettie.

His hands had lost their tenderness. Urgent and fierce and thrusting . . .

Postie's bell clanging across the yard hustled them to their feet.

'Get that straw out of your hair!' Alex Ewan said, staring at her as if she was somebody he had never set eyes on before. 'And for God's sake, tidy yourself up a bit! Get a *move* on!' he urged, as she stood shamed into immobility. Her knickers dangling below her knees shamed her far more than his hand groping up them in the darkness had done. 'Postie will be on us in a minute.' He warned, flicking his trousers down with his hands, and whistling towards the byre door. Suddenly an ordinary man, shouting an ordinary greeting on an ordinary morning.

'Aye, Postie. Another fine day again, then!'

'It could be worse,' Postie admitted. 'I thought I might find you round here. Has the calf come, then?'

'Only just, Postie. A real fine beastie.'

'You've got company, I see.' Postie halted at the Byre door. 'Isabel. Isabel Emslie.'

'O aye.' Alex Ewan glanced at her, as if he, himself had just become aware that he had company. 'She's just been with my milk. She wanted to see the new calf.'

'A bull calf,' Postie said, peering down into the calf's box. 'Man, Alex. But that'll be *another* subsidy for you. Still.' Postie straightened up to consider it. 'Still. Subsidy or no subsidy, there's a lot to be said for a little heifer! Would you not agree, now, Alex?'

The laughter, rising up around her, seemed to derive itself from her. But did not include her.

'You should make your feet your friends, Isabel!' Alex Ewan advised, when the laughter died down. 'Your mother will be wondering where you've got to all this time!'

Juggling with time. Losing herself in the recollected safety of last Tuesday's silent reading period.

It was the best of times. It was the worst of times. A fair haired queen . . .

Thrusting herself forward into the oblivion of the days that were still to come. Getting down off the stile and walking into and through the days. Proud and elusive. Past the forge where the men all gathered on Friday nights. Past Alex Ewan. Most of *all*, past Alex Ewan. Stockings straight. Hair sleek and shining. Skirt swinging in a high wind blowing. Showing the seductive sheen of *silken* knickers!

A cool miss *that* one's turned into! They'd murmur together, as she passed. The way they spoke of the doctor's daughter, when she came home on holiday from the university.

I wouldn't mind getting her in amongst the whins for five minutes! I'd soon take the fire out of her!

For never. Never again would she stand not knowing what

to do. Crumpled and sticky and dirty, with her knickers dangling around her knees. And herself be told to 'tidy up'.

Walking furtively through the field that lay fallow at the back of the house. Time slipping out of her control altogether. Forcing her feet into the almost forgotten habit of side stepping the clusters of the last of the summer's daisies. Shamefulness falling away from her in the intense, absorbed recollection of early praise from morning memory

> Daisies are
> our *silver*
> *buttercups* our
> gold
> *this* is
> *all*
> the treasure
> *we*
> can *have*
> or hold.

'She should have been home long by *this* time!' her mother's voice drifted complainingly out, from the scullery window. 'But she's been on the simmer this past day or two. No settle in her. No settle at all!'

'It's youngness, woman!' – her father was insisting. 'Youngness just. And that's an ill we all get cured of. If we live long enough.'

'You took your time!' Her mother swivelled round from the baking board and searched her face for the reason. Davy and her father turning to join her in the search.

'I got lost – '

It surprised herself, that she could look at them. And lie so calmly.

'I'd an awful job finding Alex Ewan's place.'

'Oh that's easily enough done!' her father said, turning round to the fire again, and accepting the lie for them all. 'Yon's the kind of place where you could meet yourself coming back.'

'The new calfie came!' She remembered. Seeing it sudden and clear, as she had never been aware of seeing it in the byre.

'A wee bull calfie, a bonnie wee thing it was! It's funny, isn't it? It's got teeth. But it sucks your fingers without hurting them. The way the foster lambs suck.'

'*That!*' her mother said, thumping the rolling pin down on the oat cakes, 'will mean *another* subsidy for Alex Ewan. That man just *lives* on subsidies!'

'I swear to God!' her father chuckled in agreement, 'yon's a man can always pick himself a cow that will only throw bull calves!'

'A heifer's best though,' Isabel remembered. 'They say a heifer's best.'

'A heifer doesn't bring in the ready cash!' her mother pointed out. 'And speaking about cash, Nell Simmers called in by when you was out. She'd just been down to see the flowers on Helen Mavor's grave. Same old Nell! Grumbling away as usual. Said the cost of the flowers on yon grave would have keepit *her* feet shod for a year! But, as I pointed out to her,' her mother's hand paused in its careful division of her oatcakes, as if it was important to consider *precisely* what she had pointed out. 'As I pointed out. If Helen Mavor had gotten the chance she would willingly have given up *all* the flowers on her grave. For sake of running barefoot again.'

> *Buttercups*
> our gold
> *this* is

WHERE THE APPLE RIPENS

all
the treasure
we
can *have*

Stormy Weather

'You lot gone deaf! First bell's gone!'

Bertha stood at the dormitory door. Cocooned within a subtle 'insolence of office', recently acquired when she had been promoted from being 'one of the orphanage girls' to 'orphanage servant'.

'Lying steaming there!'

'Steaming', uttered in Bertha's voice, sounded an obscenity. Nobody, Chris remembered from her vigil at the window, had 'steamed' more than Bertha herself, when she had occupied a bed in the dormitory.

Fat! Oozing! Pimply! The remembered image flashed through Chris's mind – a dirk unsheathed . . .

'And *you*!' Bertha said, directing her attention to Chris.

'I'm up and dressed,' Chris pointed out, cool, logically, without turning her face from the window.

'ANYHOW!' Bertha withdrew herself on a word which, although bereft of meaning, she could always infuse with threat.

'Little children love ye one another . . .'

Despite long acquaintance with the command on the large

text on the wall, signed by St Paul, the girls in the dormitory had never truly 'loved one another'. Self-preservation was their first priority. Urgent, yet fragile and easily shattered.

'First bell's gone,' Chris felt in honour bound to remind her still recumbent colleagues. But without emphasis. Without insistence. Reluctant to let go of the rare moments of privacy that only early morning could bring. Desired always, but essential on Fridays. Band of Hope night.

Hope was indeed the operative word. It had taken the minister time and patience to persuade matron to let the older girls 'out' on Friday evenings on a two-mile walk to the church hall for the weekly temperance meeting.

Matron was no doubt aware that whatever fate the future held for the girls, none of them, at least in this period of their lives, was in any danger of 'drinking themselves to death'. A realist, Matron sensed that there was more danger in a two-mile unchaperoned evening 'outing'.

On top of which, she was a strategist of the first order; with a dash of the subtle, delaying tactics of the first Elizabeth.

Since the minister was also a trustee of the orphanage, his requests were almost impossible to deny. Matron had conceded, 'allowing' the girls to attend the Band of Hope. But with one proviso – depending on the weather!

It was this proviso that kept Chris glued to her position in front of the window, searching for signs in the morning sky. For it didn't need rain itself to cancel the weekly outing. The 'threat' of rain was enough for Matron to defy the minister, and the whole United Free Kirk of Scotland.

Oh! Never had a small girl of fourteen been up against such a powerful adversary. And never was an autumn and winter so full of Fridays which 'threatened rain'! Nor even more the runes of childhood so fervently invoked could diminish the threat:

Rainie, rainie rattlestanes
dinna rain on me
rain on Johnnie Groat's hoose
far across the sea . . .

Second bell clanging through the dormitory stirred the sleepers into disgruntled wakefulness, and filled the room with
complaint. Alice, unaware at last of Chris keeping vigil, and
of the reason for such a vigil, shuffled towards the window.

'It's going to rain,' she prophesied. 'It's going to pour! We
won't get to the Band of Hope tonight.'

'It could clear up before night,' Chris said, ignoring the
gloat that had sounded in Alice's voice. 'It sometimes does,'
she reflected, taking a last lingering look at the skyline, before
making her way out of the dormitory.

'And,' she reminded Alice, in an attempt to get a little of
her own back, 'it's *your* turn to empty all the chamber-pots
– except the boys'. I emptied them all yesterday.

'I always get the dirty jobs,' Alice protested, 'always me!'

'Not always,' Chris pointed out, reaching for the door,
anxious to escape the 'my-turn-your-turn' arguments that
began each day – '*I* get landed with *most* of the dirty jobs.'

She did too! A fact confirmed when she reached the boys'
dormitory for her first task of the morning – stripping their
beds, examining the mattresses of the incontinent boys.

No Hamlet was ever forced into reaching a decision such
as the one that confronted Chris. To report or not to report
that large, damp stain that spread itself across James Dobie's
mattress? No thought of nobility troubled her mind. It was
the pact that caused her dilemma. Formed between herself
and James Dobie in their early years in the orphanage.

'I can't find no bottom to your hunger,' Matron had said

403

of them, anxious, puzzled as if the fault was her own. 'There never seems to be enough for you.'

'Table manners' which they had to memorise in their first weeks in the orphanage had no 'small print' as warning!

In silence I must take my seat
and say my Grace before I eat
Must for my food with patience wait
Till I am asked to hand my plate
Must turn my head to cough or sneeze
And when I ask, say 'if you please'.

I must not speak a useless word
For children should be seen not heard
I must not talk about my food
Nor fret if I don't think it good.
My mouth with food I must not crowd
Nor while I'm eating speak aloud.

When told to rise then I must put
My chair away with noiseless foot
and lift my heart to God above
In praise for all His wondrous love

It never mentioned porridge! Nor the fact that if you didn't eat your porridge you got no tea and bread and butter to follow.

Orphanage porridge, made the night before, so that by morning you could cut it up into thick, lukewarm slices, sent even Chris's voracious, indiscriminate stomach rising up in revolt. James Dobie became her eager and willing receptacle. Thus, the pact was formed. Wolfing down his own portion, while Chris picked warily round the edge of her plate. The transference of plates, with years of practice behind it, was a miracle of dexterity and timing!

All such subterfuges, Chris reflected, never escaped the gimlet eyes of her fellow-orphans, and had to be paid for – help with their home lessons, the coin in demand.

Engulfed in a passing moment of self-pity, assailed by the long-lost, but still remembered freedom of home, Chris struggled towards a decision.

Had James been less incontinent this morning, she would simply have turned his mattress, concealed the 'evidence' and sent up a prayer. 'Don't let Matron be in her examining mood.'

The risk was too great. On Friday, of *all* days, when good behaviour was an unspoken, but important, proviso for attendance at the Band of Hope.

'James Dobie has wet his bed, matron.'

Nobody in the whole wide world could twist a situation with the dexterity of Matron. Chris suddenly found herself the target of Matron's displeasure.

'Did you waken James Dobie last night?'

'Yes, matron.'

'Are you sure?'

'Yes, matron.'

'Did he use his chamber pot?'

'Yes, matron.'

'How do you know he used it?'

'I heard him!'

'Oh traitor untrue,' said the king 'now thou has betrayed me thrice, who would have thought that thou . . .'

James Dobie had not yet learned *Morte D'Arthur* at school, but complete comprehension of it was held within his eyes, accusing Chris from the opposite side of the break-fast table.

The flourish with which he scraped his porridge plate

clean, before clasping it firmly to his chest and settling down and back in his chair to concentrate on Chris, dithering around the mess of congealed porridge which now confronted her – no tea, no bread – a dark beginning to an already cloud-threatened day.

'Christina Forbes!'

Bertha's voice broke through the argumentative 'whose-turn-to-do-what' claims that always preceded washing up, and halted Chris in her assertions. For full titles were used amongst themselves only on formal – or foreboding – occasions.

'Matron wants to see you in her sitting-room – at once!'

'It's for something bad?' Her question, tentatively put, was purely rhetorical since it would not be answered by Bertha in her official capacity.

'I *know* it's for something bad.'

Chris flicked swiftly through her memory for recent, but so far undiscovered sins of omission and/or commission. 'I know. By the sound of your voice.'

'So this,' Matron stood guardian over Chris's opened schoolbag on her desk, waving aloft a small, oft-creased bundle of jotter pages, '*this* is why you are always so keen on the Band of Hope. I might have suspected it. Who is this boy who writes that he "can't wait for Friday night"?'

'Till I see you again' – silently Chris completed the sentence for Matron, and, in the doing, recollected every word written on the pages. The lines of 'X's for kisses, the P.S. of regret 'wish they were not on paper, but were real . . .', embarrassment negated by the inner certainty.

'At least there's not one dirty thing in the letters . . .'

'A boy at school, Matron – he lives with his grandfather, he's *nearly* an orphan!' Chris volunteered the information in the hope that such a common cause might influence Matron.

'He's got navy stockings with yellow tops . . .' Suddenly she heard herself sharing with Matron the few facts she herself knew about the boy. ' . . . He's got a bike. He can freewheel down Barclay's Brae without once touching his handlebars – you'd like him if you knew him. I know you would!'

Evincing no sign of a shared 'liking', Matron set the pages down on her desk.

'The thing is,' she concluded, after long consideration, 'you're getting too old for the Band of Hope. It's time we were thinking of your *future*. Getting ready for it, when you go into service. There's the old sewing-machine – we could make a start on Friday nights, teaching you to use it – underwear, night-dresses, petticoats, things you'll need when you start your job . . .'

'What punishment?'

Her colleagues clustered around her in the scullery, avid for her downfall.

'None.'

'*No* punishment?' The disbelief in Bertha's voice atoned for much.

'None,' Chris confirmed, thrusting up her sleeves to attack the washing-up. 'I can't be bothered going to the Band of Hope tonight,' she informed them casually. 'I'm getting too old for it, it's for children, Matron says. She's going to teach me to use her *new* sewing-machine.'

'*Her* new sewing-machine?' Bertha asked aghast.

'Her new sewing-machine. To sew my frocks for leaving.'

'Frocks!' Bertha grumbled, 'all I had to make was night-gowns and petticoats!'

'You're not *me*,' Chris reminded her, plunging her hands into the sink, '*are* you now?'

It's raining
It's pouring
The old man is snoring.

'Once in Royal . . .'

'I**T'S** *Christmas!*'
The jungle drums beat out the information from Hill Street to Lady Lane.

'It's Christmas in Higgins!'

'*Halloween* hasn't even come yet,' Sarah protested. 'Christmas is *ages*.'

'If we don't join now,' Ellen, her best friend of the moment, pointed out, 'the Club Cards will be all gone, and we won't get nothing.'

'*I* haven't got a sixpence to join,' Sarah said.

'Me neither,' Ellen admitted. 'Not till my dad gets his broo money. But we can go up and *look*.'

'Join our Christmas Club NOW!'

The notice in Higgins's window justified Ellen's urgency. The window itself held Sarah entrapped in a confusion of time. As if time had gone back on itself, had whirled towards Christmas before coming to a stop in Higgins's window.

King George and Queen Mary stared as severely from

their thrones on the tin tea caddy as they had done in all the remembered Christmases of Sarah's short life.

The toy train in front of the window still looked as if it might whistle off to somewhere, but had not yet decided on its destination.

The doll presiding in the centre of the window had not yet found a mother.

'*Her* shoes are only painted on,' Ellen said. 'Not like *real* shoes. You can't take them off.'

'Not like Mina Scobie's "walkie-talkie" doll,' Sarah agreed. 'It can sleep. Higgins's doll can't. But,' she admitted, 'I've always wanted that doll!'

Unaware as yet, that the doll, the train, the tea caddy were beyond personal possession, reappearing briefly at Christmas time in Higgins's window.

For as the weeks passed, and club members' payments began to falter, until they stopped altogether, an ominous notice appeared in Higgins's window: 'NO REFUND ON LAPSED PAYMENTS'.

'Owing to *clerical* work involved,' Mrs Higgins had once pointed out to Sarah's mother, when she had the temerity to 'object'. '*Clerical* work!' she had snorted to her more timid neighbours, awaiting the outcome of the 'objection', 'some *clerical* work! That old Irish biddy knows how to make two and two into five! That's all she *does* know!'

'She wants *doing!*' was always the unaminous verdict of the grown-ups. But their threat was never fulfilled. For, although the figures on Higgins's slate seldom reached an accurate total – 'clerical work' again covering a multitude of Higgins's sins – it had to be endured. Their slate was indispensable.

Nevertheless, Higgins's window always gave timely warning

of the spade work that had to be done if Christmas was to
be Christmas.

You didn't need sixpence to join the Mission Hall Sunday
School nor the junior corps of the Salvation Army. It was
timing that counted. Timing, that was important – 'at least
a *month* before Christmas,' Ellen insisted. 'For attendance,
or we won't be members – and won't get to the Christmas
parties!'

'Only cocoa and stale buns,' Sarah said.

'And games!' Sally reminded her, putting in a bit of
immediate practice.

> . . . Oh! The grand old Duke of York!
> He had ten thousand men
> He marched them up to the top of the hill
> And he marched them down again.
> As they raced together towards the lane.

> 'And when they were up, They were UP!
> And when they were down, They were DOWN!
> And when they were only half way up
> They were neither up nor down!'

'The Hill Street bobby's taking down names!' Sarah raced
down to the lane to herald the glad tidings. 'I've just seen
him. In Kimmer's Wynd. With his red book. The kids are
all round him.'

The information needed some consideration: had to be
weighed in the balance, since their relationship with the Hill
Street bobby was delicate, tenuous when fleetness of foot
became their strongest weapon in the small war of attrition
that waged between themselves and the bobby – when their
song of triumph pursued their pursuer:

. . . . Who would like to be a bobby?
Dressed up in other people's clothes.
Wi' a great big tarry hat
and a belly full o' fat!
And a great big mealie puddin'
for a nose!'

But that was when time was normal. The imminent approach
of Christmas, when the Chief Constable's Christmas dinner
for poor children was just weeks away, confounded the situation. The bobby's red book, and his threat to take down
your name no longer held its menace. Indeed, the thing to
be desired was to get your name taken down in the red book,
with all possible speed, for the annual Christmas dinner.
The far of your name being omitted – yourself forgotten –
cancelled out all other considerations.

'We'd best get ourselves up to Kimmer's Wynd,' Sarah
urged the others, 'so's the bobby can *see* us!'

'The "H"s to "M"s the night. And I'm "M"!'

'Me too,' Ellen affirmed. 'I'm Menzie. That's an "M".'

'*You're* all right then,' Betsy Kelly assured Ellen. She
informed Sarah that 'You're a "Mac" – MacVean – it's the
letter that comes after "Mac" that counts. "V" – you'll be
about last – there's *hundreds* of "Macs".'

Betsy was right, Sarah realised, as she stood with the other
children crowding the court yard behind the police station.

'Blue tickets this year!'

Ellen separated now, on the other side of the yard, by
virtue of sure and certain possession of her ticket, held it
aloft, waving it across at Sarah.

'*Yellow* tickets last year,' she shouted.

'*Red!*' Cis Tindall contradicted. '*Red* last year.'

'*Yellow!*'

The argument conjoined, rose in tempo until brought to a halt by the ticket bobby –

'NO tickets of any colour till you all SHUT UP!'

MacKenzie . . . MacKellar . . . McKinley . . . McRimmon . . . Macrivey . . . MacRobert . . . MacTavish . . . Her section, thinning out now, increased the panic rising up in Sarah – the feeling of being the last 'M' in the world and apt to be forgotten . . . MacVean . . . Sarah . . .

'*Blue tickets!*' she shouted, squeezing through the crowd in search of Ellen, '*blue tickets,* right enough!'

The ultimate possession of tickets brought a subtle change to the street's inhabitants. Dividing its elders into those who claimed that they 'had *still* some pride left', and ticket-holders whom they accused of 'putting on a poor mouth'.

Friends of a lifetime becoming foes for a fortnight. An attitude which influenced the children.

'We can't play "hoist the green flag"!' Ellen lamented. 'There's not enough for sides. Mina Scobie and Jean Campbell don't play with us any more. Not since we got tickets for the Christmas Dinner!'

'They still play with *me*,' Sarah claimed.

'You're *different*,' Ellen said.

A difference which allowed Sarah a foot in both camps, by virtue of the consensus of opinion of the street's elders: ' . . . she's a poor, wee soul. Bless her. No father . . .' A difference which confused Sarah, confronted by an image completely alien to herself. For she had never thought of herself as 'a poor, wee soul'. Nevertheless! The role now thrust upon her was well within her histrionic abilities, albeit hard to act up to when boredom overtook herself and Ellen, and the temptation to disrupt the elders, by playing 'catch as can' along the street, overcame them.

' . . . . *You* didn't rap on Annie Frigg's door!' Ellen accused. 'Nor on old Balaclava's door *either*!'

Sarah had begun to realise that obligations could be limiting. She could no longer afford to alienate her champions.

'A *new* frock!' Sarah's mother protested. 'If that's the way of it you'll just have to go without the Christmas Dinner, or else make your way there in your birthday suit!'

The recurring problem of a new frock had raised its anxious head and had once again been resolved, since a new frock simply meant a frock that was new to you! Tentatively donned in the prayerful hope that its original owner would make no further claim on it, accosting you with a shame-making shout – *'my* frock!'

Awkward, wordless. Those brief moments of appraisal of each other. Burnished in finery, lent or given, before lining up in your hundreds behind the kilted pipers for the triumphant march to the town hall through the main streets of the city. Elders and parents, feuds forgotten. Cheering their offspring on as they stepped it out to the music of Scotland the Brave, surging round, then rising up, bearing yourselves within it to some high and proud place of the mind. So that you felt you had really done something fine and brave, though you couldn't quite think what it was. Aware only that getting yourself there at all merited a touch of self esteem!

Racing home together in the early dusk, discarding *all* superfluous things. Fruit, a taste not yet fully acquired, flung to and fro with reckless largess.

'Want an *orange*?'

'Like an *apple*?'

Holding grimly on to the poke of sweeties. And to the newly minted penny. That talisman, with its shining, never-ending mystery. Proclaiming the date of a year that had not yet arrived.

'It's for *next* year!' Sarah reaffirmed as herself and Ellen stood examining their new pennies in the light of the street lamp. 'Nineteen twenty-four, it says, and it hasn't even come yet!'

'We can't spend it then,' Ellen said. 'Not till next year.'

'I'm not going to spend it!' Sarah vowed, as they raced towards the lane.

'I'm *never* going to spend *mine*!'

'Did you get a fine dinner then?' her mother wanted to know. 'I'm *asking* you! Did you get a fine dinner?'

The dinner itself, although consumed, remained elusive. Untasted in recollection.

'We got an orange,' Sarah said. 'And an apple, a poke of sweeties, and a new penny. Oh!' she remembered. And we all sang "Once in Royal".'

' "David's City",' her mother reminded her. 'It's "Once in Royal *David's City*"!'

THE GOWK

You'd felt pity for the Gowk, when yourself was young.
And he was a boy – debarred. Clutching the school
gates. Engrossed in the rough and tumble of the playground.

In manhood, this on-looking compulsion was still with
him. But you had outgrown pity. Revulsion, tinged with
apprehension, had taken its place. Until you thought about
it, and realised that maybe, maybe the half-witted dribbling
boy was now imprisoned grotesquely in the flesh of manhood.

But you didn't often think about that. And certainly the
boys on the inside of the school playground never thought
about it at all. Ettling always to get out, and within taunting
distance of the Gowk.

> We saw Gowkit Jockie
> We saw him run awa
> We saw Gowkit Jockie
> And his nakit Bum and a'!

'Come *inside*, Rob! *And* you, Peter!' Jean Aitken shouted from her kitchen window.

'And stop tormenting the life out of that poor bloody Gowk!' Her father admonished, over her shoulder.

'That "Poor Gowk", as you call him,' Jean Aitken shrugged, 'should have been lockit up and away a long time ago. Terrifying the life out of the bairns.'

'Jockie's harmless enough,' the old man defended. 'He wouldna mind *them*. If they didna keep tormenting him!'

'You try telling Kate Riddrie that, Father. She's had her bellyful of the Gowk!'

'That's true enough,' her father agreed. 'But not until the Gowk's father put the wedding ring on her hand!'

'And she's living to regret *that!*' Jean Aitken pointed out. 'Forbye, the Gowk was but a bairn, then. He's a man. Full-grown, now.'

. . . and the older he grows, the worse he grows,' Kate Riddrie was complaining. 'He's started to abuse himself again. In broad daylight now! You'd think he hadn't got the wit for *that* even!'

'Maybe it's the instinct he's gotten,' Hugh Riddrie said. 'Even the brute beasts have gotten *that*.'

He had long since found that words failed to justify to himself the existence of his idiot son. And was beginning to discover that they failed even to protect him.

'I could *cope*,' his wife claimed. 'I could cope when he was young. But he's getting beyond me now.'

'You could never cope, Kate.' Hugh Riddrie reached above the dresser for his bonnet. 'You could only pretend he wasna there at all.'

'*Better!*' Kate Riddrie flared. 'Than pretending he wasn't an idiot *born!* But then, of course, he's your son.

'So you aye keep reminding me, Kate.'

'And you *need* reminding! Do you know something?'

Hugh Riddrie shook his head. 'No. But I know you're just about to *tell* me something.'

'High time somebody did! You puzzle me,' Kate Riddrie admitted. 'Where other folk would try to keep a Gowk out of sight, you seem to like flaunting him in the face of the world.'

'Letting everybody share the *shame*, like, Kate?'

'I don't know what you'd call it!' Kate Riddrie snapped. 'But Nell Crombie was saying that she gets a red face, every time she puts her foot across this door!'

'She would,' Hugh Riddrie agreed. 'A very modest woman, Nell. Forever bragging that her man has never seen her nakit. In his life. Come to think of it,' he reflected, 'neither have you! What the hell is it makes you all so feared to *look*!'

'Decency!' Kate Riddrie said. 'Just plain *decency*!'

'Is *that* the name they've gotten for't? Ah well. I'm aye learning.

'Not fast enough!' Kate Riddrie shouted, as he made for the door. '*Something's* got to be done. About the Gowk!'

'*Jockie!* You mean. Don't you, Kate?' Hugh Riddrie spun round on his heel. '*Jockie!*'

'I meant *Jockie*.' She flustered. 'It was just . . . it was just that everybody else calls him . . .

'*THE GOWK*!' Hugh Riddrie finished the sentence for her. His quiet anger rising loud. Out of control. 'What do you suggest I do with him, Kate? *Lib* the poor bugger! The way I'd lib a young calf! Or would you have rather I had thrappled him at *birth!* With my bare hands! . . . I've killed a calf for less. For just being shargered . . .'

He could hear the school bairns taunting in the distance. Forcing his forefingers between his teeth, the shrillness of his whistle brought the taunting to a halt. And evoked the memories of the workers on their way home from the farm.

Old Riddrie. Whistling his Gowk again. Poor bugger. Other men had dogs to whistle for. Still. The man himself could be more sociable. Oh, but they minded on Riddrie, young. Another man then. Another man, altogether. That, of course, was before the Gowk was born. They themselves found little enough wrong with the Gowk! A pat on the head. A word in his ear, in the passing. A chew of tobacco slippit into his hand. And God! The Gowk was as happy as if he was in his right mind!

The shrill whistle halted their wives on their way back from the baker's van. Myth and memory blending in a confusion of truth.

The *minute* the Gowk was born. The *instant* the doctor set eyes on him . . . 'Poultice Jimmy', as he was known. For he believed that a bread poultice could cure anything from a blind boil on your bottom to a broken heart. Though a poultice was of little use to the Gowk. But at least the doctor knew *something* was far wrong.

It was the midwife, of course, that had let the cat out of the bag. *In confidence,* mind you! Though she should never have done the like. Not in a job like hers. According to her, the doctor cursed and swore like a tinker when he set eyes on the Gowk. Roaring away at the midwife. To pay heed to the *mother* . . . The midwife swore to the day she died, that Poultice Jimmy *knew.* That he hopit, if they paid no attention to the bairn, it might just dwine away. But the Gowk had survived. Never a day's illness in his life. To the great regret of Mistress Riddrie the Second.

Still. There was nothing on the *women's* consciences. The Gowk, young, had never been debarred from *their* games as girls. Always willing to be 'poor Gracie' lying dead and in her grave. While they circled mournfully around him . . .

> We planted an Apple-tree
> Over his head
> Over his head
> We planted an Apple-tree . . .

. . . 'Did you not hear me the *first* time? I'll comb your hair for you!' Jean Aitken threatened. 'If you don't come inside. And stop crying after that Gowk!'

'The Gowk was following our Liz. Young Rob dodged his mother's upraised hand. 'Liz didn't see him. That's why Peter and me was shouting. They were going down Sue Tatt's road.'

'Sue Tatt's road!' The information halted Jean Aitken's enraged intention.

'There you are, then!' Dod Aitken laughed. '*There's* something for you to pick your teeth on! We know Sue's not all that particular. But even Sue Tatt would draw the line at the Gowk!'

'Are you sure, Rob?' His mother demanded.

'Positive!'

'*Certain!*' Peter added. Enjoying the effect the information had produced. 'We was trying to warn Liz. That's why we was shouting.'

'Our Liz,' Jean Aitken remembered. 'Should have been home by *this* time! The school bus gets in at the back of five. What on earth would Liz be seeking down Sue Tatt's road?'

Liz Aitken, herself, knew what she was seeking. But was not sure whether it was to be found.

'Sue Tatt will know what to do,' Chris Forbes had

informed Liz. 'They say she's had more men than we've had suppers.'

That had sounded reassuring enough, last night. But then night had always brought reassurance to Liz. Expecting its very privacy to produce the dark, quiet miracle. And herself waking up. To confirm it, in the morning.

'I've *often* been late,' Chris had said. Sounding it like some special privilege rather than a comfort. 'Sometimes a whole *week* late.'

But then Chris Forbes had never been enticed up into the woods. How glad Liz had always been that she was herself. And not Chris Forbes. Never Chris Forbes. Now, she could have torn Chris right out of her skin. And gone inside it. To be safe. Like Chris was safe.

The rumours surrounding Sue Tatt were such that her house, itself, should have imparted an aura. Secret. Erotic. Its ordinariness disappointed Liz. But then the ordinariness of familiar things had begun to confuse her.

They should *know*. They should look *different*. The thing that had happened to herself should lie distorted, reflected in everything she set eyes on. The skeleton of Rob's bike, stripped of essentials, lying out in the shed. The handles of her father's old plough, curving high above the nettles.

But it was her landscape that was the ultimate traitor. Lochnagar couldn't *stand* there. The Dee it should flood . . .

> The sky it should fall
> Since I am with bairn
> Unwedded and all . . .

'This *friend* . . . this friend of yours, Liz,' Sue Tatt asked. 'About how old would she be, then?'

'Sixteen-and-a-half. Nearly seventeen!' Liz extended her

age, thinking somehow that it might advance her cause. 'Chris Forbes said you could help!'

'Oh she *did,* did she? It could be nothing, Liz,' Sue Tatt concluded, transforming her irritation with Chris Forbes into an attempt to reassure Liz Aitken. 'That whiles happens to young lassies. Till they become regular, like.'

'But I *am* regular!' Liz protested. 'I've always been regular. Till *now.*'

'Oh Liz! Liz Aitken. Not *You!*'

The roof at home would have fallen in, under such an admission. It was the echo of its fall that sounded in Sue Tatt's voice.

'But you could *help!*' Liz urged. 'Everybody says . . .'

'Everything except their prayers, Liz. The thing is,' Sue stood pondering the paradox. 'Everybody knows the cure. Till the ailment happens. Syne, they know nothing. For *myself,*' Sue recollected, 'I just fell back on the old Penny Royal. Quinine. And the skin of my legs peeling off in a pail of hot water and mustard. Knowing they were all useless. But always just . . . hoping. Nothing ever budged mine an inch! Not until they were good and ready to be born. But cheer up, Liz! It *could* be a "wrong spy"! And I've had my share of them! You might just waken up the morn's morning to find that everything's just fine, again. And oh, whatten a fine feeling that is, Liz, stroking yourself under the sheet. As if your hands loved your body again. And the sweat pouring out of you. With relief, just. And thanking God. Even though you're not a Christian. Because you cannot think of anybody else to thank. And promising never to do it again. Not as long as you live . . . But of course you'll do it again, Liz!' Sue Tatt bent towards her, laughing. Pressing her hands on Liz's shoulders, as if they might leap up, and dance together, to a bright reel of Sue's composing. 'Again. And again, Liz! And it will be *right* then. And fine. For some lad will have *wedded* you! There's no chance of this lad wedding you?' Sue asked, as if the music itself had ended, and the bright bubble of hope drifted high up. Out of mind's reach.

'*None!*' That was a certainty. And Liz merely confirmed it. 'He's sitting his Highers,' she explained, 'and I'm trying for a Bursary. I'm going to the University. My mother's *set* on that. And my father will kill me. You'll not tell!' she urged. For, although hope had gone, secrecy still seemed essential. 'You'll never tell.'

'I'll not tell,' Sue Tatt promised. 'But you should, Liz. Tell your mother. And tell quick! Before other folk get in there first. That's what "gets" mothers. Not having the time to get their faces ready. To look on the world again.'

'It's my father!' Liz rose to go. 'He'll kill me. When he finds out.'

'I doubt that, Liz. I very much doubt that!'

'You don't know my father.'

Liz Aitken could well be right, Sue Tatt thought, as she watched Liz turn the bend of the road. But still Sue doubted. It was with the *mothers* of the parish that she had a mere 'nodding acquaintance'.

'A fine night, again, Jockie!' Sue Tatt cried out to the Gowk, as he shambled past her gate. Poor silly creature, he wouldn't understand a word she was saying. But he might just know that somebody was speaking to him. 'Another fine night again, Jockie!'

The brambles down in the King's Howe were always the first to ripen. Liz Aitken stood amongst the bushes, caught up once more in a deceptive sense of security. The taste of childhood on her tongue. The colour of it staining her mouth. Savouring a fallacy.

The reeshling in the bushes behind her didn't disturb her

peace of mind. It was the unseen hands that gripped her shoulders, that sent her cry rising across the Howe.

Such cries breaking the silence of the quiet Howe were common enough. Easily enough analysed by listeners in the passing. A screaming rabbit cornered at last by the watchful weasel. A bleating ewe worried by a stray dog. The black sweep of the Hoodie Crow. And the rising protest of its victim. Distress traced easily enough to its unseen source. It was the source, itself, that could always momentarily stop the listening heart.

The Gowk was no solitary. Hugh Riddrie nearly always knew where to find him. The smiddy, the general shop, the bus stop. For Jockie liked to be amongst folk. A pity, that. For folk either ignored his presence. Or acknowledged it, the way they acknowledged old Moss, the shepherd's dog. With a pat on the head.

In all the years, Hugh Riddrie had never got rid of the ache that caught at him at the sight of his son, standing with, but not of, normal men. It was rare. But easier, at times like now, when they came upon each other alone. In the naked-ness of their relationship. When communication, though primitive, was natural. When tone of voice transcended interpretation. And monologue, comprehended by the list-ener, gave release to the speaker.

'*There* you are, Mannie! I've been whistling on you all night.
What have you been up to, Jockie?
Riving head first amongst the bushes!
Steady! Steady now! Till I get you wipit down.
Let's see your mouth now! You've been dribbling again!
The moustache of you's all slavers!
Steady now! Steady on!

Your flies are wide open again! Will you *never* learn to
    button yourself up!
You know fine that drives her clean mad.
She's gotten such a spite to flies.
Especially open flies. STILL!
You're *fine*, now!
In you go, then, Jockie.
Up the stairs. As nippit as you can!
Hold it! Hold it, Jockie. Till I get the boots off you.
That's *it! That's* it!
She'll not hear you, now.
We'll better her, this time!
Eh, Jockie? Eh, Mannie!
In you go, then! You're fine, now.
All present and correct!
NO! Jockie, NO!
Let my hand *go.*
I'm *coming* in! Right *behind* you.
Let my hand go!
Do you not *see,* Jockie?
You've got to go in *first!*
As if you'd been a *good* mannie!
And come all the way home. By *yourself!*
It's easier, that way, Jockie.
In you go then. We'll be all right!'

'It's all *wrong!* All wrong, I tell you!' Jean Aitken insisted.
'That Gowk should never be allowed to roam the countryside. Just look at the state Liz has come home in. Are you
all *right,* Liz? What did that mad bugger of a Gowk *do* to
you?'

  'We tried to warn Liz,' Young Rob remembered. '*And*
me!' Peter confirmed. 'We was shouting after the Gowk.'

'Off up to your beds! The pair of you!' Jean Aitken commanded. 'Are you sure you're all right, Liz? Are you *sure*!'

'Liz will be all right.' Rob Aitken said. 'She got a fleg just.'

'She's gotten more than a fleg! She's looking *terrible*.'

'He grabbed me,' Liz explained. 'And I didn't see him. *That's* what it was. I didn't *see* him. I ran all the way from the King's Howe. But I thought I'd never get out of the spot.'

'What took you down to the King's Howe, like?' her father asked. 'That's bit out of your road, isn't it?'

'My homework. I forgot to take it down. I went over to get it from Chris Forbes.'

'I wouldn't bother about homework the night,' Jean Aitken advised. 'You should hold straight on up to your bed. You've had a gey shake-up.'

'I'll be all right. I couldn't sleep if I went to my bed.'

'Liz is right!' her Father agreed. 'Stop fussing her, woman!'

'Well then!' Jean Aitken turned in attack on both of them. 'If she's all right, and can't go up to her bed, and can't sleep, she's *not* going to sit molloching here all night! She can just take herself through to the sink. And make a start to the washing-up!'

She would 'tell them on Saturday'. The decision taken, Liz leant against the sink, comforted by the postponement of time that lately she had begun to allow herself, when days could seem almost normal.

'I could have sworn I put preserving ginger down on the grocer's list.' Her mother's voice drifted through to the scullery. 'I'm sure I noticed some at the back of the press, the other day . . .'

There *couldn't* be anything wrong with Liz! Her mother would *know*. She would never be worrying about preserving ginger, if there was something wrong . . .

'But I think it's *last* year's preserving ginger that's in the press. The strength will have gone out of it . . .'

If there was something wrong, her mother would stop going on about preserving ginger forever . . .

'I could be speaking to *myself!*' her mother was complaining to her father. 'I *told* you she would be better off in her bed! Standing through there in a dwam. She's had a bigger upset than she'll admit. And if it's the last thing I do, I'll make Hugh Riddrie's ears blister! Him and that Gowk of his.'

The Gowk, himself, was beginning to take on a subtle new dimension in the eyes of the Howe. A curious kind of normality. An ability to share in the venial sins of ordinary men. It was Liz Aitken who began to lose dimension to its inhabitants.

You could have 'knocked them all down with a feather', they swore. Liz Aitken of *all* people. And her set to sit for the Bursary. She was just about the *last!* Not that anybody was perfect, of course. But Liz Aitken was . . .

'As liable as the *next* one!' Teen Rait had snapped, in an attempt to keep her own image of perfection intact. God help whoever was the father, they agreed. It was bound to be somebody. *That* was for certain. Though it had happened *once*. Just once. But that was two thousand years ago. And, though they were regular kirk-goers, and believed in every word the psalms uttered, they'd just never quite managed to 'swallow *that* one'. It was for papes. Although Cis Coutts, the simple creature, had tried it on when *she* was pregnant. And syne forgot. And admitted to the doctor that she 'had pink knickers on at the time'. Still, and seriously, though, God help whoever was the father when Rob Aitken got his hands on him. He couldn't get a word out of Liz herself. She wouldn't say a cheep. There was a rumour. Only a rumour, mind you! But then, there always was. They would have died without one. A 'speak'. Oh! A *whisper* just. That it was – *the Gowk*.

'You haven't got Liz to admit it, yet, then?' Kate Riddrie asked.

'No.' Jean Aitken shook her head. 'But she will. The state Liz came home in, that night. Her jumper torn, her legs scratit. And herself, nearly hysterical . . .'

'I can believe that! Your Liz would never have had the strength against a brute-beast like the Gowk!'

'Never a one for the lads, Liz. Her head aye buried in some book, just . . .'

'I was saying Liz would never have had the strength! Something will have to be done about the Gowk, now! And you've gotten witnesses!'

'Aye some book, just . . .'

'You've gotten witnesses!' Kate Riddrie urged.

'Young Rob. And Peter. They were trying to warn Liz.'

'WELL! THEN! That's it!'

'She never crossed the door at night. Except whiles. Down to Chris Forbes for her homework.'

'You've gotten *witnesses!* All it needs now, is to testify before the board!'

'But Liz. Liz is so unwilling. So unwilling to do that! Do you think? Do you think, maybe . . . . . . Jean Aitken hesitated, unable to put her own apprehension into words. 'Maybe, it's because he is a *Gowk*?'

'That's where you've *got* him!' Kate Riddrie got to her feet, in triumph. 'That's what I'm trying to *tell* you. It's Liz's word against a Gowk's word. And he's got none. At least none that anybody could make any sense out of. Forbye! The whole Howe can testify that the Gowk's forever shambling all over the place. *Exposing* himself!'

'You'll be satisfied *now* then Kate. You've gotten your will. You've gotten rid of Jockie, at last . . .'

'*My* first job. The first fine day. Will be to get that stinking mattress of his outside. And set fire to it.'

'That was what you always wanted, Kate . . .'

'It stank the house to high heaven.' 'Wasn't it, Kate?'

'At least we'll get a bit of fresh air into the house, at last . . .'

'Speak! You *bitch!* Or have you lost your tongue! A damned pity you don't lose it in front of the board!'

'It wasn't *me* that got rid of the . . . *Jockie.*'

'NO! But you said damn all to prevent it!'

'What could I say to prevent it? The board could see for themselves. Liz Aitken's belly was getting big enough!'

'Jockie didn't make it so. 'You've got no *proof* of that.'

'Nor of the *t'other!*' Hugh Riddrie concluded, making for the door. 'All that Jockie ever wanted was for somebody to *speak* to him.'

'*Speak* to him!' Kate Riddrie snorted. 'What on earth can anybody say to a GOWK!'

'I'll tell you what they can say to a Gowk, Kate! I'll *tell* you.'

Hugh Riddrie turned to face her. Searching dumbly for words, that could be put into words. *Knowing* them. Thousands of them. Words that often weren't words at all, but instincts. Transmitted by tone and touch. A language acquired and mastered in a confusion of pain and frustration.

'You can say *anything* to a Gowk, Kate!' The realisation took him by surprise. 'Anything at all. That's the best thing about Gowks. They never tell. And that's the worst thing about them. They cannot tell. But I'll find somebody, Kate. I'll find somebody who *can* tell!'

. . . Liz Aitken O Liz Aitken . . .

'Come on, Liz! Come on, lass,' her mother persuaded. 'Moping around the house like this is doing you no good. No good at all. And it such a fine night. Why don't you take yourself off for a bit walk?'

'Because she's feart!' Young Rob blurted out. Unable to contain his knowledge.

'*FEART?*'

'That's right!' Peter confirmed. '*Feart!*'

... Liz Aitken O Liz Aitken ...

'Feart of what, Liz!' It was her own fear that Jean Aitken probed. Convinced that such a fear had not touched her daughter. Oh, but the young were lucky. One danger at a time. Clear and cut. Over and done with. With little hindsight – and not very much foresight. If only the father had been a normal lad. And not a Gowk. 'Feart of *what*, Liz?'

'Nothing. Nothing, just.'

... Liz Aitken O Liz Aitken ...

'Well then!' Jean Aitken urged. 'Off into the fresh air with you. Young Rob and Peter will go with you for company.

'Never *ME!*'

'*ME neither!*' Peter echoed his brother's determination. 'The other bairns will cry after us! "Gowk's bairn! Gowk's bairn!" *That's* what they'll cry.'

'Is that right, Liz?' her Father asked. 'Is that what they cry?'

'Sometimes. It's only the bairns, though.'

... Liz Aitken O Liz Aitken ...

'I wouldn't let that worry you, Liz. Folk have always needed somebody to cry after. And they've got no Gowk, now.'

'If only it had been some other lad . . .' Regret slipped out of Jean Aitken's control. And sounded itself in her voice.

'Some *other* lad!'

Her father's astonishment confirmed Liz's own certainty.

'If it had been some *other* lad, Liz would have been out of here. *Bag* and *baggage!* What happened was no fault of her own. It took half a dozen of us grown men, to hold the Gowk down, till they got him off to the asylum.'

'Come on, Liz. Up you get.' Her mother piloted her towards the door. 'Just you take a turn round the steading. I used to like fine a walk when darkness was coming down,' her mother confided, as they stood on the doorstep. 'I suppose I felt ashamed in daylight. *Not* because I was carrying a bairn, Liz. But just I felt so ungainly. And ugly in myself. Still!' her arm found her daughter's shoulder. 'Every creature's *bonnie* when it's little, Liz.'

A daft thing to say, Jean Aitken thought, as she watched Liz from the door. The wrong words sometimes came out. When you couldn't find the right ones to say.

'Just the length of the steading, Liz!' she called out, reminding her daughter . . .

But the Gowk's father roamed freely enough. On the prowl. Night after night. They said. Neither Gowk to whistle on, nor dog for company. His croft running to wreck and ruin. His oats rotting in the stack. And the threshing mill had gone long since past his road end. His turnips neither howked nor stored for his cattle beasts. And winter nearly on top of the man. Bad enough when his first wife died, and the Gowk was born. Worse than ever *now* since they'd carted the Gowk off to the asylum.

Come to think of it, they themselves missed the Gowk.

You would never believe *that!* But they'd just got used to him, like. Popping up here and there. And everywhere around the Howe. Still. It was an ill wind. And it had fair suited *Katie Riddrie!*

'I'm not so sure that it did!' Meg Tait informed them. 'I'm not so sure at all! Kate Riddrie *herself* was telling me only the other day . . .'

'There's no living with him. No living with him at all. On the prowl all night. And sitting amongst my feet all day. Never taking his eyes off me. And never opening his mouth to me. Just mumbling away yonder to himself. He aye maintained that his first wife was at fault for the bairn being born a Gowk. But I'm beginning to have my doubts. The way he sits mumbling to himself. He'd aye gotten such an *obsession* with that Gowk.'

. . . Liz Aitken O Liz Aitken . . .

LIZ!

So it hadn't been merely in her imagination. Or, maybe it had been created out of her imagination.

LIZ AITKEN!

Strange how prepared she . . . . 'I'm in a hurry, Mr Riddrie.'

'Aye, Liz. You've been in a great hurry this past few weeks!

What is it that you're running from like?

Hold on, Liz! Just hold on, there!

You're not *feart* are you, Liz?

No! Of course you're not feart!

You know fine that the *Gowk* canna jump out on you the night.

No. He canna do that. He's far enough away, the night.
You made sure of that!
You *all* made sure of it. The whole bloody jing bang of
    you!
No! No! Liz! Hold on!
It wasn't Jockie? Was it, now?'

'I told the board . . .'

'I know damned fine what you told the *board!*
You try telling *ME!*
Struck suddenly dumb are you, Liz?
It's some late in the day for that.
It was never Jockie, Liz. *Never* Jockie.
You see Liz, he wouldn't even have kent *where* to PUT
    the bloody thing.
But I ken, Liz.

I ken *for* him.'

THE BRIDGE

FOR the first time in his eight years, he had caught the biggest tiddler. A beezer it was. Even Mike – the tiddler champ – grudgingly admitted its superiority.

'But maybe it's the jam jar that makes it look so big,' Mike qualified.

'Some kinds of glass makes things look bigger.

It *wasn't* the glass that made it look bigger. He had urged Mike to look inside the jam jar. And there swam surely – the king of tiddlers.

'*I* don't reckon it much.'

Anxious to keep on Mike's side, Tich McCabe peered into the jar. 'And Mungrel doesn't reckon it much either. Do you, Mung?'

Mungrel, who never spoke until somebody else put words into his mouth, agreed with Tich, 'S'right. I don't reckon it much neither.'

'Could easy not be a tiddler at *all*!'

Dave Lomax shouted from his perch on the branch of the tree. 'Could just be a trout. A wee trout!'

' – Could be . . .' Mung echoed; for although he had never

set eyes on a trout he was in agreement with the others to 'disqualify' the tiddler.

'Let's *go* men!' Mike commanded. Suddenly tiring of the discussion.

'Scarper! First to reach the chain bridge. Is the *greatest*!'

'You're not some kind of wee trout.' He protested. Running to catch up with them.

'You're *not* . . . .'

He stopped running to peer into his jam jar to reassure its occupant.

'You're a *tiddler*. And you're the *biggest* tiddler we've catched the day.'

'*Hold* it, men!' he shouted to the others. 'Wait for me.'

The authority in his voice surprised himself. Usually he was content enough to lag behind the others. Tolerated by them, because he was handy for doing all the things they didn't like to do themselves. Like swiping his big brother's fag ends. And ringing the bell of the school caretaker's door. Or handing over his pocket money to 'make up the odds' for a bottle of 'juice'. But *today* he was one of them. He had caught the biggest tiddler.

It was when he caught up with them at the bridge that his newly found feeling of triumph began to desert him.

'O.K. tiddler champ,' Mike said.

'Gi' us the jar. We'll guard the tiddler.'

'Yeah. Give,' Mung echoed.

'It's *your* turn to span the bridge,' Dave said.

He grasped his jar firmly against his anorak. He didn't need anybody to guard his tiddler. He didn't want to span the bridge either! *Nobody* spanned the bridge until they were *ten* at least! The others had never before expected *him* to span the bridge. He had always raced across it – the safe way – keeping guard over all the tiddlers while the others spanned it.

'*Your* turn,' Mike was insisting. 'We have spanned it. Hundreds of times.'

'*Thousands* of times!' Dave amended.

'Even *Mungrel* spans it,' Tich reminded him. 'Don't you Mung? And Mungrel's even tichier than me!'

'Mungrel's *eleven*,' he pointed out. 'I'm not even nine yet.'

'Only . . . Mungrel's not *chicken!*' Mike said. 'Are you, Mung? You're not chicken.'

'I'm not chicken *neither!*' he protested. 'I'm not chicken.'

'O.K. O.K.!' they said. Beginning to close in on him. 'O.K.! So you're not chicken! . . . *Prove* it . . . just prove it . . . that's *all!* Span the bridge and *prove* it.'

He knew how to span the bridge all right. Sometimes – sometimes kidding on that he was only 'mucking around' he practised a little. Spanning the part of the bridge that stood above the footpath. Knowing that even if he fell he would still be safe – safe as he felt *now*. Knowing that the ground was under his dangling legs.

Left hand over right – left over right – all his fear seemed to have gone into his hands. All his mind's urgings could scarcely get them to keep their grip of the girder.

Left over right – left over –

The river's bank was beneath him now. Dark pools flowed under the bank, he remembered. Pools where the tiddlers often hid – the *biggest* tiddlers. Sometimes he had caught them just sitting bent forward on the bank. Holding his jam jar between his legs. His bare feet scarcely touching the water. He'd felt afraid then, too. A *different* kind of fear. Not for himself. Just of things which his eyes couldn't see. But which his hands could feel. Things that brushed against them . . . Grasping and slimy.

He would never have been surprised, if, when he brought up his jam jar to examine its contents, he discovered neither tiddler nor tadpole inside it, but some strange creature, for which nobody had yet found a name.

Left over – right – left-

The shallows were beneath him now. Looking, even from this height, as safe as they had always looked. His *feet* had always told him how safe the shallows were. A safety – perfect in itself – because it was intensified by surrounding danger.

You could stand, he remembered, with one foot in the shallows, your toes curling round the small stones. While your other foot sank into the sand – down and down . . .

Left over right, left over right – over –

He had a feeling that his body would fall away from his arms and hands long before he reached the end of the bridge.

Left over right – over.

It might be easier that way. Easier just to drop down into the water. And leave his hands and arms clinging to the bridge. All by themselves.

Left over – right.

He was at the middle of the river now. That part of it which they said had no bottom. That could be *true*, he realised. Remembering how, when they skimmed their stones across the water, into the middle, the stones would disappear. But you could never hear them *sound* against the depths into which they fell.

Mike had once said that, though the water *looked* as quiet as anything – far down, where you couldn't see, it just kept whirling round and round, waiting to suck anybody at all down inside it .

– over – right – left –

He wouldn't look down again. He wouldn't look down *once*. He would count up to fifty. The way he always counted to himself – when bad things were about to happen.

One two three four five six . . . Better to count in tens, he wouldn't lose his 'place' so easily that way –

One . . . two . . . three . . . four . . . five . . . six seven eight.

He thought he could hear the voice of the others. He must be past the middle of the bridge, now – the water beneath him was still black but he could see shapes within it.

The voices were coming nearer. He knew that they were *real*.

'CHARGE! MEN!' Mike was shouting. '*CHARGE!*'

He could hear them reeshling up the river's bank. And their feet clanking along the footpath. They were running away . . . Ever since he could remember the days had ended with them all running away. Only *this* time, his tiddler would be with them too. And Mike would boast that *he* had catched it. He had almost forgotten about the tiddler. And it no longer seemed to matter.

Green and safe, the bank lay below him. He could jump down now. But he wouldn't. Not yet! It was only tiches like Mungrel, that leapt down from the girder, the moment they saw the bank beneath them.

Mike never did that. He could see, clear as anything in his mind's eye, how Mike always finished spanning the bridge, one hand clinging to the girder, the other gesturing, high, for a clear runway for himself before swooping down to earth again with cries of triumph!

'*Bat* Man! *Bat* Man!'

UNTIL SUCH TIMES

'THEY'RE coming the day.' Grandmother bustled into the kitchen, waving a letter aloft. 'Postie's just brought a line. Now! If,' she said, pausing to consider the matter, '*if* they were to catch the through train, they should manage to win here in time for a bite of dinner.'

'I'd be the better of a clean shawl, then,' the Invalid Aunt suggested, 'if they're coming the day.'

– A suggestion that stripped Grandmother clean of the good humour that had been over her. 'My hands are never out of the wash tub!' she snapped. 'The shawl that's on you is clean enough! It's barely been on your back a week! And, as for *you!* . . .' Grandmother's face bent down till it was level with your own. '*You* can just sup up your porridge! There's a lot of work to be got through. If they're coming the day. Your Aunt Millie and Cousin Alice.'

'A lot of help she'll be to you. That one!' the Invalid Aunt said. 'Her Cousin Alice is a different kettle of fish. Another bairn altogether. Well brought up. And biddable.'

'Alice is neither better nor worse than any other bairn!' Grandmother snorted, before turning in attack on you again.

'And there's no call for you to start banging the teapot on the table!'

'The din that one makes,' the Invalid Aunt grumbled, 'is enough to bring on one of my heads!'

'For pity's sake, Edith! She's only a bairn.'

Times like these, you loved Grandmother. Knowing she was on your side. Times like these, you hated the Invalid Aunt. Sat huddled in her shawl on the bed-chair by the window. The smell of disinfectant always around her. And that other smell of commode. The medicine bottles along the window-sill for when 'the head came on her' or 'the heart took her'. Even the Invalid Aunt's medicine bottles had taken on malevolence, getting you off to a bad start with Grandmother, at the very beginning of your stay.

'You *understand!* You understand, bairn. I'm telling you NOW! And I don't want to have to tell you again! You must never touch your Aunt Edith's medicine bottles. Never! Ever!'

'But she said the heart took her!'

'Not even when the heart takes her,' Grandmother had insisted. 'Mind you on that! you must never touch Aunt Edith's medicine bottles. Not as long as you are here!'

But you weren't here to stay forever! Your Aunt Ailsa had promised you that. You was only here to stay ... 'Until Such Times', Aunt Ailsa had said on the day she took you to Grandmother's house ... 'Until Such Times as I can find a proper place for you and me to bide. For you should be at school. But the authorities would just go clean mad if they found out they had a scholar who lived in a Corporation lodging house. And spent most of her time in the Corporation stables. Sat between the two dust cart horses! SO You are going to school. And biding with Grandmother ... Until Such Times ...' You could never tell when Until Such

Times had passed. But you began to recognise its passing. With Grandmother bringing each week to an end, always on the scold, on Sunday mornings.

'Learning your catechism on the *Sabbath!* Five minutes before you set off for the Sunday School! I told you to learn it last night!'

But you had learned it 'last night'. You knew it 'last night'. 'It's just . . .' you tried to explain to Grandmother, 'it's just the words. They might all change in the night. I'm looking up to make *sure!*'

'It's just . . .' Grandmother always maintained, 'it's just that you didn't put your mind to it, last night! So! Let's hear it now, then! What is the Chief End of Man?'

'Man's Chief End is to glorify God and enjoy Him forever . . .'

It was the coming of the dark night that told you summer was at an end. 'A *candle*!!! A candle up to her *bed!*' The Invalid Aunt had protested, prophesying that 'They would all be burned alive in their sleep!' And so paving the way for Grandmother's instant rejection of your request for a candle. 'It was only,' Grandmother had pointed out, 'the shadows of the fir trees that you've seen, moving against your window, and you should be used to that by this time! There was nothing,' she tried to assure, 'nothing to be feared of in the wood. It's a blithe place for a bairn. Wait you!' she had exhorted. 'Just wait you till summer comes round again!' – an exhortation that had dismayed you, that had extended time beyond all comprehension of its passing self.

'I'm *saying!*' Grandmother grabbed the teapot from your hands. 'I'm saying there's a lot of work to be got through. With your Aunt Millie and Cousin Alice already on their road!'

'If it had been *Ailsa* that was coming,' the Invalid Aunt

said, 'she would have jumped to it! My word! She would that!'

But it *wasn't* your Aunt Ailsa that was coming. She never 'dropped a line'. She just arrived. Unexpected. Unannounced.

How you wished that she could have arrived unseen. That the wood, which hid everything else, could have hidden Aunt Ailsa, too. But the kitchen window looked out on the road, and on all who passed along it, and the Invalid Aunt's voice was always the first to rise up in forewarning. 'God help us! *She's* on her way! Ailsa! Her ladyship! Taking up the whole of the road. Looks like she went into the Broadstraik Inn. And didn't come out till closing time!'

How you wanted to leap up off your stool, and hurtle yourself down the road to warn Aunt Ailsa. 'Walk straight, my Aunt Ailsa. Walk as straight as you can! They've seen you coming. They're all watching behind the curtains.'

'Thank God it's not Ailsa that's coming,' the Invalid Aunt concluded. 'We can do fine without her company!'

For once, you found yourself in agreement with the Invalid Aunt. Albeit with a sense of betrayal, and a pain for which you had not found the source, hidden somewhere, within the memory of your Aunt Ailsa's last – and first – 'official' visit.

You had recognised the man and his pony and trap, waiting at the small wayside railway station, but had not realised that he, too, was awaiting the arrival of your Aunt Ailsa. Not until he came towards you, in greeting . . . 'You mind on me? Surely you mind on me!' he had insisted, flummoxed by your silence. 'You'll mind on the pony then! I'll warrant you've forgotten the pony's name.'

'He's Donaldie,' you said, willing enough to claim acquaintance with the pony. 'He's Donaldie. His name's Donaldie.'

The cat, Aunt Ailsa grumbled, as the man elbowed her towards the trap, must have got her tongue, for this was a poor welcome, considering Aunt Ailsa had come all this way.

It was the man! you protested. HIM. Donaldie's dad. 'He belongs to his pony! Not to US. Not to you and me!'

It was only when they reached the wood that the old intimacy warmed up between them. Whoaing Donaldie to a halt, Aunt Ailsa spoke in the tone of time remembered, when the world was small enough to hold what she used to describe as . . . you and me. Ourselves two. And the both of us . . .

'You know,' Aunt Ailsa had confided, 'how Grandmother hates me smoking my pipe. So we're just going to take a turn up the wood for a smoke. I want you to do a small thing for me. To. bide here, and keep an eye on Donaldie. We'll not be long. About five minutes just,' she emphasised, presenting you with another aspect of time.

'Five minutes *must* be up now, Donaldie,' you confided to the pony, munching away on the grass verge. His calm acceptance of passing time beginning to distress you, since animals differed from yourself in appearance only, never in understanding. 'It must be up, Donaldie. I've counted up to hundreds.'

'*I* know something about you, Donaldie,' you boasted, beginning to be irritated by the pony's indifference. 'Something about all horses. Something my Aunt Ailsa once told me. All horsemen have a secret word of command. 'The horseman's *knacking* word,' she called it. But no horseman will ever tell the secret word. He would lose his power, that way of it. I don't know the secret word,' she admitted to the pony. 'But you might know it, Donaldie. If I could just find it.'

Time poised upon, and passing within, all the words you

could remember. Tried out and tested, with no reaction from the pony.

'Maybe,' you suggested at last, 'maybe the secret word's in Gaelic . . . Ay Roh. Ay Roh

'El Alooran
El Alooran

Ay Roh Ay Roh
Ay Roh'

'Stop wheebering away to yourself, there!' Aunt Ailsa commanded, as they turned up the track to Grandmother's house. 'And pay attention to what I am telling you! Not a word out of your head to Grandmother. Not one word about Donaldie's dad! We never saw him the day. We never set *eyes* on him. Just you mind on that.'

'Mind now,' Grandmother was saying, 'When your Cousin Alice comes the day, just you play quiet in the clearing. You know how her mother hates Alice getting her clothes all sossed up in the wood.'

'That one wouldn't worry,' the Invalid Aunt assured Grandmother. 'She would rive in the bushes till she hadn't a stitch to her back. It's high time she took herself through to the scullery and made a start on the dishes!'

'You cannot expect her to be stood out in the cold scullery all morning!' Grandmother snapped.

'But I'm needing the commode!' the Invalid Aunt protested. 'I'm needing to pay a big visit. And I can't do a thing! Not with that one. Stood there. All eyes!'

'She's taking no notice, Edith! She's got better things to look at, than you sat stuck there on the commode. Come on, bairn!' Grandmother said, elbowing you out of the kitchen. It's time you and me took a turn up the wood for a burthen of kindlers. And a breath of fresh air!'

'I'm needing the commode.' The Invalid Aunt's whine followed them to the porch door. 'I'm leaking! You know fine I can't contain!'

> I can contain
> I've never wet myself
> Nor ever will again

'*That!*' Grandmother said, when she caught up with you at the clearing, 'is a bad thing to say. And a worse thing to *think*!'

'I beg pardon.' Your apology was instant. And genuine. Moments shared alone with Grandmother were too rare, too precious, to be wasted in acrimony.

'I grant you grace,' Grandmother acknowledged, spreading herself down and across the log. 'But, if that's what they're learning you at the school . . .'

School, like Grandmother herself, was a separate thing, and shared only at times like these, beyond influence of the house and the Invalid Aunt.

'If,' you said, squeezing yourself down on the log beside her, 'if we were sitting out in the porch, on a fine summer evening, and a weary, thirsty traveller came by and begged us for a drink of milk. And he had wings instead of ears. And wings instead of feet. Do you know what that man's name would be?'

'Wings instead of ears, did you say!'

'And wings instead of feet!' you reminded Grandmother.

'No,' she admitted. 'You've gotten me fair beat there! I've never heard tell of that man before!'

'His name would be Mercury. He's in my school reader. He can fly all round the world in a minute!'

'I can well believe that!' she conceded. 'With all that wings he's gotten.'

In moments like that, with the mood of acceptance over Grandmother, a positive admission of time, and its passing, seemed feasible.

'I wouldn't need a candle at night, now,' you boasted. 'I'm not feared of the wood, now.'

'Of course you're not feared,' Grandmother agreed. 'The nights are stretching out, now.'

'I still wouldn't need a candle!' you insisted. 'But that's one thing! I won't be here when the dark nights come again. That's *one* thing!' you claimed, jumping down off the log. 'I won't be here when the dark nights come again. Do *you* think I'll still be here when the dark nights come again?'

'That's hard to say,' Grandmother pulled herself up off the log, and stood, considering. 'Hard to tell. But no! she decided at last. 'No. I should hardly think you'd still be here, when the dark nights come again.'

> Until Such Times
> As we go home
> A Hundred Hundred miles
> And all the People
> They bow down
> And everybody smiles . . .

'I know,' Cousin Alice claimed, when they reached the clearing, 'I know why Grandfather says we mustn't go down through the woods where the men are working.'

'So do I though,' you assured her. 'It's because they *swear!* Something cruel! Grandmother says it's because they come from the south. And I know the swear the men say! It's a terrible swear. It begins with F! But mind!' you urged Cousin

Alice. 'Don't you say it. *Ever!* They would just murder me! For telling!'

She hadn't heard that word before, Cousin Alice admitted. But you had heard it. Hundreds of times. In the Corporation lodging house. It didn't sound terrible then. Just like all the other words. It didn't sound terrible, until one day in the wood, when one of the wood men shouted it out.

'You should have seen the look on Grandfather's face!' you said to Cousin Alice. 'I wanted to cry out to him . . . it wasn't me that swore, Grandfather! It wasn't *me!* Just to make Grandfather speak to me. For once. And to let him know that I don't swear. And I wanted to stand as quiet as anything, so that the twigs wouldn't crackle, and Grandfather wouldn't see me at all. Sometimes,' you confessed to Cousin Alice, 'sometimes I'm never sure what to do . . .'

'Ankle strap shoes, like what Alice has got! Whatever would you be wanting next!' the Invalid Aunt wondered. 'Alice's Mother and Father worked hard for Alice's shoes!' she informed you. 'And Alice took good care of them when she got them!'

'Sorrow be on shoes!' Grandmother snapped. 'The lark needs no shoes to climb to heaven. Forbye!' she assured you. 'Thin shoes like yon wouldn't last you a week in this wood!'

'They wouldn't last you a day!' the Invalid Aunt said. 'But then, there's just no comparison!'

She would like you to be jealous of Alice, the Invalid Aunt. And that was the strange thing, although you envied Alice's shoes, you was never jealous of Alice herself. But glad for her. Proud of her. Willing to claim acquaintanceship. The glory that was Alice, somehow reflecting on yourself . . . Look everybody! Just look! This is Alice. She's *my* cousin! My cousin Alice. Did you ever see anybody so beautiful. So dainty. In all your life! With long golden hair. And blue ribbons. She's my cousin! *My* cousin . . . Alice.

Look! Everybody just *LOOK!* That's *my* grandfather's horses coming up the road. They're his horses . . . my grandfather.'

'My conscience, bairn!' Grandmother edged you out of her road, and away from the window. 'You should know every tree from this scullery window by heart! For I never did see anybody who could stand so long. Just looking!'

That was about all you was good for, the Invalid Aunt confided to Grandmother. It was high time, she insisted, that Ailsa found a place for herself and that bairn! But, being man-mad, a bairn on her hands would fair clip Ailsa's wings.

'Be quiet Edith!!' Grandmother admonished. 'It's your sister you're speaking about.'

'Sister or no sister,' the Invalid Aunt said, 'Ailsa died to me a long time ago.'

My Aunt Ailsa died to me
– Words of lament forming themselves in your mind –
A long long time ago

A dirge for a death, beyond your comprehension, singing in your head.

'The *world!*' Grandmother announced, 'must surely be coming to an end!' For, she informed you, this was only the second time your Aunt Ailsa had bothered to write!

'If she's bothered to write,' the Invalid Aunt said, 'she must be on the cadge for something or other. Either that, or she's lost her job again. It's my opinion . . .'

'There's a time and a place for opinions,' Grandmother declared, taking you by the hand into the scullery . . . 'Your Aunt Ailsa is coming to see you the day,' she confided. 'She might have some good news for you. So! Would it not be a good idea for you to take a turn up the wood for some dry kindlers for the fire.'

Until Such Times had maybe arrived at last. The very thought of it fixed your feet to the cement of the scullery floor. With the voices from the kitchen rising and falling to the rise and fall of your own heart beats . . .

It was to be hoped, the Invalid Aunt was saying, that this chield would marry Ailsa this time. Though any man that did that had all the Invalid Aunt's sympathy! Either that or he must be a poor, simple creature that was of him!

Neither poor nor simple, Grandmother pointed out. A decent enough chield. A disabled war soldier.

That would fit the bill! the Invalid Aunt maintained. Knowing *Ailsa*, she would have her eye on his bit pension! And lucky to get that! Better women than Ailsa had never even got the *chance of* a man! It was the Invalid Aunt's opinion that Ailsa had never 'let on' about the bairn.

O but she did! Grandmother confirmed. She said in her letter that she was bringing him to see the bairn.

And that, the Invalid Aunt concluded, would be enough to put any man clean off! Unless of course, it was somebody they didn't know.

'We know of him,' Grandmother admitted. 'Summers. Dod Summers. His father's got that croft down by the railway.'

'I'm with you now!' The Invalid Aunt's voice shrilled out in triumph. 'Peg Leg Summers.' So that's who she's gotten. Old Peg Leg Summers. And he's got no pension. He shouldn't have been in the war in the first place. Well, well! Even I can mind on him! He used to go clop, clop, cloppin round the mart on a Friday!'

'Listen now,' Grandmother urged you. 'When your Aunt Ailsa comes the day, she'll maybe be bringing somebody with her . . .'

'She wouldn't!' you protested. 'I know she wouldn't. My Aunt Ailsa never *would*!'

'Good grief, bairn! What ails you?'

'What on earth are you on about?' Grandmother insisted, puzzled by your distress.

'My Aunt Ailsa. She wouldn't. She'd *never* marry a man with a wooden leg!'

'*Listening* again!' The Invalid Aunt snorted. 'Lugs cocking at the key hole!'

'Look a here. Just you look a here, now,' Grandmother said, easing you down on your stool by the door. 'A wooden leg's nothing. Nothing at all just. Many a brave man has a wooden leg. You like biding with your Aunt Ailsa,' she reminded you. 'Who has been making sore lament to get back to her Aunt Ailsa? Well then! You'll be happier with your Aunt Ailsa than you've been here. And fine you know that . . .'

'I wish to God she'd stop blubbering,' the Invalid Aunt complained. 'She should be thankful that somebody's willing to give her a home!'

'Now, listen, bairn, just you go and wash your face,' Grandmother suggested. 'And put on a clean pinny. You want to look your best to meet your Aunt Ailsa. But, first things first. I'll away to the well for some fresh water. You can follow on with the little pail.'

'Are you still blubbering there.' The Invalid Aunt's voice, battening itself against your hearing, was powerless to reach the horror of your imagination. 'You heard your Grandmother! You could at least obey her. But no faith you! Obedience would be some much to expect! *My!* But you're stubborn! Just like Ailsa. The living spit of the mother of you . . .'

'She's my Aunt Ailsa,' you said, protective of a relationship that was acceptable. 'She's my Aunt . . . She's not my *mother!*' The implication of the Invalid Aunt's words had penetrated at last, sending you hurtling towards her bed chair. 'She's my Aunt Ailsa!' Grasping the aunt by the shoulders, you tried to shake her into understanding. *My mother* is ladies I cut out from pictures in books. Ladies I pick out passing in the street! You know fine she's not my mother! You're just saying that because . . . because you're ugly! And you smell terrible! You're just a *fucker*!

. . . It wasn't *me* that swore, Grandfather. It wasn't me . . .

'My Aunt Ailsa's coming!' you shouted to Grandmother, bent over the well at the edge of the wood. 'She's all by herself. She wouldn't. I knew she wouldn't. Marry a man with a wooden leg!'

'I doubt you're right,' Grandmother agreed, as you stood together watching Aunt Ailsa coming up the track. 'Ah well!' she sighed, 'maybe it's all for the best. Who knows! Who can tell! You'd better run on and meet her, then. You haven't even washed your face!' Grandmother admonished. 'Nor changed your pinny! Whatever keepit you so long?'

'It was Edith,' you told Grandmother. 'I think the heart took her. She was making that funny noise.'

'Heaven above! O good grief.' The water from the pail that Grandmother dropped swirling round your feet.

'I didn't touch her medicine bottles!' you reassured her retreating figure. 'I didn't *touch* them!'

Good Friday

For more than a year now you had made a bee-line, first thing every morning, to the only window that looked down on the outside world.

A vigil shared with Miss Henly, at the opposite side of the window. The lines of demarcation were clearly defined. Neither intruded on the other's vision. Miss Henly spoke seldom but laughed often. Great gusts of laughter, that caught the ward up in the force of its gale. And left it quivering in the calm of the aftermath.

The turbanned women in the Co-op dairy across from the window were already pulling down the shining levers of their bottling machines. Raising their heads now and again, to gaze across into your world. Waving frantically, when they caught a glimpse of you. The way they might wave to an infant in a pram. Emphasising their presence.

You never waved back. You weren't a daftie. Acute neurasthenia. That was all that ailed you. It had no symptoms. At least, none you yourself recognised. Except when the passing of time took hold of you like a terror. And hurry clutched at you like a panic.

'*When?*' you would burst out, the instant the doctor got himself through the ward door. '*When* will I get *out?*'

When becoming timeless. Balanced in the doctor's long, silent calculation.

'When?'

'When you stop wringing your hands.'

You weren't even aware that you had been wringing your hands.

The groups of young office girls were making their way through the back gate now. Remembering also. Looking up towards the window.

'Do you see that girl?' Miss Henly's query was directed to nobody in particular. But you responded. Without curiosity. Unable to distinguish the individual, amongst the faces, cast up like foam bells in a whirlpool.

'Do you know her, then?'

'Not in this life,' Miss Henly admitted. 'But I have known her. Somewhere. Sometime.'

That was the summer the swallows deserted you. Silently. Suddenly. As if you had betrayed them. It was *les hirondelles* out of a book of poetry the dominie had given you, that lay battered out on the tiles of the Co-op dairy. Basking like kittens in the sun. Secret birds. Exotic. Everybody else thought they were just swallows.

Light as a butterfly, the hand on your arm. But bone and sinew knew the touch of the fragile, tormented partner of your daily walk.

'He's at my neck, again! That man! My poor neck. Nip nip nippin' awa!'

'He'll go away soon,' you console. The pain in the hallucinated eyes was real enough. 'He won't come on our walk today!' you insist.

For yourself got wearied whiles of the third, invisible

tormentor, who so often thrust himself on your company. Brief moment of ease, bringing lucid recollection.

'O lassie. The milk. And cheese. And fine sweet crowdie.'

The young girl, your own age, has taken up her day-long stance by the ward door. Ready to hurl herself on the first man who enters. Whether it is the chief medical superintendent, or the clock winder.

Madge. Her hand engloved in a yellow duster, is beginning to weave her way round the ward. Dusting the bed rails. A task unending. Set upon her by Hercules.

All words uttered in Madge's hearing become relevant. Essential. Stripped down to ballad bare bones. Only when the ward is wordless does Madge infringe on copyright. And lands you with herself, on Mormon Braes.

> Where heather grows
> Where oft-times I've been cheerie

You could avoid such a fate. You could rush to the old gramophone one of the nurses gave you, and put on the two sides of your only record. But usage has blunted it. Time has scarred it, and the heather on Mormon Braes never lost its bloom.

The knitting needles began to click through the ward. The old women, their pale tongues cleaving their chins in their absorption, sat knitting furiously against time. Pink socks for male patients.

Not for you such altruism. The ancient craftswomen, skilled in the cunning art of turning the heel. Could never show you how. Or explain such intricacies.

> No wise man utters what he only knows.
> Certainty in an uncertain world
> Is far too firm a treasure

Wise man goes warily
Jealously guarding
His small particular knowledge

The nurses either didn't know how, or hadn't got time. And so your sock had gone far beyond human dimensions, in a year of weaving. Fit only for the seven-leagued legs of some footless giant. Its immensity bewildering the ancient crafts-women, and amusing the nurses.

Penelope? Athene?, aware of the futility of her task, has utterly abandoned it.

The telephone, beginning to ring through the ward, demanded instant concentration. For it never rang, but it rang for you. Even silent, cradled in its own shining aura of black magic, it never lost potential power. Some day. One day, it would ring for you.

And, although you could never visualise who the caller might be, you stood alert, always. Waiting for the summons. Strangely unprepared for it when it came.

Ginny. Your old china. Linked arm-in-arm with her new china, Meg. Giggling together at the uniqueness of their surrounding, and at their own temerity. They crowded your small austere room. It was never meant for company. It was the great confessional. Within its dark sleepless hours you made abject acknowledgement of the waste of your days. Strange noises usurped the small room. And crept about it. Shod with caution.

'You dinna *look* different!' Ginny had said, scrutinising your face. 'You dinna *look* daft!' she had concluded. Almost as if her finding had disappointed her. It was your gear that finally lived up to Ginny's horrific expectations. Your long grey flannel frock. And thick pink knitted stockings. It must have been the sight of the latter that impelled Ginny to urge you to:

'Beat it! Make a run for it! Scarper!'

No fate in all the world, it seemed to Ginny, garbed out in her black fishnets, could be worse than having to wear stockings that looked like her 'faither's combinations'.

There were no bars on the window, Ginny noticed. There was nothing to prevent you escaping.

'Dead easy,' Ginny said. Until she tried to raise the window herself!

Convinced at last that she could only leave you to your fate, combinations and all, Ginny had rushed into her next enthusiasm. 'The fella at the gate! The bloke that let us in! Mustard! A real sheik! Was he no, Meg?'

To which fact Meg had giggled her confirmation.

'*She* wadna mind a knockie doon to him!' Ginny claimed. 'You must have seen him,' she insisted. 'If not, Hen, you must have gone blind. As well as daft!'

Maybe Ginny was right. You had blinded yourself to all the outside workers, encountered on the long, crocodile walks.

They would come back to see you, again, Ginny had vowed. 'Sure we will, Meg. Sure we'll come back!'

Your heart accepted the momentary sincerity of the promise. But your mind knew that if Ginny ever did come back, it would be for another dekko of . . . the fella at the gate.

The ward door clanked open. Jean, massive behind the laundry trolley, pushed it towards the linen cupboard. In every institution in the land, you will find Jean. Hardworking, trustworthy. Too long inside to ever want to go outside. A boon, and a burden to the nurses. Nearly always a burden to her fellow-patients. Not that Jean ever considered herself a patient.

Still. It was from Jean that you learned most of the hospital's routine and its precedents. And most of what you had learned was depressing. She always seemed to get some kind

of vicarious pleasure from your reactions to her adverse
prophecies, which you knew were but the truth.

You would never, according to Jean, get out. You needed
to have somebody to sign for you. Be responsible for you,
like. That's why she herself had been here for over thirty
years. Nobody to sign for her.

Puffing with the importance of having stacked all the laundry away, Jean plumped herself down on the bed nearest the
window. She was, she said casually, thinking of having her
tea out in the tea room in the grounds. But not until 'they'
had passed. The senior doctor and the students were on their
rounds. On their way here. She'd passed them in the north
corridor.

The information sent you scurrying from the window to
sit down on the bed with Jean. The doctor couldn't see your
legs trembling when you sat down.

You might, you confided to Jean, ask the doctor today, if
you could get ground parole. And go to the tea room.

'Not a chance!' Jean assured you. 'Not a hope! Because,'
she confided in a conspiratorial whisper, 'young girls never
get it. With all the bushes. And the gardener's boys!'

Madge had caught the relevant words, and began putting
them together, in her ballad for the day:

> With the gardener's boys!
> With the gardener's boys!

She had just got it sorted out to her liking, when 'they'
unlocked the door. Slipping on her cuffs, Charge Nurse
advanced to meet them.

> In the bushes
> With the gardener's boys
> With the gardener's boys

At a passing signal from Charge Nurse, a junior removed the songstress to the kitchen. At another, two nurses untangled the young girl who had got herself enmeshed in the group of students. Miss Henly deserted the window, and laughingly pushed her way past the group, and out of focus. Caught unawares, but never unready, Jean leapt from the bed, and advanced to meet the group. Chiding the senior doctor with a familiarity which both horrified and impressed you.

'You haven't been to see me for ages! Dr Main!'

'Sorry about that, Jean. But . . .'

Charge Nurse cut short the doctor's apologies with a look. And a command.

'There's sluicing to be done, Jean! Have you forgotten?'

'And how are you this morning?'

The other walking patients had disappeared. It was you the doctor was speaking to.

'I'm fine,' you told him. Searching his face as closely as he searched yours. For this, according to Jean, was the doctor who held the keys to outside.

You could feel the sweat gathering at the roots of your hair, and beginning to trickle down your face. But you remembered not to wring your hands. And your feet, clamped firmly down on the wooden floor, kept your legs from shaking.

'I'm just fine,' you repeated. To make quite sure he had heard the first time. 'Just fine.'

The ward had become itself, again. Each of you took up your self-appointed stances. Friday. You remembered. A good day, Friday. Fish for dinner. And plum duff. Good Friday.

Senior Nurse's weekend off. Freedom. A flush of anticipation all over her. Flicking her cuffs in one hand. Rattling her keys in the other, in an impatience for the clock to strike twelve. Time had truly made you its numbering clock. You could have written out the off-duty lists yourself. But its chimes still startled you.

Rattling her keys aloft, in a final gesture of farewell, Senior Nurse admonished us cheerfully.

'Behave yourselves now, till I get back! Don't do anything I wouldn't do!'

And, uninhibited by the absence of Charge Nurse, her long, black-clad legs skated the whole length of the polished floor. Pausing to chuck Madge under the chin, she turned at the ward door, and bending down on one knee, beseeched of her watchful, wordless audience.

'Why do men adore me?'

And disappeared in a clang of doors and a flurry of white.

The ward absorbed her disappearance in complete silence. But quivered still, in the aura of her exhilaration.

You began to circle with the bed patients' trays. Madge, beginning to dust the bed rails again, took off once more for Mormon Braes.

> I'll nae go intae mourning
> I'll nae put on my gown of green
> For my true love ne'er returning

Fully in voice now, she ceased dusting. And you ceased circling to join in, and gave the ballad the crescendo it deserved.

> Ye Mormon Braes
> Where heather grows
> Where oft-times I've been cheerie . . .

The ward door clanged open. Charge Nurse stood on its threshold. Static. Knowing, no doubt, that the 'artists' – like

all true artists – could not stop in the middle of a performance, listened until we reached a shaky falsetto close:

> Fare ye weel ye Mormon Braes
> It was there I lost my dearie

'You!' It was you Charge Nurse spoke to. 'Can get down
off Mormon Braes right now! And come and have a bath!'

A bath! At dinner-time! On a Friday!

Saturday was bath night!

'A bath!' Charge Nurse repeated. 'Right now!'

It was only when you got into the bathroom that Charge
Nurse told you. 'You're getting out! They're waiting for you
round at the front. I didn't want you to know till the last
minute! You would have got over-excited. And that would
have been that!'

You couldn't be getting out. No place to go. No one to
go to.

'You're going to your domicile,' Charge Nurse said. 'To
the Highlands. The place where you were born. To work on
a croft in the hills. It will do more for you than this has
done. Besides,' she insisted, 'I never want to see your face
here again!'

It was only when you saw your own clothes folded on a
chair by the bath, that reality hit you.

'Nurse!' Charge Nurse flung open the bathroom door, and
shouted down the ward; 'Nurse! Bring a sheet for this daft
lassie, to cry into. She's crying here. Because we're letting
her *out*!'

LIFE MODEL

THEY almost knocked her flat on her face. The young students bounding up the steps of St Martin's School for Art. But then she was not so steady on her legs now, and finding stairs harder to climb. You slowed down a bit when you had crossed seventy.

'Do you know how old I am?' she would sometimes ask, in a hoarse, conspiratorial whisper, of the young students, who brought her coffee up to the cubicle, to save her legs the long trudge down to the cafeteria.

It always disappointed her that they never said, as she half hoped they *would* say,

'You don't *look* seventy-two!'

'You can't be!'

They would say instead: 'Nobody could hold a standing pose for a whole day. Not at seventy-two!'

But she *could*. And she did.

Dear God . . . she remembered, as she stood 'getting her breath' . . . *thank* you for making me strong enough to hold a standing pose. But if I *do* get a booking today, make it be just portrait or costume. So that I can just sit down and take the weight off my legs . . .

If it be *your* will, she added hastily. For although she had established a close, 'on speaking terms' relationship with God over the years, nobody ever got close enough to dictate *their* terms to *Him* . . .

Her relationship with God had started all those years ago. When she had stepped out from behind her curtain for the very first time. Naked and revealed to a blur of faces.

It was her legs that had begun to give way, before extending to a convulsion of her whole body. With sweat gathering in substance and momentum, till it dropped from her like rain, to gather in pools round her bare feet.

'Our Father . . .' she had repeated to herself, her mind grasping for something to hold on to, until her body had eased itself down into stillness again, under the intensity of her repetition: '. . . Our Father'.

And, in all the years since, she had never trembled, sweated, or felt ashamed.

' – Hallowed be Thy name . . .'

What job satisfaction can you ever get out of being an artist's model, the social security lady was always asking.

And Nella had never been able to put it into words. Not even to herself.

Maybe . . . maybe the social security lady was right. It wasn't like a 'job'. It was something different . . .

Something you became completely involved in. Something you took out with you from behind your curtain. You could never tell what it was. But you always knew when you had taken it.

You knew by the silence that fell over the students, broken by their hurried rush to capture it. By the blankness on their faces when the tutor's voice brought the strange, trance-like involvement to an end.

– Thank you, model. Rest now . . .

'It isn't as if modelling was *real* work,' the social security lady was always insisting . . .

'*Real* work,' Nella would always protest. 'It's the *hardest* work in the world. The easiest pose is agony after the first twenty minutes. Even just sitting for portrait. Your hip bones start growing into the chair. And the chair don't want them. And the battle between you is on!'

The ultimate revenge of inanimate things. Nella knew all about *that*. But had no words to describe it to the social security lady . . .

Nella!

A voice rang in her ears. And a hand grasped her shoulder. Names sometimes eluded her, faces seldom. Professor of Fine Arts now . . . But a student in the distant days of her 'block bookings'. Always a gentleman, she remembered. *Still* a gentleman. Still bought her a coffee along with his own – whenever he saw her in the cafeteria.

'What is the *secret* of your stillness, Nella?' he had once asked her. 'I never had a model who could stand so long. So still as you.

'The Lord's Prayer,' she had told him, grinning, her grin widening as the confusion on his face increased. 'Just the Lord's Prayer. Three times at a very slow pace. And I knew my hour was up. I never had to look at the clock!'

'I could draw Nella blindfold,' he was saying to the students gathering up behind him. 'I am more familiar with Nella's contours than I am with the map of England.'

Someone who *really* knew. Someone who remembered, from her first young years as 'The Pocket Venus' of St Martins, to her middle years as their 'Rubens Model', to her decline, when her body was dissolving down into nothingness. And she had become a face. A '*head*' for portrait. 'Plantaganet' they said. Something to do with history.

'Have you got a booking, Nella?' She shook her head.

'I was passing. I just popped in. On the off chance . . .

'The thing is . . .' he hesitated, '. . . the thing is . . .'

She wished she could give him the words he was searching for. She *knew* them. Young models coming up. New faces –

'I've booked a model for today. But – '

He turned, as if in appeal, to the students –

'We *could* use *two* models. Just for old time's sake . . .'

The gesture warmed her heart. But her mind rejected it. She had found the answer for the social security lady. She knew at *last* what job satisfaction meant.

'I got the chance of a booking, the other day . . .' she would say to the social security lady. 'They still *remember* me, you see! But it was for old time's sake. And I refused it – for old time's sake!'

ROAD OF NO RETURN

I found the road because I expected to find it. It was not easy, after forty years. And, as I had searched for it through memory's eyes, I was to discover that memory was misleading.

Had I so forgotten summers, then? Wind-blown anemones and stars of Bethlehem, that flitted white and furtive amongst the bracken? Or was it just that spring had out-blossomed all the other seasons of my mind?

'You must not pluck the primroses on the Sabbath,' my Aunt Teenac had commanded haltingly. Searching for 'the English' that could convey the strength of her Gaelic commandment

'You must not . . .

Yet she was a *good* woman, my Aunt Teenac. Everybody on the hill said she was. She subscribed to Dr Barnardo's Homes every Christmas. 'And never told a living soul about it,' they all said.

How then, did they all know?

I had never considered this contradiction till now. Yet she was still a good woman. Even my adult cynicism was forced to admit *that*. At least she was moved to 'subscribe', something that has never happened to me.

But she was adamant about the primroses. And I never plucked them. Somewhere, somewhen, though, my spirit must have defied her embargo, and gone flying down that hill, stumbling into that wood, and tearing and gathering unto itself all the primroses it could ever contain, for I still hold within my nostrils their faint and passing sweetness. And my fingers still know the rough and hairy texture of their leaves.

Perhaps it was not as far-fetched as all that. It may be that I plucked them on the Friday nights of spring, when we all raced down the hill to meet Neil, the grocer's van. For our hill was far too steep for his van to come up to us.

I doubt it, though. I had other things on my mind! I doubt too, if I ever was 'beautiful'. But I know for certain that I felt 'beautiful', on those far off Friday nights. My hair brushed till my scalp ached, with Aunt Teenac grumbling in the background.

'Yourself and that little bit of hair that's on you! And you haven't even boiled the rooshacs for the hens, yet.' And my legs, which *were* 'good', aching within the tightness of my garters, so that not one wrinkle should show on my stockings. My skirt as short as Aunt Teenac would allow. And hitched up that little bit shorter the moment the house was out of sight.

'*You* will come to a Bad End,' Aunt Teenac had always prophesied.

She didn't live long enough to know that I didn't. But I sometimes wonder if the knowing would have pleased her. She liked her prophecies to be proved correct. Did my Aunt Teenac.

It may be that it was but lack of opportunity on my part that disrupted her prophecies! But certain it was that my hair glinted, my stockings stayed taut, my whole being glowed in anticipation of a chance encounter with one person and one person only. 'The Boxer'. So named, not so much for the power behind his fists, as for the dexterity of his fingers on the keys of the melodeon.

> And time and tide
> Shall be nae mair.
> O gin I were the Baron's heir.
> Lassie, I was lo'e Thee

He played for his own pleasure, and was possibly almost unaware of my existence. But since all music and any melody is taken personally, and to heart, when one is sixteen, it was still a potential 'baroness' who puzzled over and deciphered Aunt Teenac's grocery list, with Neil, the vanman, knowing, if it *was* 'half a stone sugar' she wanted, it would still not be too much sweetness for so sweet a world. But yet aware that 'a quarter stone of sugar' would be lighter to carry up the hill.

The shed where 'the Boxer' played on those spring Fridays still stood at the foot of the hill. Emitting a sense of timelessness. A timelessness dispelled the moment I reached the top of the hill. For I missed something I could put no name upon. And stood for a long time, wondering what it was.

It had never been a land that sang with colour, except in late autumn. Hard to tell then whether it was the heather, or the red rocks that so assailed the skies, and made the loudest impact. At all other times it was a grey land, mottled with silver. Small burns leaping over the dun stones, and rushing down through the birch trees. Yet it had always 'smouldered' behind its greyness. The smoke of its hidden fires would catch at your throat, and envelop you forever. Even at your desk in school, ignorant of where 'the trade winds' blew. Or why they blew at all. You would hide your head between your arms, and your ignorance would find its comfort in the warm, peaty smell of your jersey's sleeves. There was no peat-reek now. The houses scattered on the slopes stood with heart-remembered names. Achullen. Balbec. Tullorach. Balmore. But you had now become aware that they were empty. Staring sightless down over Loch Ness. Blind to the tourists' caravans, and the scientific ships, searching for a monster that *they* had never glimpsed in all their window-wide and watchful years.

The school was deserted, too. But, rushing down the wind, I could hear a prayer in a Glasgow accent.

' "*Butter!*" Bu – *tt* – er! Please let me remember to say "butter." *Not* "bu'rer." Or I'll get the strap!'

'My' house was not deserted though. It was burnt to the ground. But how? And when? There was no enlightening sermon in the charred and silent stones surrounding it. No book of explanation in the running brooks that passed it. And the only immediacy, the long silent voice of Aunt Teenac, urging me to 'go west to the burn for water' and 'east to the barn for straw'.

The clump of wallflowers that straggled amongst the debris *could* have been those of my memory, growing under the scullery window. A face-length away, on summer mornings.

That smelt so heavenly sweet.
The senses *ached* at thee

Only of the rhubarb could I be sure. Itself grotesque. A great umbrella of green. Sheltering and towering above the fence that had once contained it. Outwith and far beyond Aunt Teenac's anguished lament.

'Ochone, ochone. I forgot to put the ginger for the rhubarb down on my list.'

Gone too was all trace of the sacred stairs that ascended up to Uncle Ian's bedroom. Even after his once-a-year celebration of the sale of his sheep, Uncle Ian would still 'remember his Maker', with his alarm clock in his hand, kneeling on the stairs, either through sheer inability to mount them, or genuine Christian fervour. And because he was not only a good man, but a kindly man as well, I give him the benefit of the doubt – he would pray in Gaelic, till morning came. Fortified, I like to think, to meet Aunt Teenac's tight-faced disapproval. 'What a man that's in it. And what will the neighbours be thinking of it all?'

I was not a nice child. I stood realising that.

'Uncle Ian was drunk, last night,' I would announce to all with whom I came in contact. Aware for once that I had something to tell, important enough for them to *listen* to!

'As drunk as a tinker. Aunt Teenac was just furious!'

Given the chance again, I would hug Uncle Ian's rare but intense 'remisses' to my heart. Or confide them only to laughter-lifted things, like the flying clouds and the rushing wind. And I would put it differently. Clothing it with the words and tune of Uncle Ian's favourite psalm.

> When Zion's bondage God turned back.
> As men that dreamed were we.
> Then filled with laughter was our mouth.
> Our tongues with melody

It was when I was coming down the hill, that I met the new inhabitant going up. Retired there, from Inverness. Cars could easily go up the hill now, he assured me. His own was being serviced at the moment. Yes. Television reception was quite good. The croft he had converted had all 'mod cons' now. Soon all the crofts would be 'snapped up.' Cheaper in the long run than all the caravans lining the lochside, there. An ideal place for retirement. With air like this. And scenery second to none.

No one *ever* 'retired' on the hill, my mind protested. They just died when their work was done. But he was right. Everything he said was reasonable so there was no logic for my resentment. But resentment was within me. Tangible and hard as a lump I could have put my hand on, and squeezed.

No. He hadn't known any of the former inhabitants. The crofts had been empty for a long time. Oh there was one. An old boy, turned tramp, who lived at the foot of the hill in an old hut. Found dead there from exposure last winter. Nothing at all in his hut except some old coats.

'And a melodeon,' I heard myself confirming.

If there ever *was* a melodeon, the stranger was sure it would have been sold 'for drink' long since. Everything had gone for drink. Even his social security money. Had I known the man, then?

I wasn't sure. It could have been another man I had known.

As I passed the hut at the foot of the hill I knew that I *never* would be sure. Never till

> time and tide shall be nae mair
> Gin I were the Baron's heir
> O Lassie . . .

Dear Edith . . .

Tʜᴇ Warden of Anson House – a Home for Elderly Indigent Ladies – slammed the telephone down.

'We'd best get our skates on. A new resident's coming,' she snapped to her trainee assistant. 'Struth!' she grumbled, as she led the way upstairs. 'They hardly give the old dears time to die before they pop another into their place!'

'This lot will take some clearing out,' her assistant reflected as they stood staring round the recently vacated bed-sitting-room. 'Books! Must be hundreds of them! Old Cresswell could never have read all this lot!'

'She reckoned she did.' The Warden automatically flicked her hand across the bookshelves in her compulsive search for dust. 'Nothing better to do, I suppose. And time to do it in.'

'She wasn't a bad old stick,' the assistant ventured.

'We've had worse,' the Warden conceded.

'No next of kin, had she?'

'Not that I know of. And there was no mention on her admission sheet. There was' – the Warden straightened herself up from stripping the bed – 'some woman she'd shared a flat with for years . . . what was her name again? I ought to know, didn't I? It'll come to me . . . it always does. when you're not thinking about it . . . *Edith*! I knew it would come! It was when Edith died that old Cresswell came here. Same year as myself. And that's ten years since! 'My friend Edith', on and on, as if Edith was still alive! Gave me a bit of a turn at first, being new to the work . . . "I must write to my friend Edith".'

'And did she? Write, I mean.'

'If she did,' the Warden said, '*I* never saw a letter go out from old Cresswell. Nor come in for her either.'

'I suppose they get like that, muddled . . .'

'Confused.' The Warden supplied the correct 'medical' term before bending again to strip the bed.

'Dear Edith,

The horse chestnut tree in front of my window is in full bloom now. It set me thinking about you, took me back, back to that Sunday. We had just come out from the cemetery, our usual afternoon visit. No that we had either kith or kin buried there, but as you always said since we would be longer there than anywhere else on earth, we might as well get accustomed to the place. Maybe, I don't know, maybe that was still on your mind when we sat in our usual seat in the park. The wind must have been beginning to rise, the red petals of the horse chestnut trees were fluttering down all round us, I started to play a little game – closing my eyes then opening them to see if any of the petals had landed on my shoes. 'Don't be so childish!' you said. 'Pay attention to what I am saying! When we come to be a burden to others, we will find our *own* way out . . .' That was when we put our plan into operation. Setting aside a few of our Seconal pills out of each monthly prescription. Better, you

explained, to go sleepless for a few nights, than to be unprepared *if* . . .'

'Didn't you hear me knocking, Miss Cresswell! Forgot to
put your hearing aid in *again* . . .'
  'Sorry, Miss Ainslie, I was just finishing off a letter to – '
  'Not feeling poorly again are you, dear?'
  'No – thank you – I was just . . .'
  'Anyhow! Miss Cresswell, I just popped in to tell you the
Committee Ladies have arrived to take us out for a little
"run". I thought you might like – '
  'Thank you, Miss Ainslie. Kind of you to bother, but I
. . .'
  'Don't feel *up* to it? Between *ourselves*, Miss Cresswell,
neither do I. Thing is, thing is dear, the Ladies *expect* us to
go. To show willing. They get a bit tetchy if – '
  'Yes, I see. Very well, I'll just finish off my letter.

'Oh, Edith, I have forgotten what privacy is like. The Committee Ladies have swooped down on us again . . .'

'Ah! Miss Cresswell! Come to join us for a little "spin".
That's a girl! Just the day for it. How about you, Miss Miller-
Browne. Won't you join us today? Do you a world of good!'
  'No, thank you! If *I* could go anywhere at all, with one
foot in a calliper, and the other in the grave, I would gather
up my skirts and get myself out of here – in a very rapid
manner!'

'I know, Edith, I know I should be grateful for all that the
Committee Ladies try to do for us, it's just, I get so tired of
having to feel grateful. I was cajoled into going for a run.
Helped and heaved into the car, we got stuck in a traffic jam

on the way back, I found it so hard to contain myself. As you know, I always did suffer from a weak bladder . . .

'Miss Miller-Browne refused as usual, to be cajoled. She always reminds me of you. She has such courage.'

'*Bloody-minded*! That's what *I* call Miller-Browne,' the Warden confided to her assistant, as they stood unwiring the flowers sent in from the crematorium. 'Uncooperative! Never leaves the house. Scared we get a minute to ourselves – anti-social!'

'To put our feet up,' the assistant agreed. 'This lot,' she reflected, stripping the bottom leaves from the chrysan-themums, 'must have cost a bomb!'

'*Waste*!' the Warden agreed. 'Even the *dead* don't get the good of them. Not at the crematorium!'

'A rose tree now,' her assistant said. 'That's a different thing! You can plant that in the Vale of Rest. That's what *we* did when our Aunt Freda got cremated . . . we didn't bother with *flowers*!'

'Flowers from the dead to the dying. According to Miss Ainslie, who overheard as usual . . . I wondered what *you* would make of that, Edith . . .

'I tried to imagine, to hear you, "a natural and thoughtful gesture on the part of the dead," something like that, maybe? I chose some freesias. They seemed less death-like than the other flowers. I put them into that small green vase you gave me on a birthday . . .

' "Green," you said, "will never clash with flowers of any hue. Which is why nature is so prodigal of its use." '

'What are your beads?'

'Green glass, goblin . . .'

'Remember? Strange isn't it? I can remember long ago things, they just pop into my head of their *own* accord.

'They are brighter than stars
Brighter than water
Better than voices of winds that sing
Better than any man's fair daughter
. . . your green glass beads . . .

'It's the little every day things which I *ought* to remember, that sometimes elude me. And makes the Warden annoyed with me . . .'

'*Laundry*! Miss Cresswell. Don't forget your laundry again! Bring it down when you come to supper. Van collects first thing in the morning – *laundry*, I said!'

'Yes, yes, Warden. It's my hearing-aid. The battery's finished and I . . . forgot.'

'Struth!' The Warden grumbled to her assistant as they prepared supper. 'They do go on and on. Demanding. Always demanding. Nothing ever seems to be enough for them. Almost as if' – she paused, struggling to find words to fit her thought, 'as if old age entitled them to everything . . . owed them. "I need a new hearing aid, Warden. I need a new bottom set. My lower dentures are slipping!" "I need a new Zimmer. This one's too high for me now!" And you can't tell them that their gums are shrinking. Their bodies are shrinking. They don't want to know! They don't even listen to Dr Crombie when he tells them that he hasn't got a cure for old age! You'll learn!' she assured her assistant. 'If you stick this job long enough!'

'It'll come to us all, I suppose,' the assistant said, 'if we live that long!'

'God forbid we should!' the Warden snapped. 'And don't forget to put out the mustard pot tonight!'

'*Mustard*! With *fish*, Warden? It's fish tonight!'

'With *everything*!' the Warden confirmed. 'Mustard with everything! Just goes to show,' she reflected. ' "A *bland* diet, Warden." Committee always insisting on a "bland diet". They want to cook *here* for a week! You keep your ears cocked to the serving hatch,' she advised her assistant, 'and you'll hear what the old ones think of blancmange, tapioca, semolina. No!' she asserted. 'They like a good old fry-up. And I don't blame them for *that*! A bit of "taste". I reckon it don't matter much what you eat when you're on the last lap. It's just the *mustard* I can't get over!'

'Maybe,' her assistant suggested, 'they were used to it when they were young.'

'I don't know about *that*!' the Warden admitted. 'I'd just like a word in the geriatric dietician's ears!'

'. . . I had intended to look through my book shelves in the hope of coming across one book that I haven't yet read. The mobile library comes, of course. But the choice is limited. That was *before* supper. *After* supper, Edith, I seldom feel in the mood to do anything at all. I, thankfully, cannot grumble about my health, it is reasonably good, but when we all gather together at meals, the main topic of conversation is aches and pains. By the time the meal is over, I feel that I suffer from every ill that afflicts man, as if the symptoms of the others have invaded me. What affects me, Edith, what frightens me most, is the anticipation with which what I can only describe as "medical days" are looked forward to. And when the unexpected happens, as it sometimes does – "repeat prescriptions" a day late in arriving, chiropodist's visit postponed, ambulance arriving half an hour late for the checkups – the blank that falls down on the day is filled with complaint. For the "medical days" have become the highlights of our weeks, of our existence.

'The seasons are brought in to us. Miss Ainslie told me

that she heard the Warden discussing the Harvest Festival
. . .'

'Miss Cresswell! The Vicar!'

. . . He's arrived, dear. *And* Church Sister – thought I'd
better let you know. We're all getting together in the dining-
room . . .'

'. . . And we look forward,' the Vicar was saying, 'to having
those amongst you who are able to do so, joining us in our
Harvest Home Service on Sunday morning.'

'We will, of course,' Church Sister reminded the Vicar,
'provide transport for those who are not quite so able. I have
the list here. Miss Brecon, Miss Harris, Mrs Wade, Miss
Miller-Browne . . .'

'Wait for it!' the Warden whispered to her assistant, as
they stood together, peeping through the half-closed serving
hatch. 'Miss Miller-Browne won't. She never does!'

. . . Miss Miller-Browne,' the Church Sister was persuading 'you'll try to make the effort this year, won't you?'

'I have told you *before*! I have no truck with the Church
since I was a child, and *then* under compulsion. But I *do*
know the Bible! "Remember thy Creator in the days of thy
Youth . . ." I didn't do so then! And am most unlikely to
do so in my old age!'

'I knew it,' the Warden triumphed. 'She is an old so-
and-so, Miller-Browne. Just the same,' the Warden admitted
reluctantly, she sticks to her guns. Look at her! Calliper or no
calliper! She can't half move herself out of it when something
annoys her.'

' . . . The altar looked beautiful this morning, surrounded by
autumn. Sheaves of corn intertwined with tea roses. We used
to think, you and I, Edith, that tea roses looked old. Older

than other roses. Because you said, they had their roots in a civilisation far older than ours – India? China? Persia? I forget.

'The Girl Guides sang – did I tell you? We have been "adopted" by a Girl Guide. A nice child, mine. She came to have tea with me in my room. We talked and talked, but didn't communicate. The gap was too wide to be bridged by words . . . and yet today it seemed to be bridged in an almost miraculous way. The Vicar didn't announce this hymn, you see. The Girl Guides simply stood up, and the music seemed to swell out from nowhere . . . your hymn, Edith.

> 'Choose me in my golden time
> In my dear joys . . .
> Have part . . .
> For Thee the . . .
> Fullness of my prime
> The gladness . . .'

'*Singing*! Miss Cresswell! You *are* in good spirits! I just popped up dear, to let you know – tip you the *wink*! They've just brought in the Harvest Festival Offerings from the church, and remember what happened to *you* last Harvest Festival, Miss Cresswell! Only a few russets left by the time you came down to collect your share. Miss Brecon took the lion's share of the grapes! Said apples went for her dentures!'

'I don't mind, Miss Ainslie. *Truly*, I don't.'

'You *should* mind, Miss Cresswell. We're all entitled! Warden ought to supervise the share-out. I daresay after she gets her pick, it's devil take the hindmost!'

'I doubt that. Now Miss Ainslie, if you'll excuse me . . .'

'. . . And so, Edith, autumn was brought into us and piled high on the sideboard, a pyramid of colour. We could only stand looking at it, arrested by the intensity of the colour that confronted us. Apprehensive of putting out a hand towards it, lest it should tumble down at our touch. That moment and that mood passed, and *then* . . . !'

'*Ladies*! See what I mean?' the Warden flung over her shoulder to her assistant, as she flounced out of the kitchen into the dining-room.

'Ladies! There's surely enough here for all of you! The others like grapes, too, Miss Brecon!'

'Ladies?' the Warden sniffed, perching herself up on her stool beside the serving hatch again. 'I don't know . . . Better take your pick of what's left,' she suggested to her assistant. 'And there's not much of *that* now. Not after *that* lot's had a go.

'When I first came here,' she reflected, 'ten long years since, the secretary who interviewed me for the job – a Miss Fenwick she was. Dead now – went on and on about "putting me fully in the picture". She said. "We don't accept 'God Blimmees' here", she told me. For a minute, I thought she meant *me*! And that I'd *had* the job! Till she went on to explain that they cared for women who had "seen better days", had "come down in the world". Sometimes,' the Warden sighed, 'I wish she wasn't dead. Fenwick, I mean. I could have told *her* something! There are ladies – and – *ladies*! And Brecon's not one. Nor Ainslie – '

'Miss Cresswell?' her assistant prompted.

'Cresswell?' the Warden considered the matter. 'She's not with us half the time, but she'll pass.'

'Miller-Browne?'

'She's the *real* thing. You can always tell!' the Warden claimed. 'She didn't go to their Harvest Service, but she didn't barge in here and grab all the grapes either!'

' . . . Christmas is almost upon us. How I dread it, Edith.

Cards that come. Cards that go. A contest of cards. To see which of us can lay claim to the largest number of cards received, to prove something to ourselves? That we still have friends? Are still in touch with the world outside? That we still exist? Cards which will not herald the advent of this Christmas but testify to Christmas long past from well-wishers long dead. I realised this when Miss Ainslie invited me to her room to see "all her cards". I recognised the names of residents, now gone from us, I made no mention of my discovery to Miss Ainslie. Then gifts, no longer personal, from friend to friend, but public tokens of our continued existence. Without the small surprise that sharpened and sweetened our Christmas tides, Edith, or so I feel. You see, Edith . . .'

'*Yes*! *Yes*! Miss Ainslie, I heard you knocking . . . I'm just trying to . . .'

'An artificial tree this year, Miss Cresswell. I've just seen the Council men bring it in by the back door. Not the same as a *real* tree. Not the same thing at all! To save the Warden I suppose. Always complaining about the fir needles on the carpet! *Anything* to save herself work! I thought I'd pop up to remind you that we've got to go into the sitting-room before tea. The Committee Ladies are coming.'

' . . . to put you *all* in the picture!' Miss Sherwood, the Secretary announced, flicking through the lists of her Christmas agenda.

'You must,' Miss Ainslie invited her, 'pop in for a minute to see all my cards. More than last year!'

'Yes, yes. They do seem to mount up, don't they?' The Secretary acknowledged the invitation without accepting it, or lifting her eyes from her agenda.

'First of all!' she proclaimed, handing her lists over to her assistant and trusting to memory. 'The Ladies of St Saviour's have once again risen nobly to the occasion. And will provide *and* serve tea on Christmas Eve, as usual. Then our Girl Guides, carols on Christmas morning. The Vicar himself will be along after Morning Service.'

The applause which greeted this announcement, although appreciative, was modulated. For the old ladies knew the rote. They also knew what was what, and who was who.

'Then!' the Secretary continued, 'the Rotarians' – the applause which greeted this announcement put her slightly off her stroke – 'yes the Rotarians – always so generous in their giving – will be along.' Forgetful of when exactly the Rotarians would 'be along', the Secretary, grabbing the agenda out of her assistant's hand, began to flick wildly through its pages. 'So many bits and pieces,' she complained. 'Where *did* I put the Rotarians?'

'In your handbag?' her assistant suggested.

'Of course! The Rotarians,' she announced 'will be with us to hand out their gifts, just after lunch on Christmas Day.'

'You will pop in to see my cards?' Miss Ainslie reminded her.

'Another time, dear,' the Secretary assured her, before turning to assure the Warden. 'That's everything, Miss Watson, everything under control!'

'Everything under control!' the Warden snorted, when herself and her assistant reached the safety of their kitchen again. 'She forgets how they all collapse like burst balloons *after* Christmas! You won't see hair or hide of madam then! Not when all the viruses start going around. It's you and me that have to cope then! Strange thing,' she reflected, 'how the old dears always seem to be able to hang on like grim death till Christmas. After that' – the warden shrugged – 'they just seem to let go.'

'Nothing to look forward to?' the assistant suggested.

'Could be,' the Warden agreed. 'Could be. Or that they think they mightn't reach another Christmas.

' . . . And everything was laid on, Edith. Christmas got smothered and wept to get out. But, again, the Girl Guides sang beautifully. Echoing for me, Christmas remembered. *Our* hymn. Always my favourite. Though I could never tell why. Not until you discovered the reason. "A poem," you said, "Christina Rossetti." I sang it silently. From beginning to end, with the Girl Guides. Yet, now, I cannot remember one word of it. That happens to me, sometimes. And it vexes me. Things that tremble on the edge of my mind. Eluding capture. Battering against my brain, for outlet. Tormenting me. As if I could never find release, till I find the words . . . in the bleak

'*Midwinter*!
Frosty wind made moan
Earth . . .'
Lay hard as iron
Water . . .'
Like
. . . a stone . . .'

'A ghost? No. Ghosts walk at midnight . . .'

'Miss Brecon! It's Miss Brecon, dear – ambulance has just come for her. Different when it comes for a check-up, but when it's for hospital . . .'

'That's the first of them!' the Warden announced to her assistant. 'And there's Ainslie, creeping around, spreading the Glad Tidings! Miss Ainslie!' she demanded. 'What are you hovering up there for! Keeping Miss Cresswell's door open. As if it isn't cold enough!

'Hospital always "gets" them,' she confided to her assistant.

'Frightened they never come out. But,' she admitted, 'better to happen in hospital. When it happens here, it really does affect them.'

'Wondering whose turn next!' her assistant supposed.

' . . . Miss Brecon was admitted to hospital three weeks ago. We have just heard from Warden that she died yesterday. It's when death occurs *here* that Warden doesn't discuss it with us. We are taken "out" by the back door then. As if that could conceal a fact. A virus, Warden said. It seems to be catching. Dr Comrie came this morning to Miss Miller-Browne and Miss Hardwick. I haven't been feeling too well myself. In spirit. I used to like my room, my books, and all the small mementoes of our life together, but now, Edith, now the walls of my room seem to crowd in on me, the mementoes to mock me. I feel like crashing them through the window. And pounding at the walls with my hands. I find myself wishing that I could dissolve with no trace left. I couldn't say so to the others, but I envied Miss Brecon her escape. I'm not afraid to die. But sometimes, Edith, sometimes I feel frightened to death . . .'

'That's that, then!' The Warden surveyed the empty bed-sitting-room.

'This junk,' her assistant asked, 'where does it go?'

'Basement still,' the Warden considered. 'Some of it might "come in" one day. You never know.'

'I didn't expect old Cresswell to go. Not sudden like that,' the assistant said. 'She wasn't ill. Not *properly* ill, I mean.'

'Heart! Her heart was always dicky! And old age. We all

die of *that* through time.' The Warden stood considering a philosophy that had just struck her. 'Another thing!' she remembered resentfully. 'When Dr Comrie came to sign the death certificate – going for midnight, it was. And he doesn't like late calls. But what about me! I don't like late calls either! And I had to be there too! I was jittery, I always am when they go off, sudden. Nervous. You know what I mean. You open your mouth and let anything come out of it. "Old people are living longer now Doctor," I said. Just for something to say, when he was signing the death certificate. STRUTH! You would think that I had killed old Cresswell! "Old people are *lingering* longer!" he snapped, flung down the pen, and shot out the door. I felt as if my nose had bled! That's *it* then! Have you finished clearing out the chest of drawers?'

'Just about.'

'Good, I'll see to this lot.'

'Warden! Warden!' the assistant's voice halted the Warden at the door. 'Look at this!' she urged. 'Just take a look! Writing paper. Pages and pages! "Dear Edith . . ." Nothing else. Just "Dear Edith." What a waste of paper!'

'No wonder they're always crying out for writing paper,' the Warden snapped. 'Just to waste it!'

'I could,' her assistant suggested, 'I could just cut off the tops and the others could use up the rest of the paper.'

'You're welcome to the job! If you can find time to do it.'

'Warden! She *has* written something! On this page – "Dear Edith I have changed my mind. Not about my going. The reason for it has changed, other people have become a burden to me . . ." '

THIS WASTED DAY

DAY had slipped over her head. Forcing her way through the bramble bushes, she eased herself down in the ley of the dyke. Time now for a smoke, to recover from the weariness of a wasted day, before taking the long road back to the town.

> Tinkie Tinkie
> Tarry Bags . . .'

The bairns, Just let out of school, raced chanting past her, before riving in and out amongst the bushes in search of brambles.

> Lay your eggs
> Amang your Rags!

Long since inured to their mockery, she automatically whipped the cover off her basket, to check up on her 'swag'. A profitless day. Few blanks appeared in the precise rows of tape, elastic, safety-pins, needles, reels of cotton, so carefully set out, when morning was still early. But then, most days were profitless now. Wearying in their wastefulness ... WOOLWORTH'S! *That* was what had tolled the knell of her livelihood. 'Cheaper,' country folk said. 'A better selection.' Closing their doors before she had time to whip the cover off her basket. Not that there were many country folk left now. Not *real* country folk. The rows of cottages once inhabited by her regular customers had now been taken over as week-end residences by folk from the town. New-fangled machinery had taken over from many of the farm-workers. Like herself, they had outlived their era, had become out of step with the times that had replaced it.

Aki! The Paki!
His sackie
On his backie! ...'

The bairns had found a new target. She could hear them shouting in the distance. 'God curse *you* too,' she muttered, adding to their gibes, as the Indian 'tally man' whizzed whistling past on his bicycle, his 'pack' slung across his shoulders. He and his kind had also replaced her. For what *he* offered was not to be found in the town – hand-painted cushion covers, rolls of silk, brass falderals. All the same ... The recollection warmed her, lit up her eyes, as she watched him swerving his way through a crowd of shouting bairns, his foot trailing behind him on the ground. All the same ... neither man, beast nor bairn would have tried *that* with her in the days when she took to the road with her 'sheltie' and her 'float'. Spanking along it. Her whip cracking high in the wind. Snapping in threat to anyone who dared to bar her way.

Restored to good humour, she set about clearing out the bowl of her clay pipe. Poking at it. Dunting it against her fist, preparatory to the precise, careful ritual of 'filling up'. One good thing about a clay pipe, she reflected, if you dropped it you didn't have to bother picking it up. But she was careful of her clay pipe. Hard to come by now. 'No demand for them,' according to the wife in the tobacconist's shop. Advising her to 'try the toy shop', which sometimes sold clay pipes to the bairns 'for blowing bubbles'. Come to think of it, that *might* have been a 'good going line' if she had thought of it in the days when clay pipes cost two for a tanner but she hadn't thought about it then, content enough to 'carry' birds flying on a stick, for it was essential to win access to the Mothers through an approach to their bairns – 'You'll never die as long as that bairnie lives!' she would assure the Mothers. 'For she carries you in her face. God bless her. A bonnie bairn, a bonnie bairnie right enough. And not to be wondered at, mistress! For it's a fine figure of a woman you are, *yoursel'*!'

Cursing and wheedling. The two-toned voice of her lifetime. One for her protection. T'other for her livelihood. She was not a religious woman. Not what you'd describe as 'a Christian'. Yet she had an almost 'on speaking terms' relationship with that being on whom she always laid possessive claim as '*my* maker'. His emissary, in a manner of speaking, bestowing His blessing here, His curses there. Prodigal with both.

Her tones losing something of their certitude with the passing of the years. Wheedling coming slower to the tongue. No longer setting off 'on the Toby', taking to the road in the high hope of 'wheezing the Manashees for Jowldie'. Her mind lingered momentarily, lovingly, on her own language, 'the cant'. She *herself* could still 'jan the cant.' But she had outlived her own kind who could interpret it. Their descendants couldn't. That was what compulsory education had done to *them*! Deprived them of their own language! Spitting out her contempt, sucking fiercely on the stub of her clay pipe, she listened to the clash and clang of the berry pickers' cans in the distance. Bramble time, she realised, staring at the bushes which surrounded her. The turn of the year taking her almost by surprise. Her attitude to the countryside she knew so well was one-dimensional. Not for *her* acclamation at the sight of the first snowdrop of spring, the wild briar roses of summer, the turning of the leaves, or the first fall of snow. She lived, without comment, within the whole. Brambles were but incidental. A thing in the passing. It was the wide berry-picking days of her youth that came to mind, filling it with a small, distinct, living clarity.

The mare hitched to the float, the 'sheltie' trotting behind it, taking herself, her man, her bairns, the whole caboodle of them, southwards to the lush fruit-growing lands of Blairgowrie and Dundee.

> Says I ma young lassie
> I canna weel tell ye
> I canna weel show ye
> The road ye maun gae . . .

The old ballad defied her vocal cords, but lilted in her memory.

> But if ye wull permit me
> tae walk along wi ye
> I'll show you the road
> And the miles tae Dundee . . .

If God, Himself, was to ask her happiest recollection of a long life, he answer would fall quick to her tongue – 'the berry-picking, maister'. Stripping the bushes in the warm sun. Sure of a wage at the end of a day. Her man and his ferret away in search of a rabbit for the pot, and all that was needed to accompany it that 'fell' to his hand on the way. Floury tatties fresh from the field. And a fine, sweet turnip. And aye a copper in the pocket for 'the wine that maketh glad the heart of man'. All the same, she remembered wryly, when the drink was in, the wit went out. As it always did at reunions with her own kind on their 'social' occasions. At the berry-picking. Funerals. Weddings. And the great yearly horse sale up Foggie Loan way. All ending in a 'barney', a free-for-all. No head too hard to break in *those* days. Nor too soft to heal again.

A thing of the past now, though, the berry-picking. Students had taken it over from her kind. But she could still teach *them* a trick or two of the berry-picking trade. For there was more than one way of increasing the weight of the berries in your basket before sidling up for the 'official' weigh-in. And she knew them *all*.

Still, peering through the smoke rising from her pipe, in search of some other landscape, she was certain of one thing – she'd live the same life over if she had to live again. And the chances were she'd go where most men go.

The hooter from the tweed mill, sounding its cry of Release! across the countryside, broke through her sleep and startled her into consciousness. Struggling to her feet, she began to rive her way through the maze of bramble bushes. Gasping as she reached the slope of the bank, halting to catch her breath before beginning the climb.

Kirstac.

Her name reached her mind from a long way off.
'MacWhirdie Kirstac! STAND ALOFT! HALT!' Words

that never age. Never tire. Never go doddering past in clichés. But are always sudden. And alive with blinding power.

'As sure as death', 'As God's my judge' . . . The vows of a lifetime that had fallen so easily from her tongue. Lending truth to the lie . . . *so*. Death *was* 'sure'. God *did* 'judge'. And this, she recognised, was *His* day.

'Move yourself, woman!' A man's voice snapped, as he nudged her towards his companion, who stood flicking through the pages of a large ledger.

'That's the lot for the day, Recorder,' he announced. 'But there's always the *one*,' he grumbled, rattling his keys against the old tinker's ears, 'always the one who arrives at the last minute! Holding everything and everybody up.'

'Patience, Peter,' his companion advised, without looking up from the ledger. 'Patience.'

'She was always the same!' A woman's voice rose up in accusation.

'That wife from the tobacconist's shop!' The tinker recognised the voice and the form, visible now through the mist beginning to clear before her eyes. *This* then was how she had always imagined Judgement Day to be. On the threshold of heaven – or hell – with all the people whose lives had brushed against her own. Had touched her. Affected her. For good or ill.

'Always the same!' The tobaconist's wife was grumbling on. 'Banging on my shop door the moment I put the shutters up for the night. Demanding – *demanding*, mind you! – half-an-ounce of bogie twist. No please or thank you. Never a "sorry" nor a "beg your pardon". And the *language* that was on her! Enough to blow your *ears* off!'

'Liar!' the tinker protested, before turning to the Recorder. Contemplating him. Considering the form of address most complimentary to *him*, most favourable to *herself*. Maister

... Sir ... Your Honour ... 'Your *worship*! *This* was the way of it. I'd be hawking all day for a crust. Up Moss of Barmuckity way. A Godforsaken hole of a place. As fine you know, sir. You could walk there for miles without running into a soul who could give you the time of day. So, how in God's name was I to know it would be closing-times before I got back?'

'Blaspheming again!' The man called Peter turned to the Recorder. 'Blasphemy! Take a note of that!'

'Anything you say,' the Recorder warned her, 'will be taken down and ...'

' ... used in evidence against me,' she concluded his statement for him. 'I *know*,' she admitted ruefully, memories of her 'appearances' in the police courts still in her memory, 'I know ...'

Turning her attention to the groups in front of her, she felt her heart lift in recognition of the fish wives from the Broch. 'Souls'. Their heads covered with their black shawls, bending beneath their creels. Their red flannel skirts swaying beneath their dark aprons. Of her kind. In their own way. Striding the same country roads. Supplying the same customers. Their sing-song morning greetings in passing. 'It's threatening rain.' 'It's promising fair.'

'BUY my caller Herrin!

> 'They're bonnie Fish
> And dainty Farin
> BUY
> My caller Herrin ...'

But *then*! Whoever heard of a fish wife shouting 'stinking fish'? The idea of that creased her old face into a smile. 'GOOD souls – ' Often taking time for a bit of barter on the road. Three herrings for a packet of needles. 'And here's yin *extra*. Thrown in for – hansel!' For a gift.

Even so, she noticed. Here, at heaven's gate itself, the others stood apart from the fish wives. Their 'smell', she supposed. Just as the accusation of 'smell' had always kept folk from too close an approach to herself.

'No cleaner wives walks the face of this earth than the fish wives.' She heard herself exhorting the crowd. 'So you needna all stand there clutching at your skirts! The fish wives will no contaminate you! They're *clean* folk! As clean and clear and trig as the herrins in their creels!'

'Contempt of court!' Peter rattled his keys in warning.

'AGE?' The Recorder demanded. 'Date of birth?' Her usual reply to that question was, she realised in good time, not in keeping with her present surroundings. 'As old as my tongue. And a bit older than my teeth.' Although that indeed was all she *did* know about her age. '*That*,' she admitted, 'is one thing I canna tell you. I was never registered, you see.'

'Not *baptised*!' Peter's voice shook with shock. 'This woman,' he informed the Recorder, 'has surely arrived here by some gross error on somebody's part. Not baptised!'

'It does sometimes happen,' the Recorder conceded. 'We are still somewhat fallible. Watch and pray, Peter,' he reminded the man with the keys. A small smirk crossing his face as he did so. 'We still must needs watch and pray.'

'I *can* tell you one thing though,' the tinker remembered. Anxious to please the Recorder. 'My father fought at the Battle of Balaclava. If *that's* any help to you. Or so he claimed. Though, truth to tell, you could never believe a word that came out of his head.'

'We are well aware of *that*!' Peter snapped. 'Get on with it!'

'But *you* know my age.' She turned to the Recorder in an instant of sudden awareness. 'You know everything.'

'A matter of form,' he said, irritation creeping into his tone. 'Simply a matter of form. Place of birth?' he demanded.

'The Glens of Foudland, sir!' *That* was what she *did* know. Not that she, herself, remembered. But she had heard tell of it often enough from her mother. 'At the tattie lifting. October, November that would be. *There's* a date for you, maister. A bit of a date onywye. My mother, God rest her, just flung down her pail when her pains came on her. Took herself over to the dyke. And I was born in the ley of the dyke. She washed me in the burn, wrapped me in her shawl. And was back working in the tattie drill within an hour of my birth. We never lookit on birth as an illness, you see.'

'And that's a fact!' Dod McCluskey the poacher snarled from within the crowd. 'Her kind breed like *rabbits*!'

'He kens a lot about *rabbits*!' she informed the Recorder. 'BUT!' She turned to confront the poacher. 'You ken damn all about *tinkers*! I ken enough about YOU to send you straight to HELL!' She'd said the *right* thing, but realising that she'd said it in the *wrong* place at the wrong time, she struggled to contain her rising anger.

'However mony bairns *we* brought into this weary world,' she conceded. 'And I'll no deny *that*. We lippened on no man for help to rear them. We never "signed on the broo", applied for the means test. Nor did we ever "line up" for "chits" for free boots. Free clothes for *our* bairns! As this man beside me' – she turned to the Recorder – 'can vouch for! *Our* folk never had to end their days deserted. Up yonder in the poor's house! They got the *dignity* of dying in their own beds. In the tent or wagon that was their home. Nor did *they* end up in a pauper's grave. Our tribe made sure of *that*! Each according to what he could afford!

'*Another* thing, Dod.' She paused, struggling with the anger again, threatening to overcome her. 'We *knew* that our husbands, our *men*, had fathered *our* bairns. For our women marry virgin. That was the law. And no very often broken! So that we *knew*. Aye! And our *husbands* knew. It takes a wise man to know his own, as the good man standing beside me will agree! So, you see, Dod, I wonder, I wonder if *you* ever took a good look at that last littl'un o' yours, the wee red-heided lad. Him that's the living spit o' Chae Tastard, the coalman. "Ripe ripe like a cherry, ready to burst" – *that* was aye what Chae had to say about *your* wife, in The Hole In the Wall on a Saturday night. Mind *you*! He *could* have been exaggerating! With a good drink inside o' him. He *must* have been!' The image of Dod's great slorach of a wife rising up in her vision. 'Some CHERRY!' she chuckled.

'Contempt of court.' Peter shouted, as the crowd joined in her laughter.

'*ADULTERY*!' he prompted, peering over the Recorder's shoulder to examine the ledger.

'*That*,' the Recorder pointed out, 'has just been dealt with, in some detail.'

'BEGGING?'

'Not,' the Recorder informed him, 'included in the Ten Commandments.'

'A pity that,' Peter grumbled. 'We *know* that the Defendant was guilty enough of *that*!'

'Thou shalt not covet.' COVET. Aware of the blank expression on the Tinker's face, the Recorder turned towards her in explanation. 'COVET. To want to possess that which belongs to another human being.'

'When I was a young woman, sir,' – her words came out of long, backward reflection – 'and had just got married on to Donald McWhirdie, I had a sore hankering for a van with a wooden roof. Like the one my good-mother [mother-in-law] lived in. We had just got a wagon, you see. With the old tarpaulin covering. Green, it was. But I would have liked a van with a wooden roof. "You'll manage to get one through time," my good-mother said. Oh! We *did* get one. We got one . . . "through time." But, it's the long wait through time that claws at your gut, when you're young. But Maister – Gospel Truth! – I never grudged my good-mother *her* van with a wooden roof. I never cast my eye on that!'

'FALSE WITNESS. Thou shalt not bear . . .'

'Many a time that. But,' she qualified, 'only when false witness was borne against *me*. And *that* happened more times than I can count!'

'An eye for an eye,' the Recorder murmured.

'Whiles, of course,' she continued, 'whiles, I'd stand up in the court and lie till I was blue in the face. For my man. Poachin' was *his* trouble. Oh! but he could net a salmon. Up at the Brig o' Feuch, yonder. He could *that*! And *that* was something to *see*, sir! The salmon rinnin' and leaping for life. The thing was he, himsel aye got catched! An impatient chield, my man. Reckless, when it came to poaching. Could never wait for the dark night. Never him! But up and off when the moon was full. And the countryside as bright as day. I would swear in the court that he had never left his bed, in hope of mistaken identity. But no other man born was *his* marrow! You could never *mistake* him for anybody else. You can do no *less*, maister, no less than stick up your *ain* man. And if *that's* false witness, then I'm guilty o't.'

'FALSE PRETENCES.' The Recorder turned towards her. 'Gaining money by false pretences.'

'And *that's* true enough!' A voice full of remembered grievance rose up in accusation. 'That old *tink* did *that* right enough!'

Peering forward, she recognised her accuser – Teen Slater, yon simple craittur that was servant at the farm-toun of Drumlogie.

'Many a bonnie penny she did *me* for!' Teen complained. 'Her and her promises. Her and her lies! "A bittie o' silver tae cross her palm," she'd wheedle. Forbye! Scrounging a cup of tea to read the leaves. A tall dark man she promised *me*! Weel set up wi' gear and plenishings, she said! Time and time again, at a tanner a time! She promised me! And wha did *I* end up wi'? Jeems Simmers. Yon wee bauchle. Him that was orra man at the fornet. Wi no twa coppers to jingle together!'

'And if it wasna' the teacups,' an anonymous voice cried from the crowd, 'it was the white heather! "White heather to bring you luck", was *that* one's cry. Waving it in front o' your nose. Near forcing't on you! *White* heather. Some white heather. Just a wheen faded dirt from the Moss o' Barmuckity.'

'*One* minute! A *minute* just!' The tinker's protest rang round the gates of heaven. 'One minute, sir.' She turned to the Recorder. 'Begging your pardon, maister. I *did* read the cups. But I was always persuaded, bribed, by the country lassies and wives to "read their fortunes." Mistress and her maid were the same in *that* respect. I never laid claim of having the gift to see into the future. That was forced upon me. *They* had the idea in their *ain* heads, that, being a tinker, I could read their fortunes. That's the burden of being a tinker. Folk get byordinar notions about you. And, truth to tell, as time passes you almost believe them yoursel! *One* thing though, maister. All I ever *did* tell them was the things I knew they wanted to hear. So. I'd give them good health. A handsome man. A bairn or two. And a full purse. I *never* sent them away wi' a sore heart! Surely, sir, that was worth a tanner! As for the heather, I plead guilty to that. Only I never asked a penny for my offering. Nor forced it on them. Their own superstition did that.'

'THOU SHALT NOT STEAL'.

'Many's the autumn,' the blacksmith's wife from Corrieben began to testify, '*that* one picked the gooseberries growing at the back of my house. Then had the bare-faced cheek to *sell* them at *me* front door! I never caught her at it. She'd skedaddled down the road before I noticed that my bushes were stripped clean!'

'You *must* answer,' The Recorder urged, breaking into her thoughts. '*Did* you, or did you *not*?'

'You *ken* I did! Although I never looked on it as theft *myself*. I never charged the wumman for her *ain* gooseberries. I only asked for a copper or two for *picking* them for her! That seemed to *me* a fair enough exchange.'

'NOT PROVEN!' Peter glared at the ticket in his hand. 'Impossible!' he shouted to the Recorder. 'There's a mistake on somebody's part. A *mistake*, I tell you!'

'No mistake,' the Recorder assured him. 'The verdict came direct from Himself. And, as *we* know, Peter, as we know, He works in a mysterious way.'

Wordlessly Peter handed the ticket to the old tinker. No confession, it seemed to *her*, as she twirled the ticket in her hands, was so shameful, so demanding as the one that *now* faced her. That she couldn't write had never bothered her. 'X' had covered and contained the few official documents of her lifetime. But reading, not to be able to read . . . 'Would you' – she turned to the Recorder – 'be a good soul and tell me what the ticket says. I canna see without my specs. And I've left them down in my basket.'

> Admit BEARER Heavenwards.
> East Open Stand. North End
>   Row 11
>   Seat 12

The disappointment that struck at her heart sounded itself in her voice. 'Is *that* all it is! I was hoping it was a ticket for a bed for the night in the Corporation lodging-house.'

Norman MacCaig
COLLECTED POEMS

'Norman MacCaig is an indispensable poet, and his *Collected Poems* is a wonderful book which will give years of pleasure.'
Douglas Dunn

This revised and expanded edition of Norman MacCaig's collected poems, published on his eightieth birthday, includes all the work he wishes to preserve from fourteen individual volumes, as well as over a hundred uncollected pieces: nearly seven hundred poems in all, spanning his career from the early 1950s to the present day. All are marked with the wit and wisdom, the clarity of language and observation, and the masterly lightness of touch that have earned him the admiration and affection of generations of readers in Scotland and beyond.

Robert Crawford
A SCOTTISH ASSEMBLY

'This book reveals a rising Scottish star which will, I hope, continue to spotlight us where we are, in the continuous script of our lives.'   Iain Crichton Smith

Robert Crawford's first full-length poetry collection reveals a strong, authoritative voice, an enterprising diversity of sub-ject-matter, and, above all, a deep and complex commitment to Scotland as a whole and to particular places within it. *A Scottish Assembly* is ambitious and distinctive, confident with big historical and scientific themes, and establishes Robert Crawford as one of the most imaginative and interesting writers in Scotland today.

Mick Imlah
BIRTHMARKS

'*Birthmarks* reassured me that some people are still writing verse that is a positive pleasure to read.'   David Profumo

'He is already a poet of striking originality and cunning, a genuinely distinct voice in the murmur and babble of the contemporary'   *T.L.S.*

A collection from one of our most exciting younger poets. Mick Imlah's poetry is dark, sly, cruelly funny and studded with startling effects. In these elegantly written adventures, a variety of narrators – an aspiring Cockney, a deranged zoologist, a feckless racist, an unlucky foetus, the ugly, the beautiful – suffer the vengeful nightmares of their origins and limitations. Sharp, contemporary, witty and disturbing, *Birthmarks* puts Mick Imlah in the front rank of today's writers.

Ronald Hamilton
A HOLIDAY HISTORY OF SCOTLAND

This book is the ideal companion for travelling around Scotland: entertaining, informative, one of a kind, it is indispensable for young and old alike, be they Scots born and bred, or those about to visit for the first time.

Starting at 80A.D. and taking the reader right up to the present day, this book is illustrated throughout, and provides just the right amount of historical background we crave when looking at an ancient monument or tramping a well trodden glen. It will bring pleasure to countless visitors to a beautiful country.

Ralph Glasser
The Gorbals Trilogy

Growing up in the Gorbals, Gorbals Boy at Oxford, Gorbals Voices, Siren Songs.

'Passionate, curious and straightforward, these books possess a universal and classic appeal.'   William Boyd

These three books make up a great autobiographical sequence, and are a unique testimony to the times we live in.

Growing up in the Gorbals describes Ralph Glasser's impoverished childhood and adolescence in Glasgow's notorious slum tenements and recreates a way of life that has been swept off the map forever. Born into an immigrant Jewish family, he was sent to work in a garment factory at the age of fourteen, but after years of study he managed to win a scholarship to Oxford.

Gorbals Boy at Oxford evokes Oxford in the last days before the Second World War; a world of society hostesses and upper class communists, who regarded Ralph Glasser with a mixture of interest, envy and resentment. After military service he returned to an Oxford which had become a crucible of intrigue and the management of war.

Gorbals Voices, Siren Songs recounts Ralph Glasser's ventures in the perplexing, wayward world of postwar London, through the worlds of business and bohemia, a doomed marriage to a gentile girl and a final emergence to a new, more confident life.